BATTLETECH LEGENDS
DECISION AT THUNDER RIFT
THE GRAY DEATH LEGION SAGA, BOOK ONE

BY WILLIAM H. KEITH

BATTLETECH: DECISION AT THUNDER RIFT
By William H. Keith
Cover art by Eldon Cowgur
Interior art by Alan Blackwell, Matt Plog, Anthony Scroggins
Cover design by David Kerber

Printed in USA.

Published by Catalyst Game Labs,
an imprint of InMediaRes Productions, LLC
5003 Main St. #110 • Tacoma, WA 98407

PROLOGUE

Ten thousand years of organized warfare have culminated in that fabrication of arms and armor, mobility and strength called the BattleMech.

Standing ten to twelve meters tall, the typical 'Mech is vaguely humanoid, an armored giant of myth and legend come to life. The lightest weigh 20 tons, the heaviest 95 or more, and even the smallest 'Mech bristles with lasers, particle cannons, long- and short-range missile launchers, autocannon, or machine guns. A 'Mech is striding, thundering death for any unarmored army crazy enough to stand and fight, and a formidable foe even for heavily-armored conventional units.

Traditional military tactical thought holds that the best way to fight a 'Mech is to send in another 'Mech, preferably one bigger, stronger, and more heavily armored. When evenly-matched, the monster machines pound away at one another, each waiting for that one fatal mistake by his opponent. Each waiting for that inevitable, critical failure of nerve or machine, that instant's lapse in guard or tactics that will leave the way open for a fatal strike.

This same kind of military balance exists between the five major Houses of the Successor States of the early 31st century as they war among themselves for control of known space. On one side is the Capellan Confederation of House Liao, the Free Worlds League of House Marik, and the Draconis Combine of House Kurita. Against them stands the uneasy alliance of House Davion's Federated Suns and the Lyran Commonwealth of House Steiner. Around these giants also swarm lesser houses, powers, alliances, merchants, fronts, and out-and-out bandits, whom the Successor Lords try to woo, bribe, or force to assist them when they can.

And yet, after centuries of warfare, no clear gains have been made by any single House, no fatal flaw uncovered. War continues, with the giants struggling among the ruins of what once had been a proud, galactic civilization. Like well-matched BattleMechs, the forces seemed too evenly balanced for any one to gain that vital, decisive edge.

But the powers behind the war understood a maxim of war as old as war itself. What cannot be won by force of arms can often be achieved through cunning, deceit, or by a concealed blade slipped into an enemy's back.

—Terror's Balance: A History of the Succession Wars,
by Nicolai Aristobulus

BOOK ONE

CHAPTER 1

The traitor slid out from under the tangle of cables and hard-wired circuit boards, wiping grease-stained fingers across the front of his coveralls. The watch officer behind the console above him frowned. "Aren't you done in there yet?"

"It's a peripheral circuit, boss," the traitor replied. "I can't get it from here. I'll have to check the cameras down in the repair bay." He reached back into the circuitry access and flicked a row of switches from on to off with precise deliberation. "Your monitors'll be down for a bit."

"How long?"

"Oh, not long." He began gathering his tools and stuffing them into his canvas shoulder bag. "Fifteen minutes."

The watch officer glanced at his wristcomp. "Make it fast," he said, penning a notation on the clipboard in his hand.

"Don't worry," the other man replied. "It will be."

The traitor was an astech and a native Trell, his sharp-chiseled features and black, curly hair typical of Trellwan's small native population, his complexion extraordinarily pale due to the world's UV-poor sun. The watchstation door passed the man at a touch of his fingertips to the security scanner plate, then hissed shut at his back. As he moved down the stone-walled passageway, the clatter of his footsteps echoed hollowly.

Cold stone steps led down and down, through deserted corridors and past rooms guarded by gray uniformed sentries. Twice, the Trell had to show his pass, a holographic ID pinned high on his shoulder. Other astechs passed him in stony silence or with a nodded greeting. His coveralls and heavy tool bag were pass enough to get him through most doorways, as there were few areas in the Castle where a native astech could not go.

The repair bay was part artifice and part natural cavern, a high-vaulted room whose lingering gloom was broken by isolated pools of light One wall was brown-rusted and corroded with age. At the bay's center, crisscrossed by spotlight pools and the snaking coils of power feeds and compressor lines, the 55-ton hulk of a partly disassembled 'Mech lay sprawled across an elevated rack. A tech bawled orders and gestured from the deck at a pair of astechs working on the behemoth's chest. Wearily, they stooped above the actinic flare of a wielding laser. Armor plates weighing a half-ton apiece dangled above in a tangled web work of lines and scaffolding.

The traitor looked around at the four 'Mechs that were the heart and soul of Carlyle's Commandos. Armored, ten-meter monsters, BattleMechs were all but invincible against troops or conventional armor, so powerful that only another 'Mech of equal or greater firepower had any chance at all of bringing one down. The Trell smiled to himself, thinking how he had accomplished just that with merely a forged maintenance order and fifteen minutes' work.

Disabling the lance's *Shadow Hawk* had been the first part of his two-pronged mission. He had been given explicit instructions and training, as well as a replacement circuit board to be slipped into a 'Mech's servoelectronics control nexus if he got the chance. He'd found that chance, and the board had crippled every power feed in the 'Mech's leg servoactuator series before melting itself into an anonymous lump of slag, all traces of sabotage erased. Now the Lance had but three 'Mechs—the captain's *Phoenix Hawk* and the two 20-ton *Wasps*. Without the *Shadow Hawk*'s particular balance of heavy firepower and maneuverability, the garrison would be crippled if it found itself in an all-out fight.

The Trell clutched his tool bag tighter under his arm, and hurried past to the rattletrap metal steps that led in dizzying zigzags to the Bay Control Center, a windowed booth suspended from the back wall fifteen meters above the stone floor.

The repair bay officer looked up from the glow of a monitor, lowered his feet from the console, and set his mug of chava aside. "Yes?"

"Maintenance, sir," said the small, dark man, turning his shoulder so that the officer could see his astech's card without rising from his chair. "They sent me down from Central Control to find a fault in the security camera circuitry. I think it's a bad line in here somewhere."

The officer nodded. "Damn junk," he said. "Like everything else on this sand-rotten—" Realizing too late that he was talking to a Trell, he bit off whatever else he'd been about to say and pointed at a row of dead monitors, "Access is back here," he said, then propped his feet back up and returned to the single live monitor on the console. The traitor glanced over the officer's shoulder, and noted the monitor showed the spaceport, empty ferrocrete broken by overlapping patches of shadow and light under a chill, starry sky.

So they weren't down yet. He glanced at his wristcomp, silently counting out the minutes and seconds that remained, and began laying out his tools. It wouldn't be long now.

Grayson Death Carlyle had long ago given up being sensitive about his grim middle name. He'd inherited it, so to speak, from an ancestor, Lord Grayson Death Thomas. Lord Grayson, it was said, had changed the pronunciation of his middle name's vowel from a long to short "e" after he became the Victor of Lysander and a landholder so powerful no one dared care how he pronounced his name. In a warriors' society that reveled in the deeds and exploits of heroes, the younger Grayson's name drew little more than occasional wry heckling from the other members of his father's lance.

As soon as he stepped from the electric runabout that had brought him back to the Castle, Grayson knew he was in trouble. Shedding his cold-weather gear, he dropped it into the arms of a waiting Trell orderly, who said nervously, "The Weapons Master's been looking for you, sir."

Grayson glanced at his wristcomp and winced at the time. "Yes, I expect he has."

"He seemed a bit upset," the orderly went on, sounding like someone who feared being caught any minute near ground zero of a long-expected blast.

Grayson shrugged, then turned to the electric heater the Vehicle Bay watchstanders had rigged to take the edge off the bitter air that came in whenever the Bay's outer doors were opened. Amid the grime-smeared walls of the arena-sized hall, about 20 other House troopers were about, either standing in the heater's glow, lounging with books, or playing card games. Grayson rubbed his numbed hands briskly to restore circulation. It was a typical Secondnight, 20° below, with a low-keening wind that plunged the windchill to -40° Centigrade or worse. Sergeant Griffith's reprimand was going to be worse than the cold, he decided, but the memory of Mara's caresses, the lingering warmth of her kisses, made up for it all.

A voice broke into his thoughts. "So! Master Death has deigned to join us."

"Hello, Griff," he said amicably. "Sorry I'm late."

The shadow resolved itself into the unit's warrant weapons master, Sergeant Kai Griffith. The harsh overhead lights gleamed from his hairless scalp and seemed to highlight the savage blue scar that twisted down his jaw close to his right ear.

"'Sorry,' the boy says! 'Sorry!'" Griffith's face, with its drooping mustache, wore a studied sneer. "What I want to know is where'n the bloody blue hell have you been?"

To mask his anger at being called "boy," Grayson continued to smile, but his voice was chill. "With friends," he said, thinking that someday Griffith would go too far.

"'Friends!' Off-base again, then. Seeing that Trell girl, I suppose?"

"Aw, Griff—"

"Don't give me that! You were scheduled for weapons practice *four hours ago*, and you're supposed to be in the Command Center observing right this minute. What the hell're you playing at, boy?"

Grayson touched fingertips to his shock of pale blond hair in mock salute. "Reprimand received, Sergeant Griffith."

"Your father'll receive it too, son." The bald head moved slowly from side to side, the scar rippling as jaw muscles clenched. "I can't perform my duty if you persist in ignoring yours."

Grayson turned from the heater and started up the ramp toward the Castle's main central passageway. "Look, Griff, I figured this might be my last chance to see her. We're pulling out in three days—"

The bald sergeant fell into step beside him. "We'll pull out if these negotiations come off. Until then, you'll attend your duty, Mister, or I'll know the reason why!"

Grayson scowled. He was now 20 standard years old, and the weapons master had been his personal instructor in the military arts since he'd formally joined the lance as a warrior apprentice at ten. The older he got, the less he appreciated Kai Griffith's sharp tongue or his interference in his private life. After all, Grayson wasn't a child any longer, and was both son and heir to a MechWarrior. The weapons master would not order his life forever.

"I'll attend to my duty," Grayson retorted, "but my private life is my own!"

"Still playing the loner, Master Carlyle? That attitude is going to buy you a world of trouble before you end your apprenticeship. Look, can't you get it through your skull the damned Trells aren't our friends?"

"This one is. C'mon! I just wanted to say goodbye!"

Griffith shook his head disapprovingly. "The daughter of old Stannic himself, no less!"

"What's that got to do with anything?" Grayson broke in. It was true Mara was the daughter of Trellwan's chief minister, but so what?

"You keep sneaking off to play with your girl in town, and you're going to end up dead!"

Remembering a fragment of the evening's fun, Grayson only smiled and shrugged. Kai Griffith shared the prejudice of most old-time garrison soldiers against the local civilians they were supposed to protect. He would never understand.

They paused at a massive steel door set into a wall of rough-cut stone, guarded by a gray-uniformed trooper holding his submachine gun at a stiff port arms. The door was decorated with the design of a clenched, mailed fist against a sky-blue background. Griffith shook his head resignedly, knowing the stubbornness of this boy staring at him with pale gray eyes.

"We haven't finished with this, Master Carlyle. You're being trained to con a BattleMech someday, to be a MechWarrior of Carlyle's Commandos. But warriors have to learn a damn sight more than how to pilot a walking metal mountain. Get me?"

Grayson had heard the lecture and all its variations before—about discipline and dedication to the unit and working as a part of a team. He made himself look attentive as he stifled an insistent yawn. There hadn't been much sleep for him during the past rest period.

Griffith finally stopped when he realized Grayson was simply tuning him out. "C'mon, son," he said, gesturing at the door. Let's get in there and watch the reception."

CHAPTER 2

The Combat Command Center was a bare-walled room lined with consoles and carpeted with enough power feeds and cables to make footing hazardous. Clusters of gray-uniformed men stood or lounged here and there, some talking quietly over cups of dew or hot chava, others studying the pale flicker of monitor screens or the eerie green glow of radar trackers. From somewhere overhead, a woman's amplified voice announced, "Mailai DropShip now entering atmosphere. Her captain confirms presence of the Oberon representatives on board. Estimate time to grounding at eleven minutes."

Two men sat at one near console. One was a dark-eyed senior tech in official gray-and-blue coveralls and the other a slight, swarthy-skinned man wearing a high-collared, richly worked civilian tunic. Beside them stood another civilian, silver-haired and erect, a silver-chased quarter cloak fashionable on the Inner Worlds draped across his left shoulder.

The dark-haired civilian looked up sharply at Grayson, Though his eyes were angry, he said nothing. Grayson knew Nicolai Aristobulus was keeping his reprimand silent only because of the outsider standing behind him.

"Hello, Ari," Grayson said, as though he neither saw nor felt his tutor's disapproval.

"Master Carlyle," Ari replied stiffly, with only the slightest inclination of his head. "You're late."

"What's Carlyle's boy doing here?" the silver-haired civilian asked, turning toward Griffith. "These negotiations are extremely delicate."

It was Ari who replied. "He is here at my request, my Lord, and at the direct order of Captain Carlyle."

"Indeed? And since when does a battlelance tutor set staff policy?"

"When he is charged with training the CO's successor...my Lord." Ari's hostility was barely restrained. "The boy may have to handle this someday."

"Let him stay, my Lord," Griffith interjected, nodding toward the monitor. "That trader DropShip's almost in."

Lord Olin Vogel scowled, then moved away to another monitor console, trailing his ruffled dignity. Behind Vogel's back, Griffith made a face at Ari. Seated at the communications console next to the tutor, Chief Tech Riviera could not conceal his own grin.

Grayson was completely uninterested in politics, but found Representative Vogel's presence with the Lance annoying. He had arrived from Tharkad 80-some standard days before, brimming with plans to forge an alliance with the nearby stellar empire of a troublesome Bandit King. None of the men or women in Carlyle's Commandos liked the stiff-necked and arrogant viscount, and the necessary formal etiquette of dealing with Katrina Steiner's personal emissary often failed to veil their black looks. Few in the unit agreed with Vogel's plan for pacifying this sector.

Fortunately, that had nothing to do with Grayson. He peered across Ari's shoulder at a console monitor. "So what's happening?"

"If you'd been here on time, you wouldn't have to ask. Your father is at the spaceport. The Mailai shuttle has entered atmosphere and should ground in...about ten minutes."

The monitor showed the spaceport's empty expanse of ferrocrete. The image moved in peculiar, swaying bobs and dips caused by the lurching of the transmitting camera, which rode on a BattleMech.

Grayson needed no explanation of the monitor scene. The camera transmitting that ponderously shifting image was mounted on the unit's lead BattleMech, a *Phoenix Hawk*, 45 tons of battle-scarred and endlessly patched and rewired walking combat machine. And Grayson's father was at the con.

Griffith frowned at the image. "I still wish he'd been able to take all four 'Mechs."

Riviera shrugged. "The *Shadow Hawk's* in the repair bay, and the Captain wanted the *Wasps* on patrol in town, just in case." He made a slight gesture toward Vogel still standing at a nearby console. "*That* one wasn't going to see his plan sabotaged for anything!"

Griffith watched the government representative with narrowed eyes. "Did we have to send both *Wasps* to patrol Sarghad?"

The tech made an unpleasant face. "Who knows? The natives're none too happy about this deal."

"I wouldn't be, either," Ari said. "The line between a legitimate interstellar empire and a pack of bandits can be rather fine at times. The Trells'll have to live with them when we're gone. They have a right to be nervous about old Hendrik's...intentions."

The meeting this hour would seal the hard-fought pact between the Lyran Commonwealth, which was using Carlyle's Commandos to garrison Trellwan, and the new and blossoming empire of Hendrick, the Bandit King of Oberon VI. It was unfortunate that the Trellwan natives had no love for Hendrik's legions, but that did not affect the secret negotiations one single jot.

A deep voice blared from the overhead speakers. "I'm in position."

Riviera leaned forward and touched a console plate. "Riviera, private channel. Your son's here, Captain."

Captain Durant Carlyle's voice emerged from the console's private line speaker, and it was still uncomfortably loud in the hush that had fallen across Combat Command.

"Oh, he is, is he? Tell him he's earned an extra five hours in the simulator this week."

Riviera's grinned as his eyes flicked back to Grayson. "Message received, Captain."

Grayson frowned, but said nothing. It rankled that he was as subject to discipline as any of the lance's ground troops, but he'd learned not to make a fuss about it. MechWarriors were, after all, the elite. They were like modern-day knights who held the course of battles in their charge, and he was in training to take his father's place at the con of a BattleMech one day. *That* BattleMech, in fact—the *Phoenix Hawk.*

Anyway, sim time wasn't so bad, as punishments went. Grayson not only enjoyed the simulator, he was good at it. It was the closest thing to piloting a 'Mech in combat without actually being there. The only problem was the five hours would come out of his free time with Mara. But then, he'd already said his goodbyes, hadn't he?

Funny how Mara had been so sure he wasn't going to be leaving Trellwan after all, but she'd just have to get over him, poor kid. The next stop for Carlyle's Commandos was the Commonwealth capital. Now *that* would be a piece of decent duty for a change! He'd never been to Tharkad, but the troopers who had been were more than willing to yarn about the place. Cool and rocky the world might be, but nightlife in the strip outside the capital's starport had a decidedly warm reputation. He was looking forward to *it.*

Grayson had become very tired of Trellwan, with its endless succession of long cycles of dark and light dragging through years so short that seasons came and went in mere days. "Ari, my father has this pact of his pretty well wrapped up, doesn't he? I mean...this means we'll be leaving Trellwan, right?"

"This meeting'll make it official, Master Carlyle, with nothing more to do but go through a ceremonial changing of the guard. It can't get any more wrapped up than that."

Grayson watched the monitor image. "But could anything go wrong?"

Ari shrugged expressively. "When dealing with Periphery bandits, keep one hand on your account files and the other over your eyes."

"My eyes?"

White teeth flashed in Aristobulus' dark face. "So they don't rob you blind."

"Better still, shoot the lot of 'em," Griffith said. He was obviously and gloweringly displeased at the situation.

"That would take a lot of shooting, my muscle-massed friend. And maybe with this treaty of Vogel's, we won't have to. Then you could spend your time shooting Kuritists instead."

"Ah, well, there is that! You have a way of finding the bright side of everything, Ari."

They laughed, but the Weapons Master was still troubled. Worry went with his title and rank, of course, but the situation was tricky. Consider, as Ari was fond of saying during his more pedantic moments, the Trell system lying at the ragged boundaries of the Lyran Commonwealth, an isolated sentinel against an unthinkably large and empty unknown. Inward was so-called civilized space, the Inner Sphere, where the Commonwealth of House Steiner and four other warring heirs to a sundered Star League jockeyed and scuffled for fleeting advantage of arms or diplomatic position.

At their backs lay a wilderness of unknown or long-forgotten worlds, the darkness of the void, the rabble of petty tyrants and Bandit Kings scratching ragtag empires from the ruin of a war-shattered glory-that-was.

Hendrik III was one such bandit king, and his raids for water and technological flotsam had savaged scores of worlds both in Lyran space and among the other systems of the neighboring Draconis Combine. It was those raids that had brought Carlyle's Commandos to Trellwan in the first place five standard years ago, and there'd been some sharp fights between bandit raiders and Trellwan's garrison in the meantime.

Somehow, between raids, Hendrik had forged a tottering alliance of a dozen bandit kings, an alliance that had made the man a power worthy of recognition...and caution. The coalition, which was centered at Hendrik's capital of Oberon VI, controlled the firepower and transport capacity of a minor House. That was something mere bandits could not be trusted with.

Olin Vogel had arrived from Tharkad with a plan, a plan smoothed over with the veneer of diplomatic tact. By treating Hendrik III as just another bandit king, making raid for raid and challenge for challenge, the Commonwealth would simply get more raids and challenges, requiring more garrisons strung along more dry and half-forgotten worlds clear across the Commonwealth's Periphery. But treat Hendrik as a House ruler, treat him as lord of an empire as legitimate as the Commonwealth by suggesting a mutual defense pact with generous territorial inducements and guarantees...that changed the situation, and for the better.

Vogel's maneuverings had taken the better part of two local years, which was almost three standard months. As neither side trusted the other, a local trading house, House Mailai, had been hired to ferry the negotiators between Trellwan and Oberon VI. Neither party was quite ready to allow heavily-armed DropShips from the other side to ground on home territory. Worse, Hendrik already had a treaty (or at least, a rough understanding) with the Draconis Combine, and the Combine was at war with the Lyran Commonwealth. Technically, this made Hendrik an enemy, though not a particularly active one. It had taken time, and that most fleeting of human commodities—trust—but at last a pact had been hammered out

With the Trellwan Concord, Hendrik would become the Lyran Commonwealth's partner and ally. It would now be Hendrik's JumpShips and 'Mech battalions guarding the Commonwealth's peripheral worlds in this sector, freeing up the Steiner garrisons there for duty in the Inner Sphere against the latest maneuverings of the Draconis Combine. This would discourage further bandit raids because the military arm of Oberon's minor empire was already stretched to the limit

In return, Hendrik would gain more worlds to rule, more resources to tap. Trellwan was one of those worlds, a minor pawn in a political game played out across light years. Trellwan's own native population was governed by a kinglet named Jeverid, a man with fealty sworn to House Steiner and the Commonwealth, but what of that? When worlds are traded, the wishes of individuals do not count for much. Besides, Trellwan would still technically belong to House Steiner. That was the agreement. The only difference was that the outpost's 'Mechs and troopers would now be Hendrik's instead of the Commonwealth's.

The negotiations for both sides had overcome severe obstacles to such an agreement. In fact, the worst problem had come when word of the secret negotiations had somehow leaked out to the Trells, who were the unsuspecting objects of the planned transfer of power and real estate. Captain Carlyle's staff had intended to keep the Trells ignorant of the deal until after it was achieved. After all, nothing would change for them. One garrison lance at the Castle was pretty much the same as any other. But Hendrik had raided Trellwan in the past, and the Concord might be interpreted badly by Jeverid and the more short-sighted of his people if they got wind of it too soon.

Carlyle's advisors had been correct. When news of the impending agreement reached the people of Sarghad, at the base of the mountain where the Castle stood guard, city-wide riots had broken out, and the fires had turned that hot Firstnight to day. The lance's two light 'Mechs had been tied down with patrol duty in the city almost constantly since.

House Security still hadn't been able to track down the source of that leak. It boded ill for the future, and added to Sergeant Griffith's worries.

"Odd," Riviera said, as he snapped a toggle switch back and forth. "We've lost some security cameras."

"Eh? Where?"

"Repair bay. I'm checking." He touched his right hand fingers to his ear, listening to the tiny implanted speaker there. "Officer of the Watch reports Maintenance shut those cameras down a few minutes ago. Something about a fault in the circuitry."

Griffith looked worried. "I don't like it."

"You want the Captain?" Riviera reached for the communicator panel again.

The Sergeant glanced at the monitor, where the trails of fusion flame left by the descending DropShip were illuminating the sky. "No, don't jostle him. Put out a warning to all watchstations. Internal security, yellow alert."

Grayson wondered how that would help. All stations were already on alert, watching the descent of the Mailai DropShip.

On their monitors, they could see the DropShip's stubby hydraulic legs unfold as panels blossomed open across its broad base. In a final gush of light and noise, it settled to the scorch-blackened ferrocrete 500 meters from Carlyle's position. The vessel was roughly egg-shaped and very old.

Repeated patchings and dabs of brown sealant marred its once sleek surface, and the blue X-and-circle crest of Mailai House was the only bright note on a hull faded and blistered from countless lifts and groundings.

Carlyle's voice came over the commlink. "I've got its landing ID beacon. She checks out as the Mailai freighter."

The shakiest part of the balance of trust between the two new allies was in allowing DropShips to land on home ground. Because the vessels of the major houses could mount formidable armament, could carry battalions of BattleMechs and small armies of troops and heavy combat vehicles, that trust had not been easily forged. There were weapons trained on the grounded vessel now, of course, the laser turrets and heavy missile batteries that ringed the spaceport and served as the station's inner line of defense. Nevertheless, the base defenders let out a collective sigh of relief at the sight of Mailai's newly-painted crest on the ship's curved hull plates, and at the computer-coded twitter off the ship's ID beacon. There were beam turrets nestled in the vessel's pitted armor, but not the heavy armament of a major House warship. It was only a freighter, aged, battered, and bearing the representatives of House Steiner's newest ally.

Grayson and the members of the lance staff watched as their captain's *Phoenix Hawk* began striding across the ferrocrete toward the ship that loomed above it

In the repair bay, the traitor glanced over the top of the partly disassembled console where he worked and saw the watch officer with his feet still propped up, his back toward the astech.

The monitor showed the spaceport lights, the ponderous side-to-side motion of a heavy 'Mech lurching across the pavement, the settling bulk of the grounding DropShip on pillars of white light.

The Trell checked his wristcomp, and watched the last few seconds count down to zero.

The moment for action had come.

CHAPTER 3

The traitor pulled a small, back-portable generator from his shoulder bag. Of itself, the device was innocent enough. Astechs often carried generators with them for tasks requiring light and power in tight spaces. He didn't put it on because the harness had been removed, but fastened it instead to his tool belt so that it hung free at his right hip. One end of a power feed snapped into a bayonet socket. The feed's other end clicked home at the base of a slender cylinder. A twist of the cylinder snapped the blade open and locked it down.

The Trell stood slowly, his eyes on the back of the watch officer's neck. Blade in his right hand, he groped across his body for the power switch with his free hand.

Sensing something wrong, some motion at his back, the watch officer half-turned, then whirled to his feet at the sight of the astech and his blade coming at him. As the officer's chair toppled noisily, the traitor's hand found the power switch for his lead-gray blade, and a dry hum filled the narrow room.

Vibroblades are horribly efficient for close-in fighting. Power from the backpack is transformed to ultrasonics that vibrate the paracarballoy blade faster than the eye can see. In seconds, friction turns the vibrating blade white-hot, able to slice tempered steel as though it were butter.

The officer fumbled at his holster for the pistol, but collided with the console at his back before he could free the gun and bring it up.

The Trell's humming blade slashed out and down, shearing through gunmetal, flesh, and bone. The officer shrieked, clenched bloodied fingers to his chest, then stumbled backward into the console again. The traitor advanced, the vibroblade slashing out and down once more to brutally silence a final scream.

The traitor switched off the vibroblade, looped its power feed, and tucked the weapon into an insulated belt scabbard, careful not to touch the hot blade. With rapid and precise movements, he examined the instrument console, finding at last a single white button, which he stabbed down and held.

From far off and above came the hollow grinding of machinery. Across the repair bay, on the other side of the beached-whale shape of the disabled 'Mech, the metal wall began to rumble open, splitting along a rivet-pocked seam. On the console, a red warning light flashed on and off, and a woman's voice began from somewhere, "*Warning. Warning. Security breach in repair bay. Exterior wall now open. Warning—*"

Sand whirled through the wall opening, blown in by a chill, sub-zero wind. The traitor narrowed his eyes, detecting a flicker of movement outside, then gliding shapes among the shadows. He released the switch, stepped across the gore-splattered body of the watch officer, and clattered his way down the steps to the main deck.

The tech who had been at work on the 'Mech below was running for the main passageway when something caught him in the small of the back, lifted him, and hurled him sprawling against the wall. Then, one of the astechs on the 'Mech's chest screamed and toppled five meters to the deck, while the other tried to scramble to safety behind an open access plate. Next came the sharp hiss of silenced gunfire, the jarring concussion of a hurled grenade. A scream rose up from somewhere, but was mercifully cut short by a second blast and the chattered hiss of sound-suppressed automatic fire.

By now, men in neat gray and blue uniforms had burst through a door at the far end of the repair bay, guns yammering. One black-garbed attacker lurched backward as another hurled something that bobbed across the deck. There followed a flash and a stunning blow that whipped the traitor's coveralls against his legs. The next moment, those neat gray uniforms ceased to exist, save as bloodied shreds and tatters.

The Trell stepped off the ladder and felt the blade at his throat before he sensed the man behind it. "Hunter!" he choked out "Hunter!" The attacker's grip loosened.

"You're Stefan?" The voice was curiously level.

The Trell nodded, rubbing at his throat. Squads of attackers dressed in close-fitting black garb raced past. One of them stopped before Stefan, his face totally obscured by featureless black plastic, a silenced submachine gun in his gloved fist. The black canvas bag across his back bulged with menace.

"You're the traitor?"

The Trell nodded again, uncertainly. The attacker's accent was foreign and hard to follow, his manner unexpectedly harsh.

"Come."

In the passageway, there were only twisted, blood-soaked bodies and the silent forms of black-garbed attackers. The one Stefan knew must be the leader gave nearly silent commands and signals to crouching groups of commandos, sending them off down branching corridors with lethal efficiency.

"Put this on." The leader handed Stefan a lightweight breathing mask from a pouch. It was even harder to see the black shadows in the pale amber tint of the mask's amplifier goggles. Blood, he saw, became a slick and lustrous black through the goggles, and the passageway took on an eerie quality in the ghostly light. "The command center. Lead us."

Stefan nodded. "Two levels up. This way!"

The attack was heralded by the rasp of an alarm klaxon and the shuffle of boots across bare tile floors as squads of men raced to their positions. From above, the woman's voice continued the patient announcement, *"Alert, alert. Security penetration in sectors five and six."*

"I've lost the repair bay," Riviera said. "Commlink's dead."

Griffith's scowl deepened, twisting the scar on his face as his jaw clenched, then relaxed. "Tell the Captain. Ari, let me have your chair."

Ari stood up, and Griffith slipped into his vacant chair beside Riviera.

Grayson pulled another chair from a nearby console and pushed in next to the Weapons Master. "Griff, who is it? Why are they attacking us?"

"I don't know, lad, though my first guess is the Trells. Riviera, put the garrison on full alert. Then patch me to the patrol monitors. I want to try and raise the patrol in town."

Grayson felt a numbing confusion. Certainly, the Trells had not been happy when news of the coming treaty with Oberon had leaked out, but he found it hard to believe they were storming up from the Castle's repair bay. How had they broken in? Those vast, sliding doors were proof against the hammerings of an 80-ton 'Mech. Nothing short of a small tactical nuke— long forbidden by treaty and practicality—could breach them.

He fixed his eyes on the image still being transmitted from his father's *Phoenix Hawk.* The DropShip was so close now that it filled the entire screen with black metal, though the ranging data across the bottom of the screen indicated the ship was still 90 meters away. Then he saw a port opening near the base, spilling harsh light across the ferrocrete paving.

"Griff!" The cry was torn from Grayson's throat. A ramp had dropped from the brilliantly lit opening, and soldiers were pouring out of it. The screen flared white, and the open commlink spat static as a high-energy beam swept across the 'Mech's antennae.

"Base! I'm under attack!" Captain Carlyle's words were static-blasted and harsh. "Particle beam from a turret on the ship!"

The computer readout on a nearby monitor shifted and flickered, showing a sudden surge of power within the *Phoenix Hawk,* rapid movement, a double blast from the machine's powerful, arm-mounted lasers. The 'Mech's internal heat rose four degrees in as many seconds.

The Captain shifted, blurring screen images. It was difficult to follow what was happening on the monitors. Grayson couldn't really *see* anything but gyrating snatches of the port structures and the pulsing flash of detonations. The computer readout alongside the image monitor told more of the story to those, like Grayson, trained to read it

Carlyle's *Phoenix Hawk* was a middleweight as Battle-Mechs go, and shared the humanoid pattern of most 'Mechs. It mounted a massive laser weapon in its right hand. The 'Mech also mounted smaller lasers and antipersonnel machine guns in the extended duralloy vambraces of each forearm. The readouts showed those weapons systems powered up and swinging into line, showed turrets on the grounded freighter bracketed by crosshairs and the steady flicker of range and target acquisition data.

The left arm laser beamed invisible, coherent light across the DropShip's lower hull plates and baffles, and a weapons turret fragmented in flame and hurtling chunks of metal.

"Acknowledged, Captain." Griffith's voice was steady, but beads of perspiration had broken out along his eyebrows and mustache. He paused to read a printed message flickering across one of the monitor screens. "Security Chief Xiang's on his way from our shuttle. He'll be in position to support you in two minutes!"

There was no answer as another particle beam caught the *Phoenix Hawk*, staggering the big machine and threatening to melt through already smoldering armor. Carlyle's 'Mech whirled, dissipating the killer beam, then fired a twin laser burst, tracking the enemy cannon by its infrared glow. There was a savage blast as white-hot, multi-ton fragments rained across the landing area.

Another man joined the knot of staff personnel at the console. Ernest Hauptman was the pilot of the lance's number two machine. He wore his lieutenant's blue-rimmed, gray dress uniform, with worry hung from his shoulders like a cape. Normally, he would be piloting the 55-ton *Shadow Hawk* that now lay helpless in the repair bay. At the moment, his duty station was in Combat Command, and he didn't like that at all.

"Griff, we got problems," Hauptman said. "The intruders are up to the deck below. Looks like they're making a try for Combat Command."

"Who are they, Lieutenant? Trells?"

The big man shook his head. "Can't tell. They're in combat sneak-suits. Can't get a better look until we take one."

"Then let's do it." Griffin stood, then looked over at Grayson. "Son, we'd best get you to—"

"No, Griff! Not now!" Grayson still sat before the monitor. The screen showed little more than wild zigzags of movement punctuated by the white flare of exploding missiles and stabbing beams.

"Riviera, I've got to go," the Weapons Master said tersely. "You'll get him out if it gets tight?"

"Right, Griff. We'll be okay. I can use him here on the commlink."

"Right."

Grayson turned back to the monitor as Hauptman and Griffin hurried away. The battle at the landing port was developing with savage speed. He wanted to do something, to help, but there was nothing to do but watch.

The *Phoenix Hawk* was running, taking five-meter strides that echoed thunder above the blast and crash of exploding shells. Grayson thought about how dependent a pilot was on his 'Mech's mobility on the battlefield. Even more than on his armor, for the pilot's commands to his gigantic steed could not be anticipated by fire control computers. But in a close-range battle such as this one, fire control could be of the point-in-that-direction-and-fire variety and still score hits.

A sound like a tornado's roar and light too bright to bear burst from the monitor. Carlyle's *'Hawk* was hit hard by a medium-range missile that fireballed across the right upper rear of its body and smashed the 'Mech into the ferrocrete.

"Dad!"

Grayson's involuntary scream into an open mike brought Riviera's hand down on his shoulder. "Don't clog the commlink, young sir. It can't help him."

"S-Sorry." Grayson struggled for control. For him, battle had never been so gut-wrenchingly personal. "He's hit!"

The image monitor showed the pavement swinging down and away as the 'Mech staggered back to its feet. Smoke swirled across the scene. By the unsteady light of a fire burning somewhere near, Grayson could make out the flitting shapes of troops running from shadow to shadow.

"I'm okay, son." Carlyle's voice over the commlink was steady, though Grayson heard the tightness of battle strain edging the words. "Is Griff there?"

"Griff's helping coordinate the defense," Riviera cut in. "We're being attacked here, too."

"Damn. We've been had."

"Who is it, Dad?"

The monitor image swooped, dipped, and spun. They heard the staccato rattle of the 'Hawk's heavy machine guns blazing away at half-screen targets in the smoke. Tracers floated lazily across the screen as they tracked a racing vehicle that skimmed just above the ferrocrete on howling fans. A light autofire cannon stuttered and winked in reply from the darkness.

The hovercraft vanished in smoke and shadow. "I don't know, Gray," his father replied at last. "They're not traders, though, that's for damn sure!"

"Hendrik's pirates?" Riviera said.

"I don't know. Could be. But why? By all the gods of space, why?"

Grayson looked across the room at Vogel. The Commonwealth representative was rooted to a monitor console, white-faced and stricken. The alliance with Hendrik had been *his* idea.

Riviera followed Grayson's gaze. "He's watching his career die on that screen," he said, and Grayson nodded. The man was clenching and unclenching his hands, which gave them the appearance of being gripped by some dreadful spasm.

There was a searing flash and a blast that stunned the listeners in Command Control. The *Phoenix Hawk* was down again, with a half-dozen flashing red indicators clamoring for attention. On the screen, Grayson could make out twisted metal, paint-charred and still smoldering. It took him dazed seconds to recognize in the debris half of the *Hawk*'s right arm, its steel fingers still closed across the grip of the heavy laser, now lying on the pavement in blasted ruin.

"Sergeant?" Carlyle's voice was tight now, almost inaudible across the blast of battle static.

"Sir! Are you all right?"

"Gyros hit...port servos out...having trouble stabilizing. Looks like the right arm and main gun are gone too. I'm...hit pretty bad..."

Riviera was studying another monitor. "Hang on, Captain! Xiang's on his way with the security patrol! They'll be close enough to support you in a few seconds!"

The 'Hawk was on its feet again, and telemetry readouts showed it was firing into the smoky darkness as rapidly as the single remaining heavy weapon could be recharged, stabbing invisible beams of laser light at half-glimpsed targets whenever the 'Mech's computer trackers could pick them up from IR scans. An infrared mosaic overlaid the visible light image, picking out running figures in light blue, the white-hot geysers of vehicle engines, the towering mountain of yellow heat that was the grounded DropShip a few hundred meters away. Much of the enemy fire was coming from the freighter, which was obviously much better armed than any freighter had a right to be. Carlyle had blasted at least five turrets that he could identify, and the returning fire had scarcely slackened at all. It appeared that beam weapons had been temporarily mounted in ports cut right into the hull metal.

"What's...status...in the base?" Carlyle's words came in grunts now as he gasped for air. The computer readout showed the cabin temperature was climbing steadily, blasted higher by each maneuver, by each discharged weapon and hit.

"Inside job, I think, Captain. Someone disabled some of our security cameras and opened the repair bay outer lock. The fight's pretty hot down there."

"Hauptman?"

"With Griffith, fighting the intruders."

"Tell him...he's in command. Get the lance...out of there. We...can't...stay...Trellwan any longer..."

"Dad! Hang on! Xiang's almost there!"

"I see him. His troops are spreading out across the tarmac. I..."

There was a long silence. "Captain!" Riviera shouted.

"Son of a bitch..." The words were spoken quietly, almost reverently. The image monitor was focused now on the base of the grounded freighter, at the gaping maw of an open hatch with a heavy black ramp sliding to the scarred ferrocrete. The IR overlay gave the scene a glistening, unreal quality, colored harshly where no color would normally be visible.

Something was lurching down the ramp, coal-black against the yellow glow of the freighter's hull. The imaging camera zoomed in, resolving the silhouette into gray metal and glistening joints. Targeting crosshairs snapped on, with four beads of light tracking in to meet in a pulse of light at the bullseye center. Laser scan readouts flickered on one side, showing range, height, mass, and bearing. Grayson didn't need the computer ID to tell him what he was seeing. It was a 'Mech, the kind known as a *Marauder.*

The *Marauder* did not share the humanoid appearance of most BattleMechs. Instead, its 75 tons of arms and armor were molded into a crablike body mounted on a pair of oversized legs that knifed back and down in a forward-leaning, digitigrade stance.

The machine was old, patched and etched with the signs of frequent repairs and replacements. The black and gray paint pattern was broken in places by brown rust and old battle scars. A pair of arms hung suspended from just forward of the leg joints, each mounting a heavy particle cannon and a laser in over-under mounts where hands and forearms might be expected in a living being. The massive tube of a 120mm rapid-fire autocannon balanced above the body, completing the battle machine's armament.

The *Phoenix Hawk* was 30 tons lighter, normally far more maneuverable, but still badly outclassed by the bigger machine in any 'Mech-to-'Mech slugmatch. And the '*Hawk* was already crippled...

"Dad! Do you see its insignia?"

"I see it" The image had picked up the shine of fresh paint against the scarred surface of the enemy 'Mech's left leg, a stylized animal's eye colored scarlet and black, with slit pupil and menacing brow.

It was the crest insignia of Hendrik III, King of Oberon, the bandit warlord who was supposed to sign the Trellwan pact. Behind the first enemy 'Mech, the shadowed shape of a second, smaller 'Mech appeared, followed by a third. Grayson wasn't certain, but he thought one of those shapes was a *Stinger,* the other a *Locust*—both 20-ton 'Mechs more suited to scouting or fighting infantry than tangling with heavy Mechs.

But even light scouts could gang up on a solitary *Phoenix Hawk,* especially when the *'Hawk* was barely able to stand or fire. Autocannon fire winked from the *Marauder,* and explosions stitched across the savaged *'Hawk*'s torso.

"Betrayed!" Riviera said, and his open palm smashed at the console table. "Those filthy, backstabbing..."

"I guess...that settles who's...behind this..." Carlyle said. "But why...would they attack...now?"

The *'Hawk* opened fire with its solitary laser, then spun, dodging. A tracery of twisting contrails arced through the night sky from the DropShip, short-range missiles seeking the solitary target. The image jarred and went white as at least one of the warheads struck home.

Half the readout monitor was blinking red now. The *'Hawk*'s internal circuits had been savaged by a spray of molten steel. Carlyle was having trouble keeping his 'Mech upright. The shriek of protesting servomotors keened across the audio pickup.

"*OPERATOR WARNING! HEAT CRITICAL. SUGGEST IMME-DIATE SHUTDOWN.*" The warning pulsed in crimson light across the top of the screen, and Grayson could hear the harsh bray of an onboard klaxon.

The pattern of telltale lights shifted. Carlyle had slapped his override, was dragging the 'Mech's left arm up to bear on the *Marauder.*

"Boss!" Riviera shouted into the com mike. "Eject!"

The crosshairs centered on the looming *Marauder,* and points of light tracked inward along the line to merge at target center.

"You don't have the power!" Riviera's yell was shrill.

Grayson felt a sick burning rise in his throat.

The events of the next few moments occurred in rapid-fire succession, but to Grayson, they seemed to crawl through a small eternity. The *Marauder* rushed forward, taking the *'Hawk*'s fire across its lower torso in a flare of light and heat that swamped the IR scanners and left the image broken in a dazzle of computer-enhanced color.

"Got him!" someone at another console shouted. There was a ragged cheer that faltered as the monitor image shifted up, up, to show the *Marauder* still intact and looming above the *Phoenix Hawk,* which lay helplessly on its back. Then, one massive forearm descended like an avalanche of steel. The monitor flickered to static-chopped black before eyes or minds could sort out that pell-mell confusion of images.

An animal sound caught and broke in Grayson's throat as he came to his feet, his palms grasping at the monitor frame. "No!" he screamed. *"NO!"*

Riviera's voice, meticulous in its control, rose above the hush of a room suddenly gone silent. "PXH-One, PXH-One, this is Control. Respond if you can. Over."

There was no answer, and the silence grew deeper. Grayson's eyes were burning, and he realized his face was wet with tears.

His father was dead.

CHAPTER 4

"PXH, PXH..." Riviera's voice cracked. "Boss, are you there?"

"Control, this is Xiang." The words were blurred by static and the thunder of continuing battle explosions. "The Skipper's had it. Nothing we can do. Those light 'Mechs are closing on us. We're pulling back."

The silence in Control dragged for several long seconds. Then Riviera leaned over the mike. "Okay, Rama. Fall back on the Castle. We're under heavy attack here."

"We'll try, Control, but they're between us and the Castle."

"Damn!" Riviera muttered. "Okay, fall back to the shuttle. Try to form a perimeter. I'll alert the *Wasp*s."

A hand fell on Grayson's shoulder. He shrugged it away, looked up when it fell on him again.

Griffith's face was streaked with smoke and sweat, his uniform crumpled. The hand gripping the Gunther MP-20 was dripping blood from a nasty gash.

"We've got to go, Gray. Quickly."

"He's...dead." Shock had left Grayson feeling cold and dazed, with a hollow in the pit of his stomach.

"I know. Come on."

Riviera said, "Where's the lieutenant? The...the Captain said he was to take charge, pull us off-world."

Griffith jerked his bullet head past his shoulder. "Downstairs. We're holding, I think, but there's too many of 'em."

Griffith turned and raised his voice to address the entire control room. "All right, listen up! We're going to move out down Corridor A to the vehicle bay. Lieutenant Hauptman is holding a perimeter for us there. We'll be able to board HVTs and make it to the shuttle from there!"

"What about our families?" The lone voice cracked on the question that was reflected in the eyes of many of the technicians and soldiers around the room. Wherever stationed, Carlyle's Commandos carried with it a small army of support and technical people, including the wives, husbands, and children of many of the unit's members. Most of them were also members of the Commandos' support company, serving as medics, cooks, maintenance personnel, orderlies, or tutors for the children.

"Already on their way," Griffith said. "Don't worry. We won't leave anyone behind. The Commandos take care of their own!"

There was a muffled cheer, then men and women began switching off their monitors and comgear as they filed toward the door.

Vogel stepped up beside Griffith. "Warrant, I will want a special escort and a hovercraft for myself, at once."

"Yes, sir, we'll take care of you. You'll come with the rest of us. I don't have the men for a special—"

"I expect my orders to be obeyed, Mister!" Vogel then pointed out a group of troopers standing awkwardly by the door, TK assault rifles in their hands. Their faces were grease-smeared and hollow-eyed beneath their large, plastic-visored battle helmets. "Those five. They'll do."

"They're with me, my Lord. They'll protect all of us on the way to the vehicle bay."

"Now listen here—"

The Gunther machine pistol came up, small and wicked-looking in Griffith's blood-streaked paw. "My Lord, *shut the hell up!* And get in line with the rest of them! *Move!*"

The party passed into the corridor, the uneven echoes of their running feet filling the passageway with noise. The hallway took several turns past now-abandoned and debris-strewn rooms, twisted down stairs to the bay level two floors below, and angled across toward the vehicle bay.

Grayson stayed by Griffith's side in the rear of the column, with the five young troopers. Vogel, he saw, was with Riviera and Ari up near the head of the group, but scowling at his offended dignity.

That'll mean trouble for Griff, Grayson thought. *Trouble for all of us.* His mind spun back to the explosion that had taken his father. *How and why had it happened?* The thought of his father's BattleMech lying in a twisted ruin out on the spaceport apron, a tomb for whatever remained of Durant Carlyle's body, tore at his mind. He suddenly began remembering odd little moments.

—His father presenting him with apprenticeship orders when he was ten and the surge of still-remembered pride.—

—His father's ashen face at his mother's funeral just before they'd come to Trellwan five years ago.—

—His father discussing Grayson's education schedule with Ari and Griff in the officer's lounge here in the Castle just after they'd arrived.—

Durant Carlyle had been a permanent, unchanging fixture in Grayson's life. Though always busy with the never-ending business of outfitting, supplying, and leading a House Steiner BattleMech lance, the smile and the steady warmth in those eyes had always been there for his son.

Now they were no more. Grayson had taken them for granted, and their loss tore a wound so deep and so telling that he could not yet feel it. He could only repeat inwardly, numbly, *"Dad..."*

The vehicle bay was crowded with men, women, and children waiting to board the HVTs, transport hovercraft capable of carrying 25 or 30 people at a time. The plenum chamber fans were already turning, filling the room with the high, warbling hum of many engines.

A sergeant saluted Griffith as they entered the room. "We've set scouts out down the road. It appears clear."

"IR and motion scans?"

"All clear, Weapons Master."

"Good. Maybe they didn't expect to be this successful. The road to the port may not be covered yet. But I want the convoy covered by every HVWC we have."

The weapons carriers were already moving, small hovercraft mounting missile launchers or beam weapons and carrying five or six soldiers each. The keening of hovercraft engines rose in pitch, and the first machines skimmed off their heavy rubber skirts and drifted through the open doors into the cold darkness outside.

Vogel was there. He seemed to have lost some of his bluster, but not his scowl. "I've had enough of this foolishness, Weapons Master. I want a hovercraft, a pilot, and a guard. And I want them *now*."

Griffith waved him aside with the machine pistol, then called out "Brookes! Sergeant Brookes! Are you ready to move?"

A harried, red-haired man looked up from his humming scout. It was a tiny hovercraft, a four-seater. A pair of soldiers were wrestling a lightweight laser onto an aft-deck pintle mount. "Yeah, Griff! Any time!"

"Take Master Carlyle with you."

The realization that Griffith was sending him on ahead cut through Grayson's numbness. "Griff, no! I—"

"Go on, lad. I'll catch up with you later. Quickly now!"

Grayson didn't hear Griffith's answer. The Weapons Master had turned away from him and was facing Vogel, speaking quietly. Vogel's face was turning red.

"C'mon, Master Carlyle. Old Hattie here'll have us back t' the shuttle at light speed. Here. You'll be wanting these." He handed Grayson a hooded, cold weather jacket and goggles. The scout had an open well deck, and a high-speed run would be dangerously cold in this weather.

The sharp *crack* of an ear-stunning detonation smacked across the vehicle bay, and smoke boiled from the door across the room. Grayson whirled, wide-eyed. Vogel was lying on his face, with Griffith crouched above him. The five soldiers were fanning out toward the smoking door.

Just then, several black-clad figures burst through the smoke, spewing the savage white bursts of automatic weapons fire. Griffith was on one knee now, the Gunther balanced in a classic one-hand brace right out of the BattleMech Manual. He fired in short, precise bursts, centering each burst on an attacker's chest

More attackers swarmed through the door. Grayson realized with dull shock that each wore a heavy mask, the goggles insect-like in the bay's dim red lighting. They plunged into the room in headlong dives that brought them rolling up to one shoulder, subguns chattering in sharp, short bursts before the milling crowd of techs and staff personnel could respond. Grayson saw Riviera sagging back against the skirt of an idling hovercraft, tiny scarlet explosions blossoming across his torso from right thigh to left shoulder.

One of the soldiers beside the weapons master pitched back, his face a streaming mask of red. Two more crumpled where they stood, and the two survivors turned and ran for the nearest hovercraft

"Griff!" Grayson screamed. His fingers were on a handhold on the hoverscout's side. "Come on!"

"Let's go, son!" Brooke laid a hand on Grayson's shoulder, urgency in his voice. "We've got to leave!"

Grayson shook free of the hand and dashed back toward Griffith. As long as he had known his father, he had also known Kai Griffith, with whom he had probably spent more time from day to day.

"Grayson! Come back!" Sergeant Brooke was close behind. Grayson dodged in front of a hover transport that was just rising from the ferrocrete, its skirts rattling in the overpressure of screaming fans. Air whipped Grayson's pants against his legs, and the keening fans drowned out the rattle of small arms fire from across the Bay. Black figures continued to pour from the passageway door.

Grayson spotted a TK rifle lying on the ferrocrete, close by the outflung hand of the soldier who had been carrying it. He had never fired one in combat, but he'd practiced with them often enough on the firing range under Griff's sharp eye and tongue. He checked the seating of the 80-round magazine in its slot in the stock behind the trigger hand grip, checked that the safety was off, leveled the barrel at the oncoming black figures, and squeezed the trigger.

TKs fired caseless, 3mm slivers of soft metal and high-velocity explosives that ballooned on impact into miniature, tissue-destroying suns. Almost noiseless, almost recoilless, and on full auto, it hacked through the enemy ranks like an HP laser through soft tin. Grayson hosed the weapon's flare across the attackers, saw them pitch back into the yawning doorway or forward into untidy heaps on the ferrocrete.

His finger slipped from the trigger, and the gun snapped upright. Added now to the bewildered, conflicting emotions Grayson was feeling was the realization he had just killed for the first time.

Griffith turned and seemed to see Grayson for the first time. "No, son! Go—"

As he spoke, a stream of bullets caught the bald weapons master in his side and from behind, spinning him around and slapping him onto the pavement in a sprawl of arms and legs.

"*Griff!*" Grayson screamed.

There was a soft, plopping sound, and clouds of white smoke geysered from exploding gas grenades. Grayson tasted the numbing tang of paralytic gas in his throat, choked on the acrid fumes.

The next thing he knew, he was lying on the ferrocrete deck of the vehicle bay, his muscles locked in a rigor that could not be broken. He could scarcely see now, though the departing whine of the hovercraft convoy was audible. Around him, he heard the coughs and hoarse yells coming from people in the hovercraft that had not made it away in time, as masked troopers swarmed aboard and cuffed gasping prisoners into submission. Then Grayson saw nothing more.

He decided later that he must have lost consciousness. When he opened his eyes, the air was clearer, and he could move again. The muscles in his legs and arms trembled uncontrollably, though, and Grayson felt so weak he could scarcely lift his head from the pavement.

Black uniforms moved among the few remaining hovercraft, herding small parties of prisoners toward the door to the main passageway. Cold air was pouring in from the open Bay doors, and as he gulped it down, Grayson's mind and vision cleared, and the muscle spasms eased. He pulled himself upright.

Kai Griffith was nearby, propped against a grounded hovercraft. The weapons tech appeared to be alive, though his uniform was drenched with blood and his skin paler than that of a native Trell. His chest was moving in a short, jerky rhythm, his breathing shallow and rapid. It took a moment for the realization to sink in. Griff was alive!

He also became aware of one of the attackers in particular, a tall man all in black, his face masked by a metal sensor mask. Grayson did not need to see the silver starburst at his throat to know this was the warleader of the enemy assault force. The man was attended by a small band of sneak-suited soldiers, and he seemed to be interrogating the ragged handful of prisoners. A pair of attackers hauled one prisoner to his feet, thrusting him before the warleader.

When the man said, "I am Viscount Olin Vogel," Grayson started. The prisoner was dirty, disheveled, and unrecognizable. His hands were tied behind him, and he was not wearing a cloak or other finery. "I am a Commonwealth representative, and as such, expect to be ransomed. I'm sure my principals will make a generous offer for my exchange."

The warleader paused, as if considering, though it was impossible to read expression through his blank sensor mask. It was common practice for important prisoners to be ransomed. The custom was lucrative, and prevented the out-of-hand slaughter of captured nobles or wealthy businessmen.

"I have been in close communication with your king," Vogel continued. "He will be delighted to see me. In fact—"

The warleader drew a machine pistol from the holster slung low on his hip, held it to Vogel's chest, and pulled the trigger. There was a ragged burst, and the man snapped backward in a spray of blood. Through ringing ears, Grayson heard the *thud* of the body and a last, strangled sound from Vogel. The man's feet scraped aimlessly at the pavement for a moment, then jerked and were still.

The sight of the casually murdered Vogel froze Grayson as effectively as had the paralytic gas. Why had the warleader done that? Vogel would have been worth millions to this pirate...

A hand grasped his forearm, hauling him up off the pavement, setting him on unsteady feet. Grayson stared into the smooth metal of the warleader's mask.

"That's the captain's kid," someone said. Grayson's eyes shifted. It was the astech speaking—Stefan was his name. Grayson recognized him despite the grotesque mask the man wore. He'd seen him about the Castle after the latest batch of astech recruits had arrived from Sarghad.

So, this was the betrayer, the traitor. An astech, one of the workers inside the Castle, had opened the repair bay gates and let the attackers in. And they would be in league with the 'Mechs that had inexplicably descended from the freighter DropShip. All of it had been part of some monstrous plot to take the Castle, destroy Carlyle's Commandos, and kill his father.

The warleader's machine pistol was coming up, and Grayson thought they were going to murder him as well. His foot lashed back, crumpling the kneecap of the man holding him and breaking his captor's grip. Then he lashed out again, striking for the warleader's face. The shock as his opponent blocked the kick with a down-stabbing fist nearly knocked Grayson off his feet. He whirled and lunged close inside the man's reach, using his hands to smash and grab at the helmet's blank visor.

His opponent yelled as connections broke free with a soft, sucking sound, and the faceplate hinged up and back from the chin and came away in Grayson's hand. The inner surface of that plate was lined with receptors and a high-tech enhancer that projected images directly onto the wearer's retinas. For an instant, Grayson saw an angry, black-bearded face, whose features were vaguely familiar and whose eyes seemed to promise sudden death.

A blow to Grayson's chest sent him staggering back against the ruined console, where the warleader held him with the muzzle of his pistol held steady and level one meter from Grayson's left eye.

"Singh! You animal!"

The shout had come from Grayson's right. Grayson turned, saw horror and anger and a death's-edge determination burned into Griffith's face five meters away. The weapons master was supporting himself on one blood-smeared arm, was holding a small automatic pistol in the other.

The warleader's gun fired first, three quick shots that split Griffith's straining face and opened new rivers of blood from the Weapons Master's throat and gaping mouth.

Grayson screamed mindlessly and threw himself forward. The warleader swung back to cover him, the machine pistol centimeters from his head. Grayson lurched to the right as the weapon struck him with a hammer blow of thunder and white pain. His body hit the floor an instant later.

CHAPTER 5

Grayson was aware of sound before he felt the pain. There was a low and steady roaring in his ears, like surf against a rocky coast, but with a steady, rhythmic pulse that was maddening until he recognized it as the beat of his own heart. Somehow, though, the pain had lost its knife's edge. He hurt, but not as much. Not as much as what? He struggled with the idea, a vague sense of passing time, of horror and wrenching loss, but could not remember.

The pain receded somewhat. Encouraged, Grayson opened his eyes. He winced at the sudden glare, but managed to get them open and carefully survey his surroundings. He did not recognize the room. Bare plaster walls with chipped patches high up by the wood-beamed ceiling were close around his bed. A table, a clothes chest, chairs, and a mirror completed the list of furnishings. A narrow window let him see a patch of orange sky beyond dust motes dancing in a shaft of bloody light.

Light. It must be...daylight! The long night was over!

He sat up suddenly, then sagged back onto the bed, hands clasping his dizzy, pain-wracked head. His head was wrapped in bandages, he found. Someone had carefully tended what was obviously a fairly serious head wound.

A door opened somewhere behind him, and Grayson sensed someone enter the room. "So, awake at last! I thought I heard you yell."

Grayson didn't remember yelling, but decided anything was possible with his head feeling as it did. He turned slightly, and focused on the speaker.

The man was a young Trell, somewhat shorter than Grayson's lanky stature, and stockier, with wide, stubby-fingered hands stained with grease. He had the pale skin of a native, which looked even paler next to the unruly black hair and deep, dark eyes. He wore a casual, knee-length tunic, white except for a triangular shoulder panel that caught the red light in shifting patterns of warm color.

Grayson's eyes went back to the Trell's face. Recognition clicked somewhere behind the ache in his skull. "I know you! Ah...Claydon, isn't it? Right! Senior Astech Claydon. You were on Riviera's team!"

Claydon inclined his head with a wry smile. "At your service, Lord, though I can hardly admit to the title anymore. That's not exactly healthy now."

"Not...what? Why?"

Claydon jerked a thumb over his shoulder toward the window. "It's not safe to admit to being one of the off-worlders' pets. Not any longer."

Grayson wrestled with that concept for a while, then let it go. He decided to concentrate on more immediate questions. "Where am I?"

"My father's house, of course. I brought you here after the attack."

"Your...father?"

"Yes. Berenir is his name. He's a merchant. He's done business with you folks. Doesn't share the local prejudice against you off-worlders. He's the one who got a doctor to come in and tend your wound."

Grayson touched his bandaged head. "Then I have you and your father to thank for saving me."

Claydon grimaced. "You'll be able to show your thanks by getting well and out of this house and away from here. If the neighbors knew we had *you* here..."

"What makes me so unpopular all of a sudden?"

"All of a sudden? What have you been using for eyes, Lord?"

Grayson ignored the bitterness in Claydon's voice. "Is it because of the Pact?"

"You ought to know most Trells think Captain Carlyle was betraying them to Oberon. When word of the Pact got out, off-worlders stopped being welcome around here."

Claydon's casual mention of Durant Carlyle brought tears to Grayson's eyes. Memories flooded back unbidden, memories of the battle with running, black-clad figures in the smoke-filled vehicle bay, of the horror of that instant as an enemy *Marauder* painted with the slit-eyed emblem descended toward his father's 'Mech.

Emotions clamored within him, a mix of grief, shock, and loss. "My father is dead," he mumbled.

"I know. I think they all know...now."

"It wasn't his idea...the Pact, I mean."

Claydon shrugged. "It's all the same. He was the leader up there in the Castle. The people looked to him, and when word came that we were being given over to those filthy bandits..."

"Who told you about that, anyway?"

Claydon shrugged again, and said nothing. Grayson couldn't tell if he didn't know or wasn't telling.

Betrayal. And more betrayal. There had been enemies among the Castle workers, that much was certain. Grayson remembered the astech Stefan standing at the black-garbed warleader's side, pointing him out to the enemy. Perhaps Stefan had been the one who had leaked word of the Trellwan Pact to the people of Sarghad. Grayson remembered now that the first anti-Commonwealth student riots had begun shortly after the last batch of astech recruits had arrived at the Castle, and Stefan had been among them. Grayson had been one of those assigned to guide them through their physicals and indoctrination lectures.

He felt a cold, growing resolve. That was *one* traitor he would find before he left this dustbowl planet. And after he found the man, he would kill him. If the Trell had set up the attack on the Castle, he must be involved with Durant Carlyle's ambush and death as well. It begged too much of coincidence to think the pirate landing at the spaceport and the assault on the Castle were unrelated.

There were still so many unanswered questions. *Who had laid this extensive plot? If it had been Hendrik of Oberon, then why?*

His thoughts circled back to a groove in his memory. *Who is responsible for killing my father?*

Grayson held his voice rigidly in control. "So? Why'd you save me?"

Claydon went to the window and leaned against the sill, his face and tunic catching the red-hued sunlight. He spoke quietly. "I went up there looking for Sergeant Riviera. He was...a friend. A good friend. He taught me everything I know about teching."

"I know he spoke highly of you," Grayson lied. Master Tech Sergeant Riviera had been a hard man to know, and Grayson had never been very close to him. Certainly, the lance's senior tech would not have discussed the performance of a member of his staff with anyone but the captain, not even the lance captain's son.

Grayson did remember a scene he'd happened to witness one day in the repair bay. The dark-skinned Riviera stood with his hand on Claydon's shoulder, an expression of complete and relaxed patience on his face as he explained some arcane twist of 'Mech circuitry to his protege. Most of the unit's staff techs relied on the astechs as raw muscle power and little more, acting the part of overseers more than mentors.

Evidently, Sergeant Riviera had subscribed to a markedly different philosophy.

The astech paused, then turned to face Grayson. "I wasn't in the base when the attack took place. That's what saved me. I was here, at home, on a 60-hour pass. But we could see the battle at the port even from down here, and pretty soon we could tell the Castle was under attack too.

"We knew the Oberon pirates had cleaned out the Castle. We watched what was left of your lance heading down the Avenue Coraza toward the spaceport. But by daybreak, it looked like the pirates had pulled out of the Castle and followed them. There was a lot of gunfire going on at the port.

"I figured the pirates would be back to the Castle soon, but I thought I might find out what happened, and maybe find out if the Sarge had gotten away."

Grayson saw Riviera in his mind's eye once more, kicking back in slow-motion horror across the well deck of a hovercraft transport, blood geysering from half a dozen shocking wounds. "Sergeant Riviera...he was killed. I was there."

"I know," Claydon said softly. "I found him in the vehicle bay. And then I heard you groan, and saw you were still alive.

"There was an awful lot of blood on your head. The doctor said scalp wounds bleed a lot, and I think that's why they left you. They must have thought you'd been shot clean through the head, and left you for dead. But the bullet just creased your scalp." Claydon touched the left side of Grayson's head. "Here."

Grayson repeated the gesture, and felt the burn of the grazing wound under the bandages. He remembered the sight of the attacker's submachine gun leveled at his face, and suppressed a shudder. The man must have fired only a single shot and not checked the results closely. If he'd fired that deadly little weapon on full auto...

"I put you on a skimmersled I found in a storage area and brought you out. Doc Jamis said you have a slight skull fracture, but that there was no brain damage, and you'll recover."

"Thank you," Grayson said, feeling how inadequate the words were.

Again, Claydon shrugged. "I couldn't very well just leave you there." He paced away from the window, passed close by Grayson's bed. "Like I said, if you want to thank us, you'll hurry up and get better and then get out of here. If the anti-Commonwealthers find out we're keeping you here..."

Grayson remembered the riots, the burnings, the screaming mobs of people when rumors first circulated through the city that Trellwan was being turned over to Hendrik III. "Yeah, I can imagine."

"Can you? I doubt that!" Claydon's bitterness was fully visible now. "This city, this entire planet is wide open to Hendrik's pirates now...and it's *your* fault."

"Hey! Not *mine*. I didn't have anything to do—"

"Your people then, same difference! Look, I thought Trellwan was a protectorate of the Commonwealth! Why abandon us? Why hand us over to those monsters?"

"Are they that bad?"

"I don't remember much of their last raid," Claydon said. "Just confused pictures of people running...a night sky on fire...a cave crowded with scared and screaming people...I was pretty young at the time. But I remember my mother. She was killed when they burned Sarghad...killed or carried off as a slave." He shook his head. "I prefer to think she was killed."

Grayson was silent for a long moment, eyes shut. He'd had no idea that such angry, bitter feelings ran this deep among the people of Sarghad. Finally, he opened his eyes. "Why did you help me, Claydon?"

The astech paused before answering. "I don't know. Maybe it was because of Riviera. If it hadn't been for him, I'd still be working a stall on the Street of the Merchants, maybe dreaming of following my father someday as a prosperous Sarghadian merchant. For a time...for a time...there was something better. I can't put it into words. It's gone now...all gone. But I figured I owed the sergeant this much, at least."

"Do you hate me...for what's happened?"

"Hate you? Personally? No, I don't think so. I don't even hate the Commonwealth for what happened. I do think your people were stupid for trying to bargain with those devils."

As there seemed no answer to that, Grayson decided to change the subject. "How long have I been out?"

"Seventy hours or so. The Doc had you on something to make you sleep."

"Seventy?" That was three standard days. "It's the morning after the attack?"

One of Trellwan's leisurely days was 30 standard days long. He'd returned to the Castle perhaps ten hours before Thirday dawn, which meant it must now be early morning.

Claydon nodded. "Thirday, fourth morning period. You understand our timekeeping?"

"Pretty well." Carlyle's Commandos had stuck with their own routine based on a standard 24-hour day divided into three watches. The Trellwan day-night cycles were somewhat more complex, with each 732-hour day divided into night and day segments called "Firstday," "Firstnight," and so on, with three days and nights equal to two of the planet's years. Each segment was divided into 12 periods of 15 and a quarter hours each.

Grayson still had trouble converting from standard hours to Trell time, but had taught himself enough so that he could

match his schedule with Mara's. Trells alternated work periods
with periods for sleep or recreation, but which daily period was
for what was a matter of personal choice. The city of Sarghad
was always awake, whatever the hour.

Numbers clicked into place. *Three days!*

"God! What happened to the lance? You say you saw them
moving toward the spaceport?"

"That's right. Most of them got aboard their shuttle and
took off just before dawn."

"They're...they're gone? You're sure?"

The Trell nodded. "Sure. I've pulled duty at the port. I know
what your shuttle looked like—huge, blunt-nosed, stubby
wings, with the bridge perched way up high above the prow." He
held up a clenched fist, imitating the graphic symbol of House
Steiner. "I saw the unit patches on the 'Mech exit panels. It's a
good thing Hendrik's people didn't have any fighters handy. The
pirates took some shots at them from the ground, but I think
they got away clean. They passed almost directly overhead,
jets full out, and the sonic boom when they boosted to hi-G
rattled my teeth. The firing stopped down at the port then,
though I saw lots of the bandits running around putting out
fires after that."

Grayson sagged back into the pillow. He felt a quiver of
relief in the knowledge the shuttle had gotten away. Lieutenant
Hauptman must have organized a good enough defense to keep
the enemy off the shuttle, or maybe Rama Xiang had managed
to hold a perimeter until the Castle forces had reached him.

His relief was quickly overwhelmed by a rising despair. If
Claydon was right, Grayson had been left for dead. Though
still alive, he was alone and far from safe on this hostile, god-
forsaken world.

CHAPTER 6

The city of Sarghad was laid out on the edge of the desert as concentric wheels with unevenly spaced spokes that stretched beyond the city into the encircling ocher sands. Northward, the mountains of the Crysanden Range thrust jagged ice-capped peaks against the reddish sky. The mists hung low now above Thunder Rift, while on the plain to the south, the spaceport shimmered in the growing heat. Every hour, the swollen red sun crept higher above the horizon, and the dry winds from the south turned hot. The Castle crouched on Mount Gayal's western flanks, brooding above the city and its port.

It was growing hotter, though the sun would not be overhead for another 150 hours. The searing passage of Periasteron occurred at midday of Thirday, and the time of rising heat was accompanied by the boom of temporary glaciers shattering within the Rift's narrow caverns and crevasses. To the north, distant volcanos smudged the sky as Trellwan began to feel the twisting of the sun's tidal grasp.

Most of Sarghad's streets were partially covered over by massive slabs of ferrocrete or stone, heavily reinforced by arches and buttresses against seismic tremors, and strung with lights that let business continue even through the long planetary night. The planet's sun was a red dwarf so weak in ultraviolet that humans could stare directly at it without danger or discomfort, even though its disk was over three times larger than that of Earth's sun as seen from Earth. The parent star's single danger lay in its rare but periodic flares, when patches on its mottled red surface turned white hot and scorched the surface of Trellwan with light, heat, and storms of high-energy atomic particles.

At those times, ready shade close at hand was a necessity. The design of Sarghad had originally called for it to be roofed over by a massive ferrocrete dome that would protect its inhabitants from flare radiation, and seal out the incessant sand and climatic extremes. But those plans had been drawn in a century without war, when technology promised miracles. There were places along Sarghad's rim where eggshell fragments of a partially-begun dome still rose above the sands, other places where sections of the dome had collapsed across acres of buildings now deserted or crumbling away into slums. For the most part, the people relied for shade on the protective sunscreens stretched across the city's narrow avenues and walkways.

Sarghad's usual crowds were out among the marketplace stalls that lined the Street of Merchants from the crumbling ferrocrete ruin of the Ajiani highway all the way to the fence that hedged in the palace grounds at the hub of the city. To Grayson, it seemed the crowds were quieter than usual, less boisterous. An atmosphere of fear had crept through the streets, reflected in the voices and faces of the people there. Merchants and pedestrians clustered together in the blue-ink pools of shadow under the street shades, or hurried through the red glare of daylight.

Two more 15-hour periods had passed since he'd awakened and learned of the exodus of the remnants of Carlyle's Commandos. Though his head was still bandaged, the throbbing pain and dizziness were gone, and Grayson's strength had returned enough that he'd decided to leave the house of Berenir the Merchant.

"Where will you go?" Claydon had asked when Grayson announced his intention.

"I'm not entirely sure. I have one friend in the city...the daughter of the Chief Minister. She may be able to help me, or take me to someone who can."

Berenir had frowned, stroking his stubby white beard. "It's the political ministers who've been stirring up this hate-the-off-worlders sentiment lately. I wonder if it's wise for you to visit the household of one of the planet's leading politicians."

Grayson shrugged. "It's not as though I have much choice. I can't stay here."

Berenir nodded. "I won't say I'm sorry to see you go. It is dangerous for you to stay."

"You didn't have to bring me in." Perhaps it would have better if he hadn't. Growing desperation and loss knotted Grayson's stomach.

"Don't misunderstand me, young Lord." He still used the honorific most Trells reserved for representatives of far-off Tharkad, and the near-legendary inner worlds of the Commonwealth. "I don't blame you, personally, but..."

"But there are the neighbors to consider."

"Eh, yes. As you say."

"I'm grateful for your help."

"And I'm grateful for what your people brought to Trellwan." He smiled at Grayson's startled expression. "No, I don't mean Hendrik. But technology...science to combat superstition... education. My son, Claydon, learned much in his years working at the Castle."

Clayton shrugged. "A lot of good it does me now, Father. The Commonwealth will never return."

"It did you good in the way it taught you to think, son. There are always multiple ways of looking at a problem, some good, some bad. You have learned to apply scientific method to your thoughts, to think critically, rationally. That is the treasure that these...these starmen brought with them. They will not take it away with them again."

He turned again to Grayson. "It is we who are grateful to you, young Lord."

Grayson had remained silent. Scientific method held out little hope to a people faced with raids by bandit BattleMechs. Technology and rational thought had a nasty way of vanishing in the funeral pyres of cities.

Berenir had long been an enigma to those of Carlyle's Commandos who had followed events in Sarghad. He was one of the rich city merchants who dealt with the infrequent traders who called at the spaceport, handling their cargoes and dickering with them for shipments of Trellwan's mineral woods and spices. In the wave of anti-Commonwealth rioting and propagandizing, he had kept a low profile, but continued to deal with the men from the stars, selling Carlyle's Commandos food, oil for their machines, and commodities as varied as soap and salt. None could tell whether his attitude was one of greed, practicality, or simply a cosmopolitan acceptance of the starmen as people like everyone else.

If the population learned the whereabouts of the son of the man who had engineered the Trellwan Pact with Hendrik, Grayson might well find himself facing the brunt of their simmering resentment. The Trells were not particularly vindictive or bloody-minded, but they were human. Grayson shuddered, remembering the story he'd heard of a rapist set free in the desert just as Trell began to flare.

His first thought had been to use Berenir to contact the next off-world freighter that called at Trellwan. The merchant explained that off-world traders called but rarely this far out along the Periphery, and that he was fearful of what would happen when the next one arrived. As he rubbed his hands together, the overhead lights caught at the jeweled rings on his fingers. "Business has taken a turn for the worst, I suspect."

"But a ship will come?"

"Oh, yes, eventually. But it will be a while. The trader ships do not fill the skies as they once did..."

"But they'll come?"

"Oh, certainly they'll come!"

"Will your government let them come? With this policy of hate-the-offworlder..."

Berenir made an impatient gesture. "If there's one thing I've learned in 300 threedays on the Streets of Merchants, it's that business will turn again. How long do you think Trellwan will get along without the traders from the stars, eh?"

"I don't know. You have water here...you grow your own food...you could do without them." What Grayson didn't say was that, by his standards, Trellwan's level of civilization was scarcely removed from barbarism. They had no electronics technology to speak off. Power was drawn from tidal generators powered by burning petroleum distillates. Why, transportation in the streets was as likely to be by harnessed desert laniks as it was to be self-powered.

Berenir made an impatient gesture. "The government doesn't care about food and water. It's tariffs, import duties, and taxes they're concerned about. Give the politicians oh... ten...maybe twenty threedays, and the ships will come again."

Berenir rubbed his chin ruefully. "But in the meantime, we're going to have a bit of trouble figuring out what to do with you."

Listening to all this, Grayson had suppressed a groan. Ten Trell threedays was something like two and a half standard years. In the past six months, the only commercial DropShips to set down on Trellwan had been from the Mailai trader that had been handling the runs between Oberon and Trellwan. How much longer would it be before another called? And how could he reach it, with Hendrik's bandits at the port, and the people of Sarghad ready to kill him on sight?

Berenir looked thoughtful. "I have contacts in the government," he said. "A merchant in my position has to nowadays. The Chief Minister is a friend of mine..."

"Stannic? Chief Minister Stannic?"

"Yes. Do you know him?"

"I...know his daughter. Quite well. I've met the Minister a time or two..."

"Stannic is one of King Jeverid's most trusted aides. He's also the man to know for trade licensing, that sort of thing."

"Will he help?"

Berenir pulled at his lower lip. "He has always approved of Jeverid's policies of strengthening ties with the Commonwealth. Lately, it's been Stannic and Jeverid against the rest of their government, and their desertion by the Castle garrison—no offense, young Lord—their desertion has left the government up against something of a wall. I...trust him as much as I trust any of that pack of animals. You say you know his daughter?"

Grayson nodded.

"Well, I'll see what I can do."

A meeting had been arranged at Mara's apartment to avoid attracting attention to the merchant. Berenir's son gave Grayson clothes to replace his gray Commonwealth 'Mech uniform, a plain, light brown tunic, loose-fitting pants, and halfboots that were at least a size too small. Though it was getting well on toward Periasteron and the heat was rising rapidly, he also wore a cloak and hood that covered his light hair. There had been some discussion about whether or not to dye his hair to match the glossy black of most native Trells, but Grayson had decided against it in the end. He would see Mara as himself.

The people along the Third Street of the Merchants seemed totally absorbed in their own comings and goings and ignored Grayson. The merchant stalls were lightweight, easily assembled affairs of wood and canvas. Each crowded into the street in competition with its neighbors, turning the walk along the arrow-straight avenue into a zigzag around milling shoppers, piles of produce, stacks of woven cloth, and the merchants themselves vying with one another in a cacophony of bleated pleas for attention. But Grayson noticed even the street merchants seemed to have lost something of their enthusiasm.

Sarghad was gripped by fear, waiting for Hendrik's bandits to turn their attention to the city.

Little was known about the bandit forces that now occupied the spaceport, and less was known about their intent. Berenir had said that no demands or threats had been made by the invaders, and that City Council representatives sent to the port had been turned away by sentries at the defensive perimeter that had been erected there. Hendrik's men had driven off the Commonwealth garrison lance, thrown up the perimeter, and now were simply waiting.

For what?

The hub of the wheel of Sarghad embraced the Palace grounds, with the clustered domes of the Palace itself half hidden from public view by the lush, flowering vegetation of the irrigated gardens. The household of Minister Stannic was quartered in a line of luxurious three-story row houses that fronted the Royal Circle just across from the Palace entrance.

He'd been told Mara would be home. He knew she worked for her father, serving as Stannic's social secretary since her mother's death. Berenir had promised that she would be waiting, that she and Stannic would arrange for a place for Grayson to stay out of the public eye.

He was looking forward to seeing her again, despite his having already gone through a lingering set of last goodbyes with her. She was not as shy—or as protected—as most girls on a world that made a practice of sheltering its women by denying them much freedom. Stannic and his family had lived off-world for a number of years, according to Mara, and were not so set in Trellwan's social conservatism as their neighbors.

He was just mounting the steps in front of her apartment when a voice caught him from behind. "Stop, you."

Grayson stopped, and turned slowly. He found himself facing a young man in the dress uniform of Jeverid's Palace Guard, green jacket and trousers richly chased and edged with gold, and a white helmet polished to a dull shine ringed by a transparent blast shield. He held a functional-looking automatic rifle in white-gloved hands.

"Identify yourself," the soldier said. Beyond the man's shoulder were two more green-and-gold uniforms.

"Ah...Grayson, my name's Grayson." Trells did not use patronymics, and he dared not use his. "I'm here to see Mara. She knows me...she's expecting me..."

The rifle muzzle did not waver from its position centimeters from Grayson's sternum. "But I don't." The Guard squinted at Grayson's face under the heavy cowl. "Take that thing off."

He did so, reluctantly. The Guard's eyes widened at the sight of Grayson's fair hair. "So," he said, tightening his finger on the trigger. "Looks like we've captured ourselves one of those bandits!"

CHAPTER 7

"Nonsense!" Grayson drew himself erect. "I am Grayson Carlyle of the Commonwealth garrison lance, and I'm here to see Minister Stannic...at once!"

The direct approach failed him. The rifle barrel jabbed forward, prodding Grayson in the chest and knocking him backward, off balance.

"You're not seeing anybody but the Guard Commander, off-worlder. The interrogators will want to discuss some things with you, I'm thinking..."

Grayson had heard of Jeverid's interrogators. The methods of the Sarghad's police force were a frequent topic of speculation in the garrison barracks. The fear growing in Grayson ever since he'd awakened at Berenir's house exploded. He turned and ran, panic driving him back into the street and along the Royal Circle. Even after colliding with several Trell citizens walking under the overhanging eaves, he kept running.

Behind him, Grayson heard a shouted "Halt!" and the terrifying crack of a single rifle shot. The round must have been aimed into the air, though, as the street was too crowded for indiscriminate firing. He didn't think the guards would risk killing civilians just to get him. But he ran harder nonetheless, his back muscles bunched hard, as though anticipating a rifle bullet.

Looking about wildly, he saw few options, with the palace gardens fence hemming him in to the right and the buildings crowded wall by wall along the Circle to the left. People were ducking out of his way as he ran now, which would give his pursuers a clear shot at any moment.

Could he get to the palace? The gate was close by, and he could see the alabaster curve of the main palace dome above the trees beyond the Gardens. And if he reached it, what else could he expect except to be arrested or shot? Besides, he saw the flash of gold and green on the black-surfaced drive behind the gate. The Palace Guard was there, too, at least a company of their grim-faced, white-helmeted ranks.

A ragged thunder sounded behind him, and bits of brickwork disintegrated in clouds of stinging dust and flakes of stone close by his head. A woman screamed, and people on the walkways scattered for cover. He collided with a young man in ragged street clothes, nearly knocking them both to the ground, and then he was past and running wildly down the street.

"Halt! Halt or we fire!"

They were closer! Which way? He twisted between a pair of businessmen in richly dyed formal cloaks and tunics, leaped across the legs of an old man sitting on a crate beside the alley entrance, and plunged into the shadows of a narrow alley between two buildings to his left. Behind him, Grayson heard piping whistles and the clatter and shouts of running men.

As he ran, he saw a two-meter-high fence directly in his path. Putting on even more speed, he launched himself from an overturned produce crate, throwing his arms and one knee across the top of the fence. It creaked and swayed as he pulled the other leg across, but he landed like a cat and continued racing toward the next street.

Down this street...turn...down another...turn again. Could he lose them running blindly this way? He had come to a narrow, cross lane that curved between two of the major avenues leading out from the hub of the palace gardens. It was an ill-kept area. The sunshade had collapsed in places, filling the street with flat chunks of jagged-edged ferrocrete. The rest of it was layered with wind-swirled mounds of sand, empty bottles, and garbage steaming in the sun.

There were people here, too, dozens of them stooped in the shade pools of surrounding buildings, or sprawled with their legs in the street. They wore rags and layers of caked mud and dust. Many were barefoot. Some appeared asleep or unconscious amid the litter of empty bottles of alcohol, but the rest watched Grayson with wary, shuttered eyes.

Forcing himself to slow to a walk, he picked his way along the debris-choked road. Somehow he had to find a place to hide, or at least a place where he could blend in with the background. Glancing continuously over his shoulder as he went, Grayson's heart froze, then began to hammer at his throat when something behind him moved. He relaxed then, thinking at first it was just another derelict. But no, it was the man he'd collided with on the street in front of the palace grounds. Had the man been following him? It could well be that any citizen who turned him in to the Guard would be rewarded, which certainly would be a temptation for any of this ragged lot. Grayson quickened his step. He didn't *know* he was being followed, but...

Moving down the littered street, he was so startled to feel the squish of mud against his boots that he stopped where he was for a moment. All along the street there were places where Secondnight ice had melted off roofs, flowed down rusted gutter spouts, and pooled in curbside depressions worn hollow over the years. In most spots, the surface water was sucked away by the thirsty sand, but here the meltwater was trapped in pools of black mud, where it would remain until the next freeze. The sight of it gave him an idea.

Removing his cloak as he walked, Grayson dropped it beside a half-naked derelict leaning against a worn stone wall. There was no time to hide it. The soldiers were mere seconds behind him. Then he went to work unraveling his head bandage, which he crumpled and stuffed into an already overflowing garbage bin. A bit farther ahead, there was a stretch of road unoccupied by street people or anyone else.

Kneeling by a mud pool, Grayson gathered a double handful of the stinking stuff and lathered it over his scalp. It burned like fire when it touched the inflamed wound on the side of his head. He knew he was begging for an infection, but the thought of the interrogators drove him on.

By the time he was done, Grayson's yellow hair, his face, and his tunic were generously coated with black mud. *What else?* he thought, mind racing. His clothes were nondescript enough, except for his boots, so tight his feet were aching now. They were much too shiny and new to belong to a mud-smeared derelict

After a moment's thought, Grayson pried off the boots and carefully set them together nearby, then muddied his feet as well. The final touch would be two empty liquor bottles he found in a mound of garbage across the street. Grayson then lay down with his feet sprawled well into the middle of the street, his head close by the noisome pool, with a bottle cradled in each arm. It was only seconds later that he heard the scuffing of booted feet rounding the curve of the street.

There were five of them, Palace Guards in dark green and gold, four with wicked-looking assault rifles held at port arms. They picked their way cautiously along the street, stepping around or past the worst of the mud and garbage.

"Here!" one of them shouted. "His boots!" The soldier swooped down and grabbed the shiny boots. Grayson opened his eyes in his best imitation of bleary-eyed dullness, and saw that one of the soldiers already had tucked his cast-off cloak and the bloodied strips of bandage under one arm. Another one—probably the leader, judging by his imperious hands-on-hips stance and lack of a rifle—stood over Grayson and nudged him with the toe of his boot. "You!"

Grayson clutched the bottles tighter, and gave the man a wit-befuddled smile. If he could convince the soldiers he was just a street drunk, that someone else had dropped the boots beside him as he lay there in the mud...

"You," the soldier said again. His upper lip curled even as he spoke, as though the man were trying to avoid breathing the stench of the noxious mud and garbage. "Where'd these boots come from?"

"Wha-?" Grayson slurred his speech and turned his grin idiotic.

"Sergeant!" Here was a new voice. Grayson followed its sound and saw another squad of soldiers coming up the street from the other direction. They must have sent this second patrol ahead to another main street so that they could work back, hoping to trap him between. The newcomer was an officer, his Guard's lieutenant uniform more gold than green, looped

WILLIAM H. KEITH

59

with aiguillettes and tassels that glittered in the red sunlight. "Any sign of him?"

"He came this way, sir. Look."

The two examined the cloak, bandages, and boots for a moment, their own boots only a meter from Grayson's bare, muddy feet. The lead officer shook his head. "He didn't get past us. You must have missed him."

"He might be trying to blend in with the street scum, sir," the sergeant said. At this, the bottles trembled in Grayson's hands and his heart pounded so furiously he was certain it would give him away. "We could round them up and question them all."

"Pah! Or shoot them."

"I might be able to help you, Lieutenant." That new voice sent chills along Grayson's spine. Rags moved down the street, and a filthy and unshaven man lurched into view. It was the young man he'd thought was following him. He must have been close enough behind Grayson to see him preparing his hasty disguise!

Grayson tensed, readying himself. If he jumped up and ran, the soldiers would cut him down before he made it around the curve of the road, unless he could take them by surprise. He wondered how fast his bare and tender feet could move over broken chunks of sun-baked ferrocrete.

"You see this guy?" the Lieutenant asked, holding up the boots.

"Sure did." The street dweller glanced at Grayson, his face neutral. "See that pipe?" he said, gesturing at the drainpipe above Grayson's mud pool. "Fella came tearing in here maybe a minute ago. Stripped off his boots, plopped 'em down there, and shinnied up that pipe like a leaflighter in heat." He pointed across the flat slab roofs back in the general direction of the palace. "He headed off across the roofs off that-a-way."

"Damn," the Lieutenant muttered. "He's trying to backtrack on us. You men! At the double! C'mon!"

The troop gathered into ragged ranks and clumped off down the street at a half-run. The one holding Grayson's boots tossed them aside. When the soldiers were far enough away, he sat up slowly, brushing ineffectually at the mud caked on his tunic. "Thanks."

The man glanced up and down the street, then his dirty face with its scraggly growth of beard broke into a wide, unexpected grin. "Don't mention it. You looked like you were new in town."

"Well, you might say that. Who are you?"

The man gave a sweeping, polished bow. "Renfred Tor, at your service."

"I think it should be the other way around. I'm indebted to you, sir."

"Why were they after you?"

Grayson hesitated. His first inclination urged caution. The stranger seemed friendly enough, but maybe he was just looking for more information about the fugitive before turning him in. Picking his way across the street to retrieve his boots, Grayson turned various possibilities over in his mind. If he was going to have to do any more running, he would need those painfully tight boots.

Suddenly Grayson realized the man had used two names. He couldn't possibly be a native of Trellwan! "You're an off-worlder," he said, avoiding the other's question.

"You might say that." Tor's eyes shifted down the street. "Off-worlders don't seem very popular around here."

Grayson nodded and smiled ruefully. "I'm Grayson Carlyle. I was with the Commonwealth garrison lance at the Castle."

"Pleased to meet you. Uh...you seem to have misplaced your 'Mech lance."

"They misplaced me. The bandits attacked the Castle and I was left for dead. When I came to, my unit had already pulled out"

"Ah," said Tor.

"How about you? What are you doing here?"

Tor stared at Grayson a long moment, then told him, "I'm the DropShip pilot who brought those bandits here in the first place."

CHAPTER 8

Renfred Tor was a native of Atreus, but it had been many long, standard years since he'd seen the capital of Marik's Free World League. At fourteen, he'd shipped out as cargo handler on a Tristar Lines freighter. By the time he was 20, he had worked his way up through sundry crews to deck officer. Then, he and his four brothers bought equal shares in an aging rustbucket freighter they'd named the *Invidious* by the end of an evening of drunken celebration.

The celebration turned out to be premature. A scheme to transport laser rifles and man-portable inferno launchers to an embattled revolutionary front had ended with the revolution crushed, his partners imprisoned or broke, and himself and an unhappy fifteen-man crew plotting a jump route series into the Lyran Commonwealth. Their flight had ended in the Commonwealth's Periphery, and Tor had been buying, borrowing, or scamming spare parts and new crewmembers to keep the *Invidious* going ever since. Five years of short-term contracts and one-way cargo hauls had brought him at last to Drovahchein II in the heart of the Erit Cluster.

There, the *Invidious* faced the end of her career. She needed a complete refit before she'd jump out-system again, and her station keeping drive was threatening to fail at any moment. With no money, no contracts, his crew threatening to scatter if they weren't paid soon, and no hope of repairing the faltering hauler on his own, Tor was forced to contemplate an early retirement on Drovahchein II. Not that the trading capital of the Erit Cluster was uninteresting, but future opportunities for a freighter jump pilot with a ship were slim, the open billets on outbound ships few.

That was when he'd met Proctor Sinvalie of House Mailai.

Mailai was more the ruler of the Cluster than the distant court of Katrina Steiner on Tharkad. The Cluster was a tiny island of relative prosperity and technology in a rising sea of barbarism. Proctor Sinvalie was one of the principal House traders who oversaw the fragile web of commerce that bound the Eritese systems to the Commonwealth and to systems out in the Periphery, to worlds like Trellwan, and beyond.

Sinvalie had called on Tor shortly after he'd grounded the *Invidious'* DropShip at Gharisport, on Drovahchein II's minor southern continent. The offer he'd made Tor seemed the answer to all the freighter captain's problems. Gharisport's Mailai tech crew would give the *Invidious* the refit she needed, Tor's crew would be signed on for a six-standard-month hitch and receive an advance to spend on Gharisport's nightlife, and Captain Tor would get the long-term contract he so desperately needed. All he had to do was shuttle small numbers of passengers back and forth between Oberon VI and a world beyond the Periphery, undistinguished save for its location. That world was Trell I—Trellwan, as its natives had named it.

"I should've known," Tor said as he led Grayson through the twists and odd angles of Sarghad's back alleys and side streets. "I should've known as soon as I found out old Hendrik the Great was involved."

"Known what?" Grayson asked.

"Known I wasn't going to get out with a whole skin. Old Sinvalie, he's a sharp character. He wasn't about to trust one of his precious ships and crews to the tender mercies of Hendrik's little bandit kingdom, so he hires an independent to take the risks—yours truly. They painted House Mailai's crest on the *Invidious'* DropShips, but it wasn't Mailai taking the risks!"

"What happened?"

"Hold it!" Tor hissed suddenly, pushing Grayson into the shadows as a platoon of Palace Guards trooped past. The two had come to a place where the alley opened onto one of the city's broad thoroughfares. A number of soldiers were about, standing at intersections or along the avenue, and they seemed to be searching the faces of the crowd.

Tor motioned Grayson to sit back, then continued his story. "Nothing much happened—at first. I shuttled in a Commonwealth representative named...uh..."

"Vogel."

"Yeah, Viscount Vogel. I shuttled him from Tharkad to Oberon, and then from Oberon to here. I took his assistant from here to Oberon and back a couple of times. I gather they were setting up a deal to turn Trellwan over to Hendrik's keeping, though the whole thing was supposed to be secret."

"Supposed to be," Grayson said, more to himself than Tor.

"Yeah, well, it didn't take long to leak out. The news was all over Sarghad last time I was here. You folks had riots in town?"

Grayson nodded, but kept his eyes on the street. This was all part and parcel of the betrayal that had killed his father. Someone was going to pay.

"Anyway, there was supposed to be a last meeting, with Oberon's ministers coming to Trellwan for some kind of official treaty signing. But it didn't turn out the way they'd said." Tor kept his voice low, looking around warily as he spoke. More soldiers were passing on the street, trotting with their weapons at high port. There seemed to be a stir somewhere to the north.

"I came out of jumpspace at a planetless A2 star for a navfix, and found this big, bloody JumpShip waiting for me, fighters deployed, weapons charged. Hell, I thought it was some bandit competitor of Hendrik's, but when they came aboard, they were wearing Hendrik's livery. But Hendrik's old boys aboard ship, they went out the airlock, no fuss, no ceremony. Just out they went. I don't mind telling you, I was scared."

"They killed them?"

"Right the first time. Anyway, they transferred a lance of 'Mechs and I don't know how many men and armored vehicles across to the *Invidious*'hold. A tech crew came aboard and started drilling holes in the hull of one of the DropShips, mounting heavy weapons, beam turrets, missile batteries, that sort of thing. I hollered about it, but the next thing I knew I had a bruised head and a bloody split lip, so I kept my mouth shut after that. I thought they were going to send me swimming after Hendrik's people.

"When they were finished, that black monster furled sail and jumped, and the leader of the people they'd left aboard the *Invidious* told us to be on our way. We came out at Trellwan and parked ourselves. They made me and three of my crewmen pilot the DropShip down. I made the entry to Trellwan with a gun at my head, and once we'd grounded, they put me in an afterhold for safe-keeping."

"And they let you go afterward?"

Tor grinned, and shook his head. "Not bloody likely, lad. I didn't know what was happening, but I did know that lot wasn't about to turn me loose. Not after I'd seen them mucking about swapping cargos at what should've been just a simple nav check and recharge stop."

"Why not?"

"Hey, that was a hell of a big operation. There were at least five 'Mechs working in space to transfer the four 'Mechs in the lance and all the rest of the gear over to the *Invidious*. Funny thing about that, too."

"What?"

"The 'Mechs handling the transfer, they were high-class machines, know what I mean? New paint, clean parts. One of them was a *Marauder* painted red and black, like one of those personalized mercenary jobs you run into sometimes on the Inner Worlds. That was the one conned by their leader. Big guy, but quiet, real professional. And deadly, you know? What they were loading aboard the *Invidious* was junk, old, patchwork 'Mechs that were more salvaged parts than anything else. There was a black and gray *Marauder* and one of those light 20-tonner *Locusts*. It looked to me like some sort of covert operation, something they wouldn't want outsiders knowing about. I figured I'd last just about until the shooting stopped, and then they were going to retire me permanently."

"So how'd you wind up in a back alley with the derelicts?" Grayson asked.

"Good question. Like I said, the *Invidious* was in need of repairs, and I didn't get all of them taken care of during the refit. Seems there was a loose insulation panel in that hold, one I could pry loose, then pull back in once I'd squeezed myself into the 'tween heads. I stayed there until I heard them come back to find out I was missing, then slipped out of my hidey-hole, headed aft to a hold where they were off-loading 'Mechs, and slipped off with some soldiers." He paused, seeing Grayson's lifted eyebrow. "Well, I'd acquired a uniform by that time. That helped."

"That one?" Grayson pointed at Tor's muddied tunic.

"Hardly. I'd hoped to talk with someone here, maybe the local port authority, about what I could do to get my crew freed. They...uh...don't take kindly to off-worlders here. At least, not now."

Another troop of soldiers tramped past. These were members of the planet's militia, Grayson noted, in brown uniforms instead of green. Barracks talk in the Castle had generally held Sarghad's militiamen to be superior soldiers, though few of Carlyle's Commandos held either of the two local military forces in high esteem.

What is going on? Grayson wondered. *Is the militia searching for me now, too?*

CHAPTER 9

Grayson and Tor continued watching the soldiers in the street. It didn't appear that Jeverid's Guard was engaged in anything like a serious search, but they were definitely on the alert, patrolling the major streets for...what? Off-worlders escaped from the attack at the Castle? Or suspicious characters in general? With a bandit camp so close by, the local government forces might well be watching for any gathering of armed or unpleasant-looking folks who might be the first line of a raider assault.

Why were so many of them moving north? A small convoy of ground-effect weapons carriers—HVWCs—whined past.

Grayson kept turning Tor's story over in his mind. A freighter boarded, her diplomatic passengers slain? He'd been tempted at first to dismiss the idea as outright fabrication, but why would Tor lie about something like that? Bandits engaged in deception and subtle treachery as frequently as any organized government of the Inner Worlds, but this secret transfer of cargo and personnel at a nav check sounded pointless. One of Hendrik's ships had to have stopped the *Invidious*. Only Hendrik's people would have known the freighter's exact course as she jumped from star to star on her jump series from Oberon to Trellwan.

The distance between the two systems was about 145 light years. Because JumpShips could only manage about 30 lights at a jump, they had to plot and execute a number of system-to-system transits called the jump series, often in long and roundabout fashion from star to star. Most of those stars—like the one where Tor had been ambushed—were planetless, or were circled by barren and useless worlds of dead rock and ice. The chances that a ship would just happen to be there waiting for another ship were impossibly slim. Which meant the ambushers knew the *Invidious* was coming that way. Which meant Hendrik had ordered the ambush.

Or did it? Hendrik ruled an uneasy coalition of twelve minor bandit kings and their worlds. Perhaps someone on his staff represented a dissident faction—a revolutionary faction, one working against Hendrik. That might explain the greatest mystery in Tor's story, the mystery of why Hendrik would bother to take the *Invidious* in deep space instead of right at home in the Oberon system.

But that still left so many unanswered questions. Why would anyone in Hendrik's camp bother attacking the Trellwan garrison, when the entire planet was to have been handed over to him peacefully within a few hours? Even a rebellious faction would likely have been advised to wait. Grabbing the Trell system for themselves would do nothing for dissidents in a showdown with Hendrik's forces except tie up needed men and machines.

It just doesn't make any sense, Grayson thought. There was also the question of what Tor had seen when his ship had been taken. He'd said the men who boarded her had worn Oberon livery, but the 'Mechs transferring the cargo had been better cared-for than the equipment they'd been passing over. Bandit kingdoms—even large and powerful ones like that of Hendrik III—could rarely field anything better than patched-together and many-times-salvaged 'Mechs that had been through scores of battles. From where had those gleaming, fresh-painted machines come? Could Hendrik afford to hire a mercenary lance from the Inner Sphere? From Kurita's Draconis Combine, perhaps?

And if he could manage that, why not use them in the attack? *Why the deception? Why? Why?*

"Hey!" Tor touched his shoulder, startling him. "They're clearing out!"

The Guards seemed to be withdrawing from the streets, some piling onto a rusty, six-wheeled personnel carrier, the rest hurrying up the street. Grayson could make out an officer in the

APC's hatch talking with animated gestures on a transceiver handset.

"Something sure has stirred them up," he said. "Wonder what?"

The answer came with a flash and a bang that struck Grayson like a blow to the chest, leaving him momentarily breathless. Across the avenue from where Tor and Grayson crouched, a storefront exploded like a geyser of flame, brick, glass, stone, and black smoke. People were screaming, and above the shrieks and yells came the measured rumble of heavy machinery in motion.

Grayson knew that sound. He squirmed forward on his stomach until he could peer around the corner of the sheltering building and look up the street. What he had heard was a *Marauder,* twelve meters tall and massively armored, hung with weapons that gave it a lumbering, top-heavy look. Grayson knew from experience the machine was anything but clumsy.

He saw the stylized, slit-eyed emblem brightly painted on the heat-seared metal of the left leg and knew this was the black-and-gray-painted machine that had killed his father.

A fascination born of sick horror gripped him, held him frozen there at the mouth of the alley. Almost in slow motion, the armored monster straightened slightly, then brought its right arm up as though pointing. Recessed in the swollen bulk of the forearm were a pair of the 'Mech's primary weapons, a medium laser and the massive bore of a particle cannon.

The laser flashed blue-white, a brilliant pulse that shrieked and ionized the air in its wake. The beam struck the APC, setting aflame the Guardsmen clinging to its hull. Grayson squeezed his eyes shut against the blinding light, but still saw the afterimage of a Guards officer writhing in the carrier's hatch as the steel around him blossomed into a fireball.

A chain of staccato *cracks* carried above the roar of flame and crumbling buildings. The *Marauder*'s autocannon, a tree-sized barrel mounted over the 'Mech's left shoulder, was spewing 120mm high-explosive destruction in three-round bursts that shattered the street behind the burning carrier, and transformed clumps of running green uniforms into bloodied shreds of rag.

The smoke roiling down from the APC was acrid and black, and it stank of oil and charred flesh.

Grayson felt a hand on his shoulder, tugging, insistent. "Grayson!" We've got to get clear!" C'mon!"

But, eyes locked on the *Marauder,* he couldn't move.

The 'Mech took one huge step, then another, pausing after each step as though testing the footing. Fire flickered around its crab's head from the ineffectual shoulder-portable missiles and lasers of the city's unarmored defenders. Grayson found himself willing the Sarghad fighters to concentrate their fire, to seek out the vital nexuses of control circuits and servoactuators that might—might!—give them a slim chance of bringing the giant down. There was one such nexus where the legs joined the body, under that flat head. *If they could just work together...*

The giant brushed through the fire, unconcerned. Destruction boiled in its path as it sprayed the avenue and its buildings with flashing beams of energy.

"Grayson!" Tor's scream penetrated his numbed senses, brought him back to the scene at hand and the gagging stench of the burning vehicle. He shook himself, turned, and looked into Tor's wild eyes. "Grayson, we've got to get out of here!"

He allowed himself to be pulled to his feet, then began running with clumsy strides back down the alley and away from the monster. Behind him, the 'Mech collided with the buildings at the alley mouth, and the fall of brick and stone sent debris skittering along the ground in front of them.

Grayson followed Tor through the twists and turns of Sarghad's alleys, and the sounds of cannon fire and falling buildings began to recede behind them. Eventually, Tor stopped and fell back against the wall, chest heaving as he caught his breath.

"Where now?" Grayson asked, his mind still numb. He was willing to be led, to let the decisions be made by another.

"I don't know. I'm a stranger here too, remember?"

"I...I know a place we might be able to go." Grayson thought of Berenir the Merchant, knowing the man would not be pleased to see him again, and less so if he brought along another off-worlder to hide. "I know some people, but they may not be able to help us."

"We're going to have to find a way to get up to the port." Tor looked thoughtfully in its direction. Across the roofs of low, single-storied warehouses, they could just make out the port's control tower as a tiny white saucer perched on a narrow column. And just beyond, they glimpsed the bulk of the upper third of Tor's ship.

"Are you thinking of getting your ship back?"

Tor shook his head. "No...no way. We'd never get near her, not now."

"Then why the port?"

"Because ships'll be coming in, sooner or later." Pain clouded the freighter pilot's face. "And because I have three men three... three friends. I've got to get them out, somehow."

"You can't fight *that* alone!" The sounds of fresh skirmishing broke out somewhere behind them, followed by a series of explosions.

"Maybe not. But these pirates aren't going to stay here forever. Now that they've attacked, they'll pull out, take their loot, slaves, and captured 'Mechs and haul for Oberon...or wherever. They can't stay here, not against a whole planet. Besides, how can they be sure House Steiner won't send a punitive expedition back to ram this planet down their throats?"

"My lance..."

"Maybe," Tor said thoughtfully. "Though, from what I've heard, your friends were pretty badly shot up. The point is, traders'll be coming in. Hell, even my friends with Mailai might come in to see what happened to their investment. I want to be at the port when they do, and I mean to have my people with me. And don't forget my ship is out at the jump point, with twelve more of my men aboard." Tor shook his head fiercely. "I can't just let them go!"

Grayson thought of the small community of techs and laborers quartered at one end of the spaceport. "Maybe you could get a job at the port, and find a way to help your people that way. I don't know how you'd go about getting your ship back, though."

"Neither do I, lad. Neither do I." The pain was back in Tor's face. Grayson wondered if he was feeling guilt at having abandoned his crew, or was simply afraid that they'd already been put to death.

The other man seemed to give himself a shake. "No matter what, we'll have to eat and find a way to blend in with the natives."

Yes, thought Grayson, they'd need a place to stay, a place to wait, while he figured out a way to bring down the plotters who had killed his father. Only then would he think about how to get off this forbidding world.

The battle sounds had ceased now, leaving the city unnaturally quiet. Grayson looked in all directions, orienting himself. "Let's go visit my friends. Berenir is a merchant, with contacts off-planet and at the spaceport. Maybe he can get us jobs. At least, he might have some ideas about what we should do."

"Where is he?"

"Third Street of the Merchants. This way." Grayson took the lead as they walked, but his thoughts turned back to the *Marauder* astride the street, and the memory of his father's death. That 'Mech had ambushed Durant Carlyle after his lighter *Phoenix Hawk* had been badly damaged in a hopeless duel with the hidden weapons mounted on the *Invidious'* DropShip. His father had never had a chance.

New energy was replacing the lassitude that had paralyzed Grayson's spirit since he'd regained consciousness in Berenir's house. For the first time, he felt a goal, a purpose to keep him going. He would burn that killer 'Mech or die in the attempt. The need for vengeance was like a hunger driving him on through the twisting streets of Sarghad as panicked civilians and disorganized squads of Guards and Militia streamed past him.

Although Grayson didn't know how yet, he vowed to destroy that *Marauder* and the human who piloted it.

CHAPTER 10

Ten-meter-tall death machines now stalked the narrow avenues of Sarghad. Though Grayson knew how to find the Third Street of the Merchants, four times he and Tor were forced to leave streets suddenly blocked by throngs of panicked people or by the striding nightmares of attacking 'Mechs.

Grayson tried to keep track of the types he saw. There was one *Locust,* he knew, and another that looked like one of the Commando *Wasp*s, now bearing the animal's eye insignia of Hendrik III of Oberon. Once he saw the *Marauder* again, wading through the splintered rubble of buildings. A pall of oily smoke hung suspended above Sarghad, and the air was heavy with dust from plaster turned to brick rubble, and crumbled slabs of ferrocrete.

At the mouth of an alley opening onto the Third Street of the Merchants, Tor held back, motioning Grayson behind him. Peering past the freighter pilot, Grayson saw another *Wasp,* this one leading a string of perhaps fifteen Trells toward the city borders.

"What are they doing?"

Tor looked grim. "Taking hostages, possibly. But those people don't look all that well-to-do. Slaves, more likely."

Grayson remained silent. He'd heard stories of the slave trade among the bandit kinglets of the Periphery, but hadn't given them much credence. Even Claydon's lingering fear that his mother might have been taken by Hendrik's raiders as a slave to Oberon, that was easy enough to dismiss as the xenophobic fears of an untraveled, nearly uneducated native who had never been beyond the fringes of his own world's atmosphere. The brutal truth was that among the shards of a civilization where machines and the products of technology were treasures, human labor tended to be cheap and easily harvested.

"Where will they take them?" Grayson wondered aloud.

Tor shrugged. "The spaceport, perhaps. They won't be able to use them here. Most likely they'll be corralled somewhere off-world." His voice was curiously level and remote. "They might even load them aboard the old *Invidious.*"

A rumbling crash from farther down the street caught Grayson's attention. He crawled forward, slipping his head past the shelter of the wall close to the street. What he saw shocked him to the core.

Standing there was the *Marauder,* encased in the rubble of a building in flames. A knife twisted cold in Grayson's gut. That building was the house of Berenir the merchant.

The *Marauder* lurched forward into the street, completing the destruction. The front wall of the house rippled and collapsed inward, sending a galaxy of red sparks into the smoky pall above it.

Tor was watching Grayson's face. "That was the house of your friends, I take it."

"Yes...yes, it was. But I don't understand. Why did they destroy just that one house?" Berenir's house had been eliminated with surgical precision, but none of the other buildings on the block had been touched. Grayson wondered if Claydon had survived. As the *Marauder* moved on to the north, leaving rubble and flames behind, Grayson thought it was unlikely. He watched grimly as another wall of Berenir's house collapsed in a shower of sparks.

Grayson and Tor edged back away from the street. "Sorry about your friends," Tor said.

Grayson nodded. He felt curiously empty now, drained of all but the need to strike back against the bandit 'Mechs. But how? How? A feeling of helplessness weighed heavily on him now.

"I'm heading for the port," Tor said. "Technicians are always in demand, and I've got enough ship teching skill to find me a billet. You can come along as my assistant and we'll find a way to dye your hair. Then you won't have to take mud baths, right?"

Grayson thought for a moment, then shook his head. "Go on without me, Captain. I've got something else to do."

Tor was taken back. "What?" he wanted to know. "Where?"

"I've...never mind," Grayson said, distracted by his own musings. "I've just got to do some thinking, is all. I'll find you at the port later."

"When?"

Grayson shrugged. "I don't know." He glanced down at his hand, wondering why it was not trembling. His legs and arms felt weak, as though the surge of emotions that had drained away at the sight of the *Marauder* had left him a husk, scarcely able to stand. The adrenalin high that had kept him going till now was vanishing, leaving him exhausted.

He turned to face Tor. "Just go. I'll join you when I can."

Tor grinned, but worry showed in his eyes. "Don't take too long. Us aliens have to stick together now, right?"

Go to hell and leave me alone, Grayson thought with a viciousness that surprised him. He said nothing, however, but nodded and turned away. He was going to have to find transportation to the mountains, and was not entirely sure that he had the strength to manage it.

The junior officer stood stiffly at attention and felt the sweat pooling in the collar of his black body armor. "No, Lord, he is not here."

Looking up from the paperwork on his desk, the seated man regarded his officer with a cold and level gaze. "He must be. I shot him myself. I saw him fall, right at the spot I marked on the map of the vehicle bay I gave you."

"He was not there, Lord." There was fear in the young man's face. His commander had a reputation for ruthlessness. "We have searched the Castle, and checked all the bodies. There... there is evidence that someone was moving about the Castle after our departure. Perhaps this is the boy you seek. A storage compartment door Sergeant Wynn remembers seeing closed after the battle was open when we returned, and the manifest for that room shows a hovercraft missing. Carlyle's son must have taken a machine and escaped."

Captain Lord Harimandir Singh considered himself a just man—ruthless, yes, and demanding—but not given to whims of raw emotions. He had fired the single shot that had hit the enemy commander's son in the head. It had been his order that had led the attacking party and its prisoners out of the vehicle bay to follow the surviving Commandos to their spaceport perimeter. If Grayson Death Carlyle still lived, it was Singh's responsibility, and not that of the lieutenant trying so unsuccessfully to mask his terror.

So, the fault is mine, Singh thought. *I should have sealed the matter with a second shot, or at least had someone stay and check for wounded in the bay.*

But things had been happening so fast down in that repair bay. Only rapid decisions and swift movement would have accomplished the mission.

And the mission *had* been accomplished, had it not? Carlyle's Commandos were broken, the survivors fled, and their base in Singh's hands. If this one boy had managed to escape to Sarghad, could that seriously jeopardize the grand plan? Singh's specific orders had been to make certain of the death of Carlyle's senior tech, Riviera, all MechWarriors remaining in the Castle, and Carlyle's son. The orders had been carried out—all except for the very last.

Singh considered the matter carefully. The boy had not escaped with the surviving members of Carlyle's lance, he was certain of that. If he lived, he could only be hiding somewhere in Trellwan's desert wilderness, or in that sprawling refuse heap at the foot of this mountain the indigs called Sarghad.

If he *had* made it to the wilderness, his time was running out. Periasteron would bake those deserts with killing heat in only a few more standard days. And even if the boy survived *that* by hiding in a cave somewhere, the -50 degree weather of Trellwan's brief winter would finish him by Secondnight.

That left the city. There was no way to search the entire city for one boy, and no real reason to attempt it. Young Carlyle would not be able to get off the planet, would not even be able to approach the spaceport without being challenged by the perimeter guards. He was effectively marooned on Trellwan. The rest of the Plan was proceeding smoothly, and it seemed Carlyle's son would pose no obstacle to its final stages.

Besides, there was always the chance he would be picked up by a patrol unit. Singh decided it would be best to issue a patrol order requiring that he be notified if anyone of Carlyle's approximate age were taken in Sarghad or at the spaceport... no, make that any off-worlders, whatever their age. One way or the other, he would learn the boy's whereabouts or assure himself that he was dead.

The officer was still standing at attention before him. "That will be all, Lieutenant. You have done well. Thank you for your report."

The lieutenant sagged visibly with relief, then stiffened and executed a smart right-fist-to-left-chest salute. "Yes, Lord!"

Singh watched the man turn on his heel and leave. No, Carlyle's escape should not affect the Plan at all.

He returned his attention to the work on his desk, a report he was writing for the Duke. A fast courier was scheduled to arrive at the jump point within 24 hours, and Singh's report would bring the Duke and his armada to Trellwan before another local year had passed.

Singh knew His Grace, Duke Ricol, known throughout the Successor States as The Red Hunter, was eager to begin execution of the next phase of the game.

Above Mount Gayal and the brooding, truncated pyramid of the Castle, there rose a series of jagged, cliff-faced peaks, part of the braid of rugged mountain ranges circling Trellwan's equator. The Crysander Mountains were raw and new, shaped by the incessant tidal twistings of Trellwan's very close sun, which continued to fold and refold those upthrusting layers of igneous rock and, on occasion, literally turned them inside out in lava flows and eruptions. Many of the peaks along the 35,000-kilometer-long range were enthusiastically active volcanoes, and mild seismic quakes were a daily occurrence.

Although most of Trellwan was arid, there were two small, snaking, mineral seas nestled among the equatorial mountains. The planet's human colonies had grown in the relatively fertile regions within a few hundred kilometers of these bodies. The slow tidal swell raised by red Trell once each fifteen standard days was too high to encourage seaside settlements. Also, the high sulfur and hydrogen sulfide content of those acid waters made the air for kilometers around heavy with a sour, rotten-egg stench. However, much of Trellwan's power came from unmanned tidal generator plants along the foul-smelling shores of those seas.

Periasteron marked the beginning and the end of each 45-day year. It was the time when Trellwan was closest to Trell in its slightly eccentric orbit about the star, and always occurred over the same two spots on the planet's surface. The Periasteron called Far Passage occurred on the other side of the world in the middle of each Secondnight. It was heralded in Sarghad by mild storms sweeping in from the dayside, and by gradually rising temperatures that marked the beginning of Sarghad's brief spring-summer-fall.

The Periasteron called Near Passage occurred over the Nerge, the Black Desert, 2,000 kilometers to the west of the city, and was altogether different.

Trell was in the sky at that time, just past the middle of Firstday for Sarghad's longitude. As the local temperature rocketed under the burning heat, water evaporated from the surface of the nearby sea at an accelerated rate. Clouds boiled skyward so quickly that their growth could be followed with the eye. As vast volumes of hot, wet air rushed from ground level into the chill stratosphere, they dragged in desert winds that howled across Sarghad from the mineral flats to the east.

Then the rains came, violent, rattling-wind rains that turned the ocher deserts to seas of mud and flooded the streets of Sarghad. As the planet's slow rotation continued, Sarghad gradually descended into continuous night. In that long night, the storm continued while temperatures plummeted.

By mid-Firstnight, some five or six standard days later, it was snowing in the mountains above the city. Most of the moisture deposited as snow fell in the mountains, and across the great ergs and glacial plains far to the north and south. The equatorial desert around Sarghad froze solid as temperatures plummeted to 50 degrees or more below zero, and high in the mountains, short-lived glaciers grew.

The snow lay heavy among the jagged range peaks. There were places where seismic shocks and the repeated cycles of snow, freezing, heat, and falling meltwater had cracked open the mountains, laying bare ancient, hidden faults, caverns, and the wellsprings of river leading down to the sea. Hot mineral springs rising within the caves opened caverns beneath glistening roofs of ice. Within these caverns' sheltering heat, there was the steadily echoing *plip-plip-plip* of snow melting and trickling down the fantastic dagger shapes of stalactites.

Far Passage occurred in mid-Secondnight. There were storms then, mostly wind- and duststorms born on warm winds from the antipodes, and the temperature began to rise. By mid-Thirday, the temperature was above freezing, and still climbing. Whole mountains of rapidly accumulated ice and packed snow began melting.

In places, the melt was catastrophic.

Thunder Rift was the largest and deepest of the network of fault-rifts and caverns in the mountains north of Sarghad. During cold periods, it was completely roofed over by ice hundreds of meters thick. From early Thirday until well into Firstday, meltwater created an icy cataract. The booming, cascading, white-raging waterfall fell by many-branching paths worn through ice and rock into a deep-cleft lake, from which spray rose like a cloud. During warming periods, that cloud spray hung above the V-shaped notch that marked the Rift as seen from the city plain, and the thunder of the waters could be distantly heard above the incessant murmur of street merchants and vendors.

Grayson had discovered the Rift shortly after Carlyle's Commandos had arrived on Trellwan. It had become a refuge from Kai Griffith's demands and criticisms and from the crowded barracks. At times, it had even given refuge from the the gentle but critically sharp eye of his father.

Once, several local years ago, he had brought Mara here for a few hours' gentle diversion. He'd hoped she would feel as enthralled with the cavern's beauty as he, and had been keenly disappointed by her lack of response. The mouth of the Rift was too noisy, she'd told him, the air too wild and wet, the water-worn rock too cold and hard for what they'd planned to do.

He hadn't returned for several local days after that episode, but not even Mara could long dim his enchantment with the place. Though Grayson returned many times after that day, he had always come alone.

The Rift was where he needed to be now. It had taken only a few moments to find a Sarghad Militia ground effect skimmer parked at the fringe of the churning street mob. He felt little compunction about taking the machine. It was, after all, one of the light military vehicles the Commandos had given the local militia shortly after the garrison had arrived. It had been signed over to the locals as part of the mutual military training and assistance agreement between Trellwan and the Commonwealth government.

After what Grayson had been through in the last few hours, he felt the Trells at least owed him some transportation. The skimmer carried him on a swirling trail of dust out of Sarghad and across the irrigated fields north of the city.

There was vegetation there, stubby and stained dark blue by Trellwan's copper sulfide-based analogue of chlorophyll. A single, wide, rust-crusted pipe brought water down from the mountains to the north, irrigating the patchwork of blue vegetation alternating with low, dull silver agrodomes that stretched into the desert beyond the city. Humans could not eat the local vegetation, and so grew fields of imported grains and vegetables inside the temperature and light-controlled shelter of the agrodomes. Local crops adapted to Trellwan's cyclical climate provided the spices (safe if ingested in small quantities) and the shrub-grown, mineral-dense hardwoods that were the staples of Trellwan's off-planet trade.

Grayson guided the skimmer across the fields, opening up the little craft's considerable full speed, angling toward the glacier nesting in its V-shaped notch in the mountains to the north. There were a few people about, mostly field workers urging scaly-humped laniks out of low, domed shelters. Now that the attackers had gone, work in the fields and agrodomes would continue. None of the workers took notice of the hovercraft's flight.

There were switchback paths up the face of the mountains, but eventually he had to leave the skimmer among a jumble of boulders. From there, he plunged into a network of low-ceilinged caverns that would lead him into the mountain's heart, and then into the vault of the main Rift.

Grayson was aware first of the sound of the Rift, a dull thunder audible across ten kilometers even in the streets of Sarghad. In the caverns, the booming roar rang and pounded through rock channels and drummed at his senses like something alive. The sound rang out only during the time between early Thirday and early Firstday when the icepacks were melting and pouring into the 200-meter-deep hollow of the Rift, but Grayson knew what to do. He used to bring along ear protectors, but then discovered wads of slick, waxy yellow clay from the cavern floor would work as well to protect his hearing. He carefully plugged his ears, then headed up the slanting cavern trail toward the source of the thundering roar.

There was a ledge, the remnant of some age-old convulsion of the planet's crust, which ran along the riftwall halfway up between the translucent glow of the ice ceiling and the shadowed dimness of the spray-shrouded lake below. On that ledge, he was surrounded by the mountain's exultant roar and intense vibration. The air was cool, heavy with moisture and alive with the thrumming waves of sound from the cataracts of water. The central void of the Rift was filled with water funneling from channels and water-worn passages within the ice roof overhead. From time to time, multi-ton boulders of ice would break free and fall 200 meters through spray-filled space, and plunge into the foam and fury below.

Grayson carefully traveled along the ledge to the left. There, to the south, the Rift opened up to air and light, and the ice ceiling gave way to clear sky framed by the surrounding cliffs. Through the opening, he could see the helicopter pad on the roof of the Castle five kilometers out and down. Beyond and below that was the wheel-shaped sprawl of Sarghad. At his feet, the Rift wall dropped straight down 100 meters to the edge of the lake.

That lake was very deep and quite long. Several kilometers farther into the mountain, it fell by cascades and steaming waterfalls through the northern opening of the Rift, flowed by deep and winding channels farther north, then catapulted a final 50 meters in spray and spume into the murky yellow and sulfur-stinking waters of the mountain-locked Grimheld Sea. The southern shore of the lake, sheltered on either side by the Rift walls, opened to a boulder-sprinkled ravine leading to the arid badlands south of the mountain. The irrigation pipeline was only barely visible from this altitude.

Surrounded by sound, Grayson sat down on a mist-slick boulder. From this vantage point, he could see people on the roof of the Castle, though it was impossible to tell what they were doing or to make out details. As the spaceport lay behind and below the Castle, not much of it was visible from here. Grayson did manage to distinguish part of the control tower, a ground station communication dish, and what might have been the blunt prow of the *Invidious'* DropShip. He wished he had his electronic binoculars so he could spy on workers moving among the gantry scaffolding near the ship.

Grayson studied the Castle roof. There were several helicopters there, light scouting machines he recognized from the Commandos' vehicle depot. As he watched, one of the machines lifted into the air and swung like a huge, gleaming insect toward the port. With their acquisition of the Castle and all the equipment the lance had not had time to move or destroy, the pirates had made out quite well.

Grayson's thoughts slipped back to his need, his burning desire for revenge. Right now, it seemed like a hopeless quest. Scarcely tried in battle, unarmed, what chance did he have against a *Marauder?* For vengeance, he would need a heavy 'Mech at least, one that could stand up against that 75-ton machine. He'd also need a 'Mech lance to go with it—or a small army trained and equipped to fight 'Mechs. After all, that *Marauder* wasn't alone. There were other pirate 'Mechs on Trellwan, and how many hundreds of pirate troopers?

Grayson thought about this for a moment. The attack on the Castle had been so methodical, so carefully timed and planned. It didn't fit the typical slash-and-run tactics of bandit raiders. The more he thought about it, the stranger it seemed. The pirates had had to plan and execute the capture of Tor's ship by intercepting it at one of thirty possible navigation and power bank charging points between Oberon VI and Trellwan. Then they had to transfer the men and material for the attack to the *Invidious* once they captured her—never an easy task in deep space—and then equip the DropShip with the extra weapons that had surprised and devastated his father's *Phoenix Hawk.* All of that had been timed and coordinated with what was happening on Trellwan. The pirates must have convinced or bought the astech Stefan's help (and probably others) in bypassing the Castle's security system so a commando force could get in.

There'd been dozens of them—a company at least—and probably more. It seemed they'd been divided into numerous small units, each assigned a different target within the Castle. Grayson remembered the sight of them entering the Control Center, and knew with cold certainty they were not native troops. They must have been brought in from elsewhere, probably on another freighter DropShip that had grounded at the port some hours before. That part of the operation had demanded careful preparation and precise timing to allow it to be carried out just as Carlyle's *Phoenix Hawk* approached the *Invidious'* DropShip. The entire scheme suggested a major military operation—and an expensive one. Grayson was sure there was more to it than a mutiny against Oberon by a handful of his own pirate warlords.

Unbidden, the memory of his attacker's face returned to Grayson. That lean, dark face with the trim mustache and beard. The too-bright eyes, the eyes of a fanatic. Grayson believed he had seen that face before, but where?

An important part of any apprentice MechWarrior's training required him to become familiar with other MechWarriors. Not all of them, of course, but the important ones, the brilliant ones, the successful mercenaries and warleaders who had carved names for themselves across the battlefields of a thousand war-torn worlds. Was it in the computer files of known warriors he'd studied in Trellwan that Grayson had seen that dark face?

Was it that of a MechWarrior? A ground forces officer? He covered his eyes with one hand. *Think...think!*

He opened his eyes, blinked into the light, stood and breathed deeply, but the man's identity did not come to him. Grayson knew, though, that if he had seen that face while studying the computer files, the information he needed would still be there in the central computer in the Castle.

Somehow, he thought, *somehow I have to get back inside.*

CHAPTER 11

Grayson had lost track of time since he'd left Berenir's house with the thought of contacting Mara. Not wanting to attract unwanted attention to his off-worlder origins, he'd left his wristcomp with Claydon. And, on a world where it took the sun fifteen standard days to crawl from one horizon to the other, it was impossible to guess the time.

Whatever the hour, he was hungry and dead tired. Resting on the ledge had restored him somewhat, but he was certainly in no shape to attack anybody—certainly not a 75-ton armored giant. At the moment, the need for money overshadowed his need for vengeance, indeed, overshadowed every other need. It would get him a place to sleep, something to eat, and perhaps a bottle of dye for his tell-tale hair.

Grayson wasn't entirely sure how he was going to go about getting his hands on some local currency. Mara was his only friend, and she seemed out of reach. His only possession was a stolen hovercraft that would get him arrested the moment he tried to sell it. The local militia frowned on attempts to procure and sell military hardware.

Emerging from the cavern near where he'd hidden the hovercraft, Grayson began rummaging through the open-topped cockpit and cargo area, looking for something he might turn to his advantage.

Three candy bars stashed in an underseat compartment were put to immediate service. There seemed to be little else of value, except for a metal toolbox crowded with ratchets, spanners, drivers, and various other tools for mechanical repairs and maintenance. They did not seem to be marked. If he could find a pawn shop or even a mechanical tech's supply house in Sarghad, he might be able to sell the tools for enough money to buy a meal and a room for at least one sleep period.

His only other alternative was robbery, which seemed even less promising. Unless he was able to threaten his victim with a large wrench, Grayson wouldn't be taken seriously as an armed robber, and he had no stomach for striking innocent people down from behind.

He decided to try to sell the tools, then perhaps head to the spaceport and find Captain Tor. Failing that, he might be able to get a job as a hand in one of Sarghad's agrodomes. He didn't care what the job was. All he needed was to keep alive on a hostile planet while he planned his revenge on the *Marauder* pilot. That desire was rapidly becoming the central driving force of his existence.

Leaving the skimmer behind a warehouse on the outskirts of the city, Grayson walked toward the hub, carrying the toolbox. He wasn't certain how to find what he wanted, and feared asking directions. His mud-smeared, scarecrow appearance wouldn't help his chances of getting a straight answer, and he didn't know enough about Trell culture to guess where a pawn shop or tool supply house might be located. After some thought, he decided his best chance was to try the Streets of the Merchants. With feet aching in his too-tight boots, he stumbled in the general direction of Sarghad's business quarter.

Twice he became lost, straightening out only when he realized he had reached the Hub. There were the Palace Gardens, the domes of the Palace showing above spreading, cobalt shrubs alive with short-lived flowers. If he could just reach Mara, every problem would be solved! But the green-coated soldiers still paraded inside the main gate, and the streets were thick with Palace Guards and the brown uniforms of the Militia. If he were to try scaling the three-meter fence, they would cut him down before he made it to the top.

No, the Third Street of the Merchants was back *that* way. He would try to find Mara later.

Singh stood just inside the gaping repair bay doors. As he watched the troops fall into formation, thunder boomed incessantly from the mountains above the Castle. He had four full companies, about 300 men under his direct command, as well as five 'Mechs. Two companies manned the perimeter at the spaceport. The remaining two were here, weapons and body armor red-gilt in the warming sun, their ground effect transports idling in dusty rows nearby.

Behind the ranks of faceless, armor-masked troops towered the five 'Mechs of the battalion. Lieutenant Vallendel's *Marauder* was the lead BattleMech, of course, and would head up the actual fighting, but he was in overall command.

He, Harimandir Singh, in command of a five-'Mech lance! It was a singular honor the Duke had bestowed on him. Covert operations such as Code Dragon were too sensitive, too delicate to be given into the hands of a relatively junior MechWarrior like Vallendel. It made Singh proud that the Duke had entrusted this fighting force into his care, that he had placed Code Dragon under his command until it was time for the Duke to make his own appearance. Singh savored the heady rush of power.

Four smaller 'Mechs flanked the *Marauder*: a *Stinger*, a *Locust*, and the pair of *Wasps* captured during the battle with Carlyle's lance. Singh was less certain of their pilots than he was of Vallendel. The lieutenant was one of the Duke's experienced warriors, handpicked for this mission, but three of the pilots of the four 20-tonners were green, and three were mercenaries picked up on Sigurd in Hendrik's confederacy. Those three didn't know the full extent of the Plan, of course. Nor did they realize that they would die soon, sacrificed to the Plan once the Duke arrived to take charge.

Sergeant Mendoza, the *Stinger*'s pilot, was the only one with any experience, having spent a good many years piloting 'Mechs in the service of the Duke. That one would go down fighting when the time came. Singh's dark eyes narrowed at the thought. It might be best to end his career with an assassin's blade first, to prevent unnecessary complications. That would be a pity, but in this game of stroke and counterstroke, secrecy was so essential that even Vallendel, even Singh himself, might be sacrificed to preserve it. If the Commonwealth detected even a hint of Code Dragon, the mission would fail. Singh knew failure was one option the Duke never tolerated.

The *Wasp*s were piloted by Sigurdian mercenaries, privates Enzelman and Fitzhugh, and the *Locust* by a Corporal Kalmar. All three were painfully inexperienced, fresh from their apprenticeships on one of Hendrik's worlds, but they seemed competent enough. They'd joined the unit on Sigurd just before the expedition had left to rendezvous with the Mailai freighter.

It was not, perhaps, the most skillful or best trained of 'Mech lances, but it would be more than adequate against the pathetic popinjays defending Sarghad. That single skirmish on the outskirts of the town earlier had proven that. Imagine, armored personnel carriers piled high with troopers, driving straight up to the guns of a battle-hungry *Marauder*! It had been a slaughter, and the city's defenders would be thoroughly demoralized by now. What's more, Vallendel had brought back prisoners, from whom Singh had learned the precise location of the Royal Family's battle shelters under the palace.

His forces had only just returned from Sarghad, and he could see the men were tired, their formation less than rigidly perfect. Whether the troops were tired or not, Singh intended to continue to push the indigs with all he had, as hard as he could. They would not know a moment's respite until the Plan's second phase.

Parts of the city were still sending up twisting coils of black smoke where fires raged among those barbarian shacks and hovels. Singh knew it was time to strike again, before the populace could recover from the first raid.

It was a shame, perhaps, that the *Shadow Hawk* that had been put out of action to critically weaken the Castle's defense was not yet repaired. What an armored force *that* would be. Four lights led by a *'Hawk* and a *Marauder* team! Well, no matter. The captured *'Hawk* would be repaired by the time Duke Ricol arrived. In the meantime, the force Singh had would be more than adequate against the Sarghad rabble.

He raised his hands, shouting above the distant rumble from the mountain rift. "Men! Soldiers in the service of the Red Duke! This is the climax to our part of the Grand Plan!" Of all the troops before him, only Lieutenant Vallendel knew the plan's details, of course, but all could share in the excitement and pride of playing their part in a great scheme.

"Word has been dispatched to our Lord, notifying him of the successful completion of the first phase. When he arrives to begin the second phase, our part in this glorious project will be completed...nobly and honorably so.

"For now, we have this world at our feet! I know you are hot and tired, that you have been fighting hard, but now is the time to strike again, without mercy!" Singh gestured toward the city sprawled on the plain below the Castle, helpless and inviting in the bloody sunlight.

"Lieutenant Vallendel and Sergeant Mendoza will lead the main ground forces! Their mission is to engage and obliterate the enemy ground defenses wherever they may be found. Our three Sigurdian allies, meanwhile, will attack designated targets within the Sarghad palace itself!"

He paused, eyes narrowed. It was a calculated risk, of course, assigning the attack on the palace to three youngsters... outsiders, at that. But the important part of the operation was to destroy the local defenses, and it didn't really matter whether they got through to the Royal Family or not. At worst, an attack on the palace would create a useful diversion and spread panic and hopelessness among the defenders. At best, Code Dragon's timetable might be advanced by several days. He had weighed the dangers and possible advantages, and decided to take the gamble.

"You three are to attack Sarghad, destroy local militia and guard forces where you find them, enter the palace, and take the royal family hostage. With Jeverid and his advisors as our prisoners, the rabble will surrender to us, and we will hand them over to the Duke when he arrives, a neatly wrapped present, tied up in diamond monofilament!"

The obligatory cheer went up at this obvious place for cheering, making up in volume what it lacked in spontaneity. Singh gestured again, this time toward the rows of pikes erected along the Castle parade ground outside the Repair Bay doors. The round, brown-encrusted objects impaled on the tip of each pike were already shriveled in the dry, sand blasting air of this world. Bared teeth gleamed below empty, staring eye sockets.

"Soldiers! Behold your enemies! So will fare all those stand against us! So will fare the enemies of the Duke! Hail, Duke Ricol! Hail, victory!"

Again the cheers, this time with nervous overtones. Everyone in the ranks knew the third impaled head from the right belonged to Sergeant Proller of Company C. He'd been in charge of securing the passageway in the Castle leading from Central Control to the Vehicle Bay. Somehow, he'd become lost. By the time his squad had reached their objective, the surviving defenders had secured a number of air cushion transports and escaped toward their perimeter at the spaceport.

It was time. At Lord Singh's shouted command, the ranks of men filed into their transports, which rose on dust-churning cushions of air and drifted with shrill keening down the slopes toward the city. Ahead of them, the five 'Mechs strode with lumbering, deadly purpose.

Grayson became aware of the attack as the mournful ululation of a siren rose above crowds of people gone suddenly motionless. Then came the dull *whump* of distant explosions, and the street crowds began to scatter and run in all directions, shrieking and wailing.

Another attack? Only a few hours had passed the last one—barely time for the raiders to reach the Castle and return!

He stepped to the side of the street as green and gold-clad Guardsmen clattered past at double time, their weapons held at port arms and their faces terribly young beneath visored, gold-edged helmets. Grayson could tell by the sound of the explosions that those were SRMs—short-range missiles— probably 'Mech-launched. What chance did these boys have against BattleMechs?

There was a sharp hiss overhead, an instant's glimpse of a white contrail arrowing from the sky, and the iron fence by the palace grounds across the street vanished in black earth and hurtling chunks of ferrocrete. Grayson fell on his face and clutched at the pavement as falling debris rattled and bounced around him. When he looked up, the street was littered with twisted bits of iron and rubble, and a steaming crater interrupted the curve of the fence.

He considered the hole for a moment. *My way in,* he thought, and then thought again. Mara would be on her way to a shelter by now. He had no idea where she would be, and wandering around the palace grounds during a battle would only get him shot.

The *Wasp* emerged from a hub street several hundred meters from Grayson's position. It was a sleek and elegant-looking machine, manlike in its movements and painted blue-white with black and yellow trim. Four antennae spiked back from its head like pricked ears, two on either side, giving it the look of an alert hunting animal. That head was scanning now, sweeping up and down the street. BattleMechs had nothing so crude or vulnerable as windows in their cockpits, of course, but the recessed scanner strip under the protective brow overhang gave the head the look of a visored space helmet. Its weapons included an SRM pack tucked into the hip of its left leg, and a medium laser the 'Mech swung in its right hand with deceptive, disturbing ease.

*Wasp*s were most frequently used as 'Mech unit scouts. They were fast, relatively light-armed and armored, and extremely maneuverable. With the fusion-heated jump jets tucked into legs and angular back-mounted packs, they could leap up to 180 meters—six times their own length—firing down on ground targets from the air or gaining a clear view of the surrounding terrain.

Even lying flat on his belly, Grayson recognized the machine. Though an eye had been painted over the scratched-out clenched-fist insignia on the front of the left leg, 'Mechs—especially the much-painted and battle-worn ones—were as unique as individual humans. This was a Carlyle's Commandos *Wasp,* captured during the battle that had stranded Grayson on Trellwan. His trained eye searched for new damage, but detected none. It was possible Mendelson had abandoned the machine during the evacuation, rather than lost it in battle.

Who's piloting it now? he wondered. It might be a rookie, an apprentice next in line for a newly acquired BattleMech. Or, it could just as easily be a battle-experienced MechWarrior who had lost his own 'Mech in combat. Whoever it was seemed to be handling the machine well enough. The movements were smooth, and the rapidly striding walk was natural and confident.

The *Wasp* was bearing down on him. Grayson forced himself to remain where he was, unmoving. Of all the panicked people now fleeing the invading 'Mechs, he alone had actually piloted one, and knew what it must look like to the warrior inside the cramped confinement of that tiny head. A person lying unmoving on the pavement would go unnoticed, appearing as nothing more than a stationary blur of heat-color on the IR scan. Only if he moved, or looked as though he were readying a weapon would the lightning fall...

The ferrocrete danced and jittered under him. *Wasp*s weighed only 20 tons, the lightest class of 'Mechs, but the alternating pedal pressure of 20 striding tons slammed the ground like vast pile drivers. Those long-extinct giants of old Earth known as elephants weighed only a third what a *Wasp* did, and this present-day monster bore that weight on two legs.

The massive, inverted Y of a flanged foot swung up, descended, booming. The creaks and metal-grating protests of flanges and carballoy joints piped and squeaked in the dust-filled air as the foot rose again, and the monster's shadow swept across and past Grayson's cowering form.

When he looked up, a flat but crumple-textured gray rectangle on the pavement nearby caught his attention. It took him a moment to recognize the heavy steel toolbox he'd taken from the hovercraft, crushed by the monster's tread. A scattering of tools had been driven into the tough surface of the ferrocrete, and were now like surreal decorations in the pavement. *That had been close,* he thought. *Another meter, and...*

Grayson dared to lift his head to look up...up...and up. The monster stood in the street ten meters away, its back toward him as it surveyed the steaming crater and the shredded fence. From its attitude, Grayson guessed the pilot must be reporting to other 'Mechs or troops. He could fool a passing 'Mech by playing dead, but a platoon of enemy troops was another matter.

He looked around, eyes wild, desperate for a hiding place. Doors lined the buildings facing the street, all closed, probably bolted. As if a deadbolt could stop a BattleMech that had decided it wanted to enter!

The 'Mech was moving again, striding rapidly toward the fence, and then straight into its iron bars. Grayson heard a cracking like the sound of gunshots as the iron gave way. For an instant, the monster stood entangled by the barrier almost hip-high to it. Then it kicked, shattering concrete foundations. The entire length of fencing twisted free and collapsed.

The *Wasp* strode into the palace garden, brushing aside flowering shrubs and trees with even greater ease. Then it stopped, pivoted, and brought the long, black tube of its laser cannon to bear on some unseen target to Grayson's right. The flash of the laser discharge was searing blue, intolerably bright. When his eyes could see through the dancing haze of spots before him again, the 'Mech was moving further up the hill toward the palace.

Grayson's head snapped around, following the *Wasp*'s progress. It looked as though one phase of the attackers' plan had fallen into place. That first attack earlier must have been a probing of the city defenses, organized so as to take plenty of prisoners. Grayson knew any 'Mech operation in a hostile city required plenty of intelligence. Those prisoners would have been questioned, and at least some would have known the interior layout of the palace. *If the 'Mechs are attacking the palace,* he reasoned, *they must plan to capture or kill the royal family and various members of the government.*

Mara! She would be there by now. What would happen to her? And what could he do? Unarmed, alone, the only way he could slow a 'Mech was if the machine happened to slip as it pulped his body underfoot. Grayson didn't plan on trying that tactical maneuver any time soon.

Wildly, he considered following the machine, considered trying to warn someone at the palace. But they would know the monster was approaching already, and even in the unlikely event Grayson could outrun the striding behemoth, there was no way his warning could be turned to advantage.

A high-pitched hum shrilled in Grayson's ears, and dust swirled in the street. A pair of light military ground effect hovercraft swung into the middle of the street, with soldiers piling out amid shouted orders and the clatter of weapons. One of the skimmers mounted a heavy machine gun, the other a quad-mounted autocannon. One brown-uniformed trooper slapped the heavy cassette of caseless ammo into the quad's receiver, and shouted to an officer standing with hands on hips in the street that he was ready.

"Those poor bastards open fire, and I'll be right in the line of return fire," Grayson muttered. He had only seconds to move.

The quad autocannon fired with a buzzsaw's scream, and left a sour taste of chemicals heavy in the air. Grayson saw eruptions of dirt and smoke running with explosive fury up the blue-grassed slope along the BattleMech's path. The 'Mech swung about as the stream of shells reached it, and the clang and roar of explosions smashing at its armor rang across the street above the booming of the cannon.

The 'Mech jumped, vaulting skyward with magical grace on flaring jets of superheated mercury steam. Grayson saw it twist in midair, swinging its laser down to align on the group of soldiers and vehicles in the street.

When the blast hit, Grayson was caught in it. Blue fire seemed to fill the air, as the laser beam hosed across the bricks of the building wall behind him a meter above his head. Bricks splintered as the trace of water within them vaporized. Hot shards rained on Grayson's bare neck, and the beam swept on, slicing into the hovering GEV. The explosion blotted out the sky.

CHAPTER 12

As the fireball rose in the sky, roiling orange against oily black, men leaped howling from the stricken vehicle with their clothes in flames. The quad cannon's ammo went off with a roar that sent shards of metal hurtling dozens of meters before they fell smoking to the pavement. The officer in charge of the party had been scooped up by the blast and deposited in a shredded and bloody heap a dozen meters away.

Grayson was unhurt, except for the sting of small burns on his neck and the backs of his hands. As he had been lying flat, the deadly, blast-driven shrapnel had passed above him, and he'd been far enough from the explosion to miss the worst effects.

The *Wasp* had ended its short flight with near-catastrophic results. The pilot had overbalanced his machine on landing, and it had collided with the front of a building fifty meters further down the street with the roar of mountains falling. The 'Mech was struggling to rise now, sending bricks and broken chunks of stone skittering into the street as it moved. The building had a gaping hole in it where the door and windows had been, jagged with the broken spars of the structure's frame.

The second hovercraft was still idling further out in the street. Dead or horribly mangled, its crew lay sprawled on the pavement or crumpled over the well deck's rim. They had been caught by the full violence of the first hovercraft's exploding ammo, and the blast fragments had sliced through them like a scythe. Some of those limp bundles scattered in the street were still moving, and several shrieked and screamed with shocking vigor.

Grayson lay there, terrified. There was a terrible clarity to his awareness of the stench of burning flesh, of the rough pavement under his clawed hands, of the hiss and roar of the burning GEV. Some men in the street were still alive and unhurt, soldiers as terrified as Grayson was. He saw several running down the street, their weapons and helmets abandoned on the ferrocrete behind them. Most of the survivors lay as Grayson did, hugging the street in terror-born paralysis.

"There's only one sure way to overcome panic," Kai Griffith had repeated to Grayson so many times the words had become part of his being. He heard them again now as though Griff were standing at his side. *"The only way to beat panic is to* do *something. I don't care if what you do is dead wrong, taking action is better than just sitting there getting killed!"*

Grayson felt mild surprise that he was able to think at all, but glanced around at the cowering soldiers. Militia, most of them were, with a few green-coats thrown in. They had panicked already, and were too scared to move. Griffith had words for them as well. *"If everyone else is panicking, the person who does something is the one they'll follow. So when you're up against it, don't freeze. Take command...and do something!"*

Do something...do something...

Grayson found himself running, running without thinking toward the keening GEV that still hovered, almost undamaged, at the center of the street. When he vaulted aboard, the impact of his mass sent the machine sideslipping along the street, its fans kicking up billows of dust.

The machine gun mounted on the pintle between the driver's seat and the observer's position was standard military issue, a belt-fed chopper with a cyclic rate of 1500 rounds per minute. Its grip was familiar in Grayson's hand as he checked the ammo feed. It was one of the weapons given to the Sarghad Militia by Carlyle's Commandos when the lance had arrived to bolster Trellwan's defenses.

The hovercraft was still drifting sideways when he opened fire at the 'Mech sprawled in rubble and still-falling debris, and he had to track back to stay on target. At twenty meters, Grayson could scarcely miss.

Keeping the machine gun centered on the fallen giant's head, he held down the trigger until the pulsing roar filled his ears and pounded at his hands with demon fury. Hot brass cartridges sprayed from the ejection port to fall clinking on the deck at Grayson's feet.

Heavy caliber rounds splintered and sparked across the 'Mech's shoulders and head. Grayson knew the armor on the *Wasp*'s head was thin. There was scant room in that small, squat box for the pilot, let alone room enough for heavy armor. The 'Mech tried to rise, but when the rubble shifted under its feet, it collapsed again, sliding down into the street. Piercing rounds of fire hammered and chattered as Grayson played short bursts across the machine's head. Successive rounds sought out a chink, and sent it flying in pieces that caught the sunlight as they splattered. The twin antennae on one side of the 'Mech's head were already gone, chopped away by his relentless stream of high-velocity metal.

The 'Mech slid, rolled, brought its arms underneath it. The laser lay nearby, jarred from the monster's grasp when it fell. Grayson saw the *Wasp*'s head swinging up, searching for the weapon, as he kept firing burst upon burst at the machine's armor.

Then the *Wasp* was up and moving with unexpected speed, rushing the hovercraft with gauntleted hands outstretched. Suddenly, the monster was so close Grayson could no longer angle his gun high enough to keep it trained on the head. An armored fist swung up, plunged down—

Grayson lunged across the seat and yanked the hovercraft's control stick to the side, sending the machine in a slithering glide, skimming sideways across the crater by the palace grounds fence and into the ruin of the palace garden. The 'Mech recovered from its missed swing and followed, but clumsily. The pounding from the machine gun must have rattled the pilot, might even have injured him. Letting the craft's momentum carry it crabwise up the blue slope, Grayson crouched behind the machine gun again and opened fire. Bullets smashed against the scanner plate, and the charging 'Mech staggered as though wounded, stopped, and narrowly missed falling again.

There were soldiers around Grayson, he realized, brown-uniformed Militia and a sprinkling of richly-clad Guardsmen, dirty-faced and ragged but with a growing determination in their faces. They were armed only with personal weapons, but added the volume of their firepower to the metal hosing from Grayson's machine gun. Kai Griffith had been right. The troops had responded to someone taking action. His single-handed duel with the BattleMech had rallied them, and they were forming up on his defensive line.

"The head!" He found himself screaming, his voice raw with the effort. "Aim for the head!"

There was a flash and a deep-throated explosion as a grenade detonated in black smoke and dirt by the 'Mech's foot. The *Wasp* fell, dropping to hands and knees with a clatter of armor and mass. It left raw dirt grooves in the blue sward where it moved. Grayson leaned over and adjusted the drift of his vehicle, sending it in a slow glide toward the downed 'Mech. Then he straightened up, took careful aim, and ripped out another long, rolling burst of machine gun fire.

Armor splintered, fragmenting, flashing in the air about the head of the stricken battle machine. Bullets were penetrating the head now, smashing into the cockpit and riddling it through and through. The BattleMech sagged and collapsed, face down in a junkyard heap, its metal elbows and feet akimbo, pointed at unnatural angles into the sky. Bright red blood trickled from jagged rents in the shattered cockpit.

The troops around Grayson let out a cheer that drowned the roar of battle. His hovercraft dipped and swayed as several eager troopers piled on.

"Great shooting, sir!" one yelled. Strange how they assumed he was someone in authority. He certainly could not *look* like an officer in his ragged civilian's tunic and caking of dried mud and smoke stains. Was it because he had taken the initiative? Whatever the reason, take advantage of it! "You!" His voice was hoarse, painfully raw, but he packed it with all the authority he could muster. "Drive! Get us to the palace main gate!" He could see the flash and smoke of another firefight down the curve of the avenue. "You!" he shouted at another. "Help me load."

His gun duel with the 'Mech had gone through four linked, 250-round belts. Ten rounds on the last belt dangled unfired below the feed slot. With the soldier's help, he discarded those rounds and snapped in a fresh belt.

Warm air whipped past his face as the driver gunned the GEV past the fallen 'Mech and skimmed back into the street. Troops, dozens of them, ran along behind, shouting, shaking their weapons in the air, rooting out other soldiers hiding along the street and pressing them into the column.

A second *Wasp* knelt before the entrance where the front gate had once stood. It was firing its laser with steady deliberation up the drive in the direction of the palace. Burning vehicles and dead Palace Guards littered the grass before it.

Grayson felt his newfound confidence ebbing. He had managed to catch the first *Wasp* by surprise, opening fire from close range while the 'Mech was down, helpless in a pile of spilled rubble. He could expect no such good fortune from this machine.

"Skew us, quick!" His shout to the driver saved them. The 'Mech had sensed their approach, and had dropped to the ground in a thundering shoulder roll, bringing its laser up to point as it did so. The pulse of coherent light sliced through the GEV's port skirts. Air spilled, and the vehicle tilted sharply, sliding off to the left.

Grayson opened fire, a long, stuttering burst. He could see sparks and puffs of dust as his shots struck home, but the range was too great to allow him the accuracy required to zero in on a target as small as the BattleMech's head. Paint scarred and flaked as the heavy rounds pounded along the machine's upper torso. Then, Grayson saw soldiers moving through the dense white smoke to the left. Squinting at them through burning haze, he noted black armor and helmets that enclosed their faces completely. Pirate troops!

A wild firefight had broken out on the avenue before the palace entrance. The attackers opened up on the speeding hovercraft. Feeling bullets zing just centimeters above his head, Grayson ducked involuntarily. He swung the machine gun on these new attackers, firing now in short, searching bursts that probed the piles of rubble and collapsed buildings where the black-armored figures moved. Three armored men in a line jerked like puppets and pitched off a rubble mound. The others scattered, diving for cover.

The hovercraft smashed into a pile of bricks with a shriek of protesting metal and the ragged thud and rattle of a bent fan blade. The craft pitched and spun wildly, still circling to the left as air spilled from the damaged skirt. Grayson reached out and grabbed the driver's shoulder.

"Hey, get it under control, will you?" But the driver's head lolled back, and when Grayson pulled away his hand, it was slick with blood. A bullet had entered the driver's mouth and snapped his neck cleanly at the base of the skull.

The hovercraft grated along the pavement, striking sparks from its damaged fan. Grayson muscled the dead driver out from behind the stick and pushed him onto the street, then slid into his place. The GEV was losing power, and he had to fight to keep it from circling left.

The *Wasp* was standing now, crouched in a gunfighter's stance with its laser held out before it. The weapon fired, and an eye-searing pulse arrowed down the street toward a cluster of approaching vehicles. It seemed to have forgotten about Grayson's GEV, for it was facing partly away from him as it traded shots with the approaching infantry.

Grayson yelled to his loader to jump, then gunned the little machine's engine into a yowling keen broken by the deadly thumping air, canting the vehicle to the right to haul the torn left skirt clear of the ground on a faltering cushion of air. He rammed the stick forward as hard as he could. The hovercraft leapt across the street, engines shrieking and pounding with the effort. The *Wasp*'s pilot sensed danger at the last possible moment, rose, half turning, bringing the laser around to bear.

The hovercraft hit the giant behind the right ankle at almost 200 kph, and Grayson went hurtling forward through fire and the noise of hell.

CHAPTER 13

Grayson was airborne for the eternity of a second or two, then landed with a rib-smashing blow in the blue grass. The fall had knocked the wind from his lungs, and he lay gasping for breath. Managing to roll over on his back, he saw the gleaming mountain of the *Wasp* against the green sky.

The hovercraft had smashed into the 'Mech's right ankle. Grayson had hoped to clip the back of the leg in such a way that the *Wasp* would fall, perhaps damaging itself. The hovercraft was nearly half as long as the 'Mech was tall, and packed considerable mass in its stubby frame. But it hadn't worked. The 'Mech had shifted at the last moment, taking the wrenching impact on a skirt of armor plate that protected the side of the foot. The skimmer had bounced and crumpled, spilling itself across the ground. Grayson had been lucky the crash had thrown him past that armored pillar and into the grass, and not smack into a metal wall.

His luck was rapidly becoming a moot point. The foot was lurching into the air, dropping toward him. Grayson dove to the left, rolled on his shoulder, then scrambled to his feet. The armored boot gouged a meter-wide furrow in the spot of grass where he'd just been. It surprised him to find he could still move so fast. His chest hurt, probably from a cracked rib, but the picture of himself being stepped on like a beetle gave a special impetus to his flight. Ahead, the soldier who had loaded for him waved him on.

Then he was among a number of soldiers, most of them city militia. A trio of open-topped, six-wheeled armored vehicles was driving up, with ungainly light PPCs, or particle projection cannons, mounted on their rear decks. They fired as he turned to look at the *Wasp.*

Those weapon carrier PPCs were not as heavy as the particle cannon carried by some 'Mechs, but they could do fearful damage to the most stubborn armor. Their disadvantage was that they required critical seconds to recharge after each shot. The beams carved blue-white paths of ionization through protesting air, and three thunderclaps sounded as one.

But the 'Mech was already twisting away as they fired, using its superb maneuverability to outguess the vehicles' targeting computers. White light flared from part of the *Wasp*'s back-mounted jet pack. But there was no serious damage. It would take ten seconds to recharge the PPCs.

"Scatter!" Grayson yelled. The BattleMech was turning, bringing its laser to bear. Grayson grabbed a handhold and swung aboard one of the weapons carriers as its driver accelerated in a burst of noise and spattering gravel.

The 'Mech turned, tracking, but Grayson noticed something that gave him a small thrill of hope. The *Wasp* seemed to be favoring its right leg, where its movements seemed stiff and a bit jerky.

Leaning back toward the PPC gunner, Grayson yelled above the roar of the vehicle. "When you're charged, aim for the right leg, down by his ankle! I think he's taken some damage in the actuators there!"

The soldier looked at him uncomprehendingly. Grayson pulled himself back to the weapon platform, pushed the soldier out of the way, and swung the cannon to align on the lumbering 'Mech. Target crosshairs centered on the *Wasp*'s foot, and computer readouts scrolling across the bottom of the screen confirmed a targeting lock. The charge light flashed green, and Grayson triggered the cannon.

The *Wasp*'s outer armor absorbed most of the blast, but there was a savage scar along the side of the foot now, and trailing scraps of fragmented metal. The 'Mech's jets fired as another weapons carrier fired. The shot missed, but the *Wasp*'s flight was low and wobbly. Grayson could see that the right leg jets were out of commission.

The 'Mech landed heavily overbalanced and for one moment, Grayson thought the right leg was going to collapse completely. Then the pilot recovered, and the *Wasp* lurched off into the city, traveling north as quickly as it could travel.

Grayson realized the roar he was hearing was the cheering of the soldiers around him. Next, it sunk in that they were cheering *him.*

"Wait a minute!" He yelled above the racket. "Wait a minute! It's not over! We can catch that bastard! He's damaged! We can catch him!"

It was a kind of bloodlust that drove Grayson on now, a blood lust born of the battle joy of being able at long last to strike back. The three weapons carriers raced down the street after the retreating 'Mech, soldiers clinging to handholds all around the rim of the vehicles' well decks, other troops following behind on foot. Victory had transformed them from a rabble into a fiercely determined fighting force. Grayson grinned to himself. They were still undisciplined and poorly trained, but at least they were learning they could fight!

One of the other gun carriers was ahead of Grayson's vehicle as they turned into the avenue down which the fleeing BattleMech had gone. Normally, a BattleMech could easily outdistance a wheeled armored vehicle, but the *Wasp*'s damage would have slowed it considerably. Grayson could see the machine's back. They were gaining on it.

The *Wasp* turned, brought up its laser and fired. The shot went off quickly, without careful aim, and the pulse shattered ferrocrete blocks in the sunscreen along the side of the avenue. The pursuing vehicles swerved suddenly, then bounced over scattering rubble.

"No! No! Keep going!" Grayson yelled. The lead vehicle had stopped, blocking the way, but at his not-too-gentle urging, the driver swung the steering tiller around and continued the chase.

Another 'Mech stepped into the street, its laser already trained and locked. The light pulse was followed by a blinding flash as the lead PPC carrier took a direct hit, and exploded in flame and a cascade of hot metal fragments. Grayson's driver swerved sharply to avoid the wreck, bouncing under the sunscreen to the right, and clattering through trash barrels and wooden crates crowded against the buildings.

Grayson studied the newcomer. It was another light scout 'Mech, a *Locust,* the smallest BatlleMech type he was familiar with.

The *Locust* was a peculiar departure from the typical humanoid 'Mech design. Body and head were fused into a single, flat fuselage suspended between very long, digitigrade-canted legs. The slenderness of the lower legs and the splayed, claw-like design of the flanged feet gave the *Locust* the appearance of a gigantic, flightless bird. Despite its name, the 'Mech could not jump, but it was easily the fastest of all BattleMechs, capable of speeds up to 165 kph in open terrain.

Compared to other 'Mechs, however, it was poorly armed. The sleek, long barrel of a single laser jutted from beneath the *Locust's* cockpit section, and two tiny arms extending from the belly bore a pair of heavy machine guns. The *Locust* had sacrificed weapons for the twin battlefield advantages of speed and armor. Though shorter and more compact, the *Locust* carried thicker armor than a *Wasp,* and was far more difficult to hit.

The *Locust's* body shifted slightly, whipped the long tube of its laser about to bear on Grayson's vehicle. The driver swerved again as brilliant light arced across the street, vaporizing sunshield supports and pulling the ferrocrete eaves to the ground with a splintering roar.

The third PPC vehicle emerged from the pall of smoke of the burning wreckage and fired. White fire washed across the *Locust,* which staggered back on its haunches. Struggling for balance, it took several unsteady steps backward, then straightened, swung about, and fired again. The shot cratered the avenue as the PPC carrier cut wildly to one side.

Grayson's carrier screeched to a halt 40 meters from the creature's right foot. One of the 'Mech's machine guns dropped clear of the bulk of the upper hip and stuttered death. Large-caliber rounds stitched through the carrier's side and smashed at the building behind. Two of the carrier's riders screamed and flailed backward as the other troops jumped from the well deck and scattered along the street. Grayson stayed where he was, concentrating on the targeting lock of his PPC's simple-minded computer. When the crosshairs merged and flashed red, he pressed the firing stud. Metal chips rained from the 'Mech's body where the armor had been pierced just aft of the cockpit.

The *Locust* spun and ran then, trailing a faint smudge of black smoke from its body. The Sarghadese troops jeered and cheered and followed, their popgun weapons snapping at the giant's heels.

Grayson signaled to the second vehicle's driver. "Keep on him! Make him fight!" Then he tapped his own driver's shoulder and pointed to a side street

The driver grinned and nodded, understanding. The weapons carrier careened off the main street, raced down the cross street to the next major spoke avenue, then turned north once more. Several more blocks and Grayson signaled the driver to turn back to the first avenue.

They emerged two blocks north of the *Locust,* which had stopped again to duel with its pursuer. The PPC had scored another hit, and the *Locust* was staggering in a losing battle to control its gyros. Grayson fired again from a range of 120 meters. The hit smashed into the 'Mech's rear, scattering fragments of antenna and armor casing.

It must be getting hellishly hot in there by now, he thought. The single greatest combat problem BattleMechs of any size faced was excess heat. Their tiny fusion reactors, the dozens of actuators in legs and arms, the electronic circuits that triggered weapons and controlled the polyacetene fiber bundles of its artificial musculature all released great quantities of heat. Circulating air-vent blowers called heat sinks struggled to rid the machine of excess heat under normal, routine operation. During combat, as the 'Mech ran, and fired its weapons, as it took hits from direct, high-energy beams or lost heat sinks to battle damage, the internal heat even within the shielded cockpit became ferocious. Many 'Mechs had been defeated and captured when their pilots passed out from heat exhaustion.

Grayson took a quick look to the north for the original object of their chase, but the *Wasp* had vanished, allowing the lighter-armored *Locust* to delay the hunters. *Fine.* He tapped the driver's shoulder, and the vehicle's tires kicked up a spray of rubble as it darted forward for the kill.

Machine gun fire spat from the 'Mech's tiny arms as it tried to track both vehicles on opposite sides at once. The *Locust* was no longer firing its laser. *A sure sign,* Grayson thought, *that the 'Mech is overheating.* If they could keep pressing the armored machine, they might force the 'Mech's internal systems into auto-shutdown.

He fired, trying for a crippling leg shot, and missed. The *Locust* was still fast and had back-stepped into the mouth of an alley. The two PPC carriers met at the alley's mouth.

The alley was a broad-mouthed cul-de-sac. The *Locust* had backed to the end of the alley and crouched there now, awaiting death. A chatter of machine gun fire sent the two vehicles wheeling back out of the line of fire and left two soldiers who had ventured too close to the alley mouth sprawled in the street, dead.

Grayson dismounted from the carrier, moved up to the alley mouth, and cautiously studied the situation. The 'Mech couldn't call for help because the long whip antennae mounted on the rear of the body had been sheared off. He could detect the shimmer of superheated air at heat sinks all over the machine's legs and body. Backed into that close alley, the air around the machine would become too hot to efficiently cool the 'Mech within seconds.

"We can take 'em," a voice growled at Grayson's side. He turned and looked into the dark eyes and sharp-lined features of a Militia sergeant. "We can back one of the carriers across the street. Range'll be too great for those MGs to do much while we lock a fix and give it another blast with the PPC. It can't take too much more of this, I'm thinking."

"I think the pilot knows that, Sergeant. He might chance another laser shot or two...and it'll only take one shot to take out a carrier."

"Snipe at him with infernos, then. He's a damned stationary target back in that hole!"

"You have an inferno launcher?"

"Sure. Shoulder-fired job. Back in the carrier."

"Get it."

"Yes, sir." Again, that unquestioning assumption that he was in command. Grayson smiled to himself. *If they only knew...*

The sergeant returned with a twin-tube inferno launcher. Inferno launchers were one of the few personal weapons that infantry could use effectively against 'Mechs. The problem was the infantry had to be terrifyingly close to their targets to use the things, and the chances for survival were poor enough that only heroes and fools would chance them. The launcher was a meter-long tube with rests and grips that allowed it to be fired over the shoulder. Two rotating, over-under cylinders held the inferno rockets, which allowed two missiles to be fired within a space of a second or two.

The missiles themselves were small and unpleasantly short-ranged, but they combined features of shoulder-launched missiles, shotguns, and chemical flamethrowers. They were designed to explode within a few meters of the launcher's barrel, spraying and igniting a liquid-bonded white phosphorus compound onto the target. The binding agent jelled in heat, clinging to whatever it struck with nightmarish persistence. Larger inferno missiles could be fired from standard missile launcher packs, or the warheads alone could be used with radar-triggered detonators in artillery shells.

Because of their flammability, infernos were almost never carried by 'Mechs. They were, however, a perfect anti-'Mech weapon for infantry. At least, for infantry that didn't mind closing to almost point-blank range with one of the metal monsters.

Grayson checked the weapon's loads, shouldered it, and signaled to a soldier crouched at the far side of the alley's mouth. The soldier leaned around the corner of the building and opened fire with his assault rifle. Those low-caliber rounds couldn't harm a 'Mech's armor, but the fire drew a flurry of machine gun fire from the cul-de-sac, splattering the corner of the building with brilliant white stars where the heavy rounds gouged chunks from the bricks.

With the 'Mech's attention momentarily drawn to the other side of the alley's entrance, Grayson stepped into the open. With the 'Mech looming above him thirty meters down the alley, he felt very, very small.

CHAPTER 14

"Hold it right there, Warrior!" Grayson yelled, then gulped down a breath to control the shaking in his voice. "One twitch of any of those weapons and you're cooked. Scan me and see if I'm bluffing!"

Seconds dragged on. The *Locust*'s laser was canted down at the ground some distance in front of Grayson, and its machine guns remained rigidly immobile, trained across the street at the corner of the building opposite. Grayson stood upright, in full view, with the green image of the towering *Locust* filling the crosshaired sights of his launcher, his finger tight on the trigger.

He gave the pilot a moment to scan the electronic emanations of the armed triggering circuits in his missile warheads. "You can kill me," he called again, "but you'll fry! Your heat exchangers must be up to shutdown mode by now. One round of Willie-Pete will finish you. And that's a very nasty way to go!"

The *Locust* pilot spoke, their voice electronically reproduced in a gravelly, amplified bass. "What do you want?"

"Don't touch your weapons. I want you to come out of there, unarmed. If I even *imagine* I see a weapon move in my direction, I'll fire!"

There was a pause, and Grayson could hear the sharp *ping* of hot metal cooling on the 'Mech's hull, could smell the sour-rubber stink of melted circuit insulation. The temperature inside must be...

"All right," said the pilot. "Don't shoot, I'm coming out." The electronically-produced voice couldn't register emotion, but to Grayson it sounded tired, perhaps resigned.

He remained standing as though the launcher on his shoulder were cast in bronze. From the *Locust* came the sharp *hiss* of a broken pressure seal and the rasp of a hatch winched open by hand. There was a clatter, and a metal-runged chain ladder spilled out of the hatch, jingling half a meter from the ground.

City Militia troops were entering the cul-de-sac entrance now, weapons held ready. The MechWarrior's legs appeared from the *Locust*'s belly hatch, and it became apparent that the pilot was female. Scarcely more than a girl, she was dressed only in slippers and a scrap of black panty briefs. MechWarriors generally fought scantily clad in the hothouse confines of their machines, and she had not had time to get dressed before coming out. Her long, blond hair hung in dank, wet strands across her shoulders, and her body glistened with sweat. After stepping down from the ladder, she stood facing them with arms folded across her breasts, alone and very vulnerable.

"Hey, hey," a soldier said with a nasty laugh. "Look-a-here, look-a-here! We caught us a prize, we did! Get those hands up! Behind your head!"

"Looks dangerous," another said. He shouldered his assault rifle and started toward her. "I think we'd better search her!"

"Yeah! C'mere, baby. We gotta check your uniform for concealed weapons."

Grayson set the rocket launcher aside, stepped over to where a sergeant stood watching, and pulled the pistol from the man's hip holster. It was a Stetta auto pistol, with a selector switch that let it fire single shots, bursts, or wildly inaccurate full-auto mayhem from an extended grip magazine holding 100 caseless rounds.

He snapped the selector from safe to full auto, pointed the muzzle into the air, and pulled the trigger. The snapping chatter of the deadly little weapon, shocking in the confined space between buildings, stopped the soldiers where they were, spun them around to face him.

"The first one to touch her dies." He waited, the weapon smoking in his hand. Though the challenge was a bit melodramatic, it had the desired effect. Every eye was on him. "You!" He pointed the weapon at the two who had started toward the captured pilot. "Back to the vehicles. *Move!*" They scrambled to obey. "You!" He picked another soldier at random. "There's a blanket in my vehicle. Get it."

The trooper dashed back to the PPC carrier on the double to retrieve an orange rescue blanket that had been folded on the floor of the well deck. Grayson took it from him, walked to the girl, and draped it over her shoulders. Aware of all eyes upon him, he was careful not to touch her.

"It's okay," he said, "put your hands down. We won't hurt you. I promise."

The spell was broken, as his impromptu unit began cheering and capering in the street. They had captured a 'Mech intact!

Grayson had to shout now to be heard above the clamor. "Sergeant!"

The man snapped to attention. "Sir!"

"Detail two men to guard that 'Mech!" He put the safety back on the pistol, but tucked it into the waistband of his trousers. "I'm going to borrow this, if you don't mind."

"Yes, sir!"

"Now I need someone to take me and the prisoner to your headquarters. I'd better talk to your bosses before this make-believe goes any further!"

Lord Harimandir Singh contemplated the ruin of his career. How could it have happened? Five 'Mechs and two companies of troops had stormed a defenseless city, and what had been the outcome? One 'Mech destroyed. Another captured. A third limping into the repair bay with fused pedal servoactuators and the right-leg jump jet electronics melted into scrap, the liquid-mercury fuel core leaking great silver globbets that dripped down the leg and scurried across the deck like mice. Bell, his chief tech, pursed his gloomy features and shook his head. The damage was severe. The *Wasp* might need an entire leg replacement.

And 32 of his troops had not come back. Stragglers were still checking in, though, and so perhaps the final butcher's bill might not be that high.

Three 'Mechs down out of five and ten percent casualties in his battalion. What the bloody hell had happened? It could only be that the local forces had had some help. The crippled *Wasp*'s pilot had reported that the indigs were organized differently from the way they'd fought during Singh's initial probe of the city's defense just a few hours before. *Is it possible,* he wondered, *that their earlier inept defense had been a ruse to draw me into a trap?*

He quickly rejected that line of thought. No commander would throw lives away on such a slender chance. Anyway, it would be harder to get professional troops to act stupid than the other way around. Besides, Vallendel's *Marauder* had smashed through the light assembly of armor and ground troops that met him on the city's north rim. There had been nothing different there, no new strategy or secret defense to turn the tide against the attackers. Most of those troops had scattered and fled through the city streets without even firing a shot

No, it was more likely King Jeverid had brought in mercenaries to stiffen his defenses, but Singh couldn't fathom where these forces had come from or when they had arrived. And where had they been during the earlier attack? Or during the attack on Carlyle at the Castle? It was possible a mercenary training cadre was operating in the city and that Jeverid possessed at least one competent fighter unit. Though that might explain things, Singh wouldn't feel comfortable until he learned who these mercenaries were.

Briefly, he considered withdrawing from the Castle to the ship or abandoning Trellwan entirely. But that would contradict the Red Duke's Plan, not something a member of the Duke's entourage ever did lightly. No, he must consider this a setback, but the Plan would still succeed. It had to. If it didn't, even after all these years of faithful service, it might be *his* head on a pike above the parade ground. The thought was not comforting.

Singh would contact his agents in Sarghad and learn what he could. Perhaps, in the end, it would work out best if there *was* a mercenary unit in the city. Mercenaries could always be bought. Some of history's most splendid victories were the result of carefully timed changes in a selected merc unit's loyalties.

Grayson Death Carlyle enjoyed being the hero. Forty hours after the end of what was already called the Battle of Sarghad, he was a guest at the palace, having been fussed over by grooms and servants, attended by the palace physician, and received a spectacular change of clothes. He checked the fit of the trim Guards lieutenant uniform in the wall-sized mirror in his suite. *Not bad,* he decided, tugging the short jacket into place. The ornate gold chasing and piping across the dark green, triple-looped aiguillette and the ceremonial sword were a bit gaudy, but it wasn't bad at all.

He and his female prisoner had been taken to the headquarters of General Varney, Commandant of the Sarghad Militia Military District. The girl had been hustled away into the depths of the building for questioning, but the lieutenant who was officer of the day had been less certain what to do with Grayson.

Here was a young man dressed in rags and caked with mud and grime, armed with an automatic pistol and leading a MechWarrior prisoner in a blanket. The man claimed to be a stranded member of Carlyle's Commandos, and the soldiers with him claimed he had just single-handedly won the Battle of Sarghad. The officer quickly realized immediate and confident action was called for. He called his superior officer. Let *him* decide what to make of it all!

Grayson had been passed rather quickly up the line of command from the lieutenant to a captain to a major to a colonel to General Varney's chief of staff, and finally had been introduced to the General himself. None of these officers had quite known what to do with him. The story was spreading through the city that an off-worlder, an officer of the garrison that had betrayed Trellwan, had stayed in Sarghad and organized the heroic defense of the city.

Grayson was rapidly becoming a political issue. In the end, the army officers did the safest thing. They gave him food and much-needed sleep, brought in a doctor to tape up his ribs and attend to his reopened head wound, and presented him early the next work period to King Jeverid's military council. By the end of the period, he had had a private audience with Jeverid himself, and been invited to stay in the palace as a guest of His Majesty while preparations were made for the victory celebration.

As he examined his new Guards uniform with continuing wonderment, Grayson was still not sure whether he was supposed to be an actual member of the Palace Guard now or not. He had not been formally inducted into anybody's army, but the uniform had been ordered at His Majesty's command so that he would look the part, at least, of a hero. Bureaucratic details, the king had said, could be fussed with later.

It's amazing, Grayson thought, *how quickly official government policy could be reversed.* Before the battle, off-worlders of any type had been *persona non grata.* Had he been caught by those troopers who had chased him through the alley, he would have wound up in Sarghad's prison, at best. Trellwan's constitution protected its citizens from unreasonable search, seizure, and imprisonment without cause, but his rights as a presumed hostile non-citizen would have been decidedly limited.

Now, however, he was the Victor of Sarghad, the valiant Commonwealth officer who had triumphed over the common foe. The king's publicity ministers had worked overtime the night before, preparing the story for newsheets and vid broadcasts today. And tonight, there was to be a formal ceremony and dress ball at the palace reception hall honoring his service to Trellwan.

The door chimed, breaking into Grayson's thoughts. Opening it, he was startled to see the elfin face and wide, dark eyes of Mara.

"My love," she said, pulling her arms around a bewildered Grayson. He had expected to see her at the celebration, of course, but not before. It struck him oddly, too, that she greeted him as "my love." Never, not even during their stolen moments of lovemaking, had she ever called him that. But the thought was soon forgotten.

"Mara, how did you get in here?"

She laughed. "I bribed old Salin to let me come up." Salin was the Assistant Court Chamberlain, charged with overseeing Grayson's sartorial preparations for the banquet. "I wanted to see you, wanted to have you to myself for a bit before the party began." She clung to him. "I've missed you, Gray. I heard you were trying to reach me. I'm so sorry you couldn't..."

His eyes feasted on her. If this were part and parcel of being a planetary hero, he was all for it. Mara wore a gown fashionable in Sarghadese society, an airy thing of shifting, opaque colors that turned transparent where it clung to her body. He held her close and smiled, knowing he wouldn't arrive on time at the Reception Hall.

That evening, the pleasures of being a hero evaporated somewhat when Grayson realized he didn't have the faintest idea what he was doing here. People he had never seen before bowed and smiled, nodded and smiled, asked after his health and complimented him on his victory. About all he could do was smile and nod and mumble something in return, as the currents of the crowd gently washed him into its center. This was, he learned, the premier event of Trellwan's social season. Everyone who was anyone was there.

King Jeverid was, by tradition, the last to arrive. When he finally made his entrance on the raised stage at the end of the reception hall opposite the stairs, the presentation began. Grayson felt even more out of place as he mounted the crimson-carpeted stairs to the king, accompanied by the flourish of the orchestra playing a triumphal march and a pair of sword-bearing Guards officers on either side of him. He'd already met the king privately, of course, and his own choreography in these proceedings had been elaborately explained and rehearsed. Still, Grayson struggled with an almost unendurable premonition that he was about to trip over his own ceremonial sword.

Jeverid acknowledged him with a nod and murmured, "My son." The king seemed ancient, his skin parchment, his eyes dull. Jeverid's frail body seemed lost in the crimson cloak draped across his shoulders.

"Your Majesty," was Grayson's formal reply.

"Your valor has won a great victory for Trellwan," Jeverid intoned. "What's more, our strategists have determined that the object of the attack on this palace was almost certainly our capture or murder. We recognize your bravery, young Grayson, and the fact that you have single-handedly saved the Royal House of Trellwan."

"I had the help of your soldiers, Majesty."

Grayson's reply had not been in the script, and the King's advisors stirred uncomfortably. "Oh, yes. To be sure, to be sure," replied the monarch of Trellwan. "As a token of our gratitude and appreciation, young Grayson, we award you the Order of the Crimson Star."

Jeverid gestured, and a steward brought him a flat, velvet box and opened it. The King lifted from the box an ornate starburst on a red loop of ribbon. Grayson advanced, knelt, and bowed his head while Jeverid placed the ribbon around his neck. The starburst was mounted with a small, red stone that caught and reflected the overhead light.

"Rise, Carlyle, Defender of Sarghad," said the King, setting off an echoing roar of applause from the crowd.

Jeverid set a hand on Grayson's shoulder and drew him close, speaking above the noise. "A couple of my generals want to talk to you, m'boy. Seems you impressed 'em with your...ah...tactics."

"I'll be delighted to help in any way I can, Majesty."

"Good, good. Go enjoy yourself now. They'll find you later."

CHAPTER 15

The audience ended, and the agony of the formal reception began. Grayson endured more matronly women, junior officers venturing their opinions on anti-'Mech tactics, and the inevitable social hangers-on who wanted to talk with the Court's newest light. It was almost a relief when the ball began.

The art of formal dance had not been one of the social graces instilled in him by his apprenticeship training with the Commandos, but Grayson had acquired enough basic skill to blend in with the colorful crowd. Formal dancing on this world, at least, was little more than graceful movement to slow music, with a girl held in a comfortably close embrace.

And then it was Mara in his arms, a sweet-smelling armful wearing that magical translucence that left so little to the imagination.

"I told you once before you wouldn't be leaving me yet," she whispered in his ear as they glided across the mirrored floor, their movements matched by the movements of their own inverted reflections.

The comment stung unexpectedly. His staying on Trellwan was the result of so many tragedies—Griffith, Riviera, Ari... Dad... "I wish it could be under happier circumstances."

"Pooh, don't be so gloomy!" she pouted. "I'm just glad you're here, and that you're here to stay! You belong here...with me."

"Oh?"

"You do your new uniform quite proud, Gray," she whispered, then leaned closer to whisper how they might spend the rest of the evening after the reception.

He forced a smile and drew her closer, but there was a strange emptiness where his feelings for Mara had formerly been. What was wrong with him? The passionate fire of his last meeting with her had been wiped away by all that had happened since the first attack on the Castle.

Grayson recognized that he had changed, starting with the dulling of his desire for Mara. The girl had been a pleasant diversion before the pact with Oberon, but he'd been willing enough to break off their relationship when he had learned the lance was leaving this sand-miserable world for Tharkad. There could never have been any thought of her coming with him to share the life of a warrior. He'd known her well enough to realize she would never leave the comfort and privilege of Trellwan's royal household. When he'd awakened to find himself marooned on the planet, Grayson wanted to see Mara because it was possible her influence could rescue him. Though such a mercenary attitude had brought on some nagging guilt, it had been his only ray of hope.

A tap on the shoulder and a murmured invitation from a Guard colonel interrupted Grayson's darkening thoughts. Mara was reluctant to let him go, but she whispered another steamy proposal and sealed it with a lingering kiss.

Grayson followed the Guard out of the Reception Hall, down a carpeted passageway to a richly furnished study. The room was dim, lit mainly by the greenish glow of native chaggawood logs burning in the fireplace.

Three men awaited him there. General Varney he knew, white-haired and immaculate in his plain brown uniform with the red tabs of the Militia at throat and shoulders. General Adel he had met briefly earlier. He was younger, with a black mustache that contrasted the silver at his temples. Senior Commandant of the Palace Guards, as well as Chief of Staff for His Majesty's Military Council, Adel's full-dress greens showed more gold than green.

The third man in the room remained seated by the fireplace. Grayson recognized the hawk profile of King Jeverid.

"Thank you for coming, son," said Varney. "We have a proposal to make to you."

"Yes, sir?"

Adel lowered the drink he'd been sipping. "Carlyle, we'll get right to the point. We want you to organize a 'Mech lance to be incorporated into the Palace Guard. We want a combat company of ground troops trained in anti-Mech warfare. Can you do it?"

Varney looked sharply at his Guard counterpart. "I believe the idea is for the lance to be under joint command, in a department of its own, General."

Adel nodded, his expression pained. "Yes, Varney, yes." Then, he turned to Grayson. "Well, Carlyle? What do you say?"

Grayson said nothing at first. With the eyes of all three men on him, he felt like he wanted to hide. "Sirs...Majesty...I don't really know what to say. I'm not sure I have the experience to—"

"Ha!" The king's exclamation startled him. "You've got a damn sight more experience than anyone else on this planet... except for those bastards sitting up there in the Castle."

"We need your help, son," Varney added. "We're helpless without trained soldiers and the mobile firepower and armor to back them up."

Jerevid turned to Grayson full face, and his eyes flashed as he spoke. Grayson realized with some surprise that there was more to this king than a dull mind in a frail body. The king spoke with animation. "Varney here tells me you outfought those 'Mechs practically bare-handed, because you knew how they worked, how their drivers would think. That's what we need here."

"But Majesty, what about 'Mechs?"

"What about 'em? We have two now, thanks to you. There's the one you captured and another we can repair. And anything more you capture is yours!"

Grayson considered the potential of a 'Mech lance consisting of two 20-ton 'Mechs. Typical lances contained a mix of 'Mech weights and types, ranging from 20-ton lights to the heavies like *Shadow Hawk*s and *Marauder*s. A *Locust* and a *Wasp* might last all of 20 seconds in a stand-up fight against a *Marauder*. With luck, that is.

"Just what is it this 'Mech lance is supposed to do?"

Adel took another sip from his glass. "The withdrawal of Carlyle's men has left us wide open to bandits like Hendrik." He pursed his lips judiciously. "I'm not going to comment on just what your people were trying to pull with that Pact we've heard so much about."

"Then don't," said Jeverid.

"Yes, Majesty. Be that as it may, the Commonwealth garrison is gone, and our enemies are here. We expect them to continue raiding us for supplies and perhaps to send out a call for reinforcements.

"You dealt them a terrible blow, Grayson. Our scouts report they only have two serviceable 'Mechs left now, with another damaged and another being refitted in the Castle. Why, with your skill and a pair of 'Mechs of our own, the Guards could cripple those bastards, make it so they'd never send another expedition to Trellwan again. We need a 'Mech unit of our own if we're going to protect ourselves and our sovereignty. Without it..." He shrugged expressively. "We might as well sign ourselves over to Hendrik. We're helpless."

A *Locust* and a *Wasp* against a *Marauder* and a *Stinger,* plus a *Shadow Hawk,* once the enemy repaired the machine that had been crippled before the attack. That meant a combined combat tonnage of 40 tons against 150. And perhaps more if the bandits were able to repair that leg-damaged *Wasp.* One-to-four odds, near enough.

What the hell, Grayson thought wryly. *All in a day's work...* Assuming, of course, he'd be able to find and train someone to pilot the second 'Mech. He could not simply recruit some likely private from the ranks of the Guards and turn him into a MechWarrior. Piloting that much metal required training-honed skills and talent few possessed, and even fewer could apply.

Something told him these men did not want to hear about stats and specifications, or the problems of recruiting. More emotional protests tumbled forth. "Sir, I'm afraid I'm in way over my head here. Look, I'm 20 standard years old." These people expected the impossible!

"You've piloted 'Mechs before, haven't you?" This from Varney.

"Yes, but I've never had one in combat. What happened out there was just luck. And I certainly wouldn't know how to lead a unit." That wasn't exactly accurate, Grayson knew. His training as a MechWarrior included leadership and small unit tactics. If he was to follow in the five-meter stride of his father, he would have to know how to lead men. He had been trained for the role he'd been expected to play in the event his father had been killed. But dammit, things were happening too fast! Varney said, "Son, we have the statements of the men you led in the battle for the city. When an entire GEV detachment had been cut to pieces, you were the only one there to *do* something. You rallied those troops, and you knocked out a 'Mech. That's not easy, and it *wasn't* luck!"

The reality of what these men were saying was gradually penetrating Grayson's consciousness. They wanted *him* to be a MechWarrior. More, to build a MechWarrior lance from scratch and lead it in battle. The protests gibbering in his mind were being outweighed by the single fact that more than half his life had been directed toward a single destiny—the cockpit of a BattleMech. It was an opportunity he was not likely to encounter again. Would *never* encounter again if he were unable to buy or beg passage off-planet. Without a 'Mech of his own, his chances of joining a 'Mech unit were virtually nil.

Excitement stirred within him. Perhaps there was something to Mara's conviction that he belonged here. With scant hope of getting off-planet for years to come, maybe there was a place for the Victor of Sarghad here on Trellwan after all!

Those one-to-four odds were unattractive, but not totally discouraging. The *Locust* would be a start, and with planning and a little luck...

"Tell me more," he told the generals.

King Jeverid leaned back in his chair, his old face creased by a satisfied grin.

CHAPTER 16

Sarghad's Near Passage came and went. However, the sullen red sun appeared no larger to the eye than it ever did. Trellwan was only a few percent nearer its primary at its closest point than at its farthest, but that few percent was enough to briefly bring the temperature to 40 degrees Celsius and higher. Within 20 hours, the Firstday storms had begun.

Now that the sun was directly overhead, the air over the Nerge grew warm, then hot. Low-lying air masses from the Grimheld Sea area moved across the desert and exploded skyward in a towering column of hot, moist air. From Sarghad, the column looked like a white pillar lifting beyond the mountains to the west. Its rise was so rapid that the naked eye could perceive its movement second to second across almost 2,000 kilometers.

When the column of hot, wet air hit the subzero air of the stratosphere, clouds billowed out in all directions, blocking the sun and turning the green sky white, then gray, then roiling blue-black. That was when the hail and rain and lightning began.

During the seven-standard day period known in Sarghad as the Summer Storm, people stayed indoors in a holiday commanded by the weather. To venture outdoors would have meant wading knee-deep in yellow mud while becoming soaked to the skin, at best. At worst, to leave the shelter of Sarghad's buildings on some errand usually meant being struck dead by lightning or head-sized hailstones. The wind from the east blew steadily across the city toward the Nerge. Even during those periods when the sun was still above the horizon, the landscape was plunged into complete and unrelieved darkness, save for the lightning that flashed brilliantly against the sky.

With the driving rain a constant rattle against sealed windows and eaves, with the wind thumping against outer walls like something alive, Grayson set up his headquarters in the city armory, a squat and dismal ferrocrete block building with a warehouse interior in the mechanic's district across the Hub from the palace grounds. Seated at an old desk salvaged from some government office and using an old, black plastic compad tied into the Military Records Library in the District Headquarters Annex, he began his job of recruiting and training Trellwan's first BattleMech lance.

His assistants were Sergeant Ramage of the Militia and Lieutenant Nolem of the Guards, both of whom held the title of adjutant. Their primary job was to take all the military theory and training Grayson could put into words and writing, organize it, and then teach it to the men and women who were selected for Trellwan's anti-'Mech unit. Grayson's little team had been given the rest of Firstnight, another fourteen standard days, to organize the unit. General Adel wanted it ready for combat by the end of the Secondnight storms, which gave them just about one local year of 45 days to do the job.

"Sergeant, I don't think you understand the precariousness of your position." Lieutenant Nolem's flat, nasal voice became even more grating when he was being unpleasant.

"Sir!" retorted Ramage. "My understanding of the line of command is that the Militia troops in the special unit will be accountable to Militia HQ through Lance Command. General Varney would never have consented to placing Militia personnel under the direct command of the Guards!"

"And I, Sergeant, question whether you have any understanding of the line of command at all! The Guards clearly takes precedence over the Militia in the special unit as it does in all military matters. You meddling Militiamen—"

"Gentlemen, please!" Grayson sat between the two, fingers working at his temples. He was tired, and couldn't think of much else except getting back to the officers' quarters General Varney had arranged for him. There was so much to be done, but he was beginning to regret ever hearing of a Trellwan special unit. "If you two don't stop bickering, you can forget about the generals. You'll have to answer to the new government!"

Nolem raised a querying eyebrow. "What new government?"

"The one the bandits are going to establish in the palace if you don't drop the petty quarrels over pecking-order and help me get some work done!"

"Really, Lieutenant. My position here—"

Grayson's voice was weary but firm. "Your position here is subject to MY approval, Lieutenant, do you understand?"

"You don't rank me, youngster!" Nolem was all of four standard years older than Grayson.

"I'll bloody well rank you if I have to prove it by tossing you out in the rain!" Grayson's fist came down on the stack of requisition forms on the desk. "I was put in charge of the unit, so just because your friend Adel slipped you in to pull rank on Sergeant Ramage doesn't mean I'm going to let you get away with it!"

Nolem bristled. Grayson decided the only way to break through the man's stubbornness was to change the subject. "Now, what's the status of the damaged *Wasp*?"

The question took Nolem by surprise. "Ah...uh..."

"We still don't have a tech who can supervise repairs."

"But what's the 'Mech's status?"

"Uh...the head's smashed."

"I know that, Lieutenant. I smashed it. Can it be repaired?"

"The officer in charge says we'll need a trained tech to tell us one way or the other." He shrugged. "We don't have much in the way of spare parts for 'Mechs, either. I gather the supply officers are having to dismantle second-line weapons carriers just to get scrap armor to plug the holes in the torso."

Grayson sagged back in the chair. "Maybe I can get down there next period and have a look." MechWarriors knew as much about a 'Mech's workings as did techs. But the time... God, the time!

"You have a meeting with the Military Council next period," Ramage reminded him.

"Damn, you're right. I..." Grayson paused, thoughtful.

"Sir?"

"There is an alternative...possibly."

Ramage looked at Nolem questioningly, then at Grayson. "I don't think there's a qualified tech on the planet. Not this side of the Castle, at any rate, and I don't think *they're* going to lend us one!"

He was not about to discuss his wild inspiration with these two. Nolem would resist the idea, he knew, and even Ramage was certainly doubling as a spy for the Militia staff. He wanted to spring this idea on the generals himself.

Three periods later, Grayson descended the cold stone steps of the Military District Headquarters. It was still raining outside. He'd made the trip from the armory in a GEV, skimming over the treacherous mud. The water pooled on the stone floor as he handed his compad to the brown-uniformed corporal sitting behind the desk at the bottom of the stairs.

The corporal entered a code into the terminal on his desk, then leaned back to await clearance. "Wet out, sir?"

"A bit. Getting colder, too." By the middle of Firstnight, the temperature outside had dropped nearly to freezing. The week-long Near Passage storms acted as a gigantic heat sink for the planet, and during the long, long night following Periasteron, the heat of the Passage was rapidly dissipated. Soon the storm winds would die, and it would begin snowing in the mountains.

Grayson thought of Thunder Rift. The ice would all be gone now, the waterfall dried up. When the ice roof was gone, you could see stars up through the rift from the shore of the cavern floor lake, even during daylight.

"Clearance, sir. You can go through." The corporal operated a control, and steel bars slid to one side.

"Thank you," Grayson said, and entered the long, dimly lit passageway. The cell he was looking for was at the end of the hall.

Lori Kalmar sat on the bench in her cell, leaning back against the wall with knees tucked beneath her chin, staring at the opposite wall. She was wearing a long-tailed fatigue shirt and trousers someone had given her, but still had the light slippers she'd worn aboard her 'Mech. Tall, long-legged, and slender, *the girl is quite attractive,* Grayson thought, but her expression was sullen and bitter.

Grayson approached the bars of her cell and spoke her name.

Kalmar's eye flicked across him, then back to the wall. "Oh," she said dully. "It's you." Though there were dark circles under her eyes, the girl's hair was carefully brushed, so blond it looked almost silver in the pale light.

"Are you okay? Are you being treated all right?"

"Why should you care?" she snapped.

What she didn't know was that Grayson had been feeling guilty about the *Locust's* pilot ever since he'd turned her over to the Militia headquarters. After all, he had promised she would not be hurt. The last he'd heard, she was being put through interrogation. From what he'd been able to learn, the Militia's questioning methods were more psychological and chemical than physical. The Guards, on the other hand, were rumored to take positive pleasure in inventive and enthusiastic physical interrogation, and that was what had triggered Grayson's own panic when he'd faced the sentries at Mara's house. But interrogation in any form was brutal, leaving the prisoner exhausted, haggard, and feeling very much alone.

"I'd like to talk to you," he said.

"That's nothing new," she snapped. "That's all people want to do around here...talk to me."

"Would you like to get out of here?"

Kalmar's head whipped around to face him. Her eyes, he saw, were very blue. "What is this? More interrogation?" Her voice was hard, but Grayson heard the tremble of tears hidden in it. "We've been through it all, okay? I've told you people everything I know!"

Grayson had learned Lori's story from the security dossier compiled from her long hours of interrogation. She had been born and raised on Sigurd, a bitterly cold and isolated world that was one of twelve in Hendrik's confederation. Her parents had died during one hellish night of fire and horror when the government forcibly convinced dissident forces on Sigurd that confederation with Oberon VI was in their best economic and social interests.

Lori had been saved by a neighbor, but only after seeing her parents die in the fire that gutted her apartment. About a year after becoming a state ward (at age eight, or about thirteen by standard-year reckoning), she had applied to the Sigurd Defense Forces as a 'Mech apprentice, and been accepted.

Apparently, Hendrik's confederation did not have a combined military force. Individual worlds reserved some local defense forces for themselves, an arrangement that created the feeling of greater sovereignty. Lori's unit had been the Sigurd Independent Light Assault Group, operating directly under the command of Vice Regent Alisaden, a warleader who was also Sigurd's Defense Minister.

Lori had been an apprentice for over three Sigurdian years, which made her almost 19 standard years old now. Though well along in her training, she had not expected to go on active combat duty for several years yet. One night, while standing duty as officer of the watch in the 'Mech center, the sergeant in charge of her school section had tried to persuade her to engage in "extracurricular training" on the floor. She'd resisted, he'd insisted, and she'd given him a final and definite "no" with a knee driven into a sensitive target.

One week later, her orders had come through. She was being assigned to a "Special Expeditionary Force" with three other Sigurdian trainees, under the command of a Harimandir Singh.

The circumstances were peculiar. Singh's JumpShip was unlike any she knew within the Confederacy, and the expeditionary force seemed to be part of a deal cut between Singh and Vice Regent Alisadren. So far as she could tell, the operation had nothing to do with Hendrik or Oberon VI at all. Singh himself served someone named Duke Ricol, whom she also heard referred to as the Red Duke.

Singh. Grayson had stiffened when he'd read that name. It was the word on Griffith's lips when he died. It was obvious the weapons master had recognized the bandit leader, probably from a biog data entry in the Castle computer. As for Duke Ricol, Grayson drew a blank.

Neither Lori Kalmar nor her companions, Privates Enzelman and Fitzhugh, and a corporal named Hassilik, had ever heard of Singh or the Red Duke before being assigned to their command. By the time the ship had rendezvoused with a freighter at some nameless, worldless sun and they'd transferred across, Kalmar had learned only that Singh's mission was to gather mercenaries for an operation against a world she'd never heard of. It's name was Trellwan.

She was surprised to suddenly find herself a mercenary MechWarrior. She'd been too busy to think much about it, however. Lori Kalmar and her comrades had been kept hard at work moving and installing heavy weapons aboard the freighter's DropShips. Soon after that, the vessel had resumed its mysterious voyage across the stars.

During the trip, the three Sigurdians met and learned to fear their lance commander, a Lieutenant Vallendel. Early in the voyage, they'd delegated Corporal Hassilik to go to Vallendel and protest their virtual kidnapping. They were homesick by that time, and utterly bewildered at being transported across tens of light years in the company of utter strangers. Ten minutes later, the assembled company had watched young Hassilik, naked and tied hand and foot, go out the airlock into space.

There were no more protests. They spent most of the passage working in the cargo bay where the 'Mechs—a *Marauder*, a *Stinger*, and a *Locust*—were stored. They practiced what tactics they could on holographic map tables under Vallendel's critical eye, performing maintenance checks, and going over 'Mech operating systems.

When the time came for the drop onto the night side of a world close by a mottled, dusky red sun, however, the unwilling mercenaries had not been included in the assault team. They'd watched from the freighter's DropShip as Vallendel and two of Singh's techs had disembarked into a night of fire and terror.

They'd also watched Vallendel's *Marauder* smash to pieces an aging *Phoenix Hawk* already savaged by the weapons they'd helped install in the DropShip's hull.

"Why did they bring us here, anyway?" she'd asked. But no one was giving any answers.

Once the crew transferred to their new Trellwan base in an imposing black stone edifice built on a mountainside, her new masters had begun allowing Kalmar and her companions to exercise with the *Locust,* and with a pair of 20-ton *Wasps* captured from the yet unidentified enemy. They were closely watched by the other 'Mechs: the *Stinger* was generally detailed to keep a close eye on the Sigurdian's activities during patrols. It was clear they were not trusted.

Kalmar's initiation into battle had come shortly after the first successful raid on the enemy city, where a number of prisoners had been captured and specific targets identified. It had also been her last.

Her target had been the palace. She'd received an accurate map of the palace layout and the location of shelters where important members of the enemy government were expected to be hiding during an attack. She and her two companions were to attack it, flush the ranking officers and members of the royal family and, if possible, to capture them.

It all had gone wrong from the start. Wes Fitzhugh had been killed in a battle with unarmored troops in the street, and Enzelman's *Wasp* had been damaged at the palace gates. Lori had been moving up from the rear to support them when Enzelman had limped past, heading north. "They're after me," he'd cried over the combat circuit. "Cover me!"

She tried and succeeded. Garik Enzelman had escaped to the Castle, and now she was awaiting death at the hands of her captors.

"You can drop the pretense," she told Grayson. "I know you're going to kill me...eventually. I only surrendered because... because I didn't want to burn." She shuddered. "It's a horrible way to die."

"I didn't know about your parents," Grayson said gently. "I wouldn't have threatened you like that if..." He let the words trail off, acutely aware of how foolish he sounded.

"Look," he continued. "There's no trick. I'm not going to hurt you, and I'll do my best to see that no one else does either. And I'm serious about getting you out of here. I need a tech to supervise the repair of a damaged *Wasp.*"

"That's ridiculous. I'm an apprentice."

Yeah, right, he thought. *But so am I.* He wasn't about to admit it, however. "Which puts you way ahead of everyone else in Sarghad. Will you help?"

Her eyes were guarded. "What's to stop me from slipping off to my friends up the mountain? Or wiring a C-90 charge into your 'Mech's primary power circuit?"

"Oh, there'll be safeguards." He thought of his conversation with Varney and Adel, of the arguments he had mustered, and the promises he'd had to make. Kalmar was to be considered an enemy agent. She would be guarded at all times, and the astechs assigned to help her would have training enough to know if she were deliberately sabotaging the work. They'd finally agreed to Grayson's plan only because there seemed to be no other way to get the job done.

He had accepted their conditions, and prayed the girl would agree to work with him under such restrictions. There seemed to be no alternative, for any of them.

"You'll be watched, but at least you'll be out of this place. Do you owe some oath of fealty or service to the people who brought you here?" Many peoples in the near-feudal culture of the Successor States strictly observed fealty vows and oaths. In the shifting tangles of allegiances among the states, individual warriors needed a focus for their loyalty.

Lori Kalmar closed her eyes. "No. There's...nothing. A slave's vow to her master, perhaps, nothing more."

"Will you agree?"

There was a long silence. When she spoke again, it was in a very small voice. "Yes. And...thank you."

BOOK TWO

CHAPTER 17

Harimandir Singh drew the collar of his cold weather jacket closer about his face and ears and leaned into the wind. The storms had ended, but the long dark of Firstnight continued. With the coming of the storms, temperatures had fallen. There were patches of snow across the ferrocrete apron of the spaceport, and the wind eddied small whirls of dry snow through the pools of light cast by vapor lamps on the poles overhead. At last report, it was snowing heavily in the mountains nearby.

What a dismal, brooding planet Trellwan is, he thought, *a place I will be glad to leave when the mission is complete.* Perhaps... perhaps after this, he would see again the crystal skies and gleaming salt flats of his home deserts.

The guards at the door to one of the squat, sheet metal storage buildings lining the main port area came to attention with the *slap-crack* of a weapon salute. One of them took the paper Singh handed him, studied it, and unlocked the door. The air that poured from the dimly lit room beyond the door was sour with the stench of unwashed bodies and the odors of vomit and human waste.

"How many do we have, now?" Singh asked his aide.

The soldier consulted his wristcomp. "One hundred eighty-two prisoners, Lord."

Singh nodded and tried to keep from covering his nose and mouth to block the stink. These prisoners, many of them skilled workers, were soon to be slaves, sold among labor-hungry worlds with crumbling technologies. For now, they were a source of sometimes useful information, as well as a major problem in logistics. His expedition's food supplies were limited to what was left aboard the DropShip and what little had been raided from the agrodomes north of Sarghad. If they did not find more food quickly, their prisoners would have to be shot—and hang the waste. Singh believed the primary mission had to take priority over minor economic concerns.

The guard returned, leading a shambling, ragged man with a face bruised and caked with dirt and dried blood.

"Captain Tor! How are you? Have you decided to tell us what we want to know yet?"

"I can't tell you anything." He spoke carefully through swollen lips. The beatings had produced great, puffy bruises about his eyes and mouth.

"Oh, but you can tell us a great deal, like why you were snooping about the spaceport perimeter, and what you know about mercenary activities in Sarghad. You'd be saving yourself *so* much trouble by telling us what we want to know."

Tor was shivering, his arms folded tightly in front of his body, but he managed to snap, "Go to hell!" As he was wearing only the rags of his tunic and light trousers, the cold was doing the work of a torturer's knife.

Singh frowned. "I've offered you money. I've offered you your freedom. I'm afraid all I have to offer now is a quick death."

"You murdered my men."

"Ah...the three crewmen aboard the DropShip. That was a tragedy, I admit. It's always a tragedy when skilled workers must be killed. But you made that necessary, my friend, by escaping in the first place."

"You were going to kill me anyway." Anger flashed for a moment over Tor's cold-numbed face. "You didn't have to kill them!"

"My dear Captain, you don't think I wanted to have them killed, do you? We prize men trained for starship work, especially a man like you, who is skilled in interstellar navigation. We are not barbarians!"

Tor's eyes closed, his lips trembling. "Whatever you say."

"But this mission is highly secret, Captain. So secret, I don't believe you appreciate its importance. If you did, I would have your throat slit now. When you escaped, we had to take steps to insure that no more of your people on Trellwan escaped. The rest of your crew aboard the freighter are still in good health, of course. At least, for now."

"More threats?"

"I don't threaten, Captain." He reached out and pulled Tor's head up by the hair, looking into the man's glazed eyes. "Now, let's begin again. You were in the city for a time."

Tor's voice was weak, barely audible.

"What was that? Come, come, Captain. I'm getting cold standing here talking to you."

"Yes...I was in S-Sarghad."

"And you are a military man?"

"I am a trader. I pilot a JumpShip."

"Ah, but you know as well as I that the most important commerce between the stars today are the arms and armor of military units. You must have some knowledge of the military arts."

Tor remained silent, and Singh continued. "What sign did you see in Sarghad of a mercenary cadre?"

"I d-d-don't understand."

"Outsiders, Captain...off-worlders. A military unit...perhaps training the locals to fight."

"I didn't see anything like that...no."

Singh believed the man was telling the truth. He also knew this particular method of questioning could not go on for long. Tor would reveal no information after being frozen to death. Singh gestured to the guard, who swung Tor around and led him back into the warmer prisoner's quarters.

Though Tor might not know about it, Sarghad was definitely getting help from somewhere. Singh would have to learn the source of that help before it seriously compromised the Plan. Not only would he need to learn of it, but the mercenaries would have to be eliminated once and for all.

The wind grew colder as the long dark of Firstnight dragged on. A cadre of experienced troops, including both Militia and Guards, had been gathered, trained, and drilled, and they, in turn, had been set to training and drilling the volunteers who would make up the main body of the unit. King Jeverid himself attended the unit's first mustering ceremony, and it was he who bestowed upon them their name: the First Trellwan Lancers.

Grayson could not help but compare his new unit with his old. The Lancers were raw and ungainly, with neither the precise snap and polish of a well-trained unit nor the easy professionalism and camaraderie of an experienced one. Carlyle's Commandos had had both the polish and the professionalism. As a boy, Grayson had admired the absolute precision of the unit's response to parade-ground orders, the *snap-crack* of two hundred boots clicking into place at the same instant. He'd admired too that bond of absolute trust between each man and his squadmates, and each man and the officers and NCOs above him.

This lot is eager, he decided, but that was almost all he could say for them. All were volunteers from either the Militia or the Guards, and many had years of experience, including combat experience. But they were not yet a *unit* in the sense of belonging and working well together.

The bitter rivalry between the Guards and Militia continued within the ranks. In one of his first decisions, Grayson directed his sergeants not to separate the services into different companies, but to form squads and platoons without regard to each soldier's original affiliation. If the Lancers were to have any identity of their own or any of the pride that identity would encourage, they would have to start thinking of themselves as Lancers rather than as Guards or Militia. There were eighteen fistfights and three knifings during the first standard week. The fact that each one still wore their original green or brown uniform, with only a blue armband to distinguish them as a Lancer, didn't help.

For his part, Grayson was learning there was far more to organizing a 'Mech lance than teaching thumb-fingered recruits how to pilot a BattleMech. The details of the unit's T.O. & E. threatened to drown him in extra work hours and a deluge of paperwork. The T.O. & E—the Lancers' Table of Organization and Equipment—would make or break the fledging unit, and Grayson was becoming aware of the importance of staff paperwork in a way he never had been. Always before he had wondered why his father's staff included a small army of civilian secretaries and military orderlies, and why one of the lance staff officers, Lieutenant Hanesly, had been designated as personnel officer. Now he knew why a personnel officer was needed for a 120-man company.

Grayson's days had been one fifteen-hour work period after another, with short naps grabbed on the cot behind the office in Sarghad's armory building that had been set aside for his use. Mara had called him repeatedly on the small visor installed in the office, but he had lost count of the standard days since he'd seen her. There was simply too much to do.

A BattleMech lance is much more than four 'Mechs and the men who con them. T.O.'s generally list only the pilots and techs assigned to a particular unit, but, in fact, even a small scout lance requires a platoon-sized body of support crew.

First and foremost in the Trellwan Lancers' make-up was the infantry, the groundpounders Grayson was training to take on the enemy 'Mechs. Not all 'Mech units had foot soldiers attached to them, however. Carlyle's Commandos had had ground troops because it was a garrison force, and there were garrison duties that would have been impractical for a ten-meter-tall 'Mech. The Lancers were to be ground troops trained in anti-'Mech warfare with 'Mechs for support, which reversed the usual role for a combat BattleMech unit.

The idea had been General Varney's. Grayson's skill during the Battle of Sarghad had proven to the Military Council that ground troops could be used against 'Mechs. Grayson's ten years of training supported the idea. Ground forces *could* face 'Mechs and win, but it took a remarkable blend of skill, training, and courage to do so. This combination did not occur naturally even in elite units. Grayson faced a daunting task, and he still questioned his ability to carry it out.

The Lancers' T.O. called for two combat platoons of 60 men each. Though there were more than enough volunteers available, so far Grayson had only two short platoons of 40 each, scarcely more than a pair of platoon sections. After some work and several false starts, he had decided that the experienced sergeants on his team were able to handle no more than those

80 men. Untrained and leaderless soldiers would be far worse than no help at all.

Also in training were 35 men with various degrees of technical and mechanical training. This was the beginning of what Grayson hoped would be a 60-man technical platoon, astechs able to work under the direction of the lance's techs to keep the BattleMechs armed, patched, and functioning.

Finally, there were five men in training as MechWarriors. They were under Grayson's direct command and he worked with them for hours each day, familiarizing them with the *Locust*'s controls and drilling them in tactics and procedure. One of them, a young Trell named Yarin, showed an intuitive sense of balance and motion that might produce a MechWarrior—in about ten years. Grayson thought this part of the program was worse than useless. It would take years to bring these five up to any kind of proficiency in 'Mech operations, so it seemed absurd to spend so much time training new pilots when the unit had but a single light 'Mech on its rolls. But Grayson's own orders from the Military Council were clear on that point. What good was a 'Mech unit without MechWarriors?

His work was made easier by two experienced NCOs: Sergeant Ramage from the Militia, who had fought Hendrik's raiders as a private ten years before, and a Guards Corporal named Brooke, whom he had promoted upon learning the man had worked in a machine shop before joining the army. Another Militia sergeant named Larressen had no combat experience, but seemed sharp, intelligent, and unafraid of speaking his views. Ramage and Larressen became platoon leaders for platoons A and B, while Brooke was placed in charge of the tech platoon.

With three good men in the topkick slots, Grayson had hoped the lance would begin to run itself. That did not prove to be the case. The single worst problem he faced was equipment procurement. Quite simply, there was either no equipment to procure, or else the available material was tied up in bureaucratic red tape and interdepartment squabbling.

The lists of what he needed were endless: portable power generators, tools ranging from laser cutters to microwrenches, portable and desktop computers and access to the military data files, visors and portable communications units, weapons for the combat platoons and ammo to go with them, portable and stationary lights, gantries and 'Mech repair cocoons, power feed cable, 'Mech spare parts ranging from servoactuator relay circuits and a portable laser to a new head and cockpit assembly for the captured *Wasp.* He also needed food, drinking water and wash water, quarters and mattresses for over one hundred men, vehicles—

Vehicles! Those were the special responsibility of the technical section, which was expected to procure, maintain, and service them. He needed HVTs and weapons carriers— ground effect HVWCs as well as the slower, heavier, tracked or wheeled vehicles. Unfortunately, there were only two sources of military vehicles in Sarghad, the Militia and the Royal Guard. Neither unit was prepared to release even one scout hovercraft to the newly-formed Lancers without guarantees that the unit would become the private elite of either the Militia or the Guard. Grayson wasted days just going through the mountain of official requisitions for service hovercraft and HTs before he realized what he was fighting was not bureaucratic stupidity, but inter-service politics. There was, Grayson learned, an intense and bitter rivalry between the Royal Guards and the Militia.

Trellwan's human population was divided among three cities—Sarghad, Gath, and Tremain—plus a scattering of homesteads, agrodome collectives, and mining sites that stretched along perhaps a third of the equator. Sarghad was the largest city by far, and the center of the planetary government. Each city was the center of a Militia military district, with a resident regiment to serve as tax collectors, fire department, garbage collectors, and police on a world where there was little need for a standing army on a day-to-day basis.

The Royal Guards, on the other hand, was based in Sarghad in a modern barracks beneath the palace grounds. Their function was purely military, and primarily cosmetic on a world with a single government. They served as escorts for the king, staged parades and military reviews, and generally worked to create the image that there was indeed a monarchy in Sarghad, one rich and powerful enough to provide his private guard with attractive green uniforms. Though they claimed to be an elite force, and though the Guard received the lion's share of military appropriations and equipment from the various government councils, Grayson had seen little evidence that they were any good as fighting soldiers. But they had the vehicles he needed, and they wouldn't release them until he could assure them that the First Trellwan Lancers would be designated as a part of the Royal Guards.

The Militia, in turn, controlled such essentials as distribution of water and communications within the city. They provided these services only grudgingly, while awaiting word that the Lancers would be designated as a branch of the Militia.

Grayson began his attack on the situation by giving the vehicle problem to Lieutenant Nolem, who was obviously a spy for the Guard staff command. By assigning him full-time to the task of acquiring eight hover transports, Grayson kept the lieutenant out of his hair while keeping his need on the desk of the requisition and supply officer at Guard HQ. Perhaps if the clamor was raised long enough, loud enough...

He won cooperation from the Militia by pointing out that his two combat platoon sergeants were both Militia, and that, while he had to go along with His Majesty's original idea that the Lancers should be drawn from both services, surely his choice of fighting sergeants was proof of where his loyalties really lay. That won him a steady supply of food and water, installation of half of the visors he needed, and the loan of one aging HVT for running errands throughout the city.

Perhaps most ironic was the problem of his own uniform. Grayson had been decked out in Guard full dress for the ceremony at the palace reception hall, but had never been issued any other uniforms or personal equipment. Guard uniform regulations required that he always wear the Crimson Star with full dress, which Lieutenant Nolem had tactfully pointed out when Grayson arrived for work without the heavy starburst. Though he was beginning to feel a proper popinjay in the elaborate green and gold, his requests for uniform requisitions went unanswered. At least Nolem did not protest when he refused to wear his dress sword to work.

With all that, his biggest worry was personnel. Volunteers were numerous, but painfully few were skilled as machinists, electronics techs, robotics experts, weapons handlers and armorers, mechanics, and so on. On the other hand, the troops being formed into the unit's pair of combat platoons had experience, but little equipment. Half of them were drilling with lengths of pipe. When they had been transferred to the Lancers, they'd been ordered to turn in their weapons, and so only a few had brought guns with them. There was only a handful of shoulder-fired missile launchers, heavy weapons autofire weapons, armor-piercing shells and missile warheads, plastic explosives or detonators, or fitted body armor, and no man-portable lasers at all.

Even when well-equipped and supplied, ground troops are woefully inadequate against an attacking BattleMech. If the Trellwan Lancers were to accomplish anything, they would have to assemble a working BattleMech lance. He had five men in training as MechWarriors, but so far he'd had little success. Learning to pilot one of the battle machines was an agonizing and drawn-out process. Anyone could strap himself into the cockpit and move the machine's arms and legs, but it took a whole new way of thinking to control the automatic movements through the computer-linked neurohelmet, and without that link, the best and strongest 'Mech in the galaxy was just so much inanimate metal and spare parts.

He took a major step toward solving the personnel problem when he brought Lori—now Staff Sergeant Lori Kalmar—aboard as senior tech. She could answer technical questions and showed a flair for diagnosing 'Mech problems on scant information. Though there was no way to repair the damaged *Wasp* without procuring a complete new head and cockpit assembly, she was able to ready the 'Mech for combat in every other regard. Somehow, she even managed to rig up test circuits and relays that allowed it to be handled (in clumsy fashion) by remote control. That meant it could serve as a mobile target for the five apprentice MechWarriors training under Grayson. They could practice dry-run tracking and weapons locks aboard the *Locust* without Grayson's having to try to rig a simulator.

Then a new trouble surfaced. Despite her obvious skill, many of the new astechs in the technical section refused to work for Lori Kalmar. She was, after all, from Hendrik's bandit confederacy. Her people, they contended, had killed many Trells in raids and skirmishes across the better part of a century, and she was certainly not to be trusted now. Add to that, she was a woman in the male-dominated Trellwan culture. Women held few positions of real power, were never found in either military branch other than as secretaries or clerical assistants, and there was the continuing unspoken tradition that the place for woman was at home, raising children. A young, pretty woman giving orders to men on the job was simply not taken seriously.

That problem would never go away entirely, though Lori had made some progress on her own. Once, after she gave an order to an astech, he simply ignored her. When she repeated the command, the man responded with a leer and a suggestion about what he'd like to do instead. But warrior apprentices on Sigurd were well trained in the martial disciplines. They learned not only how to pilot a 'Mech, but how to use firearms, sticks, knives, and bare hands to deadly effect. The insubordinate astech woke up to find himself a guest in Sarghad's hospital, where he was being treated for a broken jaw. From that time on, Sergeant Kalmar found her orders greeted with considerably greater enthusiasm.

Grayson was dismayed by the fact that there were no spare parts to repair machines that broke down, little oil to lubricate machinery, and the computer programs used to coordinate schedules and duty rosters and muster lists were hopelessly inadequate. A team detailed to salvage diamond monofilament wire from junked sections of boron nitride armor plate was stalled by a lack of the proper chemicals for the extraction process.

He grew short on sleep, became impatient, and drove the unit harder. Morale sagged, and five men were placed on report for fighting in one period alone. Seven enlisted men simply walked away from the barracks during another period and never returned. No one stopped them at the door because the man on sentry duty was one of the seven. When troops restricted to the post routinely showed up for work drunk or failed to show at all, Grayson had to detail three of his junior NCOs just to patrol the area for hidden caches of alcohol.

Then, a new difficulty arose with Lori. If the Lancers were to have any chance of operating against offworld forces, they needed more than the single *Locust* operational. The first step would be capturing the other *Wasp*. If necessary, they would have to destroy it and use its head to replace the shattered one on the *Wasp* now in the Lancers' possession. Lori had been troubled when Grayson had asked her about the man who would likely be piloting the *Wasp* they intended to capture or kill.

"Private Enzelman and I were never what you'd call close," she told him. "But he's a Sigurdian, and a long way from home, like me. I...I don't think I can help you to...to kill him."

The pain in her eyes touched Grayson. Many of her critics still didn't trust Lori's willingness to work for her former enemies, and she was trapped between the need to prove her loyalty and her loyalty to a fellow warrior.

"I can take you off the project," he said.

"And go back to that dungeon? That's where your General Adel wants me, you know. Him and Lieutenant Nolem." She shuddered.

Grayson leaned back, reflecting. "You know, everything depends on our taking that *Wasp* with its cockpit intact. What we need to do is develop a diversion that will let me get close enough to cripple it without touching its head or your friend Enzelman." He spread his hands. "I can't promise more than that."

She managed half a smile. "What I'd really like is to get him to come over to the Lancers. The only reason he's fighting for *them* is he doesn't know there's an alternative."

Grayson thought of his five warrior recruits and nodded gravely. During the practice session earlier that period, one of the men had tripped the *Locust* over its own feet, and it was only fool's luck that had kept the irreplaceable machine from being badly damaged. Grayson was despairing of any of those five ever taking a 'Mech into combat.

"Believe me, Lori. I intend to try to do just that. We need 'Mech pilots, and we're not going to grow them ourselves here in Sarghad."

She'd looked up at him, her eyes shining. "Do you...do you mean that? I mean, that I might con a 'Mech again?"

Grayson rubbed his eyes. "I can't promise it, not now. But damned if I know where else I can get 'Mech pilots. It takes years of apprenticeship to learn how to con one. Ha! Look at us! Apprentices half our lives, and neither of us had even graduated yet when we found ourselves...here."

Lori laid her hand on Grayson's arm, a warm and gentle touch. "I'll do whatever has to be done, Gray."

How had they slipped into a first-name basis? Grayson could not remember. He did know he felt comfortable with Lori, able to talk to her, to discuss plans, and that he missed her when she was not there. Perhaps their growing friendship had something to do with the fact that they both felt so alone here.

"We'll all do what has to be done," he said. "It's called 'survival.'"

Two periods later, Lieutenant Nolem filed a report with General Adel on "subversive elements within the unit." He named no one, but it was clear he had Lori in mind as the one directly responsible for the unit's poor morale. As the sun rose on a crisp, clear, -20 degree morning on Seconday, the First Trellwan Lancers seemed farther away from being combat ready than ever.

CHAPTER 18

The Lancers needed combat to draw them together. *More importantly,* Grayson realized, *they need a victory.*

By the time the red sun had reached its zenith in the clear, chill cold of Seconday, the Lancer T.O. & E. showed the two combat platoons as having 40 men each. This force constituted the Ground Strike Unit, and had been trained in anti-Mech infantry tactics. How well they would be able to put Grayson's lectures into practice remained to be seen. The astech support platoon now numbered 63, and Tech Sergeant Brooke—under Master Sergeant Lori Kalmar's direction—had both 'Mechs mechanically sound and operational. The *Wasp,* however, still lacked a head.

Written out on the unit T.O. & E. chart, it all looked quite impressive, but Grayson knew even a full battalion with four times as many soldiers—even well-trained and experienced soldiers—would be hard pressed to handle even one attacking 'Mech. And when one of those 'Mechs was a 75-ton *Marauder...*

The heart of any 'Mech unit was the combat lance—the 'Mechs themselves. Ideally a balance of four 'Mechs working together, sometimes accompanied by an air lance of aerospace fighters, the unit's 'Mechs were the whole reason for the existence of support combat units. Except for special units, most 'Mech lances, especially mercenary units, had no ground strike force at all, and consisted of 'Mechs and techs alone. Without 'Mechs, a unit consisting of just ground soldiers was practically defenseless.

And the Lancers had exactly one combat-ready light 'Mech.

It was a few tens of hours shy of midday Seconday, and the Trellwan Light Lancers were deploying for combat. As Grayson had explained to General Varney when he submitted his proposal, "We fight now, and win—or it's all been for nothing." There was more than the fighting morale of the Lancers at stake. Grayson needed more than one 'Mech if the lance was to have any chance at all. And the only way they were going to get another 'Mech was to take one away from the enemy.

The spaceport north of Sarghad was an unsightly sprawl of gray and white buildings across the otherwise empty countryside. The ground there was largely barren, broken by thick clumps of blue-tufted qykka and patchy swards of blue-green prairie grass. The highway that linked port and city was pocked and rutted by Trellwan's vicious weather cycle, and had been but rarely traveled even before the coming of the bandit raiders.

Below the road was a chain of arroyos, gulleys carved through the arid ground by repeated Thirday meltwater floods. Grayson had noted this particular wadi during terrain-mapping expeditions when Carlyle's Commandos had occupied the Castle some ten kilometers northeast, on the other side of the port. It had survived the last series of floods and existed now as a broad, dry channel through the desert, encrusted with frost and ice in the overhangs where the weak sun did not penetrate. In some places, it was fifteen meters deep, with steep slopes of treacherously balanced rock and shifting sand.

The *Locust* paced along the floor of the canyon with Grayson at the controls. It felt as though a lifetime had passed since he'd last strapped himself into the MechWarrior's hot seat. As he gripped the controls and leaned into the reassuring weight of the neurohelmet, he knew how right it was that he'd trained for it half of his life.

After spending endless standard days at his report-smothered desk in the dim recesses of the city armory, Grayson felt alive again.

His hands rested lightly on the weapons controls and maneuver overrides. His electrode-padded and cable-heavy helmet picked up neural impulses relating to routine movement and balance, while a sophisticated computer built into the cockpit seat translated those signals to the 'Mech's four-meter walking stride. The *Locust* was an extension of his body.

The popular warrior mythos held that MechWarriors actually *became* their 'Mechs, that there was a personality transfer from man to machine, that the machines moved and fought because the MechWarrior's mind was directly controlling them. None of this was true, though certainly the neurohelmets had been a first promising step toward combat systems doing just that. What the helmet did do was to direct the machine in such routine tasks as maintaining its balance, which left the pilot's mind free to deal with analytical tasks such as sorting out friend from foe and engaging in combat.

"Striker One, this is Striker Two, do you read?"

The voice in his helmet speakers was electronically filtered and reproduced, and required practice to understand. Transmissions were beamed on an extremely narrow frequency band in order to penetrate enemy electronic countermeasures and to defy hostile codebreakers. Often, such transmissions were made in battlespeech, an artificial coded language known only to the users, but there'd been no time to design and teach one to all who would need to know it. Computer scrambling should make the transmissions intelligible only to the Lancers. At least, that's what Grayson hoped.

He bit down hard to flex the masseter muscles below and in front of his ears. Sensors in the helmet read the flexing's electrical signature, and opened a channel.

"Striker Two, this is One. Go."

"We're in position below the fence. No patrols...no suspicious activity."

"Good. Keep alert."

The assault force's movement up the wadi in broad daylight had been a calculated risk. The raiders had helicopters, and there was no guarantee they didn't also have a military surveillance satellite capable of counting rivets on the *Locust*'s dorsal armor. The *Locust* was shrouded in folds of camouflage netting, and Grayson was operating the heat sinks at their lowest settings to cut down the 'Mech's IR signature. What the assault team was really counting on was luck. Careful observation of the bandit bases at the port and up Mount Gayal at the Castle suggested they held the Trell armed forces in very low esteem, and weren't maintaining a proper watch on the approaches to their encampments.

"Striker One, this is Three."

"Three, this is One. Go."

"No activity at the Castle. I have the *Marauder* in clear sight. It's still parked on the parade field outside the repair bay doors."

"Right, Three. Keep on them."

The *Locust's* cockpit was so small Grayson could touch the opposite bulkheads with outstretched arms. The viewscreen formed a 180-degree strip across the front of the tiny room, showing the sharply stratified layers of water-deposited sediments in the walls of the channel outside. Most of the deck was taken up by the pilot's seat and the jungle of cables, consoles, exposed circuits, and instrumentation that kept this small, walking mountain moving and fighting.

Perhaps the dominant feature of the cockpit was the smell, a sharp, sour tang that seemed to emanate from deck, bulkheads, and seat despite scrubbings and liberal dousings with chemical absorbents. The *Locust's* onboard logs and equipment installation dates showed that this particular 'Mech was over a century old. The distinctive odors of sweat, fear, and battle fury of 40-some pilots had become as much a part of the cockpit as the armor encasing it. The smell was unpleasant, but already fading from Grayson's awareness.

It was getting warm inside the cockpit. A tiny blower behind his head struggled with the impossible task of cooling the pressurized space, but before long, it would be unequal to the 'Mech's heat buildup. Grayson had already stripped to briefs and a light tunic of net fabric. Though he was not uncomfortable yet, very soon it would become much worse.

Grayson looked down through electronic eyes at the troops... *my troops*, he thought. Their TK assault rifles had come from the armory that was now the Lancers' HQ (though the proper forms had never been approved by the Militia supply staff). Grayson had only obtained the weapons because he knew a thousand of the sleek auto-fire weapons had been given to the Militia by

Carlyle's Commandos. The men were bundled against the cold in camo-mottled winter combat jackets and gloves unofficially liberated by Sergeant Ramage from the Guard supply depot across from the palace.

He worked his jaw muscles twice, opening a line. "Striker Two, this is One. Give me a feed."

"Right, One. Patch in."

An image window unrolled across the viewscreen. On the rim of the wadi above him, a scout poked the sensor end of an optical-fiber remote scanner above the edge of the gully. On the image window, Grayson saw the squat shapes of water and fuel tanks, the crosshatching of a mesh-link fence. In the far distance, the humanoid shape of a *Wasp* moved through shimmering haze. Hot air was rising from the ferrocrete apron, causing the image to boil.

"That's our target," Grayson said. He opened the channel to Striker Three. "Is the *Marauder* still staying put?"

"No alarm, sir. All quiet."

"It won't be for long. Striker Two!" He could see the tac-force strike leader, Sergeant Ramage, touching the microphone at his throat

"Yes, sir!"

"Move out! Now!"

The small body of troops surged up the slope of the wadi, using ropes that had been set from the rim by the scouts. On schedule and according to plan, Platoon A moved toward the spaceport's outer fence.

Grayson took a deep breath and tasted the sour air of the cramped *Locust* cockpit. He opened another combat channel. "Striker Four, are you ready?"

"All set here, Lieutenant!" Sergeant Larressen was shouting, the electronically-rendered tones of his voice oddly spaced. He must be yelling above the keening of his HVWCs.

"We're ready here. Let 'em know you're there."

"On our way, sir!"

It had taken a direct appeal to King Jeverid to free up much of the equipment the Lancers needed, including eight battered but serviceable hovercraft weapons carriers, five-man machines like those he had seen and ridden in the battle in Sarghad. Three of them mounted autocannons, and one a combat laser. Two more carried short-range Skorpiad anti-armor missiles, while the rest carried antipersonnel heavy machine guns. This small armada was no match for the entire enemy 'Mech force. With luck, though, they might knock out one or more of the light 'Mechs in open battle. Grayson had decided the chance was so slim that the entire convoy would better serve as a decoy force. They were racing across the desert east of the spaceport now, their fans churning up plumes of dust visible for tens of kilometers.

"Lieutenant! This is Striker Two!"

"Go ahead, Two." Grayson paced the *Locust* along the gully as he spoke. There was a place farther along where the slope was less steep than the spot where the ground assault force had scrambled up. On his viewscreen, the layered red and ocher strata of the arroyo's wall lurched and tilted as the *Locust* strode along its gravel floor.

"There's two...repeat *two* 'Mechs at the port. They're together—"

"Feed me."

The image window opened, and Grayson saw the *Wasp* had been joined by a second light 'Mech. It was difficult to see through the churning telephoto view, but the second appeared to be a *Stinger*. The pair of 20-ton scout 'Mechs were striding rapidly across the apron to the east.

"Striker Four, this is One."

"Go...ahead...One." Larressen must be screaming against the roar of the plenum fans in the weapons carriers' bellies. The transmission carried none of the background noise, but the sergeant's words were paced by the effort of shouting them.

"You've been seen. Two 'Mechs, I say again, two light 'Mechs headed your way."

"We...copy...One!"

"Striker Two...feed me range figures."

Red numbers sprang into sharp relief across the image window, ticking off range and azimuth readings as the target 'Mechs moved. The two 'Mechs were three kilometers off, moving across Grayson's line-of-sight at an angle that would bring them closer to the *Locust*'s position.

Grayson waited, sweltering in the rising heat. If it were this bad now...

He checked the *Locust's* controls one last time. His left hand gripped the con stick that emerged from the left arm of his chair and swung on jointed sliders across his lap. His right fingers closed on a black plastic D-grip on the chair's right arm. Slight movements on the grip moved the *Locust's* laser cannon up, down, back and forth, and the red button resting under his thumb triggered it. His indicators showed all systems running hot, combat-ready.

Doubt had begun to plague him as he sat in his too warm cockpit. Attacking one of the two enemy strongholds in broad daylight, with one 'Mech and half-trained men, that had to be a recipe for suicide. Grayson pushed the doubt aside, struggled to ignore it. So much depended on surprise. If they succeeded in winning surprise, the raid should succeed. It *would* succeed. If not... He pushed the doubt aside again, harder this time. *The plan will work! It* has *to!*

He fished in a webbing pouch at the side of the cockpit chair, and brought out a filmy, blue length of soft cloth. Mara had given it to him the period before they'd left.

"I've read how the Knights of Old Earth carried their lady's favors into battle," she'd said, handing him a piece of the gown she had worn at the reception. "You could carry this."

Grayson looked at the scrap of material for a few seconds, then made his decision. *Practicality over romance,* he thought. Mara would understand. He used the cloth to wipe away the layer of perspiration that had beaded on his forehead and upper lip.

Watching the readouts on the target 'Mechs, he saw the range had decreased. A quick consultation with the *Locust's* onboard computer showed if the enemy 'Mechs held their course and speed, they would be at their closest point and moving away from Grayson's position just...about...*now!*

Grayson's hand pressed the *Locust's* control stick forward, and the 'Mech leaned forward, one armored bird's foot clawing at the soft sand slope before it. The machine lurched and seemed to stumble slightly, then Grayson heard the whine of protesting servos as the 'Mech's computer drew on his own sense of balance and struggled to remain upright. One giant foot found purchase, and the other foot lifted. The 'Mech's head lurched above the rim of the canyon. Now he saw the scene directly through the *Locust*'s sensors on the 180-degree screen. He struggled with the stick, willing the machine up and forward. One flat, four-clawed foot cleared the edge, the flanges spilling sand, and then the *Locust* was up and onto the hard, flat desert surface. The 'Mech's bird-like form leaned forward and its spindly legs swung up, forward, and down with shifting, mechanical movements.

In theory, Grayson knew there was no way one 'Mech could sneak up on another across open terrain. BattleMech hulls mounted sensors that covered the entire spectrum, infrared to ultraviolet, as well as sound, laser ranging, and radar. The 'Mech's computer created a composite 360-degree scan of the entire battlefield that is instantly available to the pilot. In practice, things were not so simple. MechWarriors are human, and, caught up in the excitement of battle or the thrill of a chase, a pilot might override or ignore a computer's signals.

Grayson was counting on the humanness of the two 'Mech pilots he was stalking now. Lori had said Enzelman was less experienced than she at 'Mech operations. Though Sergeant Mendoza was experienced, his first instinct would be to focus on the decoy convoy of speeding vehicles two kilometers in front of the targets.

Grayson could see the HVWCs off to the side, turning now under a pillar of dust that mushroomed into the sky. There was a flash of light ahead. The enemy *Wasp* had fired its laser at long range with no visible effect. He touched a control. The screen shifted to battle mode, the landscape subdued, the enemy 'Mechs outlined in light and bracketed by readouts giving range and sensor-detected information. Drifting red crosshairs showed the aiming point for the laser.

The decline of technology during the Succession Wars had keenly affected the science of weapons manufacture and design. No longer could the complex control systems for fire-and-forget missiles, for long-range particle beams or lasers be packed into units small enough and cheap enough to be casually expended in combat. BattleMech engagements tended to be brutal, short-range affairs, with individual 'Mechs closing to a few tens of meters to deliver killing shots.

Theoretically, the laser under the *Locust*'s chin could hit anything in line-of-sight clear to the horizon. That range was sharply reduced, however, by the quality of the weapon control system that pointed the heavy barrel. Grayson could not count on hitting anything with that laser at ranges greater than about 300 meters. He'd begun his charge when the enemy was one kilometer away. At top speed, he would close to firing range in less than thirty seconds.

The *Wasp* was between Grayson and the *Stinger*, blocking the *Stinger*'s electronic scanners. That was a small piece of luck, for Lori had told him the *Stinger* pilot seemed to have had some combat experience. More, certainly, than her comrade in the *Wasp*.

Range: 800 meters.

For that reason, he was locking the crosshairs of his laser sight on the rear bit of the left hip joint on the *Stinger*. The experienced MechWarrior would be the more dangerous of the two.

Range: 600 meters.

Well, listen to the old hand talking, Grayson thought wryly. *This is* your *first time in 'Mech combat,* he told himself. *Even that* Wasp *pilot has seen more action in a 'Mech hotseat than you. Training is great, but remember what Griff was always telling you about there being no substitute for experience.*

Just then, a flashing blue light on his console told him he was being probed by radar.

Range: 400 meters.

The *Stinger* was slowing, dropping behind the charging *Wasp*. It pivoted on stiff legs, the long, black muzzle of its laser coming to the point.

Grayson's throat was suddenly tight, his mouth sand-dry, his nose running, his stomach twisting. *Oh God, don't let me screw up,* he prayed to he knew not who.

Range: 300 meters.

The *Stinger* fired as Grayson twisted his running 'Mech to the side. There was a momentary dazzle, but the battlemode imaging system controlled the light level, protecting his eyes. His thumb came down on the red button, and blue light pulsed across the *Stinger*'s hip joint.

Hit! Flakes of metal glittered in the midmorning sun as they scattered on the sand, and there was a trace of oily smoke near the *Stinger*'s waist. The *Stinger* sidestepped, moving rapidly to make itself a more difficult target. Grayson spun, swinging his laser up to bear on the back of the enemy *Wasp*.

The *Stinger* must have called a warning. The *Wasp* turned before Grayson could fire again, and the laser hit the 'Mech's left side instead of the broad, almost unarmored back. The *Wasp* staggered as its armor, unable to dump the heat of Grayson's beam, exploded in bright, molten globs. The beam was attenuated somewhat as the stricken machine continued to turn beneath it, creating a ragged black scar across its flank.

Lights went red on Grayson's control panel, and there was a shock that made the *Locust* shudder and twist. The *Stinger* had fired, catching him on the right torso. The armor seemed to have stopped the worst of the beam, but there was minor damage, and another hit there would certainly penetrate.

He swung and fired at the *Stinger,* aiming low. There was a flare and a whirl of sand as the *Stinger* went airborne on flaring jets. Grayson reacted without thinking with a twist and a lurch that evaded three quick-spaced shots that cratered the sand where he'd been standing. He rolled up and fired as the *Stinger* descended.

Miss!

The *Locust* swung about, targeting the *Stinger* as it dashed across his field of fire. He triggered the laser and saw liquid metal splatter. He'd hit the upper left arm. There might be some damage there.

He pressed the control stick, and the *Locust* lurched forward. A flash...and another! Two shots, almost together, had missed. With the range down to less than 80 meters, he fired at the *Wasp* and caught it square in the chest.

So far, most of the damage had been confined to the 'Mechs' armor. Very soon now, the shots would be falling on still-hot scars, burning into the delicate electronic innards of the machines, and then the issue would be settled.

Grayson wiped his hand ineffectually across his brow under the neurohelmet's rubber padding. He was drenched with sweat, and the net shirt clung to him unpleasantly. The heat in the sealed cockpit stifled him, pressed in around him, making him lightheaded.

The *Wasp* spun before him. He lined up for a quick shot at the blackened upper chest, fired, and missed. With his left hand still on the control stick, his right hand found the jointed wrist and finger control that guided the *Locust*'s twin machine guns. Machine guns were generally used for firing at enemy troops, but as he had proven in his uneven duel with the *Wasp* in Sarghad's streets, a heavy-caliber machine gun could eventually penetrate 'Mech armor, given time and a bit of luck.

Even in the padded and pressurized interior of the *Locust*'s cockpit, vibrations transmitted by his seat hammered his body. Tracers arced, crossed, and floated into the wildly twisting *Stinger.* He saw metal chips fly from the already damaged hip, saw the *Stinger*'s left leg suddenly go stiff. Hit!

Grayson charged.

The *Stinger* was slow turning to meet him, its leg dragging as it spun. The two 'Mechs collided in an ear-splitting crash, and the *Stinger* sprawled backward onto the sand.

Grayson followed it with laser fire, but the 'Mech rolled across its shoulder as the laser pulse traced a line of molten glass in the sand. The *Stinger* fired, and Grayson's viewscreen went white then black as laser fire screamed across visual sensors recessed into the armor of the *Locust*'s combined head and torso.

He jabbed viciously at the keyboard that controlled the sensor array computer, meanwhile keeping the *Locust* twisting and dodging blindly with his left hand. The screen cleared as reserve forward sensors came online. The damage to his 'Mech's head was severe; another head shot would smash through the remaining armor and kill him.

He quickly checked the scale that registered the *Locust*'s internal heat, chewing at his lip as he scanned flickering numbers. None of it was good. The temp was climbing dangerously. The computer would be asking for a shutdown soon. He'd lost heat sinks on his outer hull, and the buildup was becoming critical. But he'd worry about that when the time came.

Now...where was the *Wasp*? Damn! In his momentary blindness, he'd lost track of the—

A violent impact from behind smashed him forward. He pivoted, caught his balance and turned. The *Wasp* collided with him from behind and nearly knocked him down. He found himself staring into the muzzle of the 'Mech's laser, knew he had no time to bring his own laser to bear. But then, an explosion mushroomed at the *Wasp*'s back, slamming it forward, off balance. There was a second explosion, this one crashing into the *Wasp*'s back armor and sending it sprawling flat on its belly.

The eight hovercraft of Striker Four were racing toward the three 'Mech combatants, spreading across the desert floor. One of the missile launchers trailed puffs of smoke in the HVWC's windstream, and twin flashes caught the *Stinger* in its right shoulder. There was a blinding pulse of light, and the *Stinger*'s main weapon, along with the rest of the arm, whirled into the sand.

The *Wasp* whirled and broke into a run away from the hurtling hovercraft and toward Grayson. The *Locust*'s laser swung to track it, locked on, and fired cleanly into the 'Mech's already savaged upper torso.

The *Wasp* staggered, blue sparks playing along the visibly shattered circuits and torn wiring behind the crater in its chest. It took one step, then froze there, locked in a rigid stance from which it could not escape. Grayson turned to track the *Stinger*, which was limping toward the spaceport. At 100 meters' range, he fired again, targeting the machine's already damaged hip.

The leg gave way and the second 'Mech crashed into the sand.

The battle ended so abruptly that Grayson found himself wondering if it could really be over. The hovercraft swung up, weapons trained on the two crippled 'Mechs. With relief, Grayson saw the pilots being hauled from their cockpits, battered, but apparently able to stand and walk.

He felt relief because of Lori, who knew one of them as a friend, as well as for himself. Those two might be willing recruits to the Lancers, if properly approached. Grayson smiled ruefully at the thought, and wondered how he would convince Nolem and Adel of that.

"Striker One! Striker One! This is Three!"

"I hear you, Three. Go."

"Code Red, Chief. We've got the big boys spotted, the *Shadow Hawk* and the *Marauder* both. They're on the road coming down from the Castle, and it looks like they're headed this way!"

"The *Shadow Hawk*? You're sure?" Even as he spoke, he realized that was a silly question. How could they mistake the ID of a 55-ton armored battle machine?

"It just came out of the repair bay! It looks good as new... moving full speed!"

Grayson chewed at his lower lip, and tasted blood. The fight wasn't over yet.

CHAPTER 19

"Got it." Grayson's throat felt tight, his mouth dry. "Okay, Striker Four! Company's coming. Deploy for Code Red."

External microphones on the *Locust*'s head picked up the thutter of auto-rifle fire. He turned the 'Mech to bring telescopic sensors to bear, zooming in on where he could see flashes and running figures through the churning air above the ferrocrete apron.

A fuel tank had been blown. Black smoke smudged the northern sky, and the pavement underneath was cast into the rippling gloom of a smoke shadow.

"Striker Two! Do you read?"

"We...hear...you!" Ramage sounded like he was gasping for breath.

"We've picked off our targets, but two big brothers are on their way down the mountain. You have ten minutes!"

"I copy! We're almost...Manning, watch that warehouse... fifteen high! Get him!" The transmission was broken off for a moment. Then, "Yes, sir...we're almost wrapped up here!"

"Do you have the transport?"

"We have it. It's on the way."

One of the most important vehicles in any 'Mech lance technical platoon was a transporter, a huge, broad, powered sled used to recover and carry 'Mechs damaged on the battlefield. Until now, the Lancers did not have such a vehicle. Their only alternative had been to take one from the bandits.

The Lancers' new transporter had been brought to Trellwan as part of a trade agreement with the Commonwealth long before Carlyle's Commandos had arrived. More sophisticated models bore their loads on air cushions. This one was an older, wheeled vehicle. Each of its eighteen tires was twice the height of a man, and a single drum winch secured 2cm cross-braided diamond monofilament cables for recovery operations. Striker Two had been assigned to cause whatever damage they could to the spaceport facilities, but capturing the giant 'Mech transporter was their primary mission. And now, transporting the *Wasp* would be their first operation.

Grayson was already preparing the *Wasp* to be hoisted when the transporter arrived on the scene. The *Locust* did not have manipulative members like most humanoid 'Mechs, but there were cleats and rings cables could be attached to. Troops from the tacforce hovercraft swarmed across the downed *Wasp*, securing it with heavy cables and passing these up through the eyes of the *Locust*'s tow rings.

The transporter arrived at the apex of a gradually dispersing cloud of dust and was positioned alongside the *Wasp*. With the *Locust* supplying the muscle power, they eased the *Wasp* half up off its back until it rested on its heels, then swung around 45 degrees and lowered it back down to a ramp that extended back behind the transporter deck to the desert floor. Working swiftly, men used the vehicle's winch and three-meter pry bars to work the damaged 'Mech into place, and then the transporter's winch hauled the ramp and its 20-ton burden aboard.

Black smoke boiled into the cold green sky above the spaceport. Seconds later, a pair of dull *thumps* sounded across the desert, followed by the rattle of small arms fire in the direction of Mount Gayal. From where his 'Mech surveyed the edge of the port, Grayson could see the brooding, truncated pyramid of the Castle halfway up the slope.

"That'll be our friends," Grayson told Sergeant Larressen. "What do you think? Can we manage the *Stinger* too?"

Larressen stood close by the *Locust*'s left foot, gloved hands on his hips, puffs of white vapor issuing from his mouth in the frigid air. He was breathing hard after the struggle to raise the *Wasp*.

"We can try." He panted a bit over the radio circuit. "The question is whether we can move it once we get it up."

"Try it."

The *Locust* helped maneuver the transporter sled across the sand to the side of the fallen *Stinger*, and they repeated the loading process. The ramp was long and broad enough for only one 'Mech, and so the *Stinger* had to be piled on top of the *Wasp*. As the *Locust* backed the *Stinger* onto the heap, Larressen detailed eight men to retrieve the 'Mech's arm from the sand 50 meters away.

"Striker One, this is Three."

"Yeah, Three, Go."

"Can't hold 'em much longer. We ambushed 'em with rocket launchers, but it didn't slow 'em down. The *Shadow Hawk* is closing on us, while the *Marauder* is still headed toward you... and we can't do a damn thing about it."

"Right. Scatter your mines and withdraw. We're rolling."

"On our way."

Grayson gave the go-ahead to the transporter's driver, who was perched in the vehicle's cab high above the desert, almost at shoulder level with Grayson's 'Mech. The vehicle was rated for 60 tons, but the pair of 20-tonners on its salvage deck were so precariously fitted Grayson didn't want to trust even diamond monofilament lashings when the accelerating vehicle hit rough ground.

Grayson opened a combat channel to all units. "All Strikers, this is One. Mission accomplished! Pack it in, we're going home!"

"Striker One, this is Two!"

"Go ahead, Two."

"Ramage, Lieutenant. We've got a bit of a problem here."

Grayson closed his eyes. Problems were what they did not need just now. "What is it?"

"Civilians, sir! A couple hundred of them! We got into a firefight with some sentries. Turned out they were guarding a quonset hut full of prisoners."

"What's the problem?"

"God, Lieutenant, how're we supposed to get them out of here? Half of 'em are sick, and none of 'em fit to run ten klicks back to town!"

Suddenly, Grayson had a mind's eye image of the prisoners—shocked, weak, tired, and nowhere to go. He remembered Renfred Tor saying the bandits' prisoners would end up as slaves, remembered Claydon's pain at the memory of his mother. He couldn't leave those people to the mercy of the bandits.

Twisting the *Locust*'s control stick, he urged the machine into a lurching, thudding run. Once across the shredded remnants of the spaceport fence, he pressed toward the sound of gunfire.

Machine gun fire howled and whined from the damaged armor of the *Locust*'s head. Grayson swung his 'Mech, tracing IR shadows of hidden men. The *Locust*'s machine guns stretched out with lazy, probing streams of tracers, then ignited a hastily constructed barricade of fuel drums and wooden crates. As the barricade exploded into dust and splinters, Grayson's external mike picked up a ragged cheer from men trotting out from cover. Their tired faces were blackened with grime, and many were missing helmets and other gear. Several were being helped along by unwounded comrades, but his men still had the strength to cheer.

The former prisoners, however, were dazed and uncomprehending. The assault team had liberated a half-dozen scout hovercraft from somewhere in the port, and these were crowded to overflowing with the weakest and sickest of the ex-prisoners, and with some of the women. From the shattered windows of the port control tower, tracers flashed and spat, seeking the refugees. A soldier screamed, thrashing on the ferrocrete. The *Locust*'s machine guns fired again, and broken glass and fragments of stone showered from the tower to the ground.

"Sergeant Ramage!"

"Sir!"

"Check those buildings over there." From his higher vantage point, Grayson could see what looked like storage sheds to the north. The *Locust* gestured with a gun arm. "See if you can round up more vehicles."

"Sir!"

"Striker Four!"

"We're here!"

"You're going to have to run interference for us. Go for the *Marauder*! Slow him down!"

There was no response, but Grayson didn't have time to pursue it. The hovercraft carrier's commander must be in shock with orders like that

"Transporter!"

"Yes, sir!"

"Change of plan! Swing north toward the port. You'll have some passengers to pick up."

"Yes, sir!"

His console warned him of probing radar. "Move it men! We're out of time!" Explosions echoed across the desert. The *Marauder* was there, four kilometers off and closing with ponderous, slow-motion strides. The hovercraft peeled off to meet this new menace, snarling low across the wastes to loose missiles and pulses of laser light.

Grayson had a new worry now. None of the ex-prisoners had cold-weather gear. The sub-zero temperature would quickly kill them if they weren't moved to shelter fast. It was also possible the *Marauder* might get them.

Grayson tracked and fired with his laser. At over three klicks, he thought he had scored hits, but could not be sure. At such ranges, even the most powerful 'Mech-borne lasers were practically useless.

The *Marauder*'s autocannon winked fire in return. Flame gushed from a striken GEV, strewing metal, plastic, and bodies across the sand. The other hovercraft circled around, seeking to strike their target from the rear, where the armor was thinnest. The *Marauder* slowed, paused, searching for ambush or concealed attackers.

The transporter ground to a rumbling halt, and the freed prisoners swarmed up along the sides, grabbing handholds and being pulled up by troopers onto the broad deck. Heavily laden hovercraft thrummed past, racing for Sarghad. Others deposited their passengers beside the transport, then swung north to gather more stragglers.

The ferrocrete emptied, except for the littered debris of battle. Grayson called all units. "That's it! Fall back! Striker Four, drop your mines and break off! Rendezvous at Sarghad!"

Autocannon shells probed and followed, falling short.

They were well underway when the *Marauder*, perhaps suspecting an ambush, broke off the chase.

Thirty hours after the battle at the wadi, Harimandir Singh stared at an image of the boy he'd thought was dead.

"So," he said. The word held calm acceptance, as well as grim anticipation. He fingered the 2-D photo his spy had handed him. "So Carlyle's son is alive. And you say *he's* the one behind this...this situation?"

Stefan nodded jerkily. Singh terrified him. He never knew how the Red Duke's man would react to the news he brought, and the uncertainty was wearing on him.

Stefan had been recruited by one of Singh's agents in Viscount Vogel's staff shortly after the Commonwealth representative had arrived at the Castle. The young Trell was proud and ambitious, and had bridled under the subtleties of custom and prejudice that separated the off-worlder starmen from the "indigs," the locals. That agent had played on both Stefan's pride and his greed. Stefan now had more money in one of Sarghad's banks than he'd ever seen in his life, and had been promised even larger rewards for continued loyalty in service to the Red Duke.

Stefan swallowed hard. "I was at the celebration, Lord. The King gave him a medal—his second, I believe—and made a speech. He called Carlyle's son 'the Deliverer of Sarghad.'"

Singh's eyes flashed, sharp and cold. "He didn't see you?"

"No, Lord. I was in the back of the room. The light on the stage was bright. He couldn't have seen me, not in that crowd. I think everyone in Sarghad must have been there."

"That's good. Otherwise he might recognize you from our assault on the Castle."

"Yes, Lord."

"Carlyle will have to die, of course. The question is what to do with this new unit he's forming." Singh looked thoughtful. "They have a full lance now. Four 'Mechs."

"Only three, Lord. I overheard two astechs talking at the reception. One of the *Wasps* cannot be repaired, and they're using it for salvaged parts."

"Three 'Mechs or four, it does not matter. Light 'Mechs are no match for a *Marauder* and a *Shadow Hawk*." He flipped Grayson's photograph aside. "Carlyle knows he cannot win. Perhaps he will try something desperate." Singh smiled. "Now, *that* would be...pleasant."

"You will attack, then, Lord?" Singh's relaxed and talkative mood made Stefan more bold.

"Eh? Not while they remain in that city. Those narrow streets and alleys are deathtraps for 'Mechs. No, we will remain here, and wait."

"But Lord, how will you bring them out to fight?"

"We won't need to. They cannot attack us here in the Castle, and very soon we will no longer need to attack them."

"I don't understand, Lord."

"And it is not desirable that you do. If you knew the Plan, I would kill you now."

Stefan paled, and remained silent.

"I want you to return to Sarghad. You've been my eyes and ears there, Stefan. Now you will be my hand." Singh smiled at Stefan in his icy fashion, and the young Trell found the expression horrifying.

Sarghad's hospital complex lay mostly below ground in the southern part of the city. Its ground level was domed-over against Trellwan's extremes of climate, but an open patient lounge and exercise area was bathed in ruddy light through wall transparencies during the day. Trell was westering. The spaceport battle was a standard week in the past.

Captain Renfred Tor shook Grayson's hand.

"I take it you didn't get the job you were looking for," Grayson said.

"They refused rather bluntly, I must say." Tor was well on the way to recovery, though he remained in a wheelchair while tissue grafts healed on his toes. He had been carried to the transporter by another escaping prisoner when his frostbitten feet had given out. The bruises on his face had healed, but there was still a haunted look to the man, some secret horror he would not discuss.

"Well, things have changed in Sarghad. I've got a job for you, if you want it."

Tor eyed Grayson's dress greens with exaggerated distaste. "Your choice of tailors seems to have changed for the worse. You're a soldier now?"

Grayson shrugged. "They haven't signed me up formally, but yeah, I guess I am. We've been putting together a 'Mech unit. We're listed as a regiment on the staff command's T.O., but that's wishful thinking so far. One working 'Mech, some captures, and three companies of eager but very raw recruits. We could use you."

The freighter pilot looked thoughtful. "Doing what? I'm not a military man."

Grayson walked to the wall transparency and gazed out at the frost glittering on the sand outside, which was red in Trell's westering light.

"Helping us get a ship, for one thing. Piloting us to Tharkad for another."

Tor's eyebrows climbed his forehead. "Tharkad?"

"Well, maybe to a Commonwealth base, first. Drune II is a possibility. It's only about 90 light years in." Grayson turned suddenly to face Tor. "We've beaten the pirates a couple of times, but we can't expect that to continue. What we need to do is get Commonwealth forces back here to help fight them. Carlyle's Commandos...what's left of them...probably went to Tharkad. Maybe we could join up with them."

"If they're still in commission," Tor said gently. "With no 'Mechs to their name, and precious little equipment, where could they go?"

"The Commonwealth has to know what's happening here," Grayson continued, stubbornly ignoring what Tor had said. "They could dispatch a 'Mech regiment and mop those pirates right off Mount Gayal."

"From what I've heard, your Commonwealth was more than happy to turn this cinder over to Hendrik in the first place. Why should they bother?" Tor stirred in the wheelchair. "But that's really all beside the point, because you need a ship before you need a ship's captain."

"Exactly! And *that's* why I need you. Your DropShip is still at the port. Your freighter must still be parked at the jump point. If we could capture the DropShip, pack it with soldiers..."

"And have them all flamed by the *Invidious'* meteor defenses the moment they get within 500 klicks of her. Lad, I don't think you know what you're up against."

Grayson felt discouraged, but rallied with an effort of will. It was too early yet to know what might work and what would not. "But you'll help us? When you get up and around? I'll make you my advisor, put you on my staff."

Tor sighed. "There's no stopping you, I see." Then he grinned. "I always did love a good fight, youngster, and I sure as hell don't know how I'm going to pay for my room and board here!"

Grayson knew the government had already promised to pay the hospitalization expenses of those the Lancers had rescued from the spaceport. But Tor was an outsider in the same curious limbo as Grayson, and belonged nowhere on Trellwan.

With a shrug, Tor added, "Besides, you need someone to keep you out of trouble."

It was not so easy to convince Claydon, however. He had been among the 180-odd civilians and soldiers freed during the spaceport raid. Grayson saw him as the group disembarked at the Militia HQ, and had run up to him with a shout and a grin. But his greeting was rebuffed. "I should be glad to see you?" The Trell asked bitterly. "After what happened to my home... to Father?"

"I—I'm sorry, Claydon." What could Grayson possibly say to bridge that rift? "Look...it wasn't my fault!"

"Not *your fault*?" Claydon's pale face flushed. "Listen, young Lord, you have a marvelous faculty for using people, for riding them like 'Mechs until they break down or you get where you're going. I'll have no more of it."

"Claydon, we need you!" With another tech of Claydon's qualifications, the technical platoon would have half a chance to get the captured 'Mechs in fighting order. But, gods of the old League, the anger in him!

"But I don't need you! Leave me alone!" Claydon had turned on his heel, leaving Grayson standing by the massive wheel of the transporter.

He mused about Claydon as he headed through Sarghad's streets toward Mara's apartment. He'd decided to walk despite the cold, because he needed the time to do some thinking. Anyway, his cold-weather gear kept him warm enough. The streets were filled with the usual merchants, civilians, and soldiers going about their business, though there were no crowds this far from the merchants' quarter.

Grayson had not seen Mara in more periods than he could count, and schedule or no schedule, he'd promised her that during his next rest period they would get, in her words, reacquainted. Somehow he could not keep his mind on Mara, though, because something Claydon had said continued to echo in his mind. Use people? Of course he used people! As lance commander, he had to use them daily to get anything done, trading favors for favors, bolstering egos to get work done, pulling strings on juniors and superiors alike. And the job *had* to be done.

But Grayson was becoming uncomfortable, certain that Claydon had been referring not to what he was doing, but why. In his heart, Grayson knew he was working to create an anti-'Mech infantry unit, not merely to guard Trellwan, but as a tool for bringing down the black and gray *Marauder*. But revenge or not, if what he did also benefited Trellwan's people, what was the wrong?

A four-wheeled transport squeaked to a stop on the road beside him.

"Grayson! Wait!" Lori climbed out of the transport's cab. "It's all right," she said to the driver. "I'll be with him."

Grayson caught the green-coated driver's answer. "My orders, Sergeant. I'm to stay with you."

Lori's expression was one of frustration as she approached Grayson. A soldier, usually a Royal Guard, watched her whenever she went beyond the Lance HQ or the apartment that had been assigned to her.

"Hello, Lori. What can I do for you?"

"I need to...talk." She glanced over her shoulder at the driver, who had parked the vehicle and stood beside it now, just out of hearing.

Oh, hell, not now, he thought, but managed a half-smile. "Sure. Walk with me?"

She nodded and fell into step. Her guard followed at a discreet distance.

"What's the problem?"

"What isn't? Grayson, this just isn't going to work!"

"Ah. Cultural problems again?" That was their private code for the difficulties Lori faced working with men from a culture that did not accept women in leadership or military positions.

"And then some! I've been trying to requisition ammo reloads, and those red tape-stuffed bureaucrats won't even talk to me. Insist they want to talk to a quote responsible officer or NCO unquote."

"You show them your warrant?" It had taken a special pass with Jeverid's seal and signature on it to let Lori accomplish much of what she'd had to do.

"Of course. And now there's the problem with Garik."

Garik Enzelman was Lori's former comrade, captured with his *Wasp* at the battle for the spaceport. After talking with Lori, he had agreed to join Grayson's command, but staff officers and even other members of the unit had ferociously resisted the idea.

"Did you get him sprung?"

She nodded. "Finally. They have watchdogs following him around, too."

"I can't really help that, Lori. You have to admit you two could do a lot of damage if you set your minds to it."

"But they don't seem to understand that we owe Harimandir Singh and his bandits nothing! Nothing! He practically kidnapped us, killed one of our people on the way here..."

Grayson knew this really wasn't the right moment for the discussion. "Look, I'll talk to someone next work period—"

"Gray, I can't take this anymore! Either they let me do my job, or I'm—"

He put his hand out. "Wait."

A noise, a low-pitched hum from behind, had alerted him. He turned just in time to see a small, dark-haired man stepping up behind him.

For a frozen instant, Grayson tried to place where he'd seen the man before. But there was no time to pursue the thought. The vibroblade in the man's hand was white hot.

CHAPTER 20

Grayson stepped back as the blade swept up past his face, leaving a trail of heat and the odor of scorched metal. The man swung again, Grayson dodged again, and felt a stone wall press into his back.

Lori shouted a warning and stepped between Grayson and the attacker. The attacker stiff-armed Lori to the side. "Out of the way!" But she had grabbed the man's wrist and elbow as her booted foot smashed into his knee.

The blade hummed through the air toward this new target, but Grayson took the man's right arm in an elbow lock as Lori spun him headfirst into the wall with a sound like eggs cracking. The vibroblade danced on the pavement, gouging out a chunk of ferrocrete as it fell. Then Grayson had pulled the power pack lead and the glowing menace died. His attacker slumped to the ground.

Grayson crouched and probed the man's throat, feeling for a pulse. "He's dead. Neck's broken."

"Damn," Lori said.

"What is it?"

"I didn't mean to kill him. Now we can't find out who he is."

"No matter. I know him."

"Oh?" One eyebrow arched. "Friend of yours?"

He shook his head. "His name is Stefan. He was an astech with the Commandos. The spy who let the bandits into the Castle. He must be working for...who'd you say their leader was?"

"Harimandir Singh. You must be getting on his nerves if he's singled you out for this kind of special attention."

"Yes," Grayson said softly. "Singh." The name settled cold and hard in his heart. He'd vowed to kill the traitor who had opened the Castle's gates to the enemy. Though it had been Lori who had delivered the killing blow, what mattered was that the man was dead. Yet, Grayson did not feel the satisfaction he'd expected. Instead, the need for revenge was rising again, a blood-burning lust. Stefan had been merely Singh's tool, so Singh was the man he really wanted. But how?

Lori's guard appeared, automatic pistol in hand. "What happened?"

"I might ask you the same thing, trooper. Where the hell were you?"

"It...it happened so fast..."

The adrenaline surge had passed, leaving Grayson suddenly weak, tired. He closed his eyes to the guard's incompetence. "Never mind. You'd better take the sergeant back to her quarters."

"Yes, sir."

"No, Gray, let me stay with you."

Grayson frowned. He was already late for his meeting with Mara. "No," he told her. "Go with him. I'll see you next work period. I've...got an appointment."

Lori's mouth set into a hard line. "Yes, sir. Good night, sir." She climbed into the front seat of the transport without another glance at Grayson. He knew she was upset, knew she wanted to talk more, but he felt so weak and suddenly tired.

Did Singh want his death as much as Grayson wanted Singh's? Perhaps the man did not realize Grayson's death would not stop the Trellwan Lancers. Though their training was still far below Commonwealth regular military standards or the standards Kai Griffith would have set, the cadre of trained and experienced troops was growing. Even if the bureaucrats wouldn't let Lori drive a 'Mech, several MechWarrior apprentices showed promise, especially the youngest one, Yarin.

Grayson clenched his hands into white-knuckled fists to keep them from trembling. It was just now dawning on him that he'd only very narrowly escaped death. It was the fact that Stefan had ignored Lori because he didn't consider her a threat—probably because she was a woman—that had saved him.

The transport pulled away from the curb and hurried off down the street. Grayson watched it go, then quickened his stride toward Mara's apartment.

"We don't dare attack, General. It would be suicide, and the end of everything we've built here."

Grayson paced the room before the desk where Varney sat. General Adel watched him from a chair in the corner. Chief Minister Stannic stood by the windows, his back to the group, a glass of something red and potent in his hand.

Grayson was afraid of Stannic. The planet's defense minister had a sharp, abrupt manner, a way of rapping out questions like autocannon fire. And Grayson did not know how much he knew about his daughter's liaison with the off-worlder leader of the Trellwan Lancers. Trells were fiercely protective of their wives and daughters, and meetings between the sexes were usually supervised by a matronly female relative called a *duennsha*. Mara had more freedom and more unsupervised free time than most Trell girls. She had her own apartment next to her father's place on the Hub, and even walked unescorted to her place of work at the Palace offices. *Does he know I've been sleeping with her?*

Through the windows behind Stannic, the green sky and red sun cast long shadows into the room. Seconday was passing with dragging hours. Outside, laborers worked to secure insulating panels to the windows. With the advent of Secondnight, the temperature would plunge in the final chill before the hemisphere's warming trend. In the distance, clouds hung gray and heavy over the mountains. *It's still snowing up there,* Grayson thought.

Adel stirred in his chair. "You lack confidence yet, youngster. Surely the Deliverer of Sarghad can be certain of his own accomplishments?"

Grayson turned to him with scarcely concealed impatience. "I can be certain we've been lucky so far, General. I can also be certain three light 'Mechs are not going to get very far in a contest with heavies. General, do you have any idea what you're asking of us?"

"The people are expecting victory, Grayson," Stannic said. "In a way, your successes are working against you. After the capture of those two 'Mechs at the spaceport, they're wondering why you haven't gone on to take the Castle."

"Take the Castle!" Grayson hadn't expected that one. "Take the Castle—with three 20-ton 'Mechs?"

Varney stirred, his expression concerned. "What would you need to storm the Castle, Grayson?"

Adel snorted. "Seems to me the Castle was taken away from the Commonwealth garrison by three 'Mechs...and with four 'Mechs guarding it!"

"General, I don't think we need to get into needless recriminations," Varney said. He glanced at Stannic, then back to Grayson. "We're not ordering you to attack, Grayson. But we would like to see some plan of action, some constructive use for the Lancers. See if you can work up a study, and have it on my desk in, shall we say, 70 hours?"

"But General—"

"Now, son. When you become a leader of men, you find out everything you touch becomes political."

"Political? What do politics have to do with it?" Grayson had never cared for politics, had always been impatient with any system that produced more words and paperwork than anything else.

"I don't know if you realize it, son, but you and your Lancers are the focus of a lot of controversy just now."

Grayson shook his head. "I've been too busy."

"I should think so. But there are people who call themselves the Peace Party, and they have support on the Ministerial Council...people who argue that we have to make terms with the bandits."

"T-Terms!"

"Don't sputter, boy," Adel said. "You'll get spots on the furniture."

Varney cast a disapproving glance at Adel. "General, if you don't mind, I wonder if you would excuse us for a moment?"

The General's jaw set in a hard line, but he relaxed after a moment, stood, and nodded to Stannic and Varney. "Very well. This is all nonsense anyway...you realize that, don't you? Stannic, you, of all people, ought to know better! You were a Guards officer before you became a politician! The Lancers must be put under a single, unified command, and it is the Guards who have the political clout to oversee their operation."

When Adel had left, Grayson said, "He doesn't like me, does he?"

Varney shrugged with a twitch at the corner of his mouth. "He's powerful, with powerful friends. He would like to control the 'Mech lance."

"Why?"

"Because it represents more power. Grayson, I asked him to leave so I could tell you frankly, without getting into a debate with General Adel, that there's a lot of trouble in the Defense Ministry over the Lancers. There are factions upset about the presence of off-worlders in the unit—"

"*I'm* an off-worlder, General!"

"—and many who protest your use of known bandits. This woman—Kalmar—her presence on your staff is generating one hell of a storm. And now I understand you have a requisition in to use another captured bandit...Enzman?"

"Garik Enzelman. He knows as much about 'Mechs as Sergeant Kalmar does."

Varney shook his head. "I tell you now, Grayson, the government is not going to be able to tolerate your use of prisoners of war in such an important military capacity. Really, son, you've got to see it our way."

"And with all respect, sir, you've got to see it mine! Kalmar and Enzelman represent valuable, tech-trained resources. They know 'Mechs inside and out, as well as any tech! We'd be stupid not to use them. General, I don't have anything else to work with!"

"That may be...that may well be. Grayson, I'm giving you all the support I can, but what I'm trying to say is you've made enemies, powerful enemies who would like to see the Lancers handled differently...or eliminated completely. You've generated one hell of a lot of problems in the Palace with these off-worlders. It gives the opposition ammunition...know what I mean?"

"What the general is trying to say," Stannic said, "is there are political careers at stake here, people who will rise or fall depending on whether your Trellwan Lancers succeed, fail, or just sit on their backsides and do nothing. We need action, successful action, and we need it fast, or we can't justify the expense or the controversy over this off-worlder thing at the Ministerial Hall."

"I thought the King himself was behind the Lancers!"

Stannic smiled, but the look in his eyes was grim. "Even the king couldn't buck the tide if it turned on us. And son, if we lose this fight, so do you. Your Lancers won't survive if the government cuts its support. God help you if you screw up! Got me?"

Grayson wasn't sure what it was he had gotten, but its touch was ice-cold.

The cold was bitter, an iridium blade borne on a keening wind, carving through sneak suits and bone and marrow. The air was so dry it leached moisture from exposed skin, but intermittent flashes of distant lightning revealed heavy snow clouds above the mountains to the north. It was the dark of mid-Secondnight. Trellwan was approaching the sun again, but this would be a Far Passage, with the sun high in the sky on the far hemisphere, while Sarghad remained gripped in sub-zero night.

With Far Passage would come the Secondnight storms, and then the gradual warming of Thirday. But that was a week of standard days away.

The team of men clothed in night-black slipped along a frost-rimed ridge on the perimeter of the parade ground below the Castle. Lights on poles strung along the fenced perimeter cast stark illumination over the ferrocrete apron, and isolated the looming black mass of the truncated stone pyramid above them. There was activity in the open repair bay. Figures moved there, visible through the broad glass walls bathed in red light.

Grayson signaled to Sergeant Ramage: *Move up.* He used no words, as there might be sonic detectors nearby, listening with computer-controlled filters to eliminate the yowling wind and pick up a whispered conversation. Ramage nodded and moved forward with cautious, uneven actions calculated to fool sensors set to detect the sounds of ordinary movement

Grayson's mouth was very dry, and only partly because of the bitter dryness of the air. He realized that never, not even during the firefight in the Castle's central control, had he ever been so scared.

He had come up with the plan Jeverid's general staff and the council ministers wanted, having worked it out during long sessions with his senior staff sergeants, Lori, Ramage, and Larressen. The plan approved, the four of them had then worked even longer and harder to select and train an assault force of 50 picked men.

Their targets were the Castle and the slumbering hulk of the *Shadow Hawk.* Sarghad's military intelligence insisted the 'Mech had been damaged by thermite grenades during the delaying action at the spaceport, but was now almost repaired. Grayson's force would gain entry to the repair bay, clear it with small arms fire and grenades, plant powerful thermite melters at key points on the *Shadow Hawk*'s armor, then withdraw into the darkness. With luck, the 'Mech would be hopelessly ruined for anything but spare parts. Even enough damage to require another few hundred hours of repair time would be worth almost any cost in men and equipment. And when he thought of it that way, Grayson knew he had to lead the mission himself.

"You can't," Varney had said. "You're the whole reason for this lance! Without your specialized knowledge of 'Mechs and 'Mech tactics—"

"Lori Kalmar has precisely the same knowledge," he'd said. That was not entirely true, for she hadn't had Kai Griffith to train her in small unit tactics, but this wasn't the moment to quibble. "She can carry on if I don't come back."

"No woman is going to lead this unit, Grayson. Especially not an off-worlder!"

Varney had continued to protest, but in the end, Grayson simply insisted on going, and that was that. They would have gotten no work from him locked into a District HQ cell, and nothing short of that would keep him from leading his team. He reasoned his training suited him for the mission, while troops would respond with an extra measure of effort if their CO was in the fight with them.

Thanks to Griffith, Grayson was an expert in commando tactics, but the men in his command were still green. As recently as four standard-day weeks ago, most of the soldiers on the team could not properly use camouflage, could not sneak-stalk an enemy sentry, could not even load and fire an automatic weapon in anything less than five seconds. Grayson had been training in small unit tactics and techniques when he was fifteen, and training under the sharp eye and sharper tongue of Sergeant Griffith. He'd balanced the risk of letting them proceed with the mission on their own with the risk that he would be killed, then decided the gamble was worth it. The chance of success would be increased by his presence, his direction, and the steadying influence of knowing the CO was watching.

Grayson's training had included a wide variety of weapons, martial arts training that blended several very old and effective fighting traditions, as well as training in moving swiftly, silently, and with precise navigation. He was sure of his skills, even glad of the opportunity to exercise them again. Why, then, was he terrified?

He licked his lips, and the pain of the cold on wetted lips steadied him. He had been scared in the firefight in the Castle, but numbed almost into insensibility by his father's death. He had been frightened during the street battle when he'd dueled with the *Wasp*, when he'd stalked and confronted the *Locust*, but he'd been sustained by the hunger for revenge. The desire had dulled, become lost in the piles of administrative details that needed Grayson's attention. He had been afraid during the one-against-one 'Mech battle, but real 'Mech combat was so like simulator combat that, except for the heat, it had been easy to lose himself and his fear in the dance of the giant machines.

But now Grayson Death Carlyle lay on frozen ground outside the gaping maw of the Castle and trembled inwardly. The other operations had all been more or less forced on him by the needs of the moment. This mission had been ordered by the high command, and he was not yet convinced it was a necessary one. Worse was the fact he was leading 50 men against a fortress designed to repulse a battle force of laser turret-armed DropShips and a regiment of heavy 'Mechs.

That a force similar in size to his Lancers had taken the Castle before was no comfort. That attack had come as a complete surprise, and been aided by a traitor within its walls. Grayson had no traitor to assist him, nor could he be sure the enemy wasn't expecting him.

There was something else, too, something nagging at the back of his mind. He had been worried about how they would enter the Castle. Formerly, the doors had responded to his palm print, but the Castle's new occupants must have changed the computer security ID system by now. At best, doors would admit him while triggering an alarm on the screens in Central Security. They had brought explosives to breach a door, if necessary.

Strangely enough, the repair bay doors stood wide open, shimmering as the Castle's inner heat spilled into the cold air outside. It was almost too easy; a volley of fire to cut down the pair of sentries just inside the door track, a sudden rush, and they would have their target. Grayson could make out the form of the *Shadow Hawk* lying flat on the work pedestal below the tangled webwork of the repair bay gantry.

Maybe that's what the worry was. It looked too easy. Griffith had always warned him to expect the unexpected, to be convinced that danger usually existed where one least expected it. What hidden danger might be gnawing at his awareness here? There was always the danger of betrayal, of course. The attack on the Castle had burned that lesson into his very being. Still, the only ones who knew of the present attack were those at the highest levels of the Defense Ministry, and they were united in the need for a Lancers victory. He thought momentarily of Stefan, of other bandit agents among his own men, but dismissed the idea. That Stefan had been the one to attempt Grayson's death suggested there were very few such agents in the city. No, most of the spies among his ranks belonged to the Guards or to the Militia.

He pulled out a fist-sized transceiver, lengthened the antennae, and scratched the transmitter three times: *click,* pause, *click-click*. He waited, straining to hear above the wind. The answer came, *click-pause, click-pause, click-click*. Had he heard a rapid flurry of clicks, it would have meant the *Marauder* was no longer under Sergeant Larressen's observation as it patrolled the perimeter of the spaceport, but was on its way up the road to the Castle. The signal received indicated the *Marauder* was still where he'd watched it ten hours before. There was no way it could reach the Castle in less than ten minutes. That gave Grayson plenty of time.

A short-range tactical receiver in his left ear scratched out another code, *click-click, click-click, click-click*. That was Ramage, in position up ahead, reporting the way was clear, with no sign of traps, hidden troops, or unexpected weapon emplacements.

Listening to the signal, Grayson watched the silhouette of a heavy-coated sentry shrug and slap himself, as though trying to get warm. The enemy might decide to close the bay doors any moment, so the Lancers had to move *now*.

Grayson pulled his weapon around on its strap into position in front of his chest. It was a Rugan submachine gun that fired large, slow rounds at 1000 rounds per minute from a blackened magazine protruding far below the handgrip. The weapon was of local manufacture, and not as trustworthy as the Commonwealth weapons Carlyle's Commandos had carried. Long hours on a firing range behind the armory had convinced him it would be a serviceable general weapon for a sneak raid. Grayson remembered to set the selector for three-round bursts. The Rugan packed 80 caseless rounds into that long magazine, but those would be gone in five seconds on full auto.

According to the plan, it was Grayson's shots that would signal the attack. That left it in his hands whether to go ahead with the operation or not. An abort would be signaled over the radios each man wore. An attack would be launched by the death of the two sentries.

He took a moment to slow his breathing, to swallow the dryness in his throat, to blink the sting of the wind and the fear from his eyes. He didn't care about the victory the Sarghadian government needed. This would be another strike against the people who had killed his father, slaughtered his friends, betrayed a trust.

He brought the bulky, suppressor-muffled snout of the Rugan to the point, sighted, and tightened his finger on the trigger.

The gun spat, and the sentry 70 meters away jerked backward like a puppet on a string. Grayson swung the weapon toward the other sentry, but it was already too late.

Fire from a dozen submachine guns rattled and shrieked through the arctic air. The blast hit a second sentry and a running bandit tech, whirled them about and hurled them down. Then, black shapes rose from the shadows on either side of Grayson's position and surged toward the open bay doors.

They were committed.

CHAPTER 21

Fifty black shapes ran across the parade field lit by the pole-mounted floods, firing as they went. Their suppressed SMG bursts snapped and hissed, sending those in and around the repair bay scrambling for cover or knocking them to the ground where they had been standing.

Grayson stepped across the boundary between the parade ground and the bay. The familiar cavern, red-lit and murky, yawned above and around him. Directly before him was the ten-meter form of the damaged *Shadow Hawk*.

"Collier!" He yelled, waving. "Senkins and Burke! The door! Demo team...move!"

Three soldiers raced for the door leading to the Castle's central passageways. Five men shouldering heavy satchels pounded past him and up to the raised deck supporting the disabled 'Mech. A burst of fire spat from above, and something whipped through the air beside his head. Before Grayson could react, the shots were answered by the harsh chatter of a subgun close by. A figure pitched off the top landing of the spindly ladder zigzagging up to the bay control booth and fell with a dull *splat* on the ferrocrete 20 meters below.

Grayson turned to the man who had just fired. It was Larressen. "Thanks," he said. "Go with the Demo Team, Sergeant. I'll be with the security force."

Larressen nodded and scrambled up a ladder to where the demolition team was heading toward the torso of the grounded 'Mech. Grayson trotted across the floor to where three privates crouched by the door to the passageway. Steel chocks had been driven into the door guides to keep it open, and a squad-portable, bipod-mounted machine gun sat with its barrel probing across the door sill into the corridor beyond. Burke lay flat, the MG stock at his shoulder. The others covered him with automatic rifles. "Anything?"

"No, sir." Corporal Collier was the security team leader. He gestured down the corridor to the next sealed, airtight door. "Just let them poke the tip of their noses through there and we'll nail 'em!" He paused, fumbled, and added a belated "sir." Collier looked younger than Grayson, but seemed to have the knack of handling men. Grayson patted him on the shoulder, then turned to go.

Rumbling thunder crashed from the repair deck, a groaning, tearing-metal protest, as men scattered and someone screamed. Grayson stopped in his tracks, paralyzed by shock and dawning horror. The *Shadow Hawk,* a sleeping giant under the glint of red lamps, was stirring, trembling, slowly raising itself upright. The black-clad figures of the demo team were leaping from that suddenly shifting torso. Sprawled on the ferrocrete where the huge machine's movement had flung him lay the man who had screamed.

What had been a carefully planned and orchestrated set of missions and movements dissolved now into panicked chaos. One of his men stood on the bay floor spraying full-auto fire up at the looming monster, while others stood rooted where they stood, mouths open. One threw his gun aside and ran screaming, and then others followed. Too late, for the bay doors were grinding shut with hollow rumblings.

This can't be happening, Grayson thought, but the half-upright battle machine proved otherwise. A vast metal hand swept out, down, and across to bat the lone soldier armed with the auto-rifle across the room. The gory shape that slid into the wall no longer resembled anything human.

The *Shadow Hawk* stood, terrifyingly large in the confined space of the Castle's repair bay. Grayson noted with some detached portion of his mind that the 'Mech's over-the-shoulder autocannon had been removed, the backpack that mounted the cannon and life support gear was off, and panels on its chest and legs had been opened, all contributing to its damaged, half-repaired look. But the machine was powered and under control.

He watched the head—tiny in comparison to the bulky torso—snap around, its sensors tracking a group of fleeing soldiers. The right arm came up, the medium laser strapped along the forearm flashed once, twice, and the ferrocrete was scorched black by swaths of high-energy destruction that turned running men into twisting, shrieking torches, or left them in charred and blackened heaps.

Carefully planted explosive charges could have destroyed that 'Mech, but there was no way to plant them *while* the *Shadow Hawk* was moving and in combat mode. The bay doors were still closing, grinding shut with agonizing slowness.

"Burke!" Grayson yelled. "Come on!"

The security team scrambled back from the open door. The 'Mech stooped and turned, possibly seeking the source of a voice shouting orders. Its laser flashed again, and Grayson dove behind a stack of wooden crates. Collier was burned as he ran, his blackened corpse unrecognizable except for the half-melted wreckage of the machine gun still cradled against the charred, smoldering husk of his body. The beams tracked relentlessly. Senkins, too, vanished in fire and oily smoke, his assault rifle spinning across the floor in clattering bounces.

The bay doors clanged shut with mournful finality. The 'Mech's left hand descended, crushing a soldier cowering in the shadows under the raised repair deck. *The man had forgotten 'Mechs can see by heat,* Grayson thought.

Somewhere, someone was screaming in an agony of burned flesh.

The situation was hopeless. He considered calling his unit leaders to get a clearer picture, but rejected the idea. The enemy would certainly be listening in on radio frequencies, and the information would help the bandits more than it would Grayson.

The *Shadow Hawk* stood scanning the room. Grayson could hear the click of mechanical relays in that squat head, and knew the 'Mech pilot was scanning IR, motion-sensitive, and visible light images for signs of his human prey. All around the bay were stacks of boxes behind which men had taken cover. The 'Mech gave the uncanny impression of a dull-witted metal giant considering how to find the fugitives without burning valuable equipment. Soon it would begin to move the crates one at a time, and anyone it flushed would be burned down or smashed.

Grayson eyed the interlocking tooth pattern of the sealed door behind him. If he could get the door open, the survivors of the attack team might have a chance, could scatter into the darkness down the slope of the mountain. But the only way to open those doors was to throw a switch in the bay control booth. His eyes traveled past the now motionless 'Mech to the lighted booth, fifteen meters above the deck.

What he needed was a diversion.

Lying near him was a body with one arm outflung, an almost undamaged hand clenched around the strap of a canvas satchel. Grayson knew it was one of Larressen's people, someone from the demo team sent to destroy the *Shadow Hawk*.

The satchel contained explosives—five packets of high-velocity plastique, each weighing two kilos—clipped to magnetic backing, and already primed with a timer-activated detonator. Properly placed over selected circuits and servoactuators, those packets could destroy a 'Mech. There was no way to place them now, but they might provide the distraction he needed.

Grayson set his teeth, wiped sweat from his face, then lunged into the open. Though he kept his eyes off the metal mountain above him, he could hear the click of relays, could feel the slow turn of the head, the ponderous movement of the right arm as the laser was brought up to bear.

He reached across the man's body for the satchel, and tugged it toward him. The corpse's hand remained stubbornly attached, and Grayson found himself in a deadly tug-of-war with the unrecognizable form of one of his own men. Worse, he could feel the laser almost in line.

Giving a last, despairing tug, he felt the strap pull free from the clenched, dead fingers as he tumbled over backward with the satchel clutched to his chest. The 'Mech's laser fired, washing white heat and sharp odor across Grayson as he rolled across the ferrocrete to cover. The crate where he had been hiding burst into flames. In its light Grayson was up and running toward the massive armored feet of the *Shadow Hawk*.

The 'Mech shifted, tracking him. He dodged right, then left, his hand reaching into the satchel and pulling out one of the two-kilo packets. Slinging the satchel, he used his free hand to set the timer for five seconds and flung it—not at the monster, but onto the ferrocrete between himself and the BattleMech's foot

Then he was running again, weaving toward the metal ladder below the control booth. The explosion at his back an instant later picked him up and flung him toward the booth, but then dumped him flat on his face with blood smearing his arms, and a hideous, dizzying ring in his ears.

The 'Mech paused, its heat and light sensors momentarily blinded by the explosion's flash. Grayson used the delay to arm two more packets and hurl them at the monster's head. The explosions did scant damage, but they kept the 'Mech's pilot blinded for precious seconds. Grayson mounted the ladder and bounded up the rattling steps three at a time.

As another explosion sounded from below, the ladder pitched wildly. He turned, his gloved hands gripping the steps alongside his head. Below, a solitary figure waved, then hurled another packet that exploded at the *Shadow Hawk's* feet.

"Go on, Lieutenant!" The figure shouted as the explosion's roar subsided. "We'll keep him busy!"

Grayson recognized Larressen's voice. Lurching to the top of the ladder, he shouldered aside the half-open door. Waiting there was a bearded man in green fatigues, a TK assault rifle in his hands.

Grayson's own machine pistol was gone, lost somewhere on the floor of the bay.

There was another explosion below, and the *Shadow Hawk* twisted, scraping against the metal ladder with a high-pitched screech of metal.

The bearded soldier's eyes left Grayson's for a half-instant, giving him the chance to swing the canvas bag into the man's face. He threw his body after it, grappling for the man's gun, thrusting him back. In the struggle, the two knocked over a chair and smashed into the monitor console. When Grayson brought his knee up sharply, the soldier grunted and loosened his grip. Grayson smashed the butt of the TK across the side of the man's skull.

He stabbed at the flat, white button that would open the bay doors. He stood there, holding the circuit open as the interlocking teeth of the doors pulled apart, spilling light into the outer darkness. Then he grabbed the soldier's TK and the canvas satchel and ran through the door of the booth.

The 'Mech was there, its head just two meters below Grayson's feet, the laser on its arm swinging up to demolish the control booth. There was nothing Grayson could do but jump.

He landed on the *Hawk*'s shoulder with a clattering scramble, and clung to the stub of a field guide antennae projecting from the side of its head. The 'Mech turned clumsily, its right hand lifting to swat him like a gnat. Grayson twisted behind the 'Mech's head, riding the wire-tangled scar where the autocannon and backpack life support system should have been, safely beyond the machine's reach.

He fumbled with the satchel. The 'Mech turned again, crashing into the control booth ladder and through to the stone wall beyond. The concussion jarred Grayson severely, tearing at his hand. He managed to keep his grip, but the TK went spinning off wildly.

His free hand closed on the last remaining packet of explosive. He clamped it to the side of the monster's head, and set the timer for ten seconds.

The machine smashed against the wall again, rolling, trying to crush Grayson between the bay wall and its own 55-ton bulk. Grayson found handholds—tack-welded grips along the *Shadow Hawk*'s back used for service access—and climbed down the monster's flank toward the ground. When the 'Mech crashed into the wall again, Grayson was shaken loose. He fell the last five meters and landed with a crash among the crumpled ruins of the control booth ladder.

Grayson's right leg felt like it had taken a blow from a sledgehammer, and his head was throbbing. He blinked open his eyes, saw the 'Mech staggering above him wreathed in smoke...falling...Then, rough hands dug under his armpits and hauled him from the wreckage of the ladder. The 'Mech's fall was a storm of crash upon crash, and black smoke poured from an ugly scar across its head.

For one wild moment, Grayson exulted. *I killed it! His* exultation faded fast as the 'Mech rolled, pulled its arms under its body, and hauled itself partly upright. The pilot was obviously stunned, possibly hurt, but the blast had not pierced that tough armor.

Cold air hit Grayson's face and an arm exposed by a tear in his jacket sleeve as his rescuer dragged him through the open bay door and onto the parade ground. Other dark shapes scattered through the night.

Somehow, Grayson managed to click the radio at his throat. "Evade and escape! Rendezvous when you can back at the arsenal! Quickly!" Then the night lit up with fire and death as gunners on the Castle's flanks opened fire with tracers and turret-mounted lasers, sweeping death and horror across the parade ground.

"Let's get out of here, Larressen."

"Larressen's had it, Lieutenant."

Only then did Grayson look at his rescuer. For some reason he'd assumed it was Larressen, but it was the blackened face of a private from the demo team that stared back at him with concern. What was the name? Greer, that was it. He was one of the new 'Mech pilot recruits.

"That...that thing...stepped on him—" Greer was saying haltingly, "—like he was an insect."

"Let's go. We'll even the score later." Even with the pain in his leg, Grayson found he could run with a free-swinging limp. With a party of four other survivors, he headed down the mountain.

CHAPTER 22

General Adel flung the printouts down on his desk and nailed Grayson with a hard look. "Twenty-eight dead or missing," he said. "Twenty-eight out of fifty. This is not what we've come to expect of your unit here at the palace, you know. Well? What do you have to say about it, Lieutenant?"

"It...It was a trap, General."

"Indeed?"

"They had that *Shadow Hawk* rigged to look like it was under repair. They must've had the pilot stuffed in the cockpit, flat on his back for hours just to—"

"I am not interested in the *Shadow Hawk* pilot's comfort, Lieutenant! I am interested in what I'm going to put into the report I must submit to His Majesty."

"Yes, sir."

"This does not bode well for the First Lancers, you understand. I know that the Royal Guards in particular has gone out of its way to provide your unit with weapons and equipment already in short supply. Critics will point out that this effort was wasted, thrown away to no purpose."

"But General! You—"

"*Silence!*"

Grayson remained rigidly at attention, clamping down on the emotions boiling within him. *This is unfair!* He had had nothing but trouble getting requisitions through the Guards supply bureaucracy, and now...

"I have never approved of this project, Carlyle. You know that, don't you?"

"Yes, sir."

"I certainly never expected His Majesty would establish anything like an elite unit elsewhere than within the structure of the Guards. I expect General Varney was responsible for this idiotic notion of having the Lancers be an independent unit. Eh? Well?"

"I wouldn't know, sir."

"Hmm, no, I expect not." Adel leaned back in his chair, carefully crossing one leg over the other. "Well, be advised that that's all changing, as of right now."

"Sir?"

"That surprises you, eh? Well, Varney is out of the picture, Carlyle, and the First Trellwan Lancers are, as of this period, being redesignated as E Company, Tenth Royal Guards. They will be under my direct command."

The room swam in Grayson's eyes. What Adel was saying did not make sense. "Sir...I..."

"You will turn over all records and files to your successor, Captain Nolem." Adel looked up from his desk at Carlyle, astonishment softening his voice. "You didn't think you'd actually keep the lance, did you? You're young, Carlyle, too young for a command of such responsibility. The job was just too big for you. Try not to feel too—"

"Do you mean the Lancers aren't mine anymore?" Grayson cut in dully.

"That's exactly what I mean, Lieutenant. You are relieved. As you were never actually a member of the Trellwan armed forces other than through a special act by the King, I fail to see how they ever could have been...yours.

"At any rate, a company rates a captain, and you can't expect us to twist the whole structure of military command around just to accommodate you, do you? You will be retained as special advisor. Your knowledge of 'Mechs and 'Mech tactics makes you invaluable to us." Adel's eyebrows came together, his eyes narrowing. "That means no more of your gallivanting around in a combat zone. I will not risk having you killed and losing your expertise!"

"Sir, Sergeant Kalmar is—"

"That young lady is an enemy alien. She should never have been given rank or position within our armed forces! You were the one responsible for that gaff, I believe? Well, don't worry. As I said, you are young, inexperienced."

"What will happen to her?"

"That, Lieutenant, is none of your business."

"General, I demand—"

"You'll demand nothing, Lieutenant!"

"But—"

"*Enough!* I've wasted more time with you than I can spare. Dismissed!"

With that, a sentry ushered Grayson out and into the marble corridors of the Palace.

General Adel stared after Grayson for long, hard seconds after he'd been escorted out. The young Commonwealther would have to be watched, and watched closely. It was always dangerous to allow any one man too much power.

And control of the Lancers? *No,* he reminded himself, *not the Lancers.* It was control of the Tenth Regiment that meant power. Men would do anything to win power, and to hold it. Young Carlyle was very popular with his men. General Adel believed popular military commanders were never to be trusted.

Perhaps it would be best if Carlyle's career ended soon. A knife in the dark had solved such problems many times before in human history. He knew there had been a previous attempt, but no one in his command would have botched the job by hiring such untrustworthy personnel.

Mara drew Grayson closer, her hands moving delicately at his ears, at the back of his neck. "But what are you going to *do?*" she asked, her dark eyes wide.

"I don't know, Mara. I really don't know." The shock of his talk with Adel had worn off, leaving him with a profound sense of emptiness, as though some inner part of his spirit had died. "It's kind of hard to say. You know, when I started out... When I said I'd start an anti-'Mech unit for your people, I was doing it for just one reason."

Her fingers moved along his chest, brushing at the few strands of hair there. "What was that?"

"Revenge. Revenge, pure and simple. I wanted to get back at the people who murdered my father, and I sure wasn't going to be able to do that on my own." He managed a smile. "Someone told me once I'd get into trouble on my own. I wish he could see me now."

"But you're not alone, Gray. You have me."

He pulled her close, and kissed her. "Thank you, love, but I needed help to fight back against those bandits, against that *Marauder*."

He lay back on the bed, his eyes staring, unseeing, past the ceiling. "You know, those weeks building the Lancers, I think they were the best of my life. I was...building something...doing something only I could do. And I had a purpose. I was going to destroy the 'Mech...and the MechWarrior who killed Dad."

"Maybe you were just trying to prove something to yourself."

He shrugged. "I don't know. Maybe at first. I know I still want revenge. Want it more than anything else." He turned to Mara, probing his own feelings. "But after a while, I had something more, something that pushed the whole question of revenge into the background.

"I had a purpose, a direction, and felt something like belonging. I was never so alone as when I found out all my people were gone...that I was marooned on Trellwan. The Lancers were like having a family again...and that was special."

He paused again, working to control his voice. *Don't think about that,* he told himself. *Not that. It was revenge you wanted. Revenge and nothing more.*

"You know, with the Lancers, there was at least a slim chance that I might someday bring that *Marauder* down. But now..."

Her eyes showed fear. "Then what hope is there for us?"

"Oh, things'll be okay here. Now that Sarghad's got three 'Mechs, the bandits won't attack the city anymore. There'd be too much chance they'd get trapped in the streets, like that *Locust* was when we captured it. It's possible they might raid the agrodomes, but they won't come into the city anymore."

Adel and his staff must have come to the same conclusion, Grayson realized with a new surge of bitterness. With three 'Mechs and a trained anti-Mech ground force, Sarghad was reasonably safe. They probably wouldn't be able to destroy the *Marauder* and *Shadow Hawk*—not without a remarkable stroke of good fortune—but the enemy could no longer get at them.

And wasn't that why they'd had him assemble the Lancers in the first place? So far as the Trellwanese government was concerned, his job was done. *They'd* never said anything about his using the Lancers to further his personal vendetta against the bandits.

"Silly, there's really nothing to worry about." Mara nuzzled his ear, her hands roving. "We have each other, and that's all we need. And next period, I'll talk to Daddy. I'll bet he can help."

He smiled, and surrendered to her caresses. But the hurt within did not cease.

Sometime later, he came wide awake. A siren was sounding outside from the roof of the palace, its strident rise and fall cutting through the air above Sarghad.

Mara was sitting up, the covers clutched in front of her. "What is it, Gray...an attack?"

Grayson stepped to the window and looked out, but could see only surging crowds of people in the streets. He scanned the horizon for 'Mechs, saw nothing. "I don't know, Mara. *Something's* stirring the people up, that's certain."

Mara used a remote to click on the room's wall visor. Grayson turned and stared at the screen. The entertainment channels had been overridden by a government newscast. A man in a Guards colonel uniform was directing the people of Sarghad to stay indoors, to keep their visors on, and listen for continued updates.

Then the scene cut to a long-range view of the spaceport, and to massive gray shapes settling out of the sky. Ships were landing, the speaker's voice explained, and Grayson was shocked to see that their insignia was the sinuous black and red dragon crest of House Kurita. Ships of the Draconis Combine, under the command of Duke Ricol, were landing on Trellwan to rid the world once and for all of the Oberon bandit menace. The bandits, the voice asserted, had already surrendered to Ricol. Now, at last, there would be peace.

CHAPTER 23

The city of Sarghad had gone mad. Dressed in cold-weather jackets, swarms of people gathered under the harsh overhead lights that kept the long night at bay, their breath making clouds of steam in the chill, Secondnight air. The cheers, the sight of people waving, leaping, dancing in the streets, were broadcast on the huge visor that curved out from one wall of the palace reception hall. A convoy was heading toward the palace past cheering throngs on streets lit bright as day. On a staff on the lead hovercraft in the convoy fluttered the black and red dragon flag of the Draconis Combine.

Grayson had dressed and hurried across to the palace as soon as he heard the news. The Guards colonel reporting the scene had sounded buoyant, almost jubilant, at the news that Kurita forces had arrived to save Trellwan from Hendrik of Oberon. Could these people possibly be so overjoyed at what was clearly an out-and-out invasion? The Combine was not known to be particularly charitable toward independent planets. Couldn't the Trells see the danger they were in?

The reception hall was crowded with people, the wealthy and powerful of Sarghad and, no doubt, other cities of Trellwan as well. When the news of the ships' arrival had broken, the people had come straight to the palace, little doubting that their future—and the future of the planet—would be settled here within the hour.

Grayson still wore his green and gold dress Guards uniform, the only one he had. He had to try to reach King Jeverid, though he knew it wouldn't be easy. Jeverid was shielded from his people by a thick bureaucratic layer of secretaries and court functionaries that had accumulated around the royal office over the past several centuries.

At that moment, curtains on the hall's platform parted, but instead of the king, General Adel and various of his staff officers appeared there. With them was Lieutenant...no, *Captain* Nolem, flanked by richly adorned Royal Guards in full dress.

Grayson scanned the crowd gathered around the platform. The Militia was conspicuous by its absence, and Varney was nowhere to be seen. Had he fallen so far from favor?

He began working his way through the throng toward the stage, where the general and his officers stood before the empty throne. *Where is Jeverid?* he wondered, when suddenly his way was blocked by a pair of helmeted and armored Guards soldiers carrying TK rifles.

"Sorry, sir," one said. "You can't go through there."

Perhaps he could use the force of his uniform. "Stand aside, soldier! I am Lieutenant Carlyle of the First Lancers. I must see His Majesty!"

Doubt crossed the soldier's face. "I'm sorry, sir, but unless you have a pass signed by General Adel—"

"If I had a pass, I would have shown it to you! I tell you, I must see His Majesty! It's vitally important!"

The soldier hesitated, and for an instant Grayson thought his bluff had worked. Then he could see the soldier resolving to do only as he was told. "I'm sorry, sir, but you'll have to go through proper channels."

"What's the problem here?" It was Adel, with Nolem close behind. The general swept cold eyes over Grayson. "What do *you* want?"

"General, sir! I must see His Majesty!"

"About what?"

"These Kuritans, sir, being welcomed like heroes. They're the enemy!"

Adel's brows beetled, a frown pulling at his face. He rubbed thoughtfully at his mustache with a finger. "Enemy? I know of no declaration of war between Trellwan and the Draconis Combine. You overstep yourself, sir."

Somehow Grayson managed to control his thoughts, to steady himself and his speech. "General, I have reason to believe this is all some kind of a plot."

Adel and Nolem both laughed. "So, it's plots now, is it?" Nolem seemed vastly amused. "We might have expected that from a Commonwealther, I suppose. Eh, General?"

"Ha! Indeed. Lord Ricol was particularly interested in what young Carlyle here might have to say."

Grayson's eyes opened wide. "This Duke Ricol knows about me? How?"

"Oh, he has ways, I'm sure. He said you might object to a Combine presence on Trellwan."

Object? Grayson could see in his mind the three-D map projection that his tutor, Ari, used to display the Cis-Peripheral sectors of Commonwealth space. The red dwarf Trell lay nearest—in astronomical terms—to stars ruled by Hendrik of Oberon and to other stars claimed by Kurita's Draconis Combine. The war, sometimes overt, sometimes covert, between the Combine and the Commonwealth, had dragged on for year after standard year. The whole purpose of Representative Vogel's Pact had been to free garrisons like Carlyle's Commandos for service against Kurita closer in toward the Inner Sphere. Hendrik was to have taken over the defense of Trellwan, and with it, defense of this entire sector against the predations of the Combine. The irony was that now Kurita was establishing himself here instead.

Trellwan would be nearly ideal as an advance base of operations against the Commonwealth. A fleet could base and refuel there, could strike deep at worlds of the Commonwealth that had never suffered Combine raids. They could strike even at the capital, at Tharkad itself.

"General." Grayson tried desperately to sound calm. These men were laughing at him! "Minister, Trellwan is so important to the security of the Commonwealth—"

"We're not interested in what is important or not important to the Commonwealth. You seem to forget, Carlyle, that this is *our* world, not yours."

"General, the Lancers...the Tenth Regiment is under your command now. You must realize that the Kuritans won't let you keep those 'Mechs."

Adel nodded agreeably. "Of course. I spoke at length with the Duke's representative just a short while ago, by visor. Trellwan will no longer need an independent 'Mech lance. Company E of the Tenth Guards Regiment is to be incorporated entirely into the personal forces of Duke Ricol. That is a singular honor, you must realize, youngster. I assumed the force would be disbanded, but when he heard of your success against the Oberon pirates, he decided the unit could be transferred to his own command."

"General, you can't let them do this!"

Adel seemed to lose patience. He gestured to Nolem, who snapped at one of the soldiers, "You. Take this man and put him under arrest."

"Sir! You're making a mistake!"

Nolem sneered. "We made a mistake the day we depended on the Commonwealthers for help! Take him away!"

As the soldiers were taking Grayson by the arms, a tall, heavy, black-bearded figure appeared at the top of the stairs. *That must be Duke Ricol,* Grayson thought.

The man wore a uniform that was of a single piece from boots to gloves, entirely red except for the black trim and silver fastenings at waist, throat, and breast. He bore on his left upper arm and shoulder the highly stylized shield cloak now stylish among worlds of the Inner Sphere. Red-trimmed with black and silver, the cloak curved from his shoulder around behind his head like the collar of a stiff-necked cape, and fastened to his right shoulder with silver chains that glittered in the light as he moved.

Behind him were his personal guards, also in red, but in uniforms and armor that looked far more military than their duke's finery. The butts of service automatic pistols rode above holsters worn low on their hips, and their faces were masked by featureless, black plastic visors beneath their helmets.

Ricol spoke, hands on hips, his voice booming across the crowd, which stood in hushed expectation. "Do I have the honor of addressing the government of Trellwan?"

Adel saluted the Red Duke. "His Majesty has been detained, my Lord. He will be with us presently."

"I don't like being kept waiting, Adel," Ricol said. He descended the stairs with an imperial air, his staff and personal guards close behind him.

Grayson stiffened. It *had* to be a plot. Where was Varney? Where was Jeverid? Whatever was afoot, Grayson was sure Adel and his Royal Guards were in on it, too. Not only that, the Lancers were to be turned over to this Kuritan duke.

With Ricol's entrance, the soldiers had loosened their hold on Grayson's arms, absorbed in the spectacle of the Red Duke. Moving softly, Grayson stepped into the crowd, headed toward a side exit in the hall.

"Stop him, idiots!" Nolem's harsh whisper was more hiss than words, but seemed louder than a shout against the Hall's shocked silence.

Hearing the step of soldiers coming after him, Grayson broke into a run, smashing past finery-clad lords and ladies of the court, and bowling over one gray-haired and stoop-shouldered man in a black cloak who stepped into his path.

There were other guards at the door to the corridor, but they couldn't fire their weapons with the crowd at Grayson's back. He lunged at one of them, smashing the helmet down across the man's eyes, pivoting, and giving him a stiff-armed blow in the chest that sent him sprawling back into the surprised arms of two of his comrades.

Then he was moving into the passageway, feet pounding against the heavy carpeting, then echoing from marble steps as the corridor ended and he was faced with nowhere to go but up. The crowd was spilling into the hallway behind him, and he heard the clatter of running boots, the predictable shouts for him to halt.

At the top of the stairs, the passageway branched. He looked both ways, frantic and unsure. Then, he got his bearings, remembering that one corridor led to the Ministerial Offices, including those of Stannic.

Grayson realized suddenly that he had not seen Stannic at the Reception Hall either. Had Jeverid and Stannic both been deposed? Or might Mara's father simply be unaware of what was occurring? If he could find the Chief Minister, if he could find Mara, who frequently worked with her father in these offices, perhaps he could warn them. Unless it was already too late...

He rounded a corner and nearly collided with a young Trell. It was Claydon! Grayson opened his mouth to speak, then noticed Claydon wore the green jacket of the Guards, with a black armband showing him to be a senior tech. So, he'd made a deal with General Adel. Or was it with Duke Ricol? Was he the new replacement tech for Lori and Grayson?

Though his head spun with questions, Grayson merely nodded curtly and hurried past. Then he heard the sound of Claydon's boots descending the stairs Grayson had just come up. Would Claydon betray him? Had he betrayed him already?

He ducked into the outer reception room of the Chief Minister's office suite, and stood with his back to the door, panting. Moments later, he heard the clatter of boots again, this time racing past the door and down the corridor. Grayson let out his breath in a long, slow sigh. He'd not been aware of holding it.

"Grayson!"

He opened his eyes and saw— "Mara! What are *you* doing here?"

"I might ask you the same question. I work here."

"Look, Mara, something terrible is going on. I think General Adel has engineered a coup. He's downstairs talking to that Kuritan duke right now, and there's no sign of General Varney or the Militia or—"

He stopped, his eyes widening. Mara had reached behind the ornate desk that dominated the room, and brought out a sleek auto-feed needler. The pistol's narrow, slit barrel was trained on his heart.

"Mara! What...?"

"You really are a fool, you know. You Commonwealthers think the galaxy revolves around you, that you can use people, use whole worlds with no more thought for their welfare than—"

"What are you talking about, Mara? I...I..."

"Quiet!" she snapped. Keeping the gun muzzle centered on his chest, Mara reached behind the desk again, and Grayson immediately heard the sound of an alarm sounding somewhere in the far distance.

Stannic appeared behind his daughter. Seeing him dressed in a resplendent gold and green uniform of the Royal Guards, Grayson recalled having heard that Stannic was a retired Guards officer. He wore a colorful cluster of medals on his chest, including the starburst of the Crimson Star. "What's all this then, Mara?"

"An intruder, Father."

"Ah, young Carlyle. I'm sorry, son, but this is for the better. We appreciated your help, but you can see it's really not necessary now. Duke Ricol will be taking care of our defense."

"Sir, you don't know what that will mean. We have fought the Draconis Combine for years, and—"

"Exactly. Your people *have* fought them for years, and you can hardly have a, shall we say, unprejudiced attitude toward them."

The door burst open behind Grayson, and armed men crowded in.

"Here's your prisoner," Mara said.

Hands closed over Grayson's arms, holding him upright when he thought he was going to keel over. He was dizzy...weak.

From far away, he heard General Adel say, "I'm sorry for the disturbance, Your Majesty."

Stannic chuckled. "No problem, General. Just see that you hang onto him now, eh?"

The only reason Lori had been awake was that she hadn't been alone. Garik Enzelman was with her, the two of them sharing memories of Sigurd with gentle touches and lingering kisses.

She'd gone to Garik after the assassination attempt. She'd known Grayson was headed for Mara's apartment that day, and her own hurt and jealousy had driven her to the one person she could talk to, remember, and feel less alone. They reminisced about life on Sigurd, the moon of a sullenly glowing gas giant. Circling its brilliant but distant F4 star, Sigurd was even more frigid and forbidding than Trellwan. They talked of their experiences in the service on Sigurd and in the time since, and they talked of their future on Trellwan.

They'd come to no certain decision, beyond the fact that the future looked dark for them. Enzelman wanted to join the Draconian forces. Then, at least, he would not have to deal with the anti-Oberon prejudice of the Trell indigs. Lori was not so sure, but she listened to him all the same.

Garik was two standard years younger than Lori. His abrupt, almost bumbling manner and studied lack of thoughtfulness made her certain she would never have been friends with the guy were it not for the fact that he was the only man within several hundred light years she could confide in.

Well...almost. She could share with him what she was not busily walling up somewhere inside her hurt and confusion. Why did she keep thinking of Grayson?

"The Dracos won't be any better."

"I don't really see what choice we have," Garik said. "If we stay on Trellwan, we have nothing to face but prison...or death. I understand they enjoy setting people loose in the desert here, unprotected."

"The Draconians might not want us." She was remembering the polish and snap of those legions debarking from their DropShips. Those were professional soldiers in every sense of the word.

"Then again, they might. Technical people are always in demand. And the fighting's over now. That means they'll be recruiting and training for their next project, whatever that is."

"Does it?" She wondered where Grayson was. This period, he'd be with Mara, no doubt, but where would he be after this shakeup in command? General Adel wasn't about to leave him in charge of so potent a force as a 'Mech lance. There had already been outbreaks of violence when Guards units had ordered the Militia to disband, and rumors were spreading that General Varney had been placed under arrest.

They both heard the whine of hovercraft outside the building at the same moment. When Lori peered out past the curtain, she saw at least fifteen Guards dismounting from military HVTs and converging on her door. Obviously, this was no social call.

With the Guards in power, with Adel calling the shots, she and Garik had become targets.

They dressed quickly, and were pulling on boots and jackets when the pounding on the door began.

"This way," Lori said. Slipping through the glass door on the other side of the apartment, they passed into the enclosed patio behind the building, and trotted rapidly across the street toward the Lancers' HQ.

There was sporadic and nagging gunfire in front of the old Militia armory, but no sign of a major assault. Troops, both Militia and Guards, were moving through streets already clogged with panicking civilians, and there seemed to be no organization to either group's movements at all.

Captain Tor met Lori and Garik at the door to the armory, an MP-20 in his hand. Behind him was Sergeant Ramage, coatless and carrying a TK. Ramage was shivering with cold.

"Lori!" Tor exclaimed. "You're safe!"

Even Ramage looked relieved. While not outwardly opposing Lori's position in the unit, the sergeant had remained carefully neutral toward her. He grinned at her now and said, "We were about to come for you. We'd heard the Guards had been sent to get you."

"But how?"

Ramage jerked his head toward the armory HQ. "We've got the *Locust* command net radio tuned into their operations frequency. It's a general uprising by the Guards. Minister Stannic has proclaimed himself king, and no one knows what's happened to Jeverid. The trouble began when Guards units began disarming the Militia."

"What about the Lancers?"

"The order came down about an hour ago. We're to stand down and wait for Captain Nolem to take charge of us. Seems we're being transferred to the Dracos."

"The Dracos!"

"Lori," Tor said, worry creasing his face. "There's worse. They've got Grayson. We intercepted a report that he was being taken to Guards HQ across from the palace."

No matter what mixture of hurt and anger she was feeling toward Grayson, she certainly wouldn't stand by while the

Guards marched him off to their cells. It was all too likely Grayson Death Carlyle would never reappear once they got him inside that HQ.

She looked up at Tor. "Ren...is the *Locust* ready?"

"We warmed her up when we started eavesdropping. Why?"

"Listen, get in touch with as many of our people as you can." Then she gave rapid-fire instructions to Ramage and Tor. The unit had to be rallied, the *Stinger* and *Wasp* both powered up and taken out of the city. She wasn't sure where they would go yet. Perhaps into the mountains. *Damn,* she thought, *if only Grayson were here.* He knew this land, knew the terrain, and where they might be able to hide. One thing was certain, however. They couldn't stay where they were.

"Sergeant, Captain Tor...I'm counting on you. Get everyone you can back here to the HQ, set up a perimeter, and hold it. Send out all the hovercraft we've got to get our people. The city is going to be up for grabs for hours yet, so you ought to be able to get through. Don't fight with the Guards. Just try to avoid them. And call Corporal Yee. Have him assemble a squad for a 'Mech ground support mission."

"Where are you going?" Ramage looked worried.

Lori didn't answer. She was already sprinting toward the *Locust.*

A Guards squad had escorted Grayson across the palace grounds and a street crowded with people to the Royal Guards headquarters building on the Hub. There were jail cells in the basement, and a platoon-strength patrol of armed and armored Guardsmen pacing the grounds outside.

As he was being led down the steps, Grayson could hear a public address system somewhere in the distance braying the news that Trellwan was now part of the glorious brotherhood of the Draconis Combine. The people were being told to disperse, to return to their homes and listen for further news on their visors. The crowds, however, showed no signs of being ready to disperse.

His cell was reasonably clean, and was furnished with a sink, toilet, bunk, chair, and table. The bare electric bulb that dangled from the cell's high ceiling cast a harsh yellow light over the thick stone walls, which were broken only by a latticework of electronically locked steel bars. Grayson knew he would not be going out that way without permission.

He sat down heavily on the bunk, feeling tiredness like a heavy pack across his shoulders. To think Stannic was now King of Trellwan! Grayson realized the Chief Minister must have been working toward that goal all along, with the Lancers and himself simply two more pawns in his struggle to consolidate power. Somehow, the knowledge he had been used did not pain him so much as his regret at not being able to continue the campaign against his father's murderers. That was what grated on his soul and left him in a rage of frustration.

Word had come that Hendrik's pirates had surrendered the Castle rather than fight the regiment of modern, well-equipped BattleMechs now disembarking at the spaceport. Even knowledge that the pirates were defeated, prisoners now, didn't help. Grayson's right fist impacted his left palm in an anguished smack. He'd wanted to take down that *Marauder* himself. It didn't help to remember that not even his three light 'Mechs could have accomplished that.

The more he thought about it, pacing his cell with the frantic circling of his thoughts, the more he wondered if the situation was quite as clear-cut as it appeared. After all, the pirates could have withdrawn into the hills, perhaps forced enough of a stalemate to negotiate for better terms. And just what was going to happen to those of Hendrik's men who'd surrendered? Somehow, he didn't think they'd have surrendered so easily if they believed they were going to be shot or sold as slaves on some market world of the Combine's dominions.

The whole package seemed entirely too neat. And it was too great a coincidence that Duke Ricol should land here *now...* just *now...* of all possible times and places.

The plot was smelling larger and deeper, making Grayson wish desperately there were some way he could check up on the Red Duke. The computers at the Castle would have the records he needed, unless Hendrik's men had done a full program dump, which was unlikely. Computer records of any kind were precious as military intelligence. Hendrik's men would be going through those records, but they wouldn't have destroyed them yet.

He slapped his hand against a dank stone wall, letting the stinging pain steady his mind. It did no good thinking in circles like that. He would not be able to think about checking records until he got out of here. Besides, if this whole thing *were* some kind of monstrous plot, it was very unlikely he would ever get out again. A walk down that corridor...a pistol shot behind his ear...that was a far more likely fate for the Deliverer of Sarghad.

He thought of Mara. Just when he'd been wondering if Claydon was going to betray him, it had been Mara all along, Mara and her father. A number of puzzle pieces were coming together. The trap the night he had led 50 men against the supposedly damaged *Shadow Hawk*—had it been Stannic who had given the attack away, set them up to be ambushed? *That* suggested some sort of three-way tie between Duke Ricol, Stannic, and the pirates. Or had Stannic been cooperating with both the pirates and the Combine to ensure he backed whoever was the winner?

And there was the destruction of Berenir's house, his death in that flaming ruin. It might have been chance, but Berenir had been speaking with Stannic moments before, telling him about Grayson. Three Royal Guards had tried to take Grayson prisoner within the hour, and Berenir's house had been singled out for attack not long after that. Perhaps Mara was the connection?

They won't keep me here long, Grayson decided, *now that I've become inconvenient.* That stroll down the passageway could come very soon. He slumped back down on the bunk, eyes burning, face wet with tears. Well, he had certainly managed to make a mess of things.

CHAPTER 24

Grayson awoke to a sound of thunder, distant but growing nearer. Somewhere beyond the darkened corridors of the cell area, he heard men running and shouts. Fully awake now, he sat up as a fine spray of plaster dust sifted down onto him from the ceiling.

The thunder came closer, a rock-splintering crash that thudded repeatedly and seemed to pound even at the wall. There was a pause in the bombardment, and then Grayson heard the harsh rattle of heavy machine guns being fired close by—perhaps just outside the building. With a start, he realized there was a battle going on out there!

There were more thundering crashes, much closer this time. Rock and shattered stone burst through the passageway outside his cell, and the lights suddenly went out. In the dark, the racket seemed even more infernal, with shouts, screams, and gunshots echoing through the corridors. Then a pair of soldiers were outside his cell, dazzling his eyes with the beam from a hand torch that probed the dust-thick air.

"Lieutenant, sir! Are you all right?"

He recognized the men. Corporal Yee and a private named Thorel. Yee used an electronic key on the lock.

"Quickly, sir! The Sarge is parked illegally upstairs!"

Dazed, Grayson let himself be led out of the cell, past rubble and shattered walls, and up a short flight of stairs to the building's main level.

The front wall had been smashed in, and was now draped around the hull of the *Locust,* which squatted in the rubble approximately where the watch sergeant's desk had been until very recently.

Lori was there, an MP-20 cradled in her arms, waving him on.

"Lori! How—"

"Later! We've got to get out of here." She turned to the corporal. "Yee! Take your squad and head back to HQ. I'll cover your withdrawal."

Grayson looked at Yee and nodded. With things happening so quickly, he'd been letting himself be swept along by them. He knew he had to pull himself together now, take charge again—of himself and then of his command. First, they needed a rendezvous, somewhere to gather the unit.

"You'll get there ahead of us, Corporal. Give Sergeant Ramage a message from me. Tell him to saddle up. Pull in the perimeter, load what he can on every available vehicle, and pull out. We'll assemble at Thunder Rift."

"Thunder Rift, sir?"

"Right. It's marked on my maps. Avoid the spaceport and the Castle, but get to Thunder Rift. Follow the eastern flank of Mount Gayal on the other side of the Castle. The 'Mechs can make it through there. Hovercraft will have to go west of the port, running at high speed and hoping they're not spotted."

Yee saluted crisply, gathered the rest of the squad, and led them into the darkness.

Grayson paced. "Now...supplies..."

Lori's teeth flashed in the dim light. "Already taken care of. We liberated a couple of HVTs behind this building when we broke in. They're on their way to HQ."

"Food?"

"We've got some. But mostly we've got ammo, some weapons, and oil."

"Okay. It'll have to do."

Running figures moved in the distance, shadows against the darkness. Light flickered with the stutter of gunfire, and bullets sighed and snapped through the air around them.

Lori jabbed a thumb toward the crouching 'Mech. "Let's move it, Lieutenant!"

Automatic rifle fire chopped at the rubble and spanged off the *Locust*'s armor. Lori propelled Grayson toward the open ventral hatch that had been brought down to within two meters of the ground. He swarmed up the chain ladder dangling below the hatch and into the 'Mech.

The *Locust* cockpit was cramped for one. With two, it was claustrophobic. Lori shrugged out of her coat and squeezed past him, slipping into the control seat and pulling the neurohelmet down over her blond hair. Grayson was forced to stand behind the seat, crouched with his head and neck brushing against the spaghetti tangle of bundled wires and power leads running across the overhead.

The 'Mech turned slowly, then lurched free of the rubble, which cascaded down in a roar of dirt and debris. The *Locust*'s IR scanners were on. Blurs of green and white light shimmered and moved through blue darkness as soldiers closed in.

With the creak of grinding metal, the *Locust* rose to its full height, pivoting to face the attackers. Lori's right hand pulled at the machine gun controls, and glowing tracers etched trails of light across the screen. One of the glowing shapes collapsed and lay still.

Grayson stooped to bring his face close beside Lori's. Even in the heat of the *Locust* cockpit, he was very aware of her warmth, her nearness. "I take it you have a plan?"

"Well...finding you, mostly."

"And now that you have?"

Something heavy and loud *whanged* off the *Locust*'s torso armor, making Grayson's ears ring and even his teeth hurt.

"I suppose the next step is staying alive," Lori said. "What was that you said about Thunder Rift?"

Grayson nodded as he clung to an overhead handhold. It was difficult to stand with the cockpit lurching from side to side with each stride the 'Mech took. "Yeah. A place I know in the mountains. A small army could hide there." Listening to the unearthly din clanging against the cockpit armor, He recognized it as the staccato rhythm of heavy machine gun fire on the outer hull.

"They may follow us."

Grayson smiled, a cold light in his eyes. "Let 'em. Hovercraft won't be able to make the trek up Gayal. Nothing else they have is fast enough."

"You've been there?"

"Many times. I know that terrain. It's broken and way too steep. Even a hoverscout wouldn't make it."

"Can we?"

"No problem."

Grayson didn't add that there were two types of vehicles that could track the *Locust* up the flank of Gayal to the Rift. Broken ground wouldn't slow aircraft. He didn't know if the Combine regiment had aerospace fighters at the port, but he knew the bandits had had helicopters. There was a good chance they were armed with anti-armor missiles at least. Or if they weren't, they soon would be.

The other vehicle that could follow them was another 'Mech.

"Better alert the rest of the unit," he said. "Yee might not get through."

Grayson saw the muscles in Lori's cheeks bunch as she opened a commline. She began speaking to some unheard listener, suggesting the rendezvous at Thunder Rift.

After the Rift, then what? Grayson asked himself. What came to mind was the conversation he'd had with Tor about capturing a ship to take them off Trellwan. He seized on the idea, feeling mingled hope and fear as he thought it through.

Capturing a ship would be a difficult undertaking. The DropShip at the spaceport was merely the shuttle for transport between a planet's surface and the *real* JumpShip, which was designed to remain close by a star's jump point without ever approaching a planet. The *Invidious* should be at Trell's jump point now, ion thrusters maintaining its position against the star's gravity. The ship might have Tor's original crew, plus an unknown number of Hendrik's pirates. Or the Red Duke may have already put his own men aboard. There was no way of knowing.

It was even possible that the *Invidious* was no more, vaporized by a missile from Duke Ricol's flotilla when he'd dropped from the jump point. That was unlikely, though. Jumpships represented a resource from the old Star League days that everyone took great care to maintain. As starships could only be built by a few remaining old League shipyards, the same practical considerations that had effectively banned the use of nuclear weapons prevented the destruction of man's last remaining starships. The starfaring vessels could be captured; they were never destroyed.

The *Invidious* would be guarded, then, either by the Duke's men or by Hendrik's. But the key to getting it was the DropShip still squatting on the tarmac of Trellwan's spaceport. A pilot—and Tor was the only pilot Grayson knew on the planet—just might be able to take an assault force close enough to storm the JumpShip.

The alternative was to remain on Trellwan until another ship called at port. With Duke Ricol in charge of the planet, it was unlikely anyone would arrive except other ships in the service of the Draconis Combine.

The third alternative was to remain in the city, where they would doubtless be hunted down and killed. Or, they could flee to the deep desert or to the wilderness beyond the mountains by the equatorial sea. There they might expect to live a few weeks or months until their food ran out, their power systems failed, and the weather or the metal-poisoned water killed them.

If they tried for a ship, at least they had a chance of surviving. Grayson was anxious to meet with Tor again so they could discuss the possibilities.

Duke Hassid Alexander Ricol looked up across steepled fingers at his warleader. "Well, Singh? What do you have to report?"

Singh stood at attention before his master, attired in a spotless black dress uniform with the blue collar and cuff tabs of the Draconian Special Forces. The Duke still wore his custom-tailored red uniform, heavy with the gold and braid that he personally found so tasteless, but that never failed to impress status-minded locals.

His own office reflected his true tastes, an almost Spartan simplicity relieved only by an extravagantly wall-sized three-D holovid of a mountain stream, blue skies, and forest green. The stream foamed and splashed its way into a pool, endlessly rippling. It occupied one side wall of the office where Ricol could watch its continuing animation.

The wall behind his desk bore a topological map of the local region of Trellwan, from south of Sarghad to the southern shores of the Grimheld Sea along the equator. The map was dominated by the twisting, tightly spaced elevation contours of the mountains north and east of the city.

"The situation in the city is satisfactory, Lord. Stannic and his people are in command, the Militia has been mostly disbanded, and our people are in control of the major communications and government centers."

"What do you mean, 'mostly disbanded'?"

"There was resistance to the order to disband, of course. Some units fought. Some are still fighting. I dispatched one lance to the palace area to quell the riots there."

"Dammit, Singh, we can't have protracted fighting down there! The whole purpose of this mission is to secure Trellwan as a friendly outpost, not as a conquered and garrisoned one! This miserable ball of excrement is of no use to us at all if we must fight to hold it!"

"Y-yes, Lord. I assure you, the incidents have been minor."

"'Minor.' And what of the Trells' 'Mechs?"

"Ah...yes, Lord." Sweat stood out on Singh's face now. He had served Duke Ricol for fifteen standard years, and still dreaded the man's wrath. "Two of the locals' 'Mechs have been taken by the rebels, my Lord, the *Locust* and the *Wasp.* We have taken a second *Wasp* that apparently has been used as a source of spare parts. Its head is missing, as well as its weapons. The *Stinger* they captured from us is missing—"

"Which means someone has taken it to the mountains as well."

"The...The mountains, Lord?"

Ricol smiled unpleasantly, and swiveled his chair about to take in the area map with a careless sweep of his hand. "Where else? There's nothing to the south or west but endless desert and mineral flats. If they want to stay out of our reach, they'll assemble in the mountains somewhere, off to the north." He leaned closer to the map, peering. "There's a major pass there, a few kilometers north of here..."

"Thunder Rift, my Lord. I've been there, and checked it out. The floor of the Rift is submerged in a glacial lake. There would be no passage there."

"Hmm, I wonder. 'Mechs can travel underwater. Slowly, to be sure, but they could make it."

"Of course, Lord."

"And the small fleet of military hovercraft that has vanished in the past 20 hours could skim across the lake's surface."

"Yes, Lord, but the north end of that lake spills out in a series of waterfalls that drop a hundred meters or more into the Grimheld Sea. Also, the lake itself receives a seasonal waterfall of considerable power that is just about to begin at this season. There will be no escape for them in *that* direction."

"Hmm...good...good." The Duke swung back to face his subordinate, his hand scratching the base of his heavy black beard. "I want those rebels, Singh. Dead or alive, I want them."

"Are they really so important, Lord?"

"One of them is. This Commonwealther you've told me about, young Carlyle. If he were to survive, get off planet, he might piece together enough of what has happened here. He could turn the Commonwealth's eyes toward Trellwan again, bring a relief fleet before we were ready to meet them. Singh, think of it! A sweep in on Tharkad from a base deep within their own Periphery that they don't even suspect. Complete surprise!

"But if Carlyle warns them, our advantage is lost, and we are reduced to defending an otherwise insignificant ball of rock blessed with unusually wretched weather for no good purpose at all. This world is useless as a base without the advantage of surprise!"

"Yes, my Lord."

Ricol turned back to the map and studied it for several moments. "You have helicopters?"

"I do, my Lord. Four are down for repairs, but there are a pair of Warrior H-7 attack ships, and a Karnov UR transport. We have been using them for reconnaissance flights and for quick trips between the Castle and the port."

"I can contribute two more Warriors. Not enough for that jagged wilderness, but they will have to do." He pointed to the mountains north of Mount Gayal, then to the plains and mountain foothills to the east. "I want these areas patrolled, starting at once. Something as large as three BattleMechs should be easy enough to spot even in rugged terrain, and they *must* be there. There is no other intelligent choice for them. When we find them, we'll flush them out with two or three 'Mech lances. We'll take them wherever they hide. And Carlyle will die."

"Yes, my Lord."

"See to it, Singh. I have work to do."

Singh saluted, fist raised to heart, then snapped it up and out, stiff-fingered. Ricol turned his attention to a small computer screen on his desk.

Carlyle was an unexpected complication in the Plan, but it was such complications that added spice to the Great Hunt. Perhaps the Red Hunter himself would lead the ground pursuit of these rebels. It had been too long since he had personally taken the controls of a 'Mech in battle.

The thought stirred Ricol's blood, and brought a dark smile to his bearded face.

CHAPTER 25

As the *Locust* proceeded up the rambling eastern slopes of Mount Gayal, the ground became progressively rockier and more broken. Trellwan's fierce, week-long storms had gouged out deep gullies that twisted and wound down the mountainsides. It was still dark, but the eastern sky showed a hint of pearl gray along the horizon, marking the beginning of the planet's long twilight. Sunrise was still two standard days away. Though still night, the temperature was rising, and had been ever since Far Passage a week before. Snow clouds hovered above the mountains, and the icy peaks glinted in the predawn light.

Inside the *Locust*, it was hot and growing hotter. Lori had boosted the power output of the 'Mech's reactor as the terrain grew steeper, and the heat sinks were struggling to keep up with the system's waste heat.

Grayson had propped open both the inner seal and the outer hatch, but the opening was not enough to cool the cockpit. He'd long since removed his uniform jacket and shirt, and Lori was down to a light, short-sleeved t-shirt and briefs. Sweat beaded her face under the neural helmet, and molded the shirt to each swell and curve of her torso. Her legs were long and sleek.

It was hard not to notice how attractive she was, even in the heat of the cramped cockpit.

Lori turned her head and caught Grayson's gaze. "Forget it, Lieutenant," she said, sounding tired. "I'm not interested."

"Neither am I, Sergeant. Neither am I. Just drive, huh?" Grayson thought he detected a flash of hurt in Lori's eyes before she turned back to face the IR imaging screen.

The *Locust* continued climbing, its broad, flanged feet picking their way up the treacherous ground using Lori's own sense of balance.

A warning light flashed on the console. "Aircraft," she said. "Coming in from the south...low and fast."

"Okay. We make like a rock." He reached behind him and pulled the hatch shut, cutting off the trace of cold air seeping in from outside. "Shut down the sinks."

The *Locust* hunkered down, its back-canted legs folding under to lower the cockpit to within a few meters of the ground. As they sank to earth, the surrounding boulders seemed to rise from the ground all around them, sheltering them.

With the heat sinks closed off, the 'Mech was no longer dumping excess heat into the cold atmosphere. Its hull would still be hotter than the surrounding boulders and detectable on an infrared scanner, but geysering plumes of heat would no longer act like white-hot flares to attract a searcher's attention.

They waited. Though the *Locust* was no longer moving, the power plant was still running, and there was no way to rid the machine of heat. The temperature soared to 45 degrees. Grayson allowed Lori and himself a swallow of tepid water from the cockpit water tank, and mopped his face with his shirt. *How much longer would this go on?*

Lori didn't look like she could take much more either. She slouched in the seat, her hand on the 'Mech's machine gun controls, her eyes half-closed and her lips parted.

"Do you want me to take the controls a while, Sergeant?" Despite himself, he whispered. There was no way that helicopter could detect their voices, but the sense of an enemy very close, listening, was hard to fight.

She shook her head. "No. I'd rather...be *doing* something. Anything."

He nodded, and sagged against the support of an overhead handhold. If only there were room in the cramped, space for him to sit down too...

The imager revealed the aircraft, a lean, streamlined Warrior helicopter. Grayson could make out the missile pods extended from the craft's flanks. It passed them, hugging the terrain as it moved up the flank of the mountain two kilometers to the east of their hiding place.

"Didn't see us," Lori said unnecessarily.

"Give it a moment. It was moving too fast to have a ground party following, but there might be a second aircraft."

Fortunately for Lori and Grayson, there was not. After a small eternity of sweltering stillness, she opened the Mech's heat dumps wide, and the machine levered to its feet and resumed its climb.

To the north, a narrow ridge spur connected Gayal with the main body of the mountains. The *Locust*'s course had taken it along the eastern flank of Gayal on the far side of the Castle, then up the ridge and along its crest. From this vantage point, they could look southwest across the valley and see the lights of the spaceport spread beyond the Castle. Beyond that were the day-brilliant lights of Sarghad.

They paused there while Grayson used the 'Mech's telephoto starlight optical scanners to zoom in on the activity at the spaceport. Even without magnification, he could see frantic activity there. Two DropShips had grounded. Huge, massive, and squat, they were larger than the *Invidious'* DropShip, which crouched by itself in a far corner of the field.

Movement was dimly visible around the base of each ship, and the silvery specks of hovercraft and other vehicles could be made out against the darker ferrocrete. At full magnification, Grayson and Lori could see steam being vented from the ships in the glare of the port lights, and the silent, purposeful confusion of repair and refueling operations. Orderly rows of troops moved among the crisscross of gantry struts and loading platforms, and Grayson counted at least twelve 'Mechs of various types and weights drawn up as if for inspection.

He zeroed in on the age-streaked body of the *Invidious'* DropShip. "That's our key to getting off this planet," he told Lori. "We have to figure out a way to take her, and then use her to take the JumpShip."

"If it's still there to be taken. What are they doing? It looks like they're loading her."

Grayson agreed. He was at the very limit of resolution for the *Locust*'s optics, but it appeared a number of people were moving up a ramp into the DropShip's holds. Vehicles seemed to be loading crates or containers of some sort, and there was an air of purposeful activity Grayson knew marked preparations for a launch.

"We'll have to hurry if we want to catch a ride on *that* one," he said. "Looks like they're planning to lift—and soon."

"We'd have to do something quickly anyway. In another 60 hours it'll be daylight."

"And then 30 standard days until it's dark again." He pulled one ear thoughtfully.

They were rapidly running out of options.

The temperature within the cavern of Thunder Rift was somewhat warmer than the near-zero chill outside. The thunder it was named for had not yet begun, but a steady spatter of milky droplets trickled from the mass of ice and snow that could be faintly made out at the Rift's opening far above. The steady, rhythmic patter of droplets falling into the black water below filled the cavern with cold, wet echoes, and the promise of the roar of an avalanche of water when the Thirday thaw began.

For the past 20 hours, the remnants and tatters of the First Trellwan Lancers had been wandering in from the dark and cold in a ragged stream. Grayson had Lori and Sergeant Ramage moving among them, taking a census and trying to bring some order to the confusion. Fires burned along the shores of the lake, each with its own cluster of men and women in Militia fatigues or, rarely, the green of the Royal Guards. Beyond the warm glow of the fires, sentries moved among the predawn shadows, watching for the approach of the enemy.

So far, the Lancers could muster a *Wasp* and the *Locust,* and radio contact had been made with the *Stinger,* which was just now coming across the ridge north of Gayal. The combined strength of the two combat companies was 51 men, while 23 astechs from the support company had made it through. Also present were the vehicles the refugees had arrived in—five armed HVWCs, a pair of HVTs, and half a dozen scout hovercraft.

It was hardly a well-equipped fighting force. Most of the combat troops had brought their weapons, but the group had almost no food. Many did not have cold weather gear, and were half-frozen by their trek up from Sarghad in open-topped hovercrafts. Ammunition was in short supply for the projectile weapons, and backpack chargers for the handful of laser weapons would have to be charged off the hovercraft power plants, for there were no portable generators at all.

Renfred Tor had arrived aboard one of the hover transports. He walked with Grayson along the lakeshore some distance away from the campfires. The movements of individuals near the fires cast gigantic, misshapen shadows across the waterworn surfaces of the Rift walls.

"Lori tells me you have an idea for how we can take the *Invidious*," Grayson said. He wore a cold weather jacket over his Guards uniform, but kept his hands tucked into its pockets. He had no gloves, and the air temperature was low enough to freeze his fingers. "Tell me about it."

Tor crossed his arms and looked down at the sand. "It's possible, but it won't be easy."

"I was sure of that too. I got a good look at the spaceport coming up."

"The problem is, we can't just fight our way through the 'Mechs they have lined up on the port tarmac. Once we get aboard the DropShip, it's going to take two standard days to reach the jump point."

"You're saying they would warn the *Invidious* before the DropShip got there."

Tor nodded. "As soon as the DropShip lifts off with our people aboard, someone in Duke Ricol's forces is going to radio the *Invidious* and let the stationkeepers up there know that we're coming. They'd have two days to prepare for us, or they could simply jump to some other system."

"What if the *Invidious* is still crewed by Hendrik's pirates?"

"We can't count on that. Hell, we don't even know whether Ricol came in at the zenith or nadir jump point, but I doubt he'd leave a potentially hostile JumpShip just floating there, undisturbed."

Grayson paced the wet sand with Tor, thinking. Every star system had two jump points, the zenith point above the star's north pole, the nadir point below the south. The distance of the point from the star depended on the star's mass. For a class M2 red dwarf like Trell, the jump points were located about seven-tenths of an astronomical unit out—a hair over 100 million kilometers. A DropShip traveling from Trellwan to the jump point at a 1G acceleration would make the trip in two-and-a-half days.

"Where is the *Invidious,* Tor?"

"Nadir point."

"And your crew?"

Tor sounded less certain. "Most of them should still be aboard. At least, there weren't that many ship handlers among the bunch of Hendrik's people who came aboard, so they'd need my people for stationkeeping, if nothing else."

"So, Duke Ricol could have put his own people aboard, but your crew is probably still there."

"Unless he spaced 'em." There was bitterness in his voice.

"They won't have had reason to do that. Not yet, anyway." Grayson decided to change the subject. "It looked like they were loading people and cargo aboard your DropShip at the port. Any idea what that might have been?"

Tor shrugged. "No idea at all. They could be loading food and loot from their raids on Sarghad. Or maybe Ricol plans to ship Hendrik's people back to Oberon." He spread his hands, exasperation pulling at his long face. "There's just no way to tell from up here!"

"Hmm, yes. But I think I know how we can work it so that we can find out what's going on, and pick up a ship for ourselves in the bargain."

Grayson and Tor continued their hike along the shores of the black lake, absorbed in plans and calculations. In the cavern, the meltwater dripped ever faster from the ceiling, the spray reflected in the firelight like falling stars.

BOOK THREE

CHAPTER 26

Local dawn was only hours away. High, cold, streaming clouds already reflected Trell's bloody light from below the eastern horizon, and the spaceport was emerging into faint visibility after days of gray predawn light.

Grayson Death Carlyle confronted his command. There were 59 combat troops now, and 28 in the technical support company, all the soldiers who'd managed to escape from Sarghad. They'd brought stories of riot, of green-coats burning homes and shooting Militiamen, or Militia forces fighting back and being dispersed by the arrival of Kurita 'Mechs. They watched Grayson now with expressions ranging from hope to despair.

Behind them, the *Wasp* and the *Stinger* crouched in silent deactivation. The *Locust,* with Lori in the cockpit, patrolled beyond the mouth of the Rift, standing sentry.

"I'll say it again!" Grayson raised his voice and caught the faint echo from the rock walls behind the assembly. "Our one hope is to get off this planet, and the only way we can do that is to take that DropShip!"

There were mutters and grumbled conversation, but most returned Grayson's direct stare with stunned and uncomprehending looks.

"Lieutenant..."

"Speak up!"

A private in a grease-stained Militia uniform edged to the front of the crowd. "Lieutenant, Trellwan is our home. For most of us, that is, we *can't* leave!"

There was a wave of muttered assent, and someone called out "That's right!" There were hostile looks on many of the faces in front of him, confusion or worry on many others.

Preoccupied with his own schemes and desires, Grayson had not really foreseen resistance from his men. "Do all of you feel that way?"

The response was more muttering, shuffling of feet, and downcast eyes.

"The situation in Sarghad is not good," Grayson said. "Our scouts who came in last period say the whole place is under martial law. The Green Coats are in total control of everything, and Militiamen are being rounded up and shot."

A disbelieving voice rang out. "All of them?"

"No, not all. Most of the Militia is confined to their barracks now, and I gather General Varney is being held prisoner in the palace. But the Militia people who are protesting the new orders—they're disappearing. And the Duke's men are helping the Green Coats. Their troops are at the Palace, the hospital, and at the visor broadcast stations—"

"Lieutenant, lots of us have family down there. We can't just abandon them!"

Grayson felt his control, his authority slipping. These men and women, most of them, had borne with him through the hardships of training and organization, and had followed him to both victory and defeat. He had been thinking of this new lance as his family, and had assumed they all felt as he did. Obviously, he had miscalculated.

Kai had once lectured Grayson on why men fight. *"A man fights for many reasons,"* he'd said. *"Most of all, he fights for his buddies on either side of him on the firing line, and that's where his loyalty lies when the heat is on. But it's home and family that puts him there on the firing line in the first place."*

Grayson could tell by the atmosphere, by the dark murmuring and darker looks, that these people were not his to the point they would abandon home and family to follow him off-planet. He'd imagined the entire lance getting off-world, of warning the Commonwealth of the dagger unsheathed at its back, of finding whatever was left of Carlyle's Commandos and rejoining them. Failing that, he and the survivors would perhaps form a mercenary unit to continue the fight against the dark coils of the Draconis Combine.

But for most of those he led, there was nothing to fight for off-world, no promise there but the very slender one of safety from Stannic's pogroms and the Red Duke's 'Mechs. And so Grayson would just have to change his strategy.

"I won't ask you to leave your homes," he said, "but if we could get off-planet, if we could capture the JumpShip, we might be able to find help, to come back with a stronger force and kick the Kuritans back to where they came from."

A single voice broke the uncomfortable silence. "And if you get your ship, how do we know you'll come back for us?"

Another Militiaman stepped in front of the crowd, half-turning to face them. "The lieutenant's always done right by us, hasn't he? If he says he'll come back, I believe him!"

"Thank you, soldier."

"Begging the lieutenant's pardon, but not all of us have ties here. I for one have no family on Trellwan, and if you're going off-planet, well, I'd like to come along."

"What's your name, soldier?"

"Manning, sir."

"You'll be more than welcome, Manning. How about the rest of you? Will you trust me in this? We can't fight a BattleMech regiment alone. Why, we wouldn't even survive in the wilderness alone for long. But if we can get off-world and reach a Commonwealth naval base, I can bring back help. Believe me, the Commonwealth doesn't want the Draconis Combine here on Trellwan!"

"The Commonwealth wasn't that interested in us when they brought Hendrik's bastards in!" cried a voice from the back of the crowd.

"No, and they won't be any more interested in you now! They've got problems of their own—elsewhere. But they're damn sure not going to want the Kuritans sitting here massing their fleets and 'Mech battalions! Now...will you help me?"

There was a terrifying silence, while Grayson thought, *My God, I've lost them.*

Then Manning waved his TK in the air. "Count me in, Lieutenant!"

Then another Militiaman stepped forward, and another. The private who'd protested that he had a family moved up, and then the cavern was ringing with the shouts and whoops of Grayson's troops.

Maybe, Grayson thought as he looked down into their shouting faces, *just maybe we'll be able to pull it off.*

Renfred Tor marched with fourteen men past the outer barracks and onto the apron of the spaceport field. Each one wore the dark green and gold of Trellwan's Royal Guards.

A number of Royal Guards had joined Grayson's ragtag unit at Thunder Rift, men who'd fled the takeover when those in power began evening old quarrels with those in their own ranks. Grayson didn't fully trust them yet, and they were also the target of black looks and unpleasant grumbling from many of the Militiamen who had lost homes or family when the Guards had taken over in Sarghad. For now, the former Guardsmen were kept within the Rift, assigned to the shrunken support company, where they could be kept out of harm's way—and watched.

Their uniforms had come in handy, though, as a disguise for the men in Tor's special party. The DropShip captain led his tiny command across the uncomfortably open field between the barracks and the *Invidious'* DropShip. There were weapons trained on the party, Tor knew. Standard operating procedure called for weapons to track any person or group approaching a grounded military ship. As they got closer, he could see the orifice-dimpled sphere of a beam turret twisting within its mount on the hull to keep them in its line of sight. He marched his men into the wind shelter of a supply shed several hundred meters from the ship, halted them, had them face front and stand at ease.

He hoped they looked like just another squad of Green Coats.

The duke was using a lot of Royal Guards, both in the city and at the port. The alliance with them made sense. If Ricol could count on the men now in power in Sarghad—Stannic and his supporters—then the Duke would be free to use his entire force elsewhere. But the Lancers knew none of the passwords or codes that might now be in effect.

Their one advantage was that the situation in Sarghad was bound to be hopelessly confused at the moment, with so many changes being put into effect so quickly. It was likely that as yet there *were* no passwords or special codes. If so, they had to move now if there was to be any chance of success at all.

Clipped to his ear, Tor wore the remote earphone to the transceiver at his belt. He was conscious of the faint background hiss of the open channel, a channel that observation over the past hours had shown was not heavily used. Everything depended on the message he would get through that earphone within the next few moments.

The DropShip loomed above them, filling the sky with the massive swell of its rounded hull. For the first time, Tor got a good look at what they'd done to the vessel when they'd installed extra weapon mounts. He winced at the carelessness with which armor plate had been burned away, but knew he couldn't dwell on that now. What Tor needed to know right now was where was that bloody signal?

The Green Coats and their Kurita allies had occupied the Castle, of course, but they hadn't moved in and set up their headquarters there. That was one stroke of luck, at least. What Grayson and his men were attempting to do would have been far more difficult, perhaps impossible, if the Duke and his staff had taken over the Command and Control Center. Ricol appeared to be still operating out of the DropShip, which bore the red chevron of his flag. That meant the Castle's Command Center should be deserted. Grayson was in there now, working to tap into the spaceport's computer net. If he could just tell the computer network that Tor and his people were expected aboard the DropShip...

But where was his signal?

Grayson waited in the corridor outside the Command Control Center. His Guards lieutenant's uniform had gotten him this far, past gangs of men installing electronics equipment throughout the Castle. Heavy power cables snaked everywhere, and heavy beam and missile weapons were being installed at strategic points across the face and upper deck of the fort. Semi-portable consoles were being hooked up in the Vehicle Bay and in a number of the Castle's larger rooms. It looked as though the Red Duke was planning on moving in to stay.

The confusion within the Castle's passageways was complete. Each party of men, each squad of soldiers seemed to have their own assigned tasks, and paid no attention at all to anyone else. No one challenged Grayson, though once a man in the red and black uniform of a Draconis captain ordered him to report to Major Kraig for a runner assignment. Grayson guessed the captain had been given the unwanted duty assignment first, and was now passing it down to the first subordinate he saw. Grayson saluted smartly with his best Guards' salute and requested permission to complete his messenger duty first... on his Lordship's business.

The captain had muttered something unintelligible and waved him on. A junior officer looking for a way to duck an assignment would not closely question anyone—even an indig—purporting to be working for the Duke.

Grayson had reached the Command Center in good time, only to find a work detail in there. He hovered outside the open door for several moments, considering what to do. There were six men inside the Center, astechs belonging to the Red Duke's 'Mech regiment, from the look of it. Their leader was a full tech wearing an armband with the black-on-red dragon of the Combine and a heavy-looking service machine pistol holstered on his hip. Considering the array of tools spread out on the floor and the way they were dismantling a communications console, it looked as though they planned to be there for a while.

Grayson walked into the Center and directly to one of the computer access consoles in the middle of the room. He kept his face impassive, worked to keep his breathing steady.

The tech noticed him. "You! What are you doing here?"

Theoretically, of course, any command officer of any service outranked full techs, who were generally sergeants or warrant specialists in rank. But Grayson knew enough of the way the

Combine worked to realize not even a Combine astech civilian was going to obey orders from an indig officer.

Grayson did his best to look unsure of himself—a young junior officer in the presence of his betters. "Yes, sir! I was sent up to check out the computer net access from here. Major..." he groped for the name. "Yes! Major Kraig wants to know if there was any damage to the banks."

The tech scowled. "That was all checked out two days ago."

"I don't know about that, sir. I have my orders—"

"Why would the major put an indig greenie like you on the job? What do *you* know about Commonwealth computers?"

He pulled himself up with what he hoped looked like pride. "I was on the astech force that helped set them up, sir. That's why the major wanted me to come down here."

Admitting he had worked for the Commonwealth garrison was a big risk, but it was the only way Grayson could explain his knowledge of these machines. He was counting on the fact that technical personnel throughout human space operated in a subculture all their own, independent of the politics of the men who gave them their orders.

The tech considered Grayson a moment with narrowed, suspicious eyes, then waved at the consoles. "Just stay out of our way. We'll be changing the access codes in the system after a while, and we'll throw you out on your head then, got me?"

"Y-Yes, sir!" The codes had not yet been changed! He might be able to pull it off!

Doing his best to ignore the workers behind him, Grayson switched on the power and tapped out the key sequences that put him into the system. He was probing the control network that kept track of ships incoming and outgoing, and kept the spaceport control tower informed of the Castle's military decisions and activities. When the Commandos had been garrisoned here, the Trells had controlled the spaceport, and the network had been used for communication and for gaining special clearance for military flights. He suspected the Combine controlled all port activities now. Yes, there was a new program controlling the network. The logo on the screen indicated that the system was under the direction of Combine Military Command.

Any computer system that will be used by many people with varying levels of training must be designed so that even inexperienced personnel can operate it. Grayson tried various words and phrases that asked the system itself for help, and found himself logged into the flight scheduling sequence as *Tower Control 1*. He caught his breath, but no alarms went off. The screen, filled with command options, waited patiently for him. Taking a deep breath, he began working.

It took Grayson ten minutes of careful searching and experimentation to find what he was after. A launch was scheduled for local dawn, 2.3 standard hours from now. The launch was identified simply as *FRTR DRPSHP ALPHA* rather than by the name of one of the Duke's warships. That must be Tor's DropShip. It was scheduled to rendezvous with *J-FRTR: NADIR* in 52 hours. The freighter's destination was listed as Luthien, capital world of the Draconis Combine.

Cargo schedule...fuel schedule...orbital windows unrestricted... transit vectors and delta V...ah! Payload manifest! The DropShip was listed as carrying 1215 tons of cargo—grain, spices, hardwood, art objects, loot from the raids on Sarghad, all of it. There were 34 passengers listed as *Supercargo - Security Detention.* Those must be more prisoners, people taken when the Duke moved into Sarghad. Hendrik's people, maybe? That didn't feel right. General Varney and other loyalists? That sounded more reasonable, but there was no way to find out. Tor would have to use his own judgment there. The security detail was five men under the command of a Gharlit, Levin; Corporal; Regimental Security Forces. Their weapons were listed as pistols and tranq guns only. Good. Firefights on board ship could be hairy.

And, what was this? A special passenger? A Captain Yorunabi, with VIP clearances and status. *Who might* that *be?* Grayson wondered. Whoever he was, the special passenger would be Tor's responsibility.

Working swiftly now, he began typing. A new unit had been assigned to board *FRTR DRPSHP ALPHA*, fourteen men under the command of *Claydon; Sergeant; Trellwan RylGds.*

He had settled on the name while discussing the plan with Renfred Tor. None of them knew how plausible it would be to have a squad of local soldiers boarding an outbound freighter, especially as they had no idea of its destination. Might it be headed for Luthien? If so, what would Trell Green Coats be doing on a ship bound for Luthien? In this, as in so much else, Grayson was relying on the studied lack of curiosity and the obedient, it's-none-of-my-affair military mind.

He entered the information, then let his breath out in a long, unsteady sigh as he saw his data appear on the screen. Grayson stole a glance across his shoulder. The astech party was hard at work dismantling the console. Keeping his back to them, he slipped a small transceiver out from under his tunic, and thumbed it to a pre-set frequency.

All he said was, "Go." They had kept it simple and noncommittal because of the danger that some listener would pick up the broadcast and triangulate its position.

A red light flashed twice on the handset: *message received.* Grayson tucked the transceiver away and turned back to the computer. With his primary mission accomplished, he began searching for one more set of data he wanted to examine, and this would be his one and only opportunity to find it.

Renfred Tor pulled out his earpiece and gave the command to his men. They'd been standing at attention in the shelter of a hydrogen tank for the past eight minutes, waiting for the word to come from Grayson. Now he had given the signal, and it was time to move.

The fifteen men swung out into the chill wind and marched toward the DropShip. The beam turret still tracked them as Tor led them into the spotlit glare from the powerful lamps casting their harsh light across the main entry hatch. Elsewhere, the lights ringing the port paled under a slowly lightening sky. The port buildings, gantries, and storage tanks were all visible now, gray shadows in the twilight.

A pair of sentries stepped from the shadows. "Hold it right there. Where do you think you're going, Green Coat?"

"Orders," Tor said. Steam boiling from the DropShip's vents fumed and churned in the spotlit pools. "We were told to report aboard before launch."

"Let's see 'em."

Tor let a trace of anger creep into his voice. These were Draco sentries, not Trells, and there was no way he could threaten or bluster his way past them. But he might be able to take advantage of the fact that the oldest of the two sentries was half Tor's age, and looked green.

"I have no written orders, soldier. I was *ordered...*" he stressed the word, "to report aboard this DropShip by the tower officer. You want to take it up with him?"

There was uncertainty in the sentry's face, the universal fear of the military's lower echelons of having screwed up somewhere. But his voice was tough. These *were* just Trell indigs, after all. "We'll just see about that."

He used a hand transceiver to call the DropShip's bridge. His muttered conversation was inaudible to Tor and his men shifting from foot to foot in the predawn chill.

The sentry looked up suddenly. "Sergeant...Claydon?"

"That's right."

"Nobody ever tells me nothin.'" The sentry waved them on as the outer hatch swung open. "Move it. Get on board. You Greenies're expected, it seems."

Too easy, Tor told himself as they filed on board. They had to be even more on guard now, for things could change at any moment.

As he entered his own ship, he reached down and unobtrusively unhooked the safety strap across the top of the Gunther MP-20 riding on his hip.

CHAPTER 27

Grayson stared down into the computer display, his hands clenched in white-knuckled fury at the data he'd retrieved. He had tapped into the biog extract files, the same files left behind by Carlyle's Commandos when they'd withdrawn from Trellwan during that night of blood and fury. Learning the information in them had been an important part of Grayson's training during the past years, but there were far too many names and faces for him to remember them all.

BattleMech combat was intensely personal warfare. The theory was a warrior would have a better chance in combat if he knew something about the man he faced. In you knew, for example, that a certain MechWarrior favored close combat, it might give you the edge if you opened fire at long range and worked to keep him at a distance. The files included the histories of thousands of MechWarriors from across known space, living and dead, friend and foe. Even friends were recorded, for it was not unusual for friends to become enemies in the era of the Successor States.

The face staring back at Grayson from the screen was one he recognized. It was a long, swarthy face with dark eyes and an abbreviated beard circling his lips and mouth, the face of the man he had seen during the attack on the Castle so many weeks before. The files identified the man as Baron Harimandir Singh, a captain of the Red Hunter Special Operations Group. His biog stated he had been born on Chekaar, was an accomplished weapons master particularly skilled in hand-to-hand and small unit tactics, and was also a renowned MechWarrior with a long list of kills.

Most important, he was the right-hand man of Hassid Alexander Ricol, Duke of Chekaar.

Even with the proof before his eyes at last, Grayson could scarcely believe it. He had first looked up the computer entry on Duke Ricol, hoping to learn more about the leader of the Kuritan invaders. The Red Duke, it turned out, was a MechWarrior well known to the enemies of Kurita's Draconis Combine. He favored a 75-ton *Marauder* painted red with black trim, and was known by friend and foe as the Red Hunter.

The background data had referred Grayson to the entry on Colonel Singh, who, it reported, had served with Ricol for at least fifteen standard years. Grayson remembered the name from Lori's story about how she had come to Trellwan, and again from Griffith's dying shout during the battle in the Castle's vehicle bay. Now he understood the connection between the face he had seen during the battle for the Castle and Duke Ricol himself.

Though Singh was a MechWarrior, he served more often in his capacity as warleader for the Duke's special ground operations group. His BattleMech was a *Crusader,* a 65-tonner, painted in the same red and black livery as Ricol's *Marauder.* The computer projected the 'Mech on the screen. It was large, humanoid, with LRM launchers and 8cm lasers packed into each arm.

So there had never been any bandits from Hendrik of Oberon at all. The entire situation—the attack on Carlyle's Commandos, the raids on Sarghad, the timely arrival of the Red Duke—had all been arranged as part of an elaborate ploy.

The reason for the hoax was easy enough to figure out. If the Red Duke had simply attacked Trellwan outright, the Commonwealth would have fought back. Even if the Kurita forces had won, they would have been ruling a conquered, hostile planet that required a sizable garrison to keep the peace.

Instead, they had sabotaged the negotiations with Hendrik and stirred up the Trell population against the Commonwealth. Thus, the Combine invaders would be transformed into liberators who arrived to save Trellwan from the ravages of Hendrik's pirates...

There had to have been Draconis agents in on it from the beginning. Stefan would have been one of Singh's men, hired by his agents. He and others like him could have spread information about the pact with Oberon among Sarghad's citizens and infiltrated the ranks of the Royal Guards. The formation of the Trellwan Lancers and the Lancers' early victories must have disrupted the fragile web of intrigue at first. But the Duke had managed to subvert even that by having the unit turned over to the Guards' control, with the officers like himself, Lori, and Tor arrested or killed.

Grayson nodded as the puzzle pieces clicked together. The Combine would win everything—a friendly base of operations deep within the Commonwealth's Cis-Peripheral sector, a new source of ground troops, water, and supplies, and a staging area for secret strikes against the heart of Commonwealth space. The plot had to be Ricol's. Which also made him the man who had planned the death of Durant Carlyle.

Almost as an afterthought, Grayson scanned the computer listings for a Lieutenant Vallendel, the *Marauder* pilot named by Lori as the one who had ambushed his father. Sure enough, Grieg Vallendel was listed as a mercenary MechWarrior who operated independently within the Draconis Combine, and who was last known to be working under contract to Duke Ricol. He usually fought in a black and gray *Marauder.*

That confirmed the plot by Ricol and Singh. And it gave Grayson three names on the list of those who had killed his father: Duke Ricol, who had planned and ordered it; Lord Singh, who had carried it out; Lieutenant Vallendel, who had committed the actual murder.

He kneaded his forehead with stiff, hard fingers. He hated Ricol, hated the entire Draconis Combine with an intensity he was only beginning to discover. In his thirst for vengeance, he wanted them all dead, dead at his hands. Grayson vowed again that he would fight them until they were...unless they killed him first.

"Hey—you!"

His head shot up, one hand stabbing for the key that would blank the screen. The tech was standing several meters away, hands on hips, a black scowl on his face. There was another man with him, an older, gray-haired officer draped in a cloak.

"S-Sir?"

"Who did you say sent you down here?"

"Major...uh...Major Kraig, sir."

The gray-haired man threw back the flap of his cloak. Beneath it he wore a black, Combine infantry major's uniform.

Fear rose gibbering in Grayson's throat. He knew what was coming.

"I am Major Kraig," the man said. "I gave you no such order, young man. I've never seen you before in my life."

"Let's see your ID," the tech said. Behind the two, the astechs gathered in an uneven line across the door. Several of them, Grayson noted, wore holstered pistols, though none carried anything larger.

Grayson was not armed. He'd decided to not carry a weapon because he'd had no way of knowing what Combine military policy toward Trells carrying guns might be. If it had been against the rules for Green Coats to carry guns and he'd been caught with one, his expedition would have ended before it began. Now, without a gun, the only way he would be able to get past that line was to catch them off guard. He turned and walked toward them, reaching under his tunic for an imaginary passbook.

"It wasn't your direct order, Major," he said as casually as he could manage. "It was one of your officers, a captain...uh..."

He launched himself, low and fast, diving past the tech and directly at the knees of the smallest of the astechs behind him. He collided with the man in a tangle of arms and legs, rolling into the open door, then bounced to his feet and ran into the passageway. A chorus of shouts to halt rose behind him, then he heard the sharp *crack* of weapons fire in the air above his head. He ran faster, twisted down a side passageway, and kept running.

Grayson's immediate concern was to put as much distance between himself and his pursuers as possible. After that, perhaps he could lose himself among the other Trell Guards in the Castle. Even that would only buy him a few minutes' time. The Castle would be sealed off and all Trells seized for interrogation. The question was, just how many minutes did he have?

Grayson had entered the Castle through the vehicle bay. Could he reach it before the doors were closed?

Renfred Tor gestured with his Gunther MP-20. "Move aside, mister. I'll take her up."

The cluster of men and officers on the DropShip's bridge watched Tor with a mixture of shock, fear, and anger. Five of his men had spread out across the bridge, their assault rifles at the ready. Meanwhile, the black-clad sentry who had been standing outside the bridge door groaned and rubbed the back of his head where one of Tor's men had brought him down with a gun butt

The man in the pilot's position was a tech wearing a black and red dragon-insignia armband, and the deck officer's elevated chair was occupied by a Combine Naval lieutenant commander.

The man in charge, however, seemed to be the civilian dressed in ornately inlaid and gilt-edged clothing. *That one has the fat and sallow-skinned look of a merchant,* Tor thought, *unless you looked at his eyes.* They were cold and dark, with just a hint of an epicanthal fold, and had the look of one used to command and authority.

Tor had seen that merchant before. It had been long ago, on Drovahchein II, in the Erit star cluster. He'd known him as Proctor Sinvalie, of House Mailai.

"Yes, we do know one another, you and I," the merchant said, smiling. He stepped forward, and Tor swung the machine pistol to cover him. They'd ordered all their captives to drop their sidearms on the deck when they'd entered, but the merchant's cloak and tunic could hide an arsenal.

"That's far enough. Keep your hands where I can see them!"

The merchant's hands appeared below his deep, loosely-draped cuffs, spread-fingered and empty. He smiled easily, but his eyes were diamond-hard. "Easy there, friend. Surely we can come to an amicable agreement, can we not? We have so much to discuss—"

"We've got nothing!" Tor was confused, and not a little frightened. The merchant had a self-assured air about him, a deadly cunning evident in his smile, his mannerisms, and the cold, hard light behind his eyes. "How the bloody hell did *you* get here?"

"I arrived with Duke Ricol, of course. His mission here is, shall we say, of great interest to my masters. As was yours."

"You arranged it so Ricol could take my ship! You arranged it with Hendrik's people!"

"Actually, I arranged things with a faction plotting against old Hendrik, people who will find political advantage in the destruction of the Trellwan Pact. They had the data on your jump series, of course. I introduced them to Ricol's man, Singh. It was necessary to have some of Hendrik's warriors involved to make this little charade...more convincing. We couldn't be sure some of them wouldn't be captured."

Sinvalie turned to the Combine commander. "This is Renford Tor, Captain—a business partner of mine. He was captain of this vessel."

"I *am* the captain of this ship, and you damn well better believe it!" Tor gestured again with the gun. "You will obey my commands, starting now."

"Of course, of course. Don't get excited, friend. Ah, may I produce some identification?"

The MP-20 hovered within centimeters of the merchant's nose. "Slowly. Very, very slowly."

The man's smile deepened, and he reached inside the folds of his thickly draped outer tunic, then brought forth a square of translucent plastic. Tor found himself looking down through layers of color to symbols that floated unsupported within the square's depths.

"ISF, Captain," the man said. "My name...my *real* name, is Captain Yorunabi. Perhaps you've heard of us? We are the investigative arm of the Draconis Combine."

Tor felt totally out of his depth. The ISF was well known, with an evil reputation that extended far beyond the Combine's borders. "I know you, yeah. Kurita's secret police."

"As you wish. I can tell you, Captain, that I am on a highly important mission, that I must get to Luthien as quickly as possible."

"That is *not* where we're going," Tor snapped.

"Captain, please. I understand you are upset over the requisitioning of your vessel. Frankly, you have shown considerable resourcefulness in taking it back." Yorunabi flourished the card. "I think you will grant that I am...shall we say...in a position to reward you well? Take myself and my companions to your JumpShip, and from there, guide us to Luthien. Think, Captain. This one commission could pay you and your crew enough for you to retire in comfort! Such an opportunity does not enter a man's life twice..."

All Tor's life, it seemed, had been a struggle for one more cargo to earn just enough money to pay his expenses or bribe the next customs agent. The payment this ISF man was offering him for a single passage would make Tor wealthy. His men, he saw, were looking at one another rather than at their prisoners. The offer was tempting. What chance, after all, did the rebels have? Or Grayson Carlyle?

Tor remembered his interrogation, the biting cold as Singh had battered him with questions. He remembered Grady, Moran, and Lathe, and his own bitter guilt at having left them behind, the pain at learning they'd been killed. What chance? What chance?

The machine pistol wavered, its muzzle dropped toward the deck—

—then whipped back up in a gray blur, smashing Yorunabi's cheek with a red-smeared slash that tore a scream from the fat man's throat.

With the toe of his boot, Tor nudged Yorunabi, who lay rolling and moaning on the deck. Then he gestured to his men. "Take these characters below...number one hold. Strap them in and watch 'em." He brought the MP-20 around to cover the pilot and deck officers. "You go, too. I'll take us up."

His men cleared the Combine men from the bridge, and Tor proceeded to check out the ship. There already were prisoners below—Trell soldiers being taken elsewhere for their technical expertise. Among them was General Varney. Varney and his

Militiamen had agreed to join Tor's crew readily enough, once the plan was explained to them.

Then Tor was able to sit down again at the familiar console, letting his hands run across the instruments. Everything was set and ready, the hydrogen tanks topped off, the fusion pile hot and running. A computer display showed that the DropShip was scheduled for launch at dawn, a little more than three standard hours from now.

They'd not come aboard a moment too soon. He pulled out his hand transceiver and clicked it on to another little-used frequency. "Ready...ready...ready," he said.

Then Tor sat back to wait.

CHAPTER 28

As Grayson entered the vehicle bay, the insistent clamor of the Castle's general alarm began its raucous shrilling. Men and women broke into trotting runs this way and that, NCOs and warrants bellowed orders, and a squad of black-uniformed Combine infantry began forming up on the ground outside the huge double doors.

His first thought of seizing a hovercraft in the bay and making off with it into the near darkness outside wasn't going to work. He'd be burned down before he got 50 meters.

They'd be rounding up the Trells next. Grayson looked down at his green dress uniform and grimaced. The only thing to do was to stop being a Trell. He snuck back into the Castle's heart, moving through familiar passageways in the general direction of the repair bay. What he needed was to find...*ha!*

A solitary Draconis soldier was hurrying toward him down the hallway, his laser rifle slung behind his shoulder. The man paid no attention to the Trell Green Coat who stood aside with proper deference to let him past, but seemed bent on hurrying up the passageway toward the vehicle bay.

Grayson's foot swept out and caught the soldier across the shins as he trotted past, and the man went down in a clatter of rifle and cumbersome backpack power unit.

The soldier came to his knees with a snarled, "You clumsy bastard—"

Grayson's foot caught him just below the point of his chin, his head snapped back, and he clattered to the floor once more, his anger scattered into darkness. Grayson felt for a pulse, but found none. He hadn't intended to kill the man, but his own fear and anger had charged that kick to the man's throat. The soldier's neck appeared to be broken.

He dragged the soldier into an adjoining room, a small storage area for office forms and clerical supplies. Working swiftly, he stripped off the man's uniform and replaced it with his own, struggling to shrug the heavy power pack onto his shoulders and get the straps adjusted securely. As a final touch, he crouched beside a metal shelving case stacked with ream upon ream of requisition and supply forms and tipped it over across the soldier's body on the floor. There was a ringing crash, then a silence broken by the rustle of skittering papers. That should at least cause a bit of confusion if the trooper's body was found. Any delay at all would win him a few precious, extra minutes.

Next he checked his laser. It was a Mark XX Starbeam, a Combine model he knew from weapons texts, but not personal experience. Still, it shouldn't be too difficult to figure out. Beam intensity would be controlled there. Power on by pulling down the handle on the backpack. A grip safety under his hand. It looked as though he could work it. Checking both directions before he stepped out of the storeroom, Grayson then trotted toward the Repair Bay.

The *Shadow Hawk* was there, standing upright on the repair platform.

The 55-ton 'Mech dominated the cavernous Bay, a vast, humanoid shape of gray and rust-streaked metal and faded paint surrounded by the metal scaffolding that had been raised around it.

Grayson appraised the 'Mech with expert eyes. From the look of things, they'd been remounting its backpack and autocannon, both of which had been removed to facilitate the trap that had nearly killed him and wiped out his entire assault force in this very room. The backpack housed the 'Mech's primary heat exchangers and the cockpit's life support systems, as well as mountings, ammunition, and the control circuitry for the 90mm autocannon that was now set in the rest position, aiming straight up. The back unit could be removed for maintenance and repair operations, but the 'Mech would not be fully combat ready without it. The BattleMech certainly looked combat-ready now.

The *Shadow Hawk* was a 'Mech of older design, and had a transparent canopy much like that of an atmospheric aircraft. Console screens gave the pilot a full range of IR through UV vision. In practice, however, the pilot generally relied on his eyes rather than the 'Mech's optical sensors, with a holographic heads-up display to project targeting information and combat intelligence above the console. The canopy was open now, and Grayson could see someone—possibly the pilot or a tech running a final check—moving about in the cockpit

Though the alarm was silent, troops were forming up on the repair bay deck, with officers pointing and yelling orders. They had gathered a milling herd of green-coated Trells at gunpoint into a far corner of the room. The round-up had begun.

Grayson thought fast. The bay doors were open, but with all those soldiers lined up near the opening, he'd be stopped or shot down before he got very far. His eyes traveled back to the *Shadow Hawk.* He had piloted that 'Mech several times during his training. It had been Lieutenant Hauptman's machine, and Grayson could still make out the man's name in faded script across the leading edge of the 'Mech's left foot. He had spent a good many hours piloting '*Hawk*s in the simulator, too. If he could get into its cockpit, he would have a good chance of escaping.

There were several potential problems, however. The 'Mech might not be as combat ready as it looked. Worse, the neurohelmet could have been set for the parameters of another pilot, and would have to be quickly reset if he was to have complete control. The only way to find out was by sitting in the cockpit himself.

Perhaps the biggest dilemma was one of tactics. Once Grayson started climbing the ladder up the side of the scaffolding, some NCO or Combine officer was certain to see him. Without some kind of diversion, he would never make it higher than the *Shadow Hawk*'s knee joint.

Lori set her jaw and shifted frequencies. "All units, I have the signal. Let's move!"

The *Locust* lurched forward, its flat-clawed feet grappling for purchase on the sandy bank as it scrambled to the top. On either side of her, the *Wasp* and the *Stinger* crawled out of the wadi and stood upright. On both flanks, the hovercraft weapons carriers hummed into life on the rim of the arroyo where the *Wasp* had carefully set them moments before. Then they began drifting toward the spaceport on eddying clouds of dust

"Just a fast raid," Lori reminded her command. "In and out. No duels! Let's see if we caught them napping!"

They had maneuvered through the wadi to within three kilometers of the spaceport, which left a long, open fire lane the various machines had to move through. The 'Mechs thundered forward at their top speeds, which quickly put the *Locust* well into the lead. Dust raised by their charge and by the fans of the hovercraft swirled and billowed to create a screening cloud.

Lori brought her laser to bear on the nearest of the Combine DropShips, targeting a laser turret in the vessel's bulging flank. The sky was just light enough for her to pick out her target optically, and the flash when the turret exploded was dazzling against the twilight

White smoke trails arced and twisted through the sky from the pair of missile-firing hovercraft. Flashes of light erupted among the grounded ships, across the curved roof of a barracks, across the side of a storage shed. The cracks and booms of exploding rockets rattled across the field.

"PBIs at 270!" Lori recognized Enzelman's voice in the *Wasp*. Garik tended to get shrill in battle as the adrenaline started flowing, and his emotions came through even the electronic filtering.

She shifted her imaging sensors, and saw a twinkle of movement. PBIs—MechWarrior slang for "Poor Bloody Infantry"—were boiling out of the stricken barracks. Many wore only bits and pieces of uniforms in the cold chill of early morning, but they all appeared to be armed.

"Okay," she transmitted. "Don't worry about them. Go for the storage tanks at 180. Hit 'em!"

The target was a tank farm, four rows of squat, massively armored storage tanks at the far side of the port. The *Stinger*'s laser probed the base of one of the tanks, searching for weakness. The blue flash of a particle beam lanced out from a DropShip and caught the *Stinger* in its glare. Lori noted with approval that the *Stinger*'s pilot, Yarin, one of Grayson's Trell recruits, held his fire steady on the stubborn armor of the tank. She targeted her *Locust*'s laser on the same spot, adding her own weapon's white fury to where the armor was softening, to where the network of pipes and conduits for fuel transfer were melting.

Those tanks held liquid hydrogen, reaction mass for the fusion impulse drives of the DropShips that called at the port. In two seconds, the valves at the tank's base slagged down, vaporizing hydrogen gushed out into the cold air, and the explosion sent a huge fireball mushrooming into the sky.

The shock knocked Yarin's *Stinger* to its knees, and Lori fought the *Locust*'s controls to keep her machine on its feet. The impact of the blast was a palpable blow, savage and deafening. The fireball climbed higher, devouring the sky. Its light illuminated the whole area, while flaming chunks of white hot metal rained onto the field and clinked across the *Locust*'s hull.

"That's it," Lori said. "They'll have the cavalry out any moment now! Fall back! Fall back!"

The diversion Grayson prayed for came as a shout from a soldier by the doors. "Hey! They're attacking the port!"

Discipline broke as soldiers turned in their ranks, craning their necks at the laser fire starkly visible against the darkened expanse of the spaceport below Mount Gayal. Several astechs ran out onto the parade ground to get a better look.

Grayson knew it was now or never.

Starting up the ladder of the gantry, he kept his eyes fixed on the *Shadow Hawk*'s head. His greatest fear was what would happen if the *Hawk* was fully powered up and ready and the pilot should spot him halfway up.

When Grayson reached the 'Mech's waist, the pilot had removed his helmet and stood in the cockpit, stretching up to see past the bulk of the 'Mech's chest to the battle outside.

Grayson climbed faster to the '*Hawk*'s chest. He was level with it when a vibration in the gantry attracted the pilot's attention. He looked down, eyes widening.

At the same instant, there was a shout from the deck eight meters below. "Hey! You up there! What the hell do you think you're doing?"

Grayson had been spotted. Above him, the pilot reached for his sidearm.

CHAPTER 29

Grayson climbed faster, scrambling out onto the narrow scaffolding walkway that ran across the bulge of the 'Mech's chest, just below the cockpit. The MechWarrior had his pistol out, aimed at Grayson's head.

"Drop that gun!" The man's voice was shrill, and a bit unsteady.

Grayson dropped his rifle, which clattered on the scaffolding. Then, he began unfastening the buckles that held his powerpack straps in place.

"This is restricted up here, fella," the warrior said. "No one comes up here but techs and—"

The last buckle slipped open, and Grayson brought the heavy laser backpack up and around in front of him like a shield. He rushed the MechWarrior, and the scaffolding jumped and rattled under his boots. The pilot fired once, his shot missing both shield and Grayson as he fell back into the cockpit

Grayson threw the bulky power unit, catching the pilot in the chest. Then Grayson was on top of him, wrestling for the gun as his feet scrabbled for a firm grip on the slick surface of the 'Mech's upper chest armor.

The two men grappled for a moment, the powerpack with the rifle dangling from its cable getting between them in the scramble. The pilot stood up, his pistol still in hand. Grayson lashed out with his foot, caught the MechWarrior on the knee, then watched as the man toppled over and fell backward with a shriek and the clatter of metal scaffolding.

The stammer of an assault rifle echoed through the bay, and bullets whined and cracked past Grayson's head. He stooped and retrieved his rifle, checked the power, then snapped off three quick shots at the soldiers advancing toward the ladder. The laser fired with a warm hum. The bolts of coherent light were invisible, but two of the soldiers below crumpled to the deck with their uniforms smoldering.

As other troops sought cover, Grayson ducked back into the *Shadow Hawk*'s cockpit. He pulled the canopy down into place, then tiwsted the handle to seat and seal it.

The canopy was heavily layered with reflective materials that transformed it into a one-way mirror, an added safety factor that prevented the pilot from being blinded if the cockpit was hit by an enemy laser beam. It darkened the cavern outside somewhat, but Grayson could still make out the scurrying shapes of Combine soldiers.

Quickly now, he told himself. His hands flicked row upon row of switches along the consoles to the right and left of his chair. Instrument readings showed his power plant active and full power available, his weapons loaded, armed, and linked to the controls.

Grayson pulled the neurohelmet down on its trailing tangle of wires and feed cables and snugged it tight against his head. With power on, he cautiously opened the feedback test circuit. First, there was the familiar wash of vertigo as circuits tuned to unfamiliar brainwave patterns fed dissonant patterns back through the nerves of his own inner ears. He found the vernier knobs that adjusted the helmet's tuning, working them back and forth as the dizziness ebbed. Out-of-step traceries on an oscilloscope resolved into a single standing wave, and he knew the *Shadow Hawk* was now set to his alpha wave patterns.

He gave the board a last scan. *Green...green...all green.*

His left hand took the conning stick, his right the weapons grip. His foot kicked off the leg locks that held the *Hawk* braced against the scaffolding, and the machine took a step forward. The gantry scaffolding exploded outward in a cloud of spinning shards and fragments. The 'Mech took another step, dragging twisted strands of aluminum alloy across the deck with a screech of tortured metal.

The bay doors were grinding shut. Grayson twisted around, searching. Sure enough, the control booth was there, the stairway back in place. He could see an astech inside the booth, frantically speaking into a microphone.

Grayson raised the 'Hawk's right arm, bringing the 6cm laser mounted to the forearm into line. His right hand tightened on the trigger. White fire burst from the booth, which spouted a stream of glass splinters and shattered metal. Half of the booth twisted away and fell to the deck, trailing black smoke and a tangle of shredded braces and metal from the stairway.

Still partly open, the bay door froze in place.

Grayson turned and strode for the opening. Men scattered before his feet, most throwing away their guns and fleeing without looking back, a pitiful few standing their ground to blaze away at the thundering 'Mech with assault rifles and pistols. Grayson ignored them, increasing speed as he exited the Castle. The laser and missile batteries mounted around the wall packed more than enough firepower to bring the *Shadow Hawk* down. His only hope was that the weapons were not yet manned and ready.

He didn't dare cut in the 'Mech's jump jets for the descent from the parade field. After piloting the *Locust*, the *Shadow Hawk* felt wildly different—huge, massive, and clumsy, as though he were attempting to walk with lead weights strapped to his hands and feet and torso. It wouldn't take long to get used to the heavier 'Mech, but Grayson was not about to risk any tricky maneuvers until he had the machine thoroughly broken to harness.

The terrain below the parade ground was broken and rough, gouged by erosion gullies and made treacherous by loose stones and gravel spills. Grayson found he had begun his descent further north than he'd intended. To the south, toward the lights of Sarghad, the slope was gentler, flat enough for hovercraft and solid enough to support running 'Mechs.

He opened his combat frequencies, and got a rasp of static and a rapidly speaking voice in his helmet phones.

"—freighter DropShip, demanding immediate clearance!"

"DropShip Alpha, this is tower. We have an emergency on the field and must deny your request for clearance."

"You idiots, it's the emergency I'm trying to avoid! Look...Captain Yorunabi, ISF, has given me orders to launch immediately. Do you read me?"

Grayson strained to catch the words, which were fuzzed by static. As these were electronic transmissions and not voices, he couldn't tell if the speaker was Tor or not. But he knew Lori would not have launched the attack on the port unless she'd had word from Captain Tor that the DropShip was secure.

When they'd made their plans, they'd not known the DropShip's launch schedule, and could only guess from the preparations around its base that it was ready to lift. DropShips were not loaded with their liquid hydrogen reaction mass until just before launch. The fuel had an unfortunate tendency to diffuse through unshielded tanks if it were left sitting for more than a few hours. It was generally cheaper and more efficient to store the fuel elsewhere, and load it just before burn time.

That was how they knew the DropShip was nearing launch time when they'd seen the astech teams fueling it, but they hadn't known how close it was. Rather than have Tor and his squad risk detection by sitting in a secretly captured DropShip for hours—possibly a standard day or more—the attack was planned to give the freighter captain an excuse to launch at once.

The DropShip pilot's frantic request was according to plan, but Grayson wondered about the presence of an ISF captain aboard. Was that Tor's bluff? Or had something gone terribly wrong?

"Alpha, this is the tower. You have clearance for immediate launch."

If it was a bluff, it had worked. A flare of light spread across the still-darkened field, and the *Invidious'* DropShip rose on a flickering pillar of white fire, moving slowly at first, then accelerating at what must have been a bone-cracking three Gs into the pearly sky.

If Tor's assault had failed somehow, there was not a thing in the universe that could be done about it now.

Grayson switched frequencies, and found the battle channel he'd assigned the Lancers.

"Lancer One, this is Grayson." They'd not arranged radio codes, because Grayson hadn't expected to be coming out of the Castle in a BattleMech.

There was a pause. "Grayson? This is Lori."

"Lori! I've liberated a *Shadow Hawk.* I'm on my way down the slope toward you. Any opposition?"

"Heavy fire from the ships, as expected. Their 'Mechs are not manned, and so far they haven't been able to scramble any against us. They'll be on us soon, though. Ground troops are moving to set up heavy static weapons on the field."

"Right. Stick with the plan. I'll see you at the rendezvous!"

Fire and shattered earth rose around him as missiles from the Castle sought across the rocky ground for the lumbering *Shadow Hawk.* Twice Grayson turned, dropped the autocannon down across the 'Mech's left shoulder, and opened a rolling barrage of explosive shells against the launchers that were tracking him, but with no noticeable result. The range was already too great for accurate placement of shells or rockets.

On the plain below, he could make out the specks of three BattleMechs retiring north toward the mountains, shielded from the grounded DropShips by the ruin of a liquid hydrogen tank. And in the sky above, a brilliant star moved rapidly toward the lightening east, trailing a white contrail plume. Success or failure?

He would learn soon enough. For now, the plan required radio silence with the spacecraft, and the pretense that Tor's part of the plan had worked perfectly.

If it had not, success would turn to failure in two short days.

JumpShips were ungainly beasts, restricted by their design and by physics to slow and extremely gentle maneuvers about that invisible abstraction in space known as a jump point. Jump points were areas spanning several tens of thousands of kilometers, depending on the mass of the star that generated them. Every star had two, the zenith point at the star's north pole, the nadir point at the south. These distances varied, of course, depending on the size of the star. With their Kearny-Fuchida drive, JumpShips could maneuver into the point, energize their drive systems, and reappear at the jump point of a star up to 30 light years away.

Energy for the jump came from the vessel's jump sail, a disk of metal fabric less than a millimeter thick and up to a kilometer wide that captured and transmitted the light and particulate radiation from a star to shipboard storage cells. Designed to absorb every photon of every wavelength that fell upon it, jump sails were black—a black so profound an old pilots' joke told of space appearing white in comparison.

Though complex in the details of operation, the basic simplicity of jump point transitions had given men the stars. Even though the war-torn civilization of the Successor States could no longer build new vessels in any appreciable quantity, ships continued to ply the lanes between stellar jump points. The *Invidious* was at least three centuries old, her drive guide laid in during the years just before the Succession Wars.

No one knew how long the power core of a JumpShip would remain charged and vital. It was a question that troubled the philosophers and warlords of every world in the human sphere.

A JumpShip's reliance on the jump points and on the huge yet delicate black jump sails meant no ship could travel far from the point at which it had entered a planetary system. The sails had to be unfurled for considerable periods of time to soak up the energy necessary for a jump, and the dust and meteoric debris that littered the orbital plane of every star could shred a sail within a few passages. Though some ships had secondary drive systems that allowed them to maneuver through a system with their sails furled, most JumpShips remained at the jump point, using their DropShips as shuttles between starship and world.

This posed another problem, however. At the jump points of any star, that star's gravity is still very much in evidence. A ship in orbit around a star would not fall, of course, but it would not remain near the jump point either. Rather, it would follow its orbital path around the star and eventually through the dust-laden plane of the system.

For this reason, JumpShips mounted ion or plasma/ fusion stationkeeping thrusters. These provided a steady, gentle thrust carefully calculated to precisely counter the pull of the star, and to maintain the spread of the jump sail at the same time. A JumpShip parked at a star's jump point is positioned with its prow aimed out-system and the sail spread perhaps ten kilometers aft, between the star and the ship. The stationkeeping thrusters are angled aft and outboard, so that their streams of charged particles will not damage the fragile sail.

Needless to say, JumpShips parked at a jump point could scarcely maneuver at all, for any lateral acceleration would distort, then shred the sail fabric. There were several ship-to-ship battles on record; ponderous affairs that had taken weeks of maneuvering to complete. Generally, when ship-to-ship combat was called for, heavily armed and maneuverable DropShips, or lighter, faster, and more maneuverable aerospace fighters were used. JumpShips were armed as a matter of course (including radar-directed lasers to defend against meteors), but a single DropShip provided enough threat against any unsupported ship that a ship captain would usually surrender immediately rather than risk damage to his precious, irreplaceable vessel.

It's a fascinating problem in space combat tactics, Tor decided. He had never paid much attention to space tactics, though any freighter captain knew enough to enable them to counter the maneuvers of a possibly hostile starship at an unfamiliar jump point. His problem here was to approach the *Invidious* without giving away the fact that the DropShip was no longer under the control of the same people. There might be passwords or approach codes he knew nothing about, though a search of the DropShip's operations programs revealed no new computer codes in the docking sequence. It *looked* as though the pirates had left everything as they'd found it. Tor could only hope that that was the case.

The tactical complication for this mission was the Draconis Combine JumpShip parked 12,000 kilometers from the *Invidious.* While this distance was great enough to keep either vessel's stationkeeping thrusters from damaging the other's sail, by space navigation standards, twelve thousand kilometers was practically next door.

Tor could feel that other ship out there. It was too distant to show optically, but he could visualize it. He was certain the warship was the same one that had stopped him en route from Sigurd to Trellwan in the first place. If it picked up even a hint that something was wrong aboard the freighter, a pair of *Union*-Class DropShips—or worse, a flight of aerospace fighters—could be positioned off the *Invidious'* sail within 30 minutes.

This particular hijacking had to be carried out with complete secrecy, or it would end almost before it had begun. Grayson and Tor had worked out the details during their walk on the shores of Thunder Rift's lake. The key to the plan was the knowledge that each JumpShip would have its directional antenna centered on Trellwan, but they almost certainly would not have them aimed at one another. Two ships at stationkeeping by a jump point, particularly a military vessel and a warship, would have little to say to one another, though the warship would keep the freighter under observation as a matter of course. An attacker like Tor would be able to tell if the *Invidious* were talking with the warship, but not if her crew were in communication with the port—and through them, with the Combine ship.

Tor's problems would begin if the *Invidious'* crew was able to alert the spaceport that he was boarding their ship. The spaceport would alert the warship, and the warship would have armed DropShips alongside almost at once. That warning would also spell trouble for Grayson on Trellwan. He was planning another raid on the port, and word that the freighter had been captured would put the spaceport defenses on their guard. That might make the attack impossible, or worse, lead his force into an ambush.

It was for this reason that Tor's mission was coordinated so precisely with Grayson's forces on Trellwan. The Lancers would be in position to attack the spaceport at the same time Tor's DropShip approached the *Invidious.* The ground attack's first target would be the spaceport control tower, which housed the communications relays to the commnet dish antenna that could warn the enemy warship of the assault on the *Invidious.*

Too, the ground attack could not be launched before the DropShip reached the freighter. If it were, someone in the tower might alert the warship, and the warship's officers might become suspicious of the timing of that lone DropShip approaching the freighter. A laser's flare could end Tor's mission just kilometers short of its goal.

Tor looked at the computer screen on his console, which showed the elapsed days, hours, and minutes since launch. Their burn time had been carefully adjusted so the DropShip would arrive at the *Invidious'* stationkeeping zone at precisely 55 hours, 30 minutes after launch.

T plus 55.5 hours was the jump-off time for both attacks. *If* everything had gone according to plan on Trellwan.

Tor and his men were about to risk their lives on the assumption it had.

More than 50 hours after local sunrise, Trell had crawled clear of the horizon and was hanging low and to one side of the black silhouette of Mount Gayal. The swollen, mottled red disk could still be looked at without discomfort, but the red light had thrown the entire western face of Gayal into shadows so deep Grayson could not make out the Castle.

The temperature was already several degrees above freezing. The faint and distant susurration the 'Mechs were picking up on their external mikes was the first roar of falling meltwater from the depths of Thunder Rift.

The assault force was approaching from the west this time, making use of the rugged and water-tortured ground to shield the 'Mechs from enemy radar and other remote sensors. Grayson was in the newly captured *Shadow Hawk* several kilometers from the rest. He had found another arroyo southwest of the port, and had moved the *'Hawk* into the shelter of an undercut bank. A computer display on his instrument console flickered with the passing seconds. Fifty-five hours, twenty-eight minutes had passed since the DropShip's launch. In two minutes, the attack would begin.

The Lancers' assault of two days ago had caught the Combine forces off guard, allowing Grayson and his men to retire to their hiding place in the Rift without being pursued. The enemy had managed to launch only one missile-firing helicopter, and that had been brought down by a salvo from one of the Lancer's missile-firing hovercrafts. There was no way to achieve such surprise a second time. In the past 50 hours, Combine forces at Sarghad had offloaded and readied two full 'Mech companies—twenty-four BattleMechs of various models and sizes. Two lances totaling eight 'Mechs had been deployed in the city around the palace grounds, and another lance had moved into the Castle shortly after Grayson's escape with the *Shadow Hawk*. The remaining company of twelve 'Mechs stood sentry at the spaceport. Eight were patrolling constantly while the remaining four were being serviced.

There was also at least one other 'Mech at the port, Lieutenant Vallendel's black-and-gray *Marauder*. Grayson wondered if Duke Ricol's own red-and-black *Marauder*, the Red Hunter, was also on Trellwan, though he'd seen no sign of it.

The Red Duke's forces also included ground troops, at least 250 soldiers equipped with a variety of hovercraft and light tracked vehicles suitable for rough mountain terrain air cushion craft couldn't manage. These troops were armed with an impressive array of assault rifles, man-portable lasers, and shoulder-fired missile launchers.

A direct attack against such a force was clearly hopeless, but it was the only way to knock out the communications relay tower. Grayson looked at another screen, whose image was coming to him from a small camera at the top of the wadi's wall. The antenna of the relay system was a 20-meter mast topped by a shallow, wire mesh dish five meters across, which was canted low toward the southeast horizon. That was the direction of the nadir jump point, the place where—if everything was on schedule—Tor should be approaching the *Invidious* in the captured DropShip at this very moment.

The tower was Grayson's special target. The other 'Mechs of the lance, the 20-ton *Locust, Stinger,* and *Wasp,* would be attacking the base, which was patrolled by at least thirteen heavy 'Mechs. With the odds they faced, the Lancers' battle plan would require a careful use of strategy.

The plan called for the light 'Mechs to attack the hydrogen tanks again, then flee. They expected most of the 'Mechs on hand to pursue the Lancers as they retreated toward the hills.

Grayson was sure the Combine forces would be determined to trap the raiders this time, chase them to their camp, and destroy them once and for all.

But while the main 'Mech force was chasing the three raiders, Grayson would slip into their rear and destroy the antenna. The Lancers' hovercraft and troops were deployed in rugged, defensible terrain halfway up the mountain slopes toward the Rift. A stubborn defense might allow the Lancers' light 'Mechs to escape, and discourage active pursuit.

Might...might...might... Grayson rubbed his hands over his face and tried to dispel the fears that plagued him. There were so many unknowns here. Was Tor really in command of the DropShip? Would he be able to take the *Invidious* without interference from the Combine warship that must be somewhere in that same area? Could three light 'Mechs and a handful of half-trained troops survive an all-out attack by three full lances of medium and heavy 'Mechs?

Once before, he had mapped out a daring battle plan against superior odds, only to watch that plan dissolve in blood and fire as the repair bay door had crashed shut behind them. Given the cunning and resourcefulness of Duke Ricol, it was entirely possible Grayson was leading his people into another trap, one even more deadly than what they'd faced before.

His first suggestion at their council of war had been that he slip into the port alone. A knapsack packed with high-velocity explosives might bring the radio tower down.

Might...might...

His men had vetoed the idea. The attack against the tower *had* to succeed—and succeed immediately. If the Duke's people managed to get a warning to either the *Invidious* or the Combine warship, they would blast Tor's DropShip into meteoric fragments. Only the *Shadow Hawk*'s firepower, consisting of medium laser, autocannon, and short-range missile clusters, could guarantee a successful strike on the tower.

Tor was depending on Grayson, who, in turn, was depending on Lori, Garik Enzelman, and Yarin to buy him the time he needed to get close enough to that tower.

CHAPTER 30

The final seconds ticked away.

And then it was time.

Grayson's external mikes picked up the *swoosh* of missiles as Enzelman's *Wasp* loosed a barrage of SRMs with smoke charges behind their warheads. They arced low and flat across the port, exploding into clouds of impenetrable white smoke. As the Duke's men returned fire with savagely interlacing beams from grounded DropShips and defensive bunkers, the air shrieked with the multiple concussions of exploding warheads.

Grayson's camera zoomed in on the low-hanging drift smoke. He could barely make out the strutting bird-shape of Lori's *Locust* as it flitted across the screen. Somewhere, a heavy autocannon yammered and howled, and pinpoint flashes erupted close by her 'Mech. The enemy would be aiming by radar in that soup, which was not as accurate as an optical or laser lock, but deadly enough at close range. He winced as a pair of bright flashes scored on the *Locust*'s hull.

More missiles arced out of the smoke as the *Wasp* laid down a second barrage. A sharp, piercing tone sounded in his ear, indicating the Lancer's ECM program was running. If the ECM did not succeed in jamming the enemy's targeting radar, all three Lancer 'Mechs would be swiftly hunted down and destroyed.

Grayson detected another movement, heavy and lumbering off to the right. He swung the camera back to the east and hit the extended zoom. *There!* Close by the squat shapes of the grounded *Union* DropShips were a pair of 'Mechs lurching toward the smoky field. The near 'Mech was a *Rifleman*, a 60-tonner with paired, over-under lasers and autocannons mounted in the place of arms.

Grayson shivered as he realized the *Rifleman* alone weighed as much as Lori's entire, three-'Mech command. And beyond it was the 55-ton bulk of a *Wolverine,* with the odd protuberance of a laser turret built high up in its massively armored chest, and a heavy autocannon carried on the right arm. In the air, the lean, shark's shape of an attack helicopter swooped down from the distant Castle.

The smoke cloud was laced with flashes and stabs of light. The DropShips seemed to be firing at random into the cloud, unsure of their targets. The radar-jamming seemed to be working the same as the smoke cloud to block the Combine forces' use of laser targeting. It did not matter much that the Lancers' targeting countermeasures also prevented them from targeting effectively. It was no part of the plan for the Lancers' three 20-ton 'Mechs to stand and tangle with the heavies now thundering across the ferrocrete landing area toward them.

Grayson's helmet crackled, then erupted in sharp, electronic tones on the Lancers' combat frequency. "Lancer One, this is Lancer Three! I've got infantry movement on our left! They're circling behind us!"

"Roger, Three. Start your retreat."

"Lancer One, this is Two. Three 'Mechs on this side, at 300 meters and closing! PBIs in support. Two...make that three HVTs!"

"Okay, Two. All units, pull back. Stick to—"

Lori's transmission was cut off by a savage burst of static. The smoke cloud lit up blue as a charged particle beam stabbed through its heart. Grayson swung the camera back and forth, trying to find the 'Mech that had fired. It had to be a big one to mount a PPC. For one horrible moment, he thought the beam had caught Lori. Then, the shrieking static of charged particles faded, and he heard her transmission again.

"—All units, stay spread out! Watch your rears!"

Grayson had lost track of their position now, though more smoke rockets were lofting down into the smoke screen to keep the heavy gray-white cloud spreading across the field. He could make out the shadowy silhouettes of at least five heavy 'Mechs moving through the smoke, heading west and north.

Grayson felt a twisting sense of guilt, lying with his 'Mech camo-netted and well out of the line of fire. It couldn't be otherwise, but that didn't ease his soul at the moment. He had to sit by while his friends were being pressed hard by vastly superior numbers.

The sounds of combat grew fainter within the smoke, but the electronic chatter among his lancemates continued. Grayson could sense a growing note of urgency in their voices even through the filtering of electronic reproduction.

"This is Three! This is Three!" That was Yarin in the *Stinger,* facing his first 'Mech combat. "Temperature's up and I've got a shutdown warning!"

"Kick in your overrides, Three, and stay cool. All units, zero check. Repeat, zero check."

Grayson reached for his controls, bringing the *Shadow Hawk* to its feet in an explosion of camouflage netting and sand. "Zero check" was the prearranged code to let him know the lance had reached the rough, boulder-strewn rise that led up the slope toward Thunder Rift. It was time to launch the next phase of their plan.

The wind was stronger high on the slopes of the Rift mountains, and was dissolving the smoke screen as quickly as Enzelman could fire his smoke rockets. The three 'Mechs had to draw in closer, too, for the rise toward the Rift was a dried-out alluvial fan that began broad and flat, but quickly narrowed as it rose.

Lori mopped sweat and strands of dripping hair from her face. The action had already been going on for almost an hour with no sign of let-up, and the internal temperatures of all three 'Mechs were rising to critical levels.

She watched as a shape materialized from the smoke 250 meters below her. Then, the targeting crosshairs of her main imager centered on that shape. Her computer read mass and power plant emissions, while a glowing, wire-outlined image appeared on her screen. It was a *Wasp.* Though certain Garik was behind her and to her left, she punched the IFF receiver to be sure.

The *Wasp*'s laser fired in the same instant she read the transponder ID. Superheated rocks exploded near the *Locust*'s leg, the fragments clattering across her hull. She squeezed the firing trigger convulsively, and saw orange flame fork from the *Wasp*'s torso armor, leaving a blackened scar across its chest. Though the 'Mech twisted away from the beam, it was trailing smoke, and Lori could see blue lightning flickering in the ragged wound.

She fired again, and again. Two more hits! The *Wasp* was having difficulty standing. One leg seemed frozen, and apparently the pilot was having trouble keeping the 'Mech balanced.

Lori urged the *Locust* forward 30 meters, then stopped and fired again. Fire gouted from the stricken *Wasp*'s torso, and there was a splatter of molten metal.

The *Wasp*'s head exploded in smoke and light as the pilot ejected. The huge hull of the machine keeled over backward, leaving a curved trail of black smoke as it went down.

Another missile blast near the leg of her *Locust* sent Lori back up the hill. The boulders were thicker here, many of them the size of a house, and the battle became a game of sight, fire, and dodge among the sheltering rocks.

"Garik!" she called on the general combat frequency. "Yarin! Where are you?"

"This is Garik! I have you in sight, Sergeant. You're 200 meters below me, and to my right. Four 'Mechs—three lights and a *Wolverine*—are heading uphill about a hundred meters to your left. Do you read them?"

She scanned in that direction, and saw only boulders and drifting smoke. "No!"

"Better fall back before you're cut off."

"Moving!"

She edged farther up the slope, the dry soil crumbling beneath the scraping claws of the *Locust*'s feet. On either side, the ground rose more sharply, creating a wide ravine that restricted movement and—worse—visibility. All three

'Mechs had to be in the first defensive line before their pursuers got there.

Another *Wasp* stepped out from among the boulders, up the hill from her position, and between Lori and her friends. She didn't need to trigger the IFF for this one. It was scarcely 50 meters away, but its paint scheme was totally unfamiliar. The orange-black tiger stripe camouflage was designed for jungle warfare, and created a stark contrast with the grays and browns of the boulder field.

Her shot caught the *Wasp* by surprise, a clean hit on its right arm that sent the 'Mech spinning back to slam into a rock. Its arm and the laser it had held lay twisted and torn in the sand.

"Good shooting!" Lori didn't know whether the voice was Enzelman's or Yarin's. She fired again, missed, then saw a lone HEAP warhead catch the *Wasp* squarely in its back.

The enemy pilot managed to stabilize his 'Mech, though, and turned to face Lori head-on. A pair of short-range missiles spat from twin launch tubes set on the 'Mech's left leg. They missed as Lori strode forward to within 30 meters and fired her laser again. The beam savaged the *Wasp*'s head, leaving a twisted, smoking, half-molten ruin where the pilot had been sitting only a second before.

Lori didn't have time to gloat. Her external mikes were picking up the grinding thud of another approaching 'Mech off to the right. She nudged the *Locust* into an ungainly but brisk trot up the hill, anxious not to be cut off from the Rift again.

Lori's 'Mech crested the top of the rise. There, it opened into a broad ravine that angled across the hill face toward a steeper, more rugged slope with vertical cliffs of striated red and ocher rock. Beyond, cliffs that were only half visible from below opened wide. They soared above her on either side of the valley, which grew narrower as its walls continued to rise like a vertical gash across the face of the mountain.

She scurried the *Locust* back among the boulders, and found a place with a good view of the slope below. Then she lowered the 'Mech into a leg-folded crouch, with the hull less than two meters above the ground and the long snout of the laser cannon protruding from beneath the cockpit.

On either side of her, several hundred meters off, she caught glimpses of the *Wasp* and the *Stinger* lying prone among the rocks with their lasers extended. There was other movement here, too, as ground troops and hovercraft weapons carriers edged forward among the barricades, falls, and fire traps hidden across the ravine.

Lori rapidly assessed their position. They'd knocked out two 'Mechs, both light scouts. That left ten, possibly eleven enemy 'Mechs. *Ah...there!*

Two more scout 'Mechs, a *Stinger* and another *Locust,* advanced into the open at the bottom of the ravine. Behind them came two more, a *Rifleman* with its odd, twin-barreled arms, and the ponderous lurch of a 55-ton *Griffin.*

Lori bit down hard, triggering a comm circuit. "Sergeant Ramage!"

"Here, Sergeant!"

"Are you ready?"

"All set, Sarge. Give the word."

Lori waited, catching her lower lip between her teeth as she studied the unfolding situation. Two more 'Mechs had appeared behind the first four. They were too distant for her to make them out by sight, but her battle computer tagged them as two more *Wasps.* The range to the nearest targets was just over half a kilometer. The attackers kept moving, struggling up the loose-packed slope, but moving quickly.

The Duke must really be anxious to catch us, Lori thought. She zoomed her telescopes in on the lead 'Mech, a *Stinger* with a dull gray camouflage pattern and the black-and-red Kurita dragon bright against its chest. She had already spotted a pair of boulders designated as markers at the base of the ravine. *Only a few meters farther...*

"Okay, Sergeant! *Now!*"

Explosions drew a curtain of hurtling rock and black smoke across the entire breadth of the ravine. They lifted the enemy *Stinger,* and hurled it with a mighty push. Meanwhile, the ground rippled under the *Locust,* creating waves of dizziness in Lori through her neurohelmet.

The wall of debris collapsed on itself like the tumble of an ocean wave, raising lighter-colored dust, and revealing a second

'Mech, the *Rifleman.* It lay on its back with the twin barrels of its right arm wrenched apart and bent back upon themselves by the force of the blasts.

The other 'Mechs were in full retreat. It was only too bad that the explosion represented nearly all the Lancers' small supply of explosives.

Someone was yelling in her helmet phones, a rolling, unending litany of "We won! We won!"

"Silence on the comm!" Lori snapped. "They're just re-grouping."

She could see the movement of men and 'Mechs through the air clearing much farther down the slope, perhaps two kilometers away. By the way they were deploying across the ravine, she could tell they had no intention of returning to the port. The Lancers were in a good defensive position, but it would not take long for a determined push by overwhelming numbers to climb back up the ravine and overwhelm them.

"Come on, Gray," she said with unexpected fervor. "Scrap that antenna and then get the hell up here."

She turned her eyes to a monitor that looked up the hill toward the vapor-wreathed opening of the Rift two kilometers behind her. Through her mikes, she could hear the muted thunder of its waterfall. Their three 'Mechs and the hovercraft defenders were rapidly running out of room to run.

CHAPTER 31

Tor let the computer direct a last correcting burn that reduced the DropShip's closing speed to just over a meter per second. The freighter *Invidious* was large on the bridge screen images from aft, under the DropShip's tubes.

Like most JumpShips, the old freighter was built around the needle-slim dagger of a central drive core. Those clean lines were broken, however, by an unsightly clutter of cargo modules, the stubby, rounded prow of the pressurized crew section, the off-center bulge of the *Invidious'* second DropShip still strapped to the aft cargo compartment, and the menacing, misshapen blisters of the ship's meteor defense particle cannon and lasers. Tor's veteran eyes searched for signs of damage or incompetence, but found none. The stationkeeping drive appeared to be functioning, though the only sign of that was the LED traceries on the DropShip's console instruments registering a magnetic flux. All the same, he had calculated this path to keep the DropShip well clear of those particle streams, which, even at a thrust measured in thousandths of a G, could kill in seconds.

Aft, far aft of the freighter, the red disk of Trell now appeared as a crescent of light caught in a black circle that seemed to be devouring the star. It was an artificial eclipse, Tor knew, brought on by the *Invidious'* jump sail ten kilometers aft.

There was a burst of field-induced static from the bridge speakers, and then a man's voice speaking. "DropShip on vector four-five, reduce speed to point five meter per second, over."

Tor touched a button, fed a correction into his computer console. There was another, almost imperceptible nudge. "Complied, freighter."

He'd kept ship-to-ship chatter to an absolute minimum on the approach for fear of giving something away. So far there had been no challenge, no order to change course or kill vector. The freighter's deck watch must be satisfied with the DropShip's IFF broadcast

The last sliver of Trell sun was swallowed by the black jump sail, and the DropShip plunged into shadow. The hull of the freighter was only a few hundred meters distant now, masked in dimness, but outlined by the glimmer and steady-paced blinks of acquisition and running lights. A green beacon pulsed at the screen's crosshair-marked center, where docking latches were blossoming open to receive the DropShip stern.

Tor touched a console key, and a flashing red light appeared on the screen well off to one side, against the backdrop of stars. That was the Kurita warship's location, 12,000 kilometers away. There was still no transmission, no indication that anyone suspected anything was wrong.

He opened the ship's intercom. "All hands...stand by. I'm going to tell them who we are."

The freighter normally carried a crew of fifteen. Three of the original crew had gone with Tor to Trellwan and died there. The memory was still an anguish of guilt inside him. He did not know how many of the remaining twelve of his crew were still alive aboard the *Invidious,* though it was unlikely—or so he prayed—that so many trained starship hands would be casually wasted.

A bigger question was how many guards might be standing watch over the ship. Tor couldn't even guess at that, though conditions would be pretty cramped with more than ten or twelve passengers.

He glanced at the screen, which was recording time. It read 55 hours, 30 minutes exactly, with the seconds flickering away to the right of those numbers.

There were a number of ways to attack a JumpShip in space. If it was unsupported, there were several positions a DropShip could take that would threaten the vessel—aft of the jump sail, for example, or close forward of the stationkeeping drives, assuming the defensive weapons had been neutralized.

If the DropShip opened fire on the *Invidious'* weapons blisters, the *Union* DropShip would detect the radiations and investigate. If the freighter suffered any damage at all—perhaps a torn sail or an explosion in a weapons pod—the DropShip would investigate. Or, at the very least, it would try to raise the freighter on a ship-to-ship frequency to find out what was happening.

Tor had been prepared to try such an attack if their approach had been discovered, but his primary plan was still on schedule so far. He knew one or more of the ship's officers would meet them at the docking lock. If he and his men moved fast enough, they might be able to storm the ship and take it before the *Invidious'* deck watch could get off a yell for help.

Might. If the watch officer was awake and on the ball, he would have at least enough time to get a message off to Trellwan. The warship might pick up a general, nondirectional broadcast, but unless the two ships were in active communication, with the frequency open, it was more likely that the warship wouldn't pick up the message.

It would take only a little over five and a half minutes for a beamed message to reach the spaceport's ground antenna at Trellwan. From there, a message would instantly go out to the DropShip, which would be alerted within the five and a half minutes it took a radio signal to travel back from Trellwan to the jump point. That was the greatest danger, and only the Lancers' attack on the spaceport antenna offered a way around it.

Then again, if the Duke had discovered the deception with the computer manifest, Tor might be met by a squad of marines with drawn guns.

The computer made a last-minute correctional burn. The DropShip's bridge rang with the clear bell tones and rattling thumps of magnetic grapples swinging home, of docking flanges clamping down to secure the vessel to its berth on the freighter's hull.

"Docked," he announced over the intercom. "Stand by, boarding party, main ship lock!"

The next few seconds would spell failure or success.

As soon as Lori's coded message had reached him, Grayson brought the hidden *Shadow Hawk* to its feet and began moving along the wadi. He was headed toward a place where the bank had partly collapsed, offering a natural ramp up and out of the gully and onto the flat ground southwest of the port.

The port itself was still masked by smoke, but the ground comm antenna stabbed up out of the haze two kilometers away. Other shapes were gradually becoming clear—the squat saucer of the control tower, the four parallel rows of liquid hydrogen tanks farther to the east, the gray shapes of the grounded Combine DropShips.

And 'Mechs. Grayson was getting moving radar images of at least eight of them, though the continuing ECM jamming was scrambling his images and making it impossible to get a hard fix. All the 'Mechs seemed to be moving toward the north end of the field, and none were closer than two kilometers away. From the look of things, the plan seemed to be working.

A light haze of smoke was drifting across the southwestern perimeter, dispersing before a light northerly breeze. The *Shadow Hawk* reached the chain-link fence at the port perimeter, and stepped over it to the ferrocrete apron. A hovercraft weapons carrier whined through the smoke a half-kilometer ahead, heading north, but it ignored Grayson.

He'd been counting on that. Though the Duke's men knew all too well that Grayson had made off with their captured *Shadow Hawk* two days ago, there was still a company of 'Mechs in the area. Any casual observer would most likely assume the battle-scarred machine moving across the southern edge of the port was friendly. The field officers who would know differently would be at the Castle monitoring combat communications, or in the field piloting their 'Mechs and with other business on their minds.

The sounds of continued combat drifted down the rising ground to the north. If the Lancers' three 'Mechs could hold out just long enough for him to destroy the antenna, he could join them by attacking the Combine forces from behind. With surprise and confusion, they might all be able to pull back into the Rift and disengage from the enemy.

After that, the Lancers would have to travel through Thunder Rift to a prearranged landing site on the shores of the Grimheld Sea. If Tor was able to recapture the *Invidious,* one of the freighter's DropShips would meet them at a beacon they planned to set two standard days from now. They would have to abandon their 'Mechs to make the passage through the Rift, because the waterfall had begun in earnest now, making any passage by water impossible. In case of his death, Grayson had drawn maps to help them pick their way through noise-blasted paths to the north opening, then down through rugged terrain to the Sea.

Once aboard the DropShip, they could head up to the *Invidious,* and from there to the nearest Commonwealth outpost Grayson could find. Those of the Lancers who wished to remain could survive for 30 standard days on the supplies the DropShip would leave them, then travel by hovercraft back to Sarghad as soon as it was dark again.

And there they would wait, with the promise that Grayson would return with a Commonwealth force large enough to smash the Combine invaders.

Grayson tore his mind away from the plan. Looking at it overall, he saw too many assumptions and premises and outright guesses, and too many little details that could so easily go wrong.

He remembered another of Kai Griffith's maxims. *"If something can go wrong,"* the Weapons Master had said, *"it will. Keep your planning simple, because the plan's certain to get a lot more complicated in practice than you thought it'd be."*

Grayson didn't see how he could have simplified it any further. With so few 'Mechs against so many, only a complex plan gave him the options and flexibility he needed.

He triggered a switch marked HUD on his console, and the green targeting bull's-eye and characters of his heads-up display snapped on at eye level. He centered the antenna mast in the target circle, and read the range as 850 meters.

Then he did a weapons check. The autocannon was still at rest, but fully loaded and ready to be brought into action. His forearm medium laser was charged and ready, and the missile launchers—a battery of LRMs set into the 'Mech's left torso and a pair of twin-tube SRMs mounted on either side of its head—were online, loaded, and showed a display of green lights on his weapons board.

All set. He pushed the con stick forward, urging the *Shadow Hawk* into a lumbering trot toward the antenna.

When the missile caught his 'Mech squarely in the back, it took Grayson completely by surprise.

CHAPTER 32

Tor arrived hand-over-hand at the docking lock, where he took a holstered vibroblade from one of his men and tied it to his thigh while the soldier strapped the powerpack across his shoulders. The fourteen Lancers who had volunteered for this mission were already there, still dressed in their Royal Guards green and carrying everything from long, keen-edged boarding knives and vibroblades to laser rifles and tranq guns. Half the prisoners they'd found aboard the DropShip were there too, armed with improvised weapons and savage determination. In the lock area's dim lighting, all their faces were pale as they clung to the lock's handholds in the dreamy weightlessness of zero-G.

Tor's eyes picked out General Varney. "Prisoners all secure, sir?"

Varney's eyes twinkled. "Secure, Captain. Aft hold and chained to their seats. There was a bit of a problem with the ISF fellow, so I had to put him out. Again."

"Good." Tor caught his lip between his teeth. "But, General—"

"Don't say it, son," Varney broke in, seeming to read Tor's mind. "You're in command here, but I *am* going along." His knuckles worked along the haft of the heavy-bladed knife he held.

Tor paused, then nodded. If he'd learned one thing about the military, it was that you don't argue with generals. "Okay, men. Remember now, don't get trigger-happy. It may still be my crew running that ship under guard, or they may even have been enlisted by these bastards. God knows what they've been told, but we'll need them to crew the ship.

"Remember, too, that our acceleration isn't going to make any difference here. When you kick into the center of a room, it'll take you two minutes to fall to the deck. You throw a punch, and it'll throw you right back. Watch yourselves! Questions? No? All right, here goes!"

The outer airlock door slid open, and they found themselves looking through the open hatch of the *Invidious* at a trio of armed, black-uniformed officers standing in the freighter's docking lock.

"Hey! What's all this?" shouted an infantry officer in a captain's uniform. The next moment, he was hit by the hurtling body of one of the Lancers, and the two were scuffled in a pinwheel of arms and legs across the cargo lock and into a far bulkhead.

General Varney crowded in ahead of the rest. Slashing out and up with his boarding knife, he caught a Combine army lieutenant low in his gut, laying the man open in a weightless spray of blood.

Tor launched himself at the third Combine trooper, but the dying lieutenant spun into his path in a welter of blood and thrashing limbs. Tor caught a glimpse of the officer—*a major,* he thought—vanishing through the cargo lock hatch and into the passageway beyond. *Damn!*

"After him!" he called out. "Get him!"

The boarding party swam through the lock and spilled into the main passageway. Tor had to orient the men so that they were heading forward in the direction of the bridge. The faint acceleration of the *Invidious* stationkeeping drive was just enough to create the impression that they were indeed swimming up through an endless tunnel. At its far end, Tor caught a flicker of movement.

"Sergeant Yee! Pick him off with your laser!"

The trooper triggered his weapon, the beam faintly visible as a red thread flickering up the corridor, but the major slipped through a hatch an instant before the shot fired.

Damn again! Tor thought as the boarding party continued up the passageway. The alert would certainly go out now. From here on, it was all going to be up to Grayson and his Lancers on Trellwan.

The explosion at his back knocked Grayson's *Shadow Hawk* to its hands and knees. He hung against the cockpit seat's straps, stabbing wildly at control switches beneath bank upon bank of suddenly flashing indicator lights. The damage didn't seem severe, but it looked like the jump jets in the *'Hawk'*s massive backpack had been put out of action. He was also getting ominous readings from the backpack environmental support system.

Grayson hauled back on the controls and let his natural sense of balance guide the computer-controlled gyro and balance systems. Pulling itself up, the *'Hawk* stood and turned to face its attacker.

A *Crusader* in red-and-black livery stood there at a range of 220 meters. Grayson knew that color pattern. He'd seen it before, on a computer data listing. The *Crusader* was Lord Harimandir Singh's 'Mech.

A console data display gave a rundown of the *Crusader*'s stats. The massively armed and armored beast weighed 65 tons, its design sacrificing speed and maneuverability for weaponry. Grayson scanned the list of weapons: medium lasers, machine guns, and LRM launchers in each arm, and SRM launchers set into the armor plate of each leg. The machine's forearms were grotesquely swollen to accommodate the strap-on packs of weaponry. It raised both arms, and strode toward Grayson like a nightmarish sleepwalker.

Adrenaline sang in Grayson's blood. He dropped the autocannon across his left shoulder and triggered a long, rolling burst of hellfire, then snapped the *'Hawk'*s right arm up to discharge three lightning-quick bolts of coherent light. Flame and minor debris splattered from the *Crusader*'s head and shoulders. A row of craters stitched across its chest, rupturing armor plate and leaving a ragged scar along one shoulder.

Grayson was moving before he could register the extent of the damage. As he plunged clumsily across the ferrocrete in a bone-jarring shoulder roll, more laser fire and missiles screamed through the air where the *'Hawk* had been standing an instant before. Grayson brought his machine to its feet with a salvo of SRM fire that rang and echoed in the confines of his cockpit as the head-mounted tubes loosed their fury in smoke and noise. Wires and charred metal dangled from a tear in the *Crusader*'s upper left arm, and an oil leak in its lower torso gave the curious impression of thick, black blood running down the scarred armor.

Tubes mounted along the *Crusader*'s hips belched fire. At this range, Grayson did not have time to react before a pair of SRMs slammed into the *'Hawk*'s torso. The ear protectors in his helmet saved him from the worst of the noise, but the shriek of tearing metal and high explosives hit Grayson's head with as much force as the shock of the blast itself.

He knew maneuverability was his single advantage over the *Crusader,* and he had to use it. Charging the *Crusader* at top speed, the *Shadow Hawk* angled across the enemy 'Mech's line of fire to work his way around to the side. The *Crusader* pivoted on its left leg, tracking him with its right arm laser.

Grayson took the laser bolt high on the *'Hawk*'s right arm, at the pauldron shield. Planting the 'Mech's left foot solidly, he whirled to the right. The *Shadow Hawk*'s left arm smashed with staggering impact into the *Crusader*'s right shoulder from behind, sending the heavier 'Mech spinning forward in a wild effort to regain its balance. Now Grayson had the *'Hawk*'s laser up and tracking. He fired two bolts into the *Crusader*'s back and side as it fell, then followed with a salvo of SRMs that struck home in a tight cluster of high-explosive mayhem.

Grayson checked the screen showing elapsed time. Fifty-five hours, thirty-three minutes. If the *Invidious*'stationkeeping crew had managed to get a message out, it would arrive in two more minutes. He had to destroy that antenna first.

Stepping past the *Crusader,* he broke into a lumbering run. Singh's machine—if that was Singh—appeared damaged, but was certainly not destroyed. It was possible the pilot had been stunned by the missile salvo, or possibly by the fall itself. Grayson thought he would have time to destroy the tower, then return for a final showdown.

From 50 meters, he launched a salvo of SRMs at the base of the antenna, then turned his laser on the struts and cables running through the mast. Metal flared and vaporized, and cables split in flashes of blue-white fire. He had probably crippled the antenna, but had to make sure.

Directing his arm up to where the mast joined with the wire mesh dish, he carefully aligned the autocannon with his HUD targeting graphics. When Grayson stabbed the firing switch, the huge weapon across the 'Hawk's shoulder bucked and roared, deafening him with an ocean of roaring sound and vibration.

Eighty-millimeter high-explosive shells shredded the dish and smashed into the mast with devastating fury. Fragments of struts and cross-braces and electronic circuitry hurtled through the air, raining a spray of debris across the field. The dish sagged, then flew apart in twisted chunks and flame. The mast itself staggered like a wounded being, then folded upon itself and collapsed in a tangled ruin.

Grayson let out a long, whistling breath. He was sure now that the antenna would never relay another message.

His next target was the spaceport control tower, which housed comm units that could handle long-range, omni-directional transmissions, and could fill the communications gap with the jump point until a new directional dish could be rigged. As the tower offered an exceptional view of the entire spaceport and the approaches to Thunder Rift, it was entirely possible the enemy was coordinating its tactics from there. It had been badly shot up during Lori's raid two days ago. Though sheets of light wood were patched over holes in the windows, Grayson could see movement there. The tower was manned and operational.

Bringing it into his HUD, he checked the range: 841 meters. That was too far for accurate fire against another BattleMech, but the tower was a considerably larger target than the largest 'Mech. Grayson triggered his autocannon, and sent a stream of high-explosive shells flying toward the brick and glass target.

Through telephoto imaging, he saw its walls burst outward, changing concrete block and bricks into hurtling gravel. At the same time, 80mm shells punched hole after hole through glass, plastic, wood, and light metal, which exploded in a roar of smoke, fragments, and licking flames.

Now for the damaged *Crusader.* Grayson swung the *Shadow Hawk* about and took eight-meter strides back toward where he'd left Singh's 'Mech. Blood roared in his ears. It would be good taking that machine apart. He would be avenged, finally, as he watched Singh die.

But the *Crusader* was no longer there. Whether Singh had recovered and moved the 'Mech under its own power, or whether another 'Mech had arrived to help, Grayson couldn't tell. He scanned the area quickly, but though the smoke was rapidly clearing, he saw no sign of another BattleMech. Perhaps one of those storage sheds ahead...

Something—some movement or noise or sixth sense— dragged Grayson's attention down to a console screen showing the view aft. The smoke showed heavier there where it was drifting down on a northerly breeze from the direction of the wrecked and burning control tower.

A shadow moved through the smoke. A large and deadly shadow, with an unforgettably familiar shape.

Grayson spun the '*Hawk* about, bringing the laser arm up to the point. The smoke eddied for a moment, then tattered away in the wind, revealing the monstrous *Marauder* striding toward Grayson's machine.

Squat and ugly, its crab's body on back-canted legs, there was no mistaking that 'Mech design. Especially with its rapid-fire cannon leveled across massive dorsal armor.

It was a *Marauder*—the same *Marauder* that had destroyed Durant Carlyle's *Phoenix Hawk.*

The *Marauder* that had killed his father.

CHAPTER 33

A long, ragged line of six heavy 'Mechs charged up the ravine. Lori shouted the first warning, and then the hull-down *Locust, Wasp,* and *Stinger* joined their firepower to that of the grounded weapons carriers sweeping the slope below them with a withering fire.

Lori's laser caught a *Griffin* squarely in its head, and other fire smashed the LRM launcher mounted over its right shoulder, leaving the heavy barrel wrenched backward on its mounting to point uselessly at the sky. But the killer machine kept coming, loosing shattering bolts from its charged particle cannon.

Next to the *Griffin,* a 45-ton *Phoenix Hawk* staggered under the combined fire from three HVWC-mounted LRM launchers. Suddenly, its right leg gave way, and the 'Mech stumbled and collapsed.

Lying prone, Enzelman was firing his *Wasp*'s laser as quickly as he could. Though he could not bring the SRM launchers in the 'Mech's leg to bear because of his position, he had the laser propped like an outsized rifle across a boulder, and was squeezing off shots with telling accuracy.

Yarin, in the *Stinger* on Lori's left, was wilder and less accurate, but he had scored at least three hits on a *Wolverine,* which was now seeking cover at the edge of the ravine, and two on a second *Phoenix Hawk,* which was now having trouble bringing its right arm weapons to bear.

"Sergeant Kalmar! This is Ramage!"

"Yeah!"

"They have flankers out, coming up on the left!"

Lori checked that side, and saw the line of tracked crawlers climbing along a ridge east of the ravine. The ridge gave out before it reached the Rift, she knew, but those vehicles carried artillery that would destroy her three 'Mechs if they got into position squarely on her flank. Firing down from that ridge, the crawlers would have no trouble picking off the 'Mechs behind their sheltering boulders.

"Pin 'em down until we can shake these people!"

"You got it, Sarge!" Two hovercraft roared into life, skittering back to the left on whirling clouds of dust. The curving contrails of an LRM salvo reached for the enemy crawlers, and return fire sizzled in among the 'Mechs amidst gouts of flame and dirt.

Two of the six enemy 'Mechs—a *Phoenix Hawk* and a *Rifleman*—were down, damaged but not destroyed. The remaining four had halted, seeming to hesitate between continuing the advance and falling back. The second *'Hawk*, already damaged in its right arm, strode rapidly toward Lori's hiding place, laser fire from its left arm stabbing at the boulder and the ground around her.

She took a hit high on the *Locust*'s torso, then another. When Lori triggered a shot in reply, the bolt washed white fire across the *Phoenix Hawk*'s head. A hovercraft to her left drifted sideways, seeking a better line of fire. Its charged particle cannon flashed once, and the *Phoenix Hawk*'s already damaged head exploded in fire and shattered metal. Unmoving, the *Hawk* stood there, a gaping crater where its head and pilot had been seconds before. Then, with smoke trailing from its deadly damage, the dead 'Mech toppled forward, landing with a deafening crash.

The hovercraft's movement had given the *Wolverine* a clear line-of-fire. When a pair of SRMs hit it from the left, the HVWC vanished in white light and a hammer-blow shock that smashed Lori's crouching *Locust*. After the shower of dirt and debris cleared, nothing remained of the weapons carrier but a smoking hole and minute fragments of hot steel.

With the *Phoenix Hawk*'s destruction, the remaining 'Mechs began pulling back. The *Griffin* and the *Wolverine* each took one of the leg-damaged *Phoenix Hawk*'s arms and dragged it down the ravine. The *Rifleman* limped down the hill on its own, trailing a tangle of disemboweled wiring and puddles of lubricant that steamed in the cold air.

"Okay, they're pulling out," Lori said. "Mechs, fall back to the next line. Ground troops...cover us...and watch those flankers."

Missiles firing blindly from extreme range landed among the retreating 'Mechs, but did no damage. The next line was at the very crest of the ridge, where cliff walls knifed skyward to an overhanging glacier. The Rift itself was a hundred-meter black slash in the mountain face behind them. The raw, majestic thunder of its waterfall sent tremors through the hulls of the 'Mechs as they cleared the rise. Verbal communication would be difficult here, and sound sensors useless.

The Lancers had dug earthworks along the ridge in the two days since the DropShip had launched. Each vehicle was positioned to give it a long, clear line-of-sight down into the ravine. Lori caught herself wishing for more explosives so that they could set off another mine blast, or another lance of 'Mechs—heavies this time.

With four *Marauders*, she could have held this hill against a BattleMech army. Watching as her remaining hovercrafts completed their withdrawal to the mouth of the Rift, she shook her head. Ammo would soon be very low, and the cabin temps of all three 'Mechs were above forty degrees. The plan had been designed to take advantage of the lake at their backs, which provided a means to cool down their 'Mechs while the attackers were forced to struggle up the hill with their internal temps rising. Beside the availability of the lake, the other advantage of the Lancers' position was the wet, cool breeze blowing steadily from the Rift mouth. As heat build-up would now be less of a problem for them than for their pursuers, Grayson had thought it might give them one slender advantage.

And they certainly needed every advantage they could get now.

For several moments, it was quiet—suspiciously so. Lori watched her screens closely, alert for any movement or heat or radar image, for any sign of the approaching enemy. She wished she could hear as well, but Thunder Rift drowned out all but voices transmitted directly to her ear.

Then her radar indicator flashed. Helicopter! *There!*

The aircraft was a large, heavy-duty transport, and was descending behind the scattered boulders beyond the bottom of the ravine. That would be reinforcements, most likely, more troops certainly, and possibly another 'Mech or two from the Castle. Lori waited with mounting dread. The attack was just beginning, she knew. That first rush had been little more than a skirmish compared with what was to come.

"Sergeant? This is Ramage, private line."

She opened a private channel. "What is it?"

"I just wanted to say that was a beautiful piece of work down there. It's...well, I never thought a woman could handle a 'Mech like that. Two targets down in as many minutes. That was some shooting!"

She smiled. "Let's save the congratulations for when we get out of this, okay?"

Just as Lori was wondering what was happening to Grayson, an explosion echoed through the cave, drowning the thunder. It was followed by another...and another. Missiles arced high up from the ravine, then came down in shattering blasts among the rocks and ice at the Rift's mouth.

The enemy 'Mechs were visible now. The four they'd seen before, plus three more. These were a *Stinger,* a *Shadow Hawk*—for one heart-leaping instant, Lori thought it was Grayson come up the hill to their rescue—and the lead 'Mech, a *Marauder* painted red with black legs and trim. *That one must have come in by helicopter,* Lori thought, remembering well Grayson's description of it. So...Duke Ricol was here in person!

There was infantry with the group too. Crawlers chewed through dust and gravel down the ridge and into the ravine, swinging north to bring the Rift's defenders into their sight.

"Fire!" Lori shouted, but the command was lost in the first volleys of laser and missile fire. Her own laser snapped off four shots, and three of them scored on the already-damaged *Griffin,* shredding armor, opening new wounds in the huge machine's arms and torso. The Duke's men were not using the scattered boulders for cover this time, but were running uphill at top speed, hoping, she realized, to overrun the Lancers' position before they took unacceptable losses.

"They're trying to swamp us!" she said. "Pour it on!"

The *Griffin* stumbled and fell, whether destroyed or damaged badly, she could not tell. Switching her sights to the *Marauder* advancing ponderously in the vanguard, Lori watched in horror as the 'Mech's head and torso absorbed bolt after bolt, seemingly without effect.

Then she realized the *Stinger*—far faster and more agile than the *Marauder*—was closer, almost on top of her position. She swung her laser up and caught the 20-ton 'Mech in the leg. Then her own 'Mech reeled as the particle cannons mounted in the *Marauder's* forearms loosed thunder and red blackness at the cockpit of her *Locust,* smashing Lori to one side in her seat and tilting the 'Mech over to its port side.

When her vision cleared, she struggled to right her machine, gasping at the sudden, stabbing pain in her side.

The *Stinger* was close now, too close, its laser leveled on her *Locust* as it pulled its metal feet under its torso and started to rise. A laser bolt from Garik's *Wasp* caught the *Stinger* on the side, spinning it around and smashing it into a house-sized rock. When Lori fired her own laser, the *Stinger* stopped moving, disabled at the very least.

But the *Marauder* was closer now, its twin cannons of high-energy death scything through the men crouched behind the shallow earthworks while the giant machines battled above them. Lori fired again, and struck the *Marauder's* head full on, without visible effect. Its 75 tons of metal death strode closer, cannons descending for a final shot. There was one long, horrible pause as the enemy's PPCs recharged.

Then an explosion caught the *Marauder* above its cockpit, followed by another and another. Dazed, Lori shook her head, struggling to clear it. The *Wasp,* Garik Enzelman's machine, stepped between her and the onrushing monster. Lori understood. The *Wasp* could not fire its missile packs while it was lying down. Garik had stood and loosed a salvo at the *Marauder,* was now trying to dart behind the slower machine to strike it from behind.

A lightning bolt of charged particles carved through the air, pummeling the *Wasp's* right arm and chest. Badly hit, the *Wasp* staggered among the smoke and hurtling fragments. A second bolt caught the light machine full across its head. Lori heard Garik's scream through the radio, saw shattered plastic and metal exploding outward in a whirling dance of death. The blast picked the light 'Mech off its feet and smashed it down among the rocks.

"Ramage!" she yelled on the com frequency, her voice raw and burning. "They're breaking through! Garik's gone!"

Three hovercraft skimmed low across the ground behind the *Marauder* as Lori snapped shot after shot at the giant 'Mech's head. This was Grayson's skill and training put to its ultimate test. Missiles slammed into the *Marauder*'s back as the trio of hovercraft howled into a tight, high-speed turn at ten meters' range.

Turning clumsily, the *Marauder* fired its autocannon, which yammered through the cave above the whine of hovercraft, the crash of explosions, and the insistent drumming of the waterfall. One of the hovercraft staggered in mid-flight, swayed sharply to the right, and smashed into the base of the cliff, vanishing in a ball of flame.

The *Locust* was on its feet, pumping laser bolts into the *Marauder*'s flank and back from 50 meters. Lori's fist cramped on the trigger as she jerked it again and again and again...

Then the *Marauder* was withdrawing. It staggered back down the ridge, followed by the other five 'Mechs that were still standing.

"Why?" Ramage questioned over the combat frequency. Lori could pick him out as he crouched at the stern of the well deck of his hovercraft, microphone in hand. "They had us cold. Why'd they retreat?"

Lori sagged back against the seat. Sweat drenched her face, chest, and shoulders, and the air inside the cabin seared hot in her lungs as she breathed. She twisted about and yanked the handle that opened the after-cabin hatch, reveling in the ghost of cold air she could feel at the opening. "Temperature, I think."

"What was that?"

"My 'Mech is so hot, it's on the verge of powering down. They must have the same problem. I think they pulled back to cool off." She pivoted the *Locust,* studying the cool, black water at their backs. The water foamed and roiled farther down the Rift, but there were only gentle ripples here by the shore.

"And that's not such a bad idea. Yarin, haul yourself into the lake and cool down. I'll mount guard until you come out. Ramage, you round up some people and check out that *Stinger* we knocked out. See if it can be enlisted."

"Right, Sarge."

But instead of moving out onto the slope where she could see the ravine, Lori parked the *Locust* above the sprawled wreckage of Enzelman's *Wasp.* A pair of soldiers had already levered open the 'Mech's cockpit and were removing Garik's shattered body. She was shocked by the amount of blood in the cockpit.

Garik was the last of those who had come with her from home. He'd been more, too. He'd been a companion and a friend when she'd needed one, and they'd been lovers—or, at least they'd shared a bed. Lori felt more alone now than at any time since coming to this bitter world.

The time readout showed a half-hour had passed since the beginning of the battle. *Where is Grayson?* If everything had gone according to plan, he should be here now, and their little band slipping back through the cold waters of the lake toward the ocean in the north. If Garik had lived, he'd have been coming with them.

Something must have gone wrong. If Grayson wasn't here, he must be lying dead inside his shattered BattleMech on the ferrocrete apron of the spaceport. And the rest of them would die, too, when the Duke's 'Mech forces cooled enough to charge again.

For a moment, Lori pondered whether they should retreat now, while they had a chance. Mopping the sweat off her face, she knew they had to wait for Grayson against all odds. She had promised. Surely, though, he should be here by now.

She glanced again at the time readout. If they could only hold out another fifteen minutes...

CHAPTER 34

The black-and-gray *Marauder*'s eight-meter legs gave it a tall and spindly look, and its dorsal-mounted autocannon rose a full two meters above Grayson's cockpit. Of all the BattleMech designs, Grayson thought the *Marauder* looked the most sinister, the most deadly. The movement of scanner antennae on either side of its low-mounted cockpit suggested the twitching mouthparts of some monstrous biped crab. Each arm, with vastly swollen vambrace and gauntlet to accommodate the paired PPCs and lasers, created an image of raw, unstoppable power.

Grayson stared at the apparition with mingled fear and hatred. Challenging a *Marauder* with a *Shadow Hawk* was a risky business. The *Marauder* outweighed him by 20 tons, and its twinned lasers and particle projection cannons seriously outweighed the *'Hawk'*s weaponry. Grayson's advantages, however, would be speed, maneuverability, and his consuming need for revenge. That need had grown to such storm-fury that he swung his *'Hawk* about to fully face the newcomer, urging it forward in a ground-eating trot.

There was a burst of static in his helmet earphones as someone sought his combat frequency. Then he heard the electronic voice of his opponent. "We knew you would come, Carlyle. We were ready for you."

Grayson did not answer. Giving his weapons systems a last check, he stepped up the feed from his power plant a notch. *Control,* he told himself. *Don't lose control and attack without thinking. He's trying to rattle you. Control...*

"My name is Vallendel," the *Marauder* pilot said. "And I've been waiting for you. I'm going to enjoy smashing you and your machine into scrap and bloody pulp. Just like I did to your father—"

At 150 meters, Grayson triggered his autocannon, a long, rolling burst that splattered explosive shells across the *Marauder*'s back and torso armor. Then he shifted his aim slightly. A *Marauder*'s "weak" points were its head and legs, but only in comparison to the massive armor of its plastron and arms.

Swinging his cannon down, Grayson probed for the complex machinery and control mechanisms at the point where the *Marauder*'s legs joined to the body. Shells hit home in smoke and flashes, but the *Marauder* was moving swiftly now, turning to present a heavily armored profile that deflected Grayson's high-explosive shells with little more than scars and scratches to the plate.

Grayson shoved the control stick all the way forward, feeling the throbbing pound of the *'Hawk*'s feet against the ferrocrete. Suddenly, the *Marauder* spun to face him, both arms up. As white fire seared close above the cockpit, Grayson dropped and rolled. His cockpit canopy momentarily went black with polarization.

Then he was up and moving again as cannon shells stitched across the ferrocrete where he had been. He opened fire as he ran, letting the stream of shells sweep across the *Marauder*'s plastron like the rush of water from a hose.

Autocannons and particle projection cannons had a serious disadvantage in close combat. At ranges of less than about 90 meters, it became increasingly hard to keep their fire trained on rapidly moving targets. If Grayson could get in close to where he could use his head-mounted SRMs, he might be able to hit without being hit back—providing, of course, he could keep from being smashed by a physical, 'Mech-to-'Mech attack.

The *Marauder*'s PPCs fired again, and the *Shadow Hawk* staggered as the armor plate on his left arm took the full brunt of the blast. Grayson fired his laser in reply, snapping off two quick shots the *Marauder* merely seemed to absorb without harm to its arm and torso.

The range was down to 50 meters now. Both 'Mechs fired, both missed as they circled, searching for an opening. Grayson waited until the *Marauder* was facing him full on, then triggered a salvo of SRMs, and loaded and fired again.

The heavier 'Mech was snapped back by the blast, but its broad feet lashed out for purchase on the ferrocrete, stabilizers cut in, and somehow the giant remained standing. Twin laser beams boiled steel where earlier damage had reeled back the outer armor of the *Shadow Hawk*'s torso. A red light signaled the loss of another heat sink, and Grayson realized the 'Mech's interior temperature was already far higher than he could stand for very long.

Circle...fire...miss...fire...hit...circle...The bizarre dance between giants continued, neither machine able to find or win advantage.

Grayson knew he couldn't continue the dance much longer. Even though neither machine was seriously damaged yet, the *Marauder* could continue to move and fight longer than Grayson's *Hawk* could. And when the *Shadow Hawk* failed, the end would follow very quickly.

He scanned his console lights, tallying damage. The armor on his left arm was almost gone, some bad holes pocked the *Hawk*'s torso, and the earlier hits to his backpack had knocked out his jump jets. The worst difficulty was the heat build-up. He'd lost a full quarter of his heat sinks, and the temperature in the cockpit was over 40 degrees. By now the shielded power core must be like an inferno.

The *Marauder* charged. Grayson snapped off two shots, then swung around and away, beyond the monster's reach, ripping off an autocannon burst as it thundered past.

"It was stupid of you to come in here alone," Vallendel said, as though the conversation had not been interrupted by brutal bursts of fire. "We've got you right where we want you now."

We? Grayson stepped back from the *Marauder*, frantically scanning his imaging screens.

Another huge and humanoid shape was moving alongside a storage warehouse. Zooming in for a telephoto enhancement, Grayson recognized the bulging forearms, the scored and pitted armor of the *Crusader.* Singh had not been put out of action after all. He had been hiding there all along, waiting for the *Marauder* to maneuver Grayson into position.

Short-range missiles arrowed in, fragmenting the ferrocrete around the *Hawk* with the fury of hellfire. The *Shadow Hawk* waded through boiling smoke, tracking this new threat and laying down a pattern of SRMs in reply.

The *Marauder* caught him dead center in the lower torso with a blast from one of its PPCs. Grayson's 'Mech staggered forward toward the *Crusader* as warning lights screamed of failing systems and dying circuits. He half-turned, struggling for balance, and a pair of missiles smashed into the already damaged backpack.

Grayson and his *Shadow Hawk* toppled helplessly to the pavement

Lori felt a strange and almost peaceful sense of detachment as she watched the black water close over the *Locust*'s cockpit. The air inside the cabin was still stifling, sour with the smells of sweat and fear, but the internal temperature of the 'Mech dropped rapidly in the cold water. She wished she could leave the cockpit to swim in the icy currents, wished she could rid herself of the layers of sweat and grime that coated her body. She didn't dare, though. The enemy would attack again very soon.

Her 'Mech cooled, she guided it sluggishly through the depths and brought it up onto the beach, water cascading from its flanks in imitation of the falls that boomed and roared farther back in the depths of the Rift.

On the beach, astechs swarmed over the carcass of the *Wasp*. She opened an external speaker. "Ramage? What's the verdict?"

The Trell sergeant looked up at her, touched his ear, and shook his head. The background noise from the waterfall was too loud to permit voice communication, even when amplified. The men on the ground outside had all stuffed clay into their ears, a trick Grayson had taught them during the planning session. Though it made communications difficult, it would save the men's hearing.

She didn't really need Ramage's report anyway. Even from the *Locust*'s cockpit, the damage looked severe. Lori knew it would not fight again—at least not without a major overhaul. The *Marauder*'s blast had savaged delicate internal systems and control circuits.

Astechs had already stripped the hulk of its laser and missile packs, however, and of every SRM left in the *Wasp*'s reload packs. Meanwhile, a detail of soldiers was working at the mouth of the cavern, trying to set up a simple fire control system that would let them add the *Wasp*'s salvaged weaponry to the firepower they still mustered. Troops and hovercraft had already dragged back the laser from the disabled *Stinger* at the front line.

"Sergeant! This is Yarin!"

Exhaustion dragged at Lori, made her slow in responding. None of them would be able to hold out much longer.

"What is it?"

"Heat readings...I think."

The *Locust* stepped up alongside the *Stinger.* She shifted through the IR frequencies, the *Locust*'s computers picking up fragmentary and inconsistent readings.

The air outside was still cool, though the day was rapidly getting warmer and was already well above freezing. Still, the heat of engines—or of living bodies—ought to be readable enough...

And then they were there. Troops, dozens of them, leaped down from the rocky crags and ridges on either side of the ravine, weapons at their shoulders, firing wildly. Bullets spanged and whined from Lori's armor as she wrenched at the machine gun controls and brought her antipersonnel weapons chattering to life.

They had crept close behind the boulders, she realized, wearing special insulated black combat suits that trapped and masked body heat so that they could sneak up without detection. Almost before she could give the alarm, dozens of enemy soldiers were swarming through the Lancers' defensive perimeter, battling with the Lancer troops at the *Locust*'s feet.

Her machine gun fire swept through a line of attacking infantry as they scrambled down a rock escarpment, pitching them into the troops struggling below. She kept firing, but clear targets were hard to find. The black-clad attackers were everywhere, mingled with her own troops too closely to risk a shot.

A missile caught the *Locust* high up on its hull. Reflexively, Lori brought the machine crouching back on its legs, absorbing the shock and keeping the 'Mech on its feet. She took several quick steps backward, getting clear of the fight. There had to be a target...had to be...

One lone, black-clad soldier in a heavy, visored helmet stood ten meters away, a heavy, double-barreled weapon at his shoulder. Lori sat rigid in the grip of paralyzing fear. That trooper was carrying a portable inferno launcher, the same weapon Grayson had once threatened her with, so long ago.

She willed her hands to move, to take the machine gun controls and fire. She willed them to move, but failed. Paralyzed, she watched the soldier's finger tighten on the trigger. As the inferno missile fired and exploded, its white fire poured across the *Locust*'s hull in a jellied wave that struck and clung, burning furiously.

Panicked, Lori began screaming, and it was Grayson's name she shrieked again and again. Then her voice failed as the air inside the cockpit seared her lungs. Smoke curled from the instrumentation, and the hull pinged and sang as violently heated metal plates warped at the center of a fire that approached 1000 degrees.

Her fist slammed down on the ejection switch. Nothing! The circuit was dead, melted by the heat! She hauled around on the con stick and set the *Locust* running. The motion, the blast of air across the burning surfaces, only fanned the flames brighter and hotter.

CHAPTER 35

The shock of impact jarred Grayson violently against his seat, but the restraining straps and mercury-cored piston mounts absorbed the worst of it. One moment there was a searing pain in his side and head. The next thing he knew, it seemed time had passed unnoticed. Had he blacked out?

The '*Hawk* was lying on its side, and Grayson could see the strutting, back-canted legs of Vallendel's *Marauder* close beside him. What were they waiting for? He craned his neck to look up through his canopy at the *Marauder* towering above him. Vallendel must have thought him dead.

His fingers found a set of hand controls on the arm of his chair. He grasped and hauled them back in a savage, swift motion. The *Shadow Hawk*'s upper leg snapped out in a whistling kick that smashed into the *Marauder*'s right leg with steel-denting force, knocking the heavier 'Mech to the side in a drunken stagger.

The *Shadow Hawk* rose to its feet as the *Marauder* toppled over in a kind of graceful slow-motion. Grayson fired the laser into the downed 'Mech's leg twice, then swung to cover the *Crusader*, which was lumbering toward him as fast as it could travel. He fired a salvo of SRMs that missed, but that turned the *Crusader*'s charge.

It might have been possible—just barely possible—that he could have taken on the *Marauder* in single combat. He was realist enough to know he would never survive if he tried to face both 'Mechs at the same time. Revenge could not be sweet if he didn't live to taste it.

The damage to the *Shadow Hawk* was extensive, especially in the back. He worked such repairs as he could manage from the cockpit. Punching the fuel dump, he felt the surge as his supply of liquid mercury reaction mass cascaded onto the ground in a spray of silver droplets. Firefighting foam surged through molten circuits, and damaged life support circuits were killed and bypassed as he brought backups on line.

With 200 meters between himself and his enemies, Grayson turned and brought the *Crusader* into his HUD sights, then triggered his autocannon.

But nothing happened. He couldn't tell from his board whether the cannon was destroyed or the ammo feed was fouled, but the mechanisms for both were stored in the *Hawk*'s shattered backpack. He fired his laser instead, catching the *Crusader* close by the damaged section of its upper left arm.

The *Marauder* was on its feet again, apparently not seriously damaged. Even at 200 meters, however, Grayson could see the dent the *Hawk*'s foot had left in the *Marauder*'s right leg, just below the knee. It made the monster move with a distinct limp as it broke into a steady jog in pursuit of Grayson's 'Mech.

Then he too was running, twisting and dodging from side to side as both enemy 'Mechs loosed bolts and missiles at his *'Hawk.* Suddenly, Grayson collided with the side of a storehouse, sending half a wall sliding down in dust and debris as he brushed past. What he needed now was cover, a place where he could separate his foes. A few hundred meters away, the squat, gray-green fuel tanks at the southeast corner of the spaceport beckoned.

The port was not deserted by any means. Black-uniformed soldiers ran singly or in small groups, and numerous hovercraft and wheeled vehicles slipped among the buildings on unknown missions. The only direct threat, however, was the pair of 'Mechs following him now among the orderly rows of storage tanks and the spaghetti tangle of pipes and feeder lines used for refueling grounded ships.

They'd stopped firing at him, but it was no wonder. Grayson had seen the result of laser bolts fired into a tank of liquid hydrogen. The shots left a crater three meters deep.

Could he perhaps trap his enemies in the blast of a hydrogen tank? Though he liked the thought of it, common sense rejected the idea. Burning hydrogen rose very quickly into the sky, restricting its range of destruction. And, though the blast could be enormously destructive, the two 'Mechs were unlikely to stand still while Grayson blazed away at a storage tank close beside them.

Ah, but here was another possibility. On the north edge of the field was a storage tank different from the others. Long and low, it had unusual pump fittings and none of the bulky refrigeration machinery required for storing liquid H. Grayson knew what had been stored in this tank before the raiders had come: aviation fuel for helicopters and the other light aircraft used for transport between the cities of Trellwan. He turned, searching among the H tanks. Though neither 'Mech was visible, he knew they were close, working their way toward him, probably moving along either edge of the hydrogen tank field in hopes of catching him between them.

Grayson slipped his hand into the snug warmth of the gauntlet controls. Flexing his fingers against the light resistance, he watched as the great fingers of the *Shadow Hawk* flexed and moved in response. BattleMechs equipped with gauntlets were capable of considerable dexterity. They could pick up vehicles, crates of supplies, and even people without damaging them.

He closed the gauntlet into a fist, then rammed it home against the fuel tank. The shock of the impact shuddered through the 'Mech's hull. As dark amber liquid gushed from the hole, he stepped back quickly. Aviation fuel was highly flammable, even explosive under the right conditions, and he did not want a chance spark to set it off. He turned and began sprinting northward.

Grayson's rear imager picked out his two pursuers as they emerged around the sides of the tank farm, but well clear of the leaking fuel tank. Both opened fire as soon as they spotted him, apparently unconcerned about the fuel tanks behind them. Though any stray shot of Grayson's might hit one, it took quite a bit to puncture one of the heavily armored H storage tanks.

Are they close enough? Grayson thought. The *Crusader* was moving in now, and was perhaps 20 meters from the tank. But was the *Marauder* near enough? *Only one way to find out,* he thought, and fired his laser at the aviation fuel tank.

The fuel on the ground took fire first. A wall of flames raced across the ferrocrete, engulfed the tank, then sent an angry orange and black fireball boiling into the morning sky. The impact of the explosion smashed the *Shadow Hawk* to the pavement, and for long seconds, the ground seemed to tremble with repeated reverberations.

When Grayson was able to lift the *'Hawk* part way up on its arms, he saw several of the hydrogen tanks had blown as well. The entire northern section of the tank farm had collapsed in a crater of rubble and flame, and the sky had become a dark pall that turned day to an eldritch night lit only by the orange flicker of burning fuel.

The *Crusader* lay on its side, one arm torn from its body, its head missing, and the torso shredded like a shoved-in plywood box. The *Marauder* had been much farther away from the blast. Though lying prone, it appeared otherwise undamaged. Grayson brought his laser up to cover the inert machine, and began closing the range.

The *'Hawk*'s computer targeted the *Marauder*'s head, locking the laser through the slowing HUD display.

The static of an open channel rasped in his ear. "Gray! I'm burning! *Gray!*"

It was Lori! That was enough to stop Grayson's charge. He hesitated, the *Marauder* his for the taking in his HUD sights. In an agony of indecision, he watched the machine stir, sliding one massive forearm under its body.

Again, Lori's screams came through on the *Hawk*'s combat frequency. Clear and shrill, she cried out, "*Grayson!* Grayson! I'm burning...*Gray!*"

The *Marauder*'s pilot was obviously stunned. The giant 'Mech remained down, partly raised on one arm as it tried to get its legs folded enough to bring them under the body to stand up.

Grayson could pepper away at the machine all day with his medium laser and might never penetrate that armor. But if he charged, he could batter the *Marauder* down, smashing it to pieces the way it had smashed his father's *Phoenix Hawk*.

He took ten more steps and picked up a tree-size length of jointed, wire-tangled metal. It had been the *Crusader*'s arm. With that as a two-handed club, Grayson would batter the *Marauder* until the plastron cracked. He would smash and kick and destroy—

"*Gray!*" Even through the impersonality of the comm circuits, he heard the naked terror in that scream.

With Vallendel at his feet, Grayson hesitated before swinging his twisted metal club. He knew he could never abandon Lori and flung the club, which spun end for end away from him. Then he swung to the north, pushing his 'Mech to the limit.

CHAPTER 36

Five and a half light minutes from Trellwan, Tor sat down at the bridge controls of the freighter *Invidious.* The enemy major had indeed managed to get a message off to Trellwan, but fifteen minutes had passed with no reaction from the warship. Tor began daring to believe the attack at the spaceport had succeeded.

The boarding party had found only eight Combine men aboard, plus all of Tor's remaining crew. The Kuritans had surrendered without a fight when dozens of armed and unarmed men had swum through the bridge hatch. Heavily outnumbered and fearing a laser firefight aboard ship, they preferred to wait and see whether the DropShip would send forces to rescue them. Now the Combine personnel were locked away below.

General Varney squinted at the main viewscreen, which was centered on the blackness of the *Invidious'* jump sail. "How do you know it's coming in?"

"I know," Tor said, indicating a bank of lights. "But it'll take some time."

"Is our...ah...friend out there going to know we're up to something?"

"Possibly, General, but that sail is awfully hard to see, even on radar. They'd have to be a lot closer to actually see the sail being furled."

Slowly, majestically, the kilometer-wide disk of black metal and plastic collapsed upon itself under the tugs of computer-directed guys and running lines. And in the JumpShip's core, the Kearny-Fuchida hyperspace field generators were channeling energies gathered and stored during the preceding weeks by the face of the jump sail turned toward Trellwan.

After several minutes, as power built within the ship's slender core, Tor turned to Varney with an apologetic smile. "Of course, there *is* the possibility they'll pick up our emissions. If they're on their toes over there, they'll know we're getting ready to jump."

"What happens then?"

"I guess we won't know that till it happens."

Something smashed into the side of Lori's flaming *Locust* with the force of a falling mountain, pitching her against the cockpit's restraining straps as the machine toppled over on its side. There was a splash, followed by a fountain of steam and white smoke. Viscous, flaming liquid spread across the surface of the water, but the 'Mech's partly submerged hull cooled quickly.

Shaken, Lori brought the *Locust* clumsily to its feet. Yarin's *Stinger* stood next to her, waist-deep in the smoking water. "Th...thank you," she told him.

The *Stinger* waved for an answer, then turned and waded ashore. The Lancers' hovercraft had rallied, and the attackers, which had not numbered more than fifteen or twenty, were pulling back, leaving their dead scattered in heaps on the sand. Several others kneeled on the sand, clutching their ears. The noise in the cavern mouth must have caught them all by surprise, helping to disorient them.

Lori checked her 'Mech for damage. One machine gun was out, whether melted or bent in the fall, she couldn't tell. Most of the ammunition had cooked off on that side of her 'Mech, so it was possible exploding machine gun rounds had damaged the gun. She had only three heat sinks left, and that was more serious. With only three operational heat exchangers, the *Locust* would overheat the first time she fired its laser—unless she could finish the battle hull-deep in the lake.

Perhaps now was the time to pull out. They could abandon the 'Mechs here and travel through the caverns to the north, following the maps Grayson had left them. With their ammunition running so perilously low, soon they would *have* to retreat if they didn't want to be overrun.

But what about Grayson? Was it possible he was still alive. If so, wouldn't he have long since arrived to join them? Lori didn't know whether he'd been able to destroy the spaceport antenna, or whether he'd been destroyed himself before getting a chance. When they'd planned this battle, they had assumed Lori would be able to see the spaceport from her position at the mouth of the Rift, and be able to tell when the antenna mast was blown. Radio silence was considered more important than a needless announcement by Grayson that his task was complete. But the Lancers had been driven all the way back inside the Rift now, and any 'Mech or human visible at the entrance drew fire from the encircling Combine forces.

Lori suddenly found her hands trembling uncontrollably— probably a delayed reaction to her terrifying brush with death. She fought to control the trembling, glad no one could see her at the moment.

Ramage was in his hovercraft, com set on his head. She opened a channel. *Keep your voice steady, Kalmar!* she told herself. "Sergeant Ramage?"

"Yes, Sarge? Are you okay?"

"Fine, Ramage. I'm fine." The shaking faded gradually, leaving her limp and weak. "What's the supply situation?"

"Not good. We've distributed the last of the ammo to the troops, and there aren't any more reloads for the 'Mechs. We have enough food for a week, maybe. No shelter, but it's warm enough right now.

"We'll definitely need shelter, though, if Captain Tor didn't get through. It will be cold by the middle of Firstnight. I don't know what we'll do then. If we don't surrender, the cold will kill us all."

Lori wondered if they shouldn't just give up now. She could see the enemy's 'Mechs moving at the bottom of the ravine, forming up for another attack. The Combine 'Mechs had been bloodied, but so far only one heavy had been positively destroyed. The rest had damage that would be completely repaired in a few days. The thought was discouraging. Every hit made the Lancers' forces weaker. At best, their own scores seemed only to slow the enemy temporarily.

Lori rubbed her eyes savagely with her hands, struggling to keep awake. There were just too many of them to hold off any longer. Two badly damaged 20-ton 'Mechs simply could not keep the fight going. She was more tired than she'd ever been. It was an effort just to grasp the conning stick and move the battered *Locust* a few steps forward.

Ramage was still there, waiting.

"We're going to have to retreat, Sergeant. Retreat or give it up now."

Ramage looked uncertain. "What about the Lieutenant?"

"He's dead, or he would've been here by now."

"Sarge!" That cry burst onto the comm frequency, interrupting them. It was a scout Ramage had posted on the ridge with binoculars and a radio. "Sarge, they're coming again! All of them!"

Their men and machines turned to face the ravine once more. Somehow, Lori found the willpower to drive the *Locust* into position, to squat the machine down in firing position.

The first LRMs came arching over from the bottom of the slope, bursting behind and in front of them and among the rocks and cliffs on either side.

"Hold your fire, people," she cautioned on the general combat circuit. How many could still hear her? "Save it till you can make it count."

Then the enemy rushed up the hill, the *Marauder* that had killed Garik in the lead. Lori opened fire on that machine, hitting it again and again! Smoke trailed now from a crater in the *Marauder*'s flank, and the autocannon perched on its back was a smashed and broken ruin. But it kept coming.

A hovercraft on Lori's right took a direct hit from a *Wolverine*'s turret laser, and a reload pack of SRMs erupted with a flash and a blast that disintegrated the vehicle. Two soldiers crouching nearby were jerked forward by the explosion and lay broken and still behind the earthworks.

The rest of the Lancer troops held their ground, using their shoulder-fired missile launchers and hand flamers to deadly effect. Three tracked vehicles were already on fire, their crews dead, and the *Shadow Hawk* was down with a crippled right leg.

But the others kept coming, but very slowly, as though forcing their way against a hurricane blast. The roar of exploding warheads blended with the steady drumming of the waterfall at the Lancers' backs.

Laser hits savaged the *Stinger,* blasting away external antennae and chunks of armor. The Duke's men were concentrating their fire on one machine. Lori knew once the *Stinger* was knocked out, it would be her turn. The *Stinger* stood up, wobbling jerkily, smoke pouring from a smashed side hull panel.

"Yarin! Get down!"

But the *Stinger* was advancing, its pilot oblivious to Lori's commands.

Maybe his radio's gone, she thought. *Or he's panicked.* Then it hit her that this might be his way of facing defeat. She had been thinking of retreat or surrender. But he—

The *Stinger* took a PPC hit full in its chest. As though time were frozen, Lori's mind held the image of Yarin's 'Mech crashing backward, arms spread, into the water.

But for three surviving weapons carriers and a handful of men crouched behind the shallow earthworks and laser-charred boulders, her *Locust* was alone now. She kept firing, but the *Marauder* was almost on her now. Range 60 meters... now 40...now 20...

Just as the attacking 'Mechs drew together at the Rift's entrance, explosions ripped into them. In a moment, the enemy's ranks were in chaos as missiles arced down from the green-tinged sky with blast after blast that echoed and re-echoed from the faces of the Rift walls.

Ramage was standing on the engine cowling of his hovercraft, waving his TK wildly. Lori caught his shouts through her external mikes. "The Lieutenant! It's the Lieutenant!"

Then she saw the *Shadow Hawk.* Though scarred, battered, and scored by laser burns, it was undeniably Grayson's 'Mech scrambling along the ridge to the east of the ravine. From that angle, LRMs came whistling down among the Duke's 'Mechs, but could not pass beyond and into the cavern mouth. The opening to the Rift was momentarily curtained off by hurtling earth and gravel, and the deafening blasts drowned out even the roar of the waterfall.

Three missiles caught the *Marauder* on the back and side, opening wider the gashes already torn into the armor plate. Its right arm now lay twisted and smoking on the cavern's sandy floor.

The *Marauder* turned then, almost sadly. It fired its surviving PPC and laser at Grayson's *Shadow Hawk,* but missed. With that, it began a shambling run back down the ridge, black smoke pouring from its hull. The surviving Combine 'Mechs broke then, each hurrying down the slope to safety, pursued by a dozen crawlers and disorganized bands of soldiers.

At the top of the ridge, the Lancers began standing, slowly, dazedly, while the remaining Combine troops dropped their weapons and raised their hands in surrender. But Lori only had eyes for Grayson's scarred *Shadow Hawk* limping to the crest of the ridge.

CHAPTER 37

At the jump point, energies flowed through the JumpShip's drive core, focused, then discharged in a space-twisting field that created something very close to a small, temporary black hole. In that instant, the *Invidious* simply vanished moments ahead of the arrival of DropShips from the enemy warship.

Aboard the *Invidious*, Tor felt the familiar crushing sensation, experienced that flash of momentary blindness as the void yawned around him, swallowing the ship in its eerie roar. The wan and distant disk of Trell, the myriad stars beyond dwindled into red, vanished into infrared, then were wiped away as if they'd never been. To be replaced by the arc-brilliant, fiercely radiating point of blue-white splendor that was their target star.

Tor found himself laughing helplessly in his relief and joy, while Varney pounded him on his back. They'd made it!

Claydon stood in the marbled corridor outside the Palace Reception Hall. He unhooked the holster strap on his Stetta automatic heavy pistol and waited.

As senior tech for the Guards 'Mech unit, he'd been assigned to Captain Nolem's personal staff. The desertion of many of the old Lancers personnel and all three working 'Mechs had left the 10th Guards without a 'Mech company—and its senior tech with nothing to do but follow Nolem.

But Claydon's thoughts were not concerned with 'Mechs now, nor with the battle raging north of the city at the spaceport, and beyond, at Thunder Rift. Like Grayson, he, too, craved revenge.

Claydon blamed Grayson for his father's death in the fire that had also destroyed their home. If it hadn't been for the young Commonwealther, Berenir would not have made the visor call that must have alerted someone in the government to his pro-Commonwealth loyalties. That someone had had connections with the bandit forces at the Castle, had been in on the betrayal of the Commandos to Singh's forces, had been behind the successful plot to bring down Trellwan's government.

Not until Claydon had met Grayson in the halls of the palace did he realize the other man was also a pawn in the hands of the giants conspiring for control of Trellwan. *That* had been what had killed Berenir. Upon learning Grayson had taken refuge with Berenir, the conspiracy had moved swiftly to take Carlyle, capture Claydon, and silence Berenir once and for all.

Though it had been Grayson Carlyle's raid on the port that had freed him, Claydon's grief and bitterness made him refuse the offer to join the Lancers. When Lieutenant Nolem approached him after the Lancers' disastrous raid on the Castle, Claydon had accepted the offer to tech for the new Lancers. The unit was being regrouped under his own command, Nolem said, and would be transferred to a Guards regiment. That he was Berenir's son carried little weight with Nolem. It was clear Claydon had no love for Grayson Carlyle. Besides, tech-trained personnel were too valuable to waste in political quibbling.

During his tour of duty with Nolem, Claydon actually spent more time going through the computer logs and comm records in the palace and at the Guards HQ than with 'Mechs. Tech Sergeant Riviera had been a master of computer programming and searches, and he'd passed that mastery on to his astech protege. By the time Claydon met Grayson again in the Palace corridor, he'd uncovered much of what he'd wanted to know.

He had learned, for example, who in the palace had been talking to Singh. And he knew Singh was a Draconian Special Forces commander, warleader for the Red Duke. He knew who had leaked word of the planned assault on the Castle to Singh's forces, who had planned the revolution to begin with Ricol's arrival, and who had ordered the murder of King Jeverid in his bed. And he knew who in the palace had betrayed his father to the enemy 'Mechs.

He'd used the time since, several standard days, watching for his opportunity to even the score.

Claydon heard steps on the far side of the great double doors of the reception hall. When the doors swung open, a pair of Royal Guards, submachine guns strapped high across their chests, stepped through and flanked the doors. General Adel and Captain Nolem followed on their heels. Behind them were more soldiers and His Majesty, King Stannic.

"Ah! Claydon!" Nolem said. "Fall in! We must get to headquarters. Things seem to be going badly for the Duke at Thunder Rift."

"Nonsense," the General said. "One lance against two companies? Don't be ridiculous!"

Claydon fell into step behind Nolem, took a deep breath, then dropped his hand to the Stetta in its holster.

A Guard shouted as the pistol came out. Claydon pivoted, bringing the heavy gun up in both hands as he swung halfway around, his finger already tightening on the trigger. Selector set to full-auto mayhem, the machine pistol spat and stitched a line of red horror across one of the Royal Guards behind him, then across the chest of King Stannic. Utter astonishment froze on Stannic's face as the force of the bullets smashed him spread-eagled onto the mirrored floor of the Reception Hall.

Claydon kept turning, the gun still barking in his hand. A second Guard clawed at his face and thrashed against the splintering door frame. Captain Nolem drove for the floor as General Adel bellowed a command to fire, then died, his last order choked in his bullet-ripped throat.

The two surviving Guards had their Rugan SMGs in hand now, spitting fire. The slugs tore through Claydon's chest and stomach, spinning him back and into the reception hall. By the time he slid to a stop in the pooling blood of the former King of Trellwan, he was dead.

Grayson sat in Duke Ricol's office, a spartan cabin in the *Alpha,* a DropShip of the Combine warship *Huntress.* The flag of truce that had brought him this far rested in one corner. With narrowed eyes, he studied the Red Duke, one of the three men he had wanted so desperately to kill. Of those, only Singh was dead, burned in his *Crusader* by the exploding fuel tank. As for Grayson's duel with Ricol, it had ended prematurely on the slope of Thunder Rift, with both 'Mechs too damaged to continue fighting. From the moment Ricol had turned away from the Rift, Grayson's passionate hunger for revenge had vanished.

"I've just had word that the *Invidious* has returned to Trellwan's jump point," Grayson said quietly, purposefully omitting the polite and proper "my Lord" and "your Grace." It was a minor spite, and served to remind this proud man who was the victor. "By now, a Commonwealth task force will be on its way."

"You don't know that, youngster."

"No, perhaps I don't. Perhaps I'm bluffing, and the *Invidious* no more than jumped out and returned to pick us up. But the question is, can you afford the chance?"

Ricol did not answer, and Grayson pursued his advantage. "You wanted this planet as a base for operations against the Commonwealth, but it doesn't do you a damn bit of good if the Commonwealth knows you're here. Your forces will be tied down by blockading fleets, your ground forces harassed by landings and fighter probes—and by my people, of course. You'll find it expensive—so expensive you'd have been better off staying home in the first place."

"What are you suggesting?" the Duke asked, proud and unbent.

"That you evacuate...now, while you can." Grayson leaned back in the chair and folded his hands across his stomach. Could he play this in a way Ricol would accept? He chafed inwardly at the need to act the peacemaker now, but there was no other choice. The Lancers could not continue this fight, not on Ricol's terms. The trick was to make the Duke see he could not continue the fight on his terms, either.

"If you stay," Grayson continued, "my people remain in the field, harassing you and making life miserable for everyone, themselves included. We'd rather see you off Trellwan, and at this point, I suspect you'd rather see that too."

"You'd let us go?"

"My word on it, your Grace. Frankly, Thunder Rift was hard on both of our forces. We have no wish to continue fighting— not unless you force us to it."

That was both an understatement and stark misrepresentation on Grayson's part. Though his astechs would soon have five 'Mechs working again from among the wrecks left on the ridge, at the moment the *Shadow Hawk* was the only fully functional BattleMech remaining. Nor could Ricol suspect that at that moment Grayson could call upon exactly 30 unwounded soldiers.

There were so many dead, and so many more wounded. And there were some injuries that seemed deeper than those of flesh and blood.

"Where were you?" Lori had asked, pain in her eyes. There'd been no anger in the words, only hurt and something like sorrow. With her 'Mech burning around her, she had called for his help. He knew how she feared death by fire, and it must have seemed like he'd abandoned her.

He had reached out for Lori, and she'd turned away. "No, Gray. Not...just...no." There had been a violation of the trust between them, and no telling if that particular wound would ever heal.

It seemed the price for revenge was high, much higher than those caught in the crossfire could afford to pay. And what vengeance was there, after all? What could restore the dead?

"You're right, of course," Ricol said. That simple admission, the sag of his shoulders, caught Grayson by surprise. "As allies, the Trell indigs would have been useful. But we can't afford to garrison a backwater desert like Trellwan, not with Stannic dead and the planet in revolt. No, the action, the real action, is elsewhere."

"The Inner Sphere."

Ricol shrugged. "So if you want Trellwan, youngster, it's yours. And welcome to it. A dreary, savage place."

Speechless, Grayson could only nod. Duke Ricol was requesting that his men and machines be allowed to leave

Trellwan, that his troops keep their guns and equipment, that everything remain as if the Duke's men had never come to Trellwan in the first place.

What of all the dead? Grayson thought. *Larressen, Enzelman, Claydon, Ari, Kai Griffith, his father...and so many more...*

"Full privileges," he said at last. "And the sooner you burn for your JumpShip, the better."

EPILOGUE

"Ten...*shun!*"

Ranks of gray-clad men snapped to attention in the sullen light of the westering sun. Master Sergeant Ramage did a sharp about-face and saluted Grayson. "*Comp'ny* all present and accounted for, *Sir!*"

Grayson let his eyes run along the rows of people, each armed, each with their duffel bag of equipment, uniforms, and personal gear at their feet.

Beyond the last rank, the 'Mechs were lined up as well, towering above the assembly. The two *Wasps* and the *Stinger* had been salvaged on the field and repaired. The *Locust* and the *Shadow Hawk* had been completely refitted. All were newly painted, too, with emblems of a death's head in gray and black against a red background on each 'Mech's left leg. Grayson's eyes strayed to the *Locust,* as though trying to see past armor and sensors to the woman inside.

"Very well, Sergeant. I will inspect the troops."

"Sir!" Ramage did another smart turn, and faced the ranks. "*Comp'ny, in-spec-tion...harms!*"

The man sounds more like a master sergeant every day, Grayson thought. For that matter, the troops were looking more like troops. With Ramage at his heels, he began walking along the line, checking men and women, uniforms, and weapons... *for what?*

Grayson shrugged off the rebellious thought. *For military appearance and readiness, of course.* For reassurance that the three platoons were tight and sharp and ready to board the DropShip at his back. And to remind them of who they were.

When the remnants of the Trellwan Lancers had emerged from Thunder Rift to meet Grayson, there had been a scant 30 soldiers unwounded and ready (after several straight periods of sleep) for duty. The *Locust,* the single surviving 'Mech, had been badly damaged, with a machine gun out, ammo storage wrecked, heat sinks gone, and large sections of the hull armor half melted away. There had been little to commend them as a victorious fighting unit.

Except for the fact that they had won.

Trellwan's Royal Guards had been somewhat taken aback by Sarghad's response to the warriors. News of the Battle of Thunder Rift was more rumor than fact, twisted and changing even as it spread. The only clearly discernible facts were that Ricol had led his army up to the Rift and been thrown back. A lone raider at the starport had destroyed the Combine force's communications station and much of their fuel. Two days later, the Combine DropShips had left, taking every 'Mech and off-world warrior with them. And then a DropShip from an incoming freighter had descended at the port, and the victors had returned to the city.

Their reception by Sarghad's citizens had been a minor revolution in its own right. With the government in total disarray after the deaths of Stannic and Adel, there'd been no one to issue an order for Carlyle's arrest. It was doubtful there were troops on Trellwan who would have carried such an order out, for the Green Coats were citizens of Sarghad as well, and totally caught up in the carnival atmosphere that surrounded the heroes' homecoming.

As for Grayson, he had not feared the government's response. Though he had had only two functional 'Mechs, the *Locust* and his battered *'Hawk,* that was more than Sarghad could muster in its own defense.

"*Comp*'ny, sling *harms!* Right *face! For*'ard *harch!*"

Many of Sarghad's troops—Militia and Guards alike—had joined the Lancers after Thunder Rift. The unit's survivors had become the experienced cadre that trained and seasoned the new troops. Grayson had already drawn up schedules so training would continue aboard the *Invidious.* There were many, it turned out, with no attachments, no reason to remain on Trellwan. When Grayson issued the call for volunteers for the new 'Mech regiment, they had come forward, this time leaving their earlier rivalries behind. The Lancers' new reputation had achieved that.

Grayson turned to face Trellwan's new leader. General Varney had taken charge of the military upon his return to the city from the DropShip. Marshaling the popular support of the now reinstated Militia and many of the Royal Guard as well, the Defense Ministers and Military Staff officers had elected Varney as military governor until a new king could be nominated.

It was entirely possible that office would also fall on Varney's shoulders. Of all Trellwan's leaders, only he had the power and authority to hold the military's openly warring factions together. The Lancers' new reputation had also achieved that.

"We wish you wouldn't go," Varney said. "There is a place for the Lancers here, you know."

"They're not the Trellwan Lancers any longer, General. Remember?"

"But you could stay! Look, Grayson, don't hold what happened against all of Trellwan! Please, reconsider! Hendrik still hangs over us, not to mention the Combine. But with your unit, we could..."

Grayson looked past Varney to where Mara watched him from the cluster of ministers and officials. The forces that had torn Trellwan's society apart were still there, for all the deaths and bloodshed.

He wondered now how could he have been such a fool in regard to Mara. He thought he'd been using her, unaware she was using him to gain useful information and to control him for the sake of her father's plans to become king.

His eyes snapped back to Varney. "Precisely, sir. They are my units now, and I will not have the Lancers be the focus of any more power struggles. We have our own destiny."

He gave the general his hand, which the old man clasped firmly. Varney would be a good leader. Trellwan might yet have a chance to combat that inner sickness of power and strife.

"The Commonwealth will be informed of the situation here," Grayson said. "I doubt the Kuritans will bother you anymore, but the Gray Death Legion will seek employment elsewhere."

He took an odd pleasure in that name, suggested by Sergeant Ramage, and made official by acclamation among the troops. As a newly formed mercenary regiment, they were small, yet—with only 5 'Mechs and 147 troops—but they had a ship and a pilot and the hope of a place among the embattled Houses of the Inner Sphere. Perhaps at Tharkad they would find whatever was left of Carlyle's Commandos. The regiment could be built to full strength elsewhere. And Grayson knew he would meet Ricol and Vallendel again one day.

"A man fights for his comrades on the firing line," Griffith had said. *"But home and family are what brings him to the firing line in the first place."* Looking across at the troops boarding the DropShip, Grayson felt a thrill of pride, of accomplishment. And of belonging.

He wanted to leave Trellwan as quickly as possible now. He needed time to assimilate what had happened here, and to examine the changes in himself.

Grayson saluted Varney with a smile. "By your leave, General."

The line of 'Mechs waited until the last of the troops filed past and up the ramp of the waiting DropShip. Grayson strode toward the *Shadow Hawk* at the end of the line and swung himself up on the chain ladder that hung down the machine's flank.

Inside the *'Hawk's* cockpit, with the neurohelmet on his head, an electronic voice sounded in his ears. "We're ready, Boss. Let's get the hell out of here!"

"Right, Lori. Lance formation...right turn...and embark." At this moment, Grayson felt content. Lori was important to him, both as a valued NCO and as a valued friend. He'd promised her the time to seek her own healing while he sought his. Meanwhile, they were still friends. In time, the wounds would heal...perhaps even before they reached Tharkad.

The DropShip's BattleMech ports gaped open. Grayson Death Carlyle's new family filed up the ramps and boarded their new home.

TRELLWAN STELLAR DATA

NSC L 4-342.
782 Star: Trell
Type: M2
Mass: 0.33 Sol
Luminosity: 0.03 Sol
Radius: 0.36 Sol
Estimated time remaining on main sequence: 4.2 x
    1010 years
Planetary System: 5 major bodies
Planet I: Trellwan
Mean orbital radius: 0.73 A.U.
Orbital eccentricity: 0.056
Periasteron: 0.164 A.U.
Apasteron: 0.182 A.U.
Period: 45.8 days
Mass: 0.68 Earth
Equatorial diameter: 11,352 km (0.89 Earth)
Mean planetary density: 5.28 g/cm3 (.96 Earth)
Mean surface gravity: 0.86 G
Escape velocity: 9.6 kps
Rotational period: 30d 11h 59m 12s (2/3 planetary year)
Axial inclination: 2° 15' 23.2"
Atmosphere: N2 -75%, O2 - 23.2%, H2O (mean) - 0.4%, CO2
    - 312ppm
Pressure: 512mm Hg at sea level
Temperature range: -80°C. (night at Apasteron) to 40°
    (midday at Periasteron)
Geology: Two small, landlocked equatorial seas total 9 percent
    of the planetary surface area. Remaining surface is divided
    into rugged mountains and uplands, and vast, arid desert
    lowlands. Tidal stresses account for the high mountain
    ranges along the equator, as well as for continuing volcanism
    and seismic activity.

Ecology: A few of the wide variety of native plants and animals
    adapted to Trellwan's dry, extreme-temperature surface
    conditions have been catalogued. Various offworld flora and

fauna have been introduced at several equatorial locations by human colonies established in approximately 2616.

Notes: Trellwan's ecology is dominated by its short orbital period and relatively long rotational period. The planet has escaped the fate of many inner worlds in close proximity to their star, and has a rotational period different from its year. However, tidal drag has slowed Trellwan's rotation until the planet is locked in a 2:3 resonance with its primary; its year is only 45 standard days, while its day is 30.5 standard days long.

The long periods of alternating darkness and light, coupled with short and climactically severe seasons, pose a serious challenge both for native forms and for the human colonies located south of the Mountains near the Grimheld Sea.

There are three principal settlements. Of these, Sarghad is the major city, the center of world government and trade, and the site of the world's only spaceport.

The planetary government is a monarchy with an appointed, unicameral legislature. Trellwan has long been a firm ally of the Lyran Commonwealth.

—Excerpt from *Pilot's Manual and Ephemeris,*
4th Quadrant, Cis-Peripheral Sector,
Lyran Commonwealth,
20th edition, published 3015, Tharkad

ABOUT THE AUTHOR

William H. Keith, is a *New York Times* bestselling author with (currently) seventy-eight novels, ten non-fiction books, and twenty short stories published, and more on the way, ranging from science fiction to action-adventure to military techno-thrillers. His first love is science fiction, however, especially military SF with a realistic, hard-science edge.

In years past, before he found out he could make more money writing about spaceships than painting them, Bill worked both as an illustrator and a game designer; he has forty games and game modules to his professional credit. His SF artwork has won fan and best-of-show awards at various SF conventions and shows, including Chicago's WindyCon and Pittsburgh's Confluence. His WWII role-playing game *Behind Enemy Lines* won the 1982 H.G. Wells Award for Best Role-Playing Game, and his *Going Home* module for *Twilight: 2000* was an Origins Award Winner as one of the Best Games of the Year in 1986. He still does artwork occasionally, and his paintings are have been on display each summer at Confluence, Pittsburgh's SF con.

Since 1984, Bill has been writing full-time. In the years since, Bill has turned out an unreasonable number of books in a psychotic effort to catch up with the late Isaac Asimov. His military fiction is written under a number of pen names, including Keith Douglass and H. Jay Riker. Most of his SF has been written under his own name, but the military-SF *Galactic Marines* series (the *Heritage* trilogy, the *Legacy* trilogy, and the *Inheritance* trilogy), the *Star Carrier* trilogy, and the *Star Corpsman* series appear on the shelves under the pseudonym Ian Douglas.

Recently he has branched out into nonfiction work, ghostwriting, and co-authoring new books with some of the brighter lights in the SF and military/thriller genres.

CRUSADER
HEAVY—60 TONS

GRIFFIN
MEDIUM—55 TONS

ACS

LOCUST
LIGHT—20 TONS

MARAUDER
HEAVY—75 TONS

PHOENIX HAWK
MEDIUM—45 TONS

PLOG19

RIFLEMAN
HEAVY—60 TONS

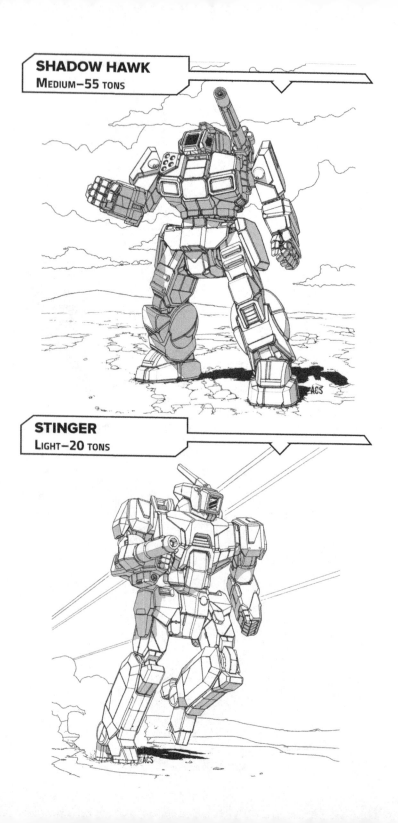

SHADOW HAWK
MEDIUM—55 TONS

STINGER
LIGHT—20 TONS

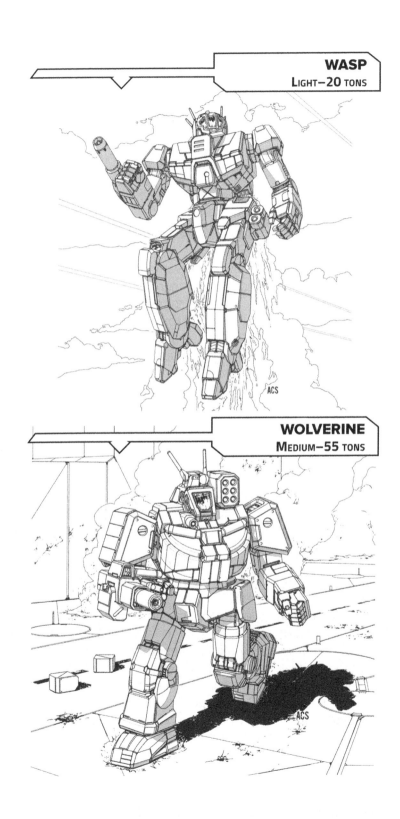

WASP
LIGHT—20 TONS

ACS

WOLVERINE
MEDIUM—55 TONS

ACS

BATTLETECH GLOSSARY

Autocannon: A rapid-firing, auto-loading cannon mounted on some 'Mechs and weapons carriers. Light vehicle autocannons have calibers ranging from 30 to 90mm, while heavy 'Mech autocannons may be 80 to 120mm or more. The weapon fires high-explosive or armor-piercing shells. Because of the limitations of 'Mech targeting technology, its range is limited to less than 600 meters.

Company: A tactical military unit consisting of three BattleMech Lances or, for infantry, three platoons with a total of 50 to 100 men. Infantry companies are generally commanded by a captain.

Crawler: A tracked, military vehicle. Various designs carry troops, cargo, or weapons.

Crusader: A heavy BattleMech, weighing 65 tons, with a top speed of 65 kph. It is heavily armed even for a 'Mech, mounting a laser, a heavy machine gun, and massed LRM batteries in each arm, and six SRM launch tubes on each leg.

ECM: Short for "Electronic Countermeasures," this is broadcast interference to disrupt enemy radar, radio, or other electronic equipment.

Hovercraft: A vehicle that travels several centimeters above the ground on a cushion of air created by large fans inside a rubber or light metal-skirted plenum chamber. Hovercraft may be designed as scouts, transports, or weapon carriers. They are fast, highly maneuverable, and can travel over land or water, but are hampered by rough or broken terrain. They are also called skimmers or GEVs (Ground Effect Vehicles).

HVT: Hovercraft Transports are a military hovercraft used to carry personnel or cargo.

HVWC: The Hovercraft Weapons Carrier is a military hovercraft, smaller than a transport, mounting a missile battery, PPC, or other heavy weapon.

IFF: Short for "Identification Friend or Foe," this is a system of signals from an onboard transponder that can be detected and used to identify the vehicle, especially in combat.

Inferno: A special, shoulder-launched missile designed as an anti-'Mech weapon. It explodes several meters from the launch tube, spraying the target with white phosphorus or a similar flammable compound in a jelly base. Infernos are not carried aboard 'Mechs because of their flammability.

IR: Infrared is light at wavelengths too long to be seen by the human eye. Infrared radiation is emitted by heat sources such as running engines or living bodies, and can be detected by equipment designed for use in the dark.

Lance: A BattleMech tactical combat group, usually consisting of four 'Mechs.

Laser: An acronym for "Light Amplification through Stimulated Emission of Radiation." As a weapon, it damages the target by concentrating extreme heat on a small area. BattleMech lasers are designated as small, medium, and large. Lasers are also available as shoulder-fired weapons operating from a portable backpack power unit. Certain range finders and targeting equipment employ low-level lasers as well.

Locust: A light, non-humanoid scout BattleMech designed for extreme speed and maneuverability. Weighing 20 tons, it has a top running speed of 130 kph. It is armed with one medium laser and a pair of heavy machine guns.

LRM: Abbreviation for "Long-Range Missiles," indirect-fire missiles with high-explosive warheads. They have a maximum extreme range of several kilometers, but are accurate only between about 150 and 700 meters.

Marauder: A heavy, non-humanoid assault BattleMech, weighing 75 tons, with a top speed of 65 kph. It is heavily armed, mounting a heavy PPC and a medium laser in each arm, and a 120mm autocannon over its back. Extremely well-armored and difficult to knock out, *Marauders* are particularly favored for the psychological advantage conveyed by their fearsome appearance.

PBI: Short for "Poor Bloody Infantry," this is BattleMech slang for non-'Mech troops.

Phoenix Hawk: A medium BattleMech weighing 45 tons, with a top speed of 100 kph. It mounts one medium laser and a heavy machine gun integral to each arm, and carries a heavy laser in an arm rifle mount. It is a particularly useful blend of speed and maneuverability in BattleMech combat

Platoon: A tactical military unit typically consisting of 50 to 60 men, commanded by a lieutenant or a platoon sergeant. A platoon may be divided into two sections.

PPC: Short for "Particle Projection Cannon," a magnetic accelerator firing high-energy proton or ion bolts, causing damage both through impact and high temperature. They are among the most effective weapons available to BattleMechs. Though they have a theoretical range limited only by line-of-sight considerations, the technology available for focusing and aiming the bolt limits effective range to less than 600 meters.

Regiment: A military unit consisting of two to four battalions, each consisting of three or four companies. A regiment is commanded by a colonel.

Rifleman: A medium BattleMech weighing 60 tons, with a top speed of 65 kph. It mounts one autocannon and a heavy laser in a twin-barrel assembly on each arm, and a pair of lasers in the torso.

Shadow Hawk: A medium BattleMech weighing 55 tons, with a top speed of 85 to 90 kph. It mounts a medium laser on its right arm, five LRM launchers in its torso, a pair of SRM launch tubes on either side of its head, and a backpack-mounted, over-the-shoulder, large-caliber autocannon.

SRM: Abbreviation for "Short-Range Missiles," direct-trajectory missiles with high-explosive or armor-piercing explosive warheads. They have a range of less than one kilometer, and are accurate only at ranges of less than 300 meters. They are more powerful, however, than LRMs.

Stinger: A light scout BattleMech, the *Stinger* weighs 20 tons, with a top running speed of 100 kph. It is armed with one medium laser and two heavy machine guns.

T.O. & E: Abbreviation for "Table of Organization and Equipment," the breakdown of a unit's personnel, order of battle, and equipment, including vehicles and weapons.

UV: Ultraviolet light is radiation at wavelengths too short to be seen by the eye. Special scanning equipment can see by UV light.

Wasp: A light scout BattleMech, weighing 20 tons, with a top running speed of 100 kph. The *Wasp* is armed with one medium laser and a pair of SRM racks.

Wolverine: A medium BattleMech weighing 55 tons, with a top speed of 85 kph. It mounts a heavy-caliber autocannon in its right arm, and six SRM tubes in its torso. High on its chest, just below the head, is a ball turret mounting a medium laser.

BATTLETECH ERAS

The *BattleTech* universe is a living, vibrant entity that grows each year as more sourcebooks and fiction are published. A dynamic universe, its setting and characters evolve over time within a highly detailed continuity framework, bringing everything to life in a way a static game universe cannot match.

To help quickly and easily convey the timeline of the universe—and to allow a player to easily "plug in" a given novel or sourcebook—we've divided *BattleTech* into eight major eras.

STAR LEAGUE
(Present–2780)

Ian Cameron, ruler of the Terran Hegemony, concludes decades of tireless effort with the creation of the Star League, a political and military alliance between all Great Houses and the Hegemony. Star League armed forces immediately launch the Reunification War, forcing the Periphery realms to join. For the next two centuries, humanity experiences a golden age across the thousand light-years of human-occupied space known as the Inner Sphere. It also sees the creation of the most powerful military in human history.

(This era also covers the centuries before the founding of the Star League in 2571, most notably the Age of War.)

SUCCESSION WARS
(2781–3049)

Every last member of First Lord Richard Cameron's family is killed during a coup launched by Stefan Amaris. Following the thirteen-year war to unseat him, the rulers of each of the five Great Houses disband the Star League. General Aleksandr Kerensky departs with eighty percent of the Star League Defense Force beyond known space and the Inner Sphere collapses into centuries of warfare known as the Succession Wars that will eventually result in a massive loss of technology across most worlds.

CLAN INVASION
(3050–3061)

A mysterious invading force strikes the coreward region of the Inner Sphere. The invaders, called the Clans, are descendants of Kerensky's SLDF troops, forged into a society dedicated to becoming the greatest fighting force in history. With vastly superior technology and warriors, the Clans conquer world after world. Eventually this outside threat will forge a new Star League, something hundreds of years of warfare failed to accomplish. In addition, the Clans will act as a catalyst for a technological renaissance.

CIVIL WAR
(3062–3067)

The Clan threat is eventually lessened with the complete destruction of a Clan. With that massive external threat apparently neutralized, internal conflicts explode around the Inner Sphere. House Liao conquers its former Commonality, the St. Ives Compact; a rebellion of military units belonging to House Kurita sparks a war with their powerful border enemy, Clan Ghost Bear; the fabulously powerful Federated Commonwealth of House Steiner and House Davion collapses into five long years of bitter civil war.

JIHAD
(3067–3080)

Following the Federated Commonwealth Civil War, the leaders of the Great Houses meet and disband the new Star League, declaring it a sham. The pseudo-religious Word of Blake—a splinter group of ComStar, the protectors and controllers of interstellar communication—launch the Jihad: an interstellar war that pits every faction against each other and even against themselves, as weapons of mass destruction are used for the first time in centuries while new and frightening technologies are also unleashed.

DARK AGE
(3081–3150)

Under the guidance of Devlin Stone, the Republic of the Sphere is born at the heart of the Inner Sphere following the Jihad. One of the more extensive periods of peace begins to break out as the 32nd century dawns. The factions, to one degree or another, embrace disarmament, and the massive armies of the Succession Wars begin to fade. However, in 3132 eighty percent of interstellar communications collapses, throwing the universe into chaos. Wars erupt almost immediately, and the factions begin rebuilding their armies.

ILCLAN
(3151–present)

The once-invulnerable Republic of the Sphere lies in ruins, torn apart by the Great Houses and the Clans as they wage war against each other on a scale not seen in nearly a century. Mercenaries flourish once more, selling their might to the highest bidder. As Fortress Republic collapses, the Clans race toward Terra to claim their long-denied birthright and create a supreme authority that will fulfill the dream of Aleksandr Kerensky and rule the Inner Sphere by any means necessary: The ilClan.

CLAN HOMEWORLDS
(2786–present)

In 2784, General Aleksandr Kerensky launched Operation Exodus, and led most of the Star League Defense Force out of the Inner Sphere in a search for a new world, far away from the strife of the Great Houses. After more than two years and thousands of light years, they arrived at the Pentagon Worlds. Over the next two-and-a-half centuries, internal dissent and civil war led to the creation of a brutal new society—the Clans. And in 3049, they returned to the Inner Sphere with one goal—the complete conquest of the Great Houses.

The march of technology across BattleTech's eras is relentless...

Some BattleMech designs never die. Each installment of *Recognition Guide: IlClan*, currently a PDF-only series, not only includes a brand new BattleMech or OmniMech, but also details Classic 'Mech designs from both the Inner Sphere and the Clans, now fully rebuilt with Dark Age technology (3085 and beyond).

RECOGNITION GUIDE: ILCLAN VOL. 01

RECOGNITION GUIDE: ILCLAN VOL. 02

RECOGNITION GUIDE: ILCLAN VOL. 03

RECOGNITION GUIDE: ILCLAN VOL. 04

RECOGNITION GUIDE: ILCLAN VOL. 05

RECOGNITION GUIDE: ILCLAN VOL. 06

BATTLETECH TLETECH TLETECH TLETECH

STORE.CATALYSTGAMELABS.COM